N O
PA

ALSO BY AARON HAMBURGER

The View from Stalin's Head

Faith for Beginners

FAITH *for* BEGINNERS

a novel

Aaron Hamburger

Random House | New York

Published in the United States by Random House,
an imprint of The Random House Publishing Group,
a division of Random House, Inc., New York.

RANDOM HOUSE and colophon are registered
trademarks of Random House, Inc.

LIBRARY OF CONGRESS CATALOGING-IN-PUBLICATION DATA
Hamburger, Aaron.
    Faith for beginners: a novel / Aaron Hamburger.
        p. cm.
    ISBN 1-4000-6298-5
    1. Americans—Israel—Fiction. 2. Middle class families—
Fiction. 3. Gay college students—Fiction. 4. Jewish families—
Fiction. 5. Terminally ill—Fiction. 6. Jewish women—Fiction.
7. Travelers—Fiction. 8. Israel—Fiction. I. Title.
PS3608.A5496F35 2005
813'.6—dc22   2004061459

Printed in the United States of America on acid-free paper

www.atrandom.com

9 8 7 6 5 4 3 2 1

FIRST EDITION

Book design by Casey Hampton

For Anthony

Faith for Beginners

one

A LIST OF PLANTS THAT GROW OUT OF THE WAILING WALL

1. HENBANE, or "SHIKARON" ("intoxication" in Hebrew). When ingested, induces a state of deep, colorful hallucination and finally a very pleasant death. Most common plant in the Wall.
2. PODOSNOMA. Roots can crack rocks to draw out water.
3. SICILIAN SNAPDRAGON. Prefers high altitudes.
4. HORSETAIL KNOTGRASS. Antidote for snakebite and the evil eye.
5. THORNY CAPER. Makes an excellent marinade for roast chicken.
6. PHAGNALON. Small and shy.

It was an intolerably hot morning near the end of June. A mother, father, and son named Michaelson floated on a cruise ship off the coast of Haifa, along with the other 251 members of the Millennium Marathon 2000. As they approached the harbor, their ship was briefly turned back by a black military helicopter, chartered to reenact the drama of Holocaust refugees sneaking into Palestine during the British Mandate. The Michiganders offered a light round of confused applause, and as if by command, the helicopter instantly swirled away.

Sweaty, bleary-eyed, and a bit deaf from the chopping of the helicopter, the Michaelsons collected their luggage and duty-free bags and streamed down the gangplanks with the other Michiganders. Aliza, the rabbinic intern, tried unsuccessfully to lead their group in a chorus of "Jerusalem of Gold." Her lavender song sheets fluttered down the side of the boat into the murky green water of the harbor.

On dry land, they received commemorative T-shirts with a handprint-shaped outline of their state and the message "THE MILLENNIUM MARATHON 2000! What's good for the goose is even better for the Michigander!"

"Isn't that a riot?" said Mrs. Michaelson, fifty-eight years old and often called handsome. She held a shirt up to the chest of her bored-looking son, who clearly did not think it was a riot. Her husband, busy emptying his nose into a hankie, had no opinion. And to tell the truth, Mrs. Michaelson herself didn't think it was a riot either. She was distracted by the heat as well as the realization that this was the first time she had ever set foot in Asia.

Before she could explore the continent further, their group was confronted by three air-conditioned buses, two unlicensed Russian photographers, who were chased away by the police, and one rabbi. His name was Rabbi Sherman, but he encouraged them to call him Rabbi Rick. He looked younger than Mrs. Michaelson had expected—though actually in his forties, he could have passed for thirty-five—and more attractive than any rabbi had a right to be. He was also unusually hairy. The top of his head, his arms, his hands, the back of his neck, and even his feet, peeking through the gaps in his brown leather sandals, were all covered in black wool.

Rabbi Sherman, riding in the first bus of their caravan, led them to their hotel, which boasted a commanding view of the harbor. Mrs. Michaelson took it in alone on the terrace after dinner. A sultry breeze blew in from the purple water of Haifa harbor, where the crescent moon was reflected as a series of white dashes on the waves. Within minutes, her dress was sticking to the skin under her arms and along the neckline.

Clutching an empty wineglass, Mrs. Michaelson closed her eyes and imagined she was having a religious moment. A trickle of sweat inched its way down between her breasts; a mosquito tickled her ear. "It's so late. . . ." she murmured.

A high, sharp voice, like a seagull, cried out, "Who's there?"

Someone moved in the shadows. Mrs. Michaelson made out the wide smile first, a wall of chiseled white teeth. The smile belonged to a short, sharp-chinned woman with pointy elbows jutting out of a glittery tissue-thin shawl. She padded up to Mrs. Michaelson in her bare feet.

"Sherry Sherman," said the stranger, her right hand thrust forward like a gun.

Mrs. Michaelson, who wasn't the type to accost strangers minding their own business, gave a bored smile, as if she were placing her order at dinner. When she smiled, her kind gray eyes pressed together so tightly it was impossible to see into them.

"I'm sort of a den mother to you folks," Sherry said. "Rabbi Rick and I live together in Tel Aviv. No, no, nothing like that. Of course, I'm much too old for him. And there's one more small matter: he's my son! By the way, your dress is stunning. Did you find it in New York City? I hope you don't mind spilling all your secrets."

"This?" Mrs. Michaelson said, holding out the material so that Sherry Sherman could admire the workmanship more easily. "It's just something I made. The pattern was easy."

"You made it?" said Sherry, fluffing her tight curls with the tips of her fingers. She was bony and spry like a cat, not a bit like the tall, strapping rabbi, who plodded ahead of their group with his shoulders thrown back like the Great White Hunter. "I don't know anyone who still sews. Maybe a button, not a whole dress. You really made it? Now that's special. But aren't I interrupting? I heard you talking to someone."

"I wasn't talking to anyone . . ." said Mrs. Michaelson, who talked to herself so often that she'd had plenty of practice making excuses.

"Hush! Do you feel that breeze? That's a typical Middle Eastern cooling breeze blowing in off the Mediterranean. Take a moment to let it soak into your skin."

Mrs. Michaelson took a moment, but didn't notice anything particularly special about the breeze. Chatty women made her feel like the chubby, soft-spoken girl she'd been in grade school, always dressed in stiff, frilly dresses suitable for antique dolls.

"You're here for an adventure. Am I right? In that case, I'll have to keep my eye on you to see how it turns out. If only I could visit Israel for the first time all over again." Sherry sighed, then recited, " 'If I forget thee, Jerusalem, let my right hand forget her cunning.' That's from Psalms."

"I've heard that one," Mrs. Michaelson said, smashing a mosquito on her neck.

" 'In Jerusalem, everyone remembers he's forgotten something, but he doesn't remember what it is.' That's by Yehuda Amichai, one of our great poets." Sherry stared directly at Mrs. Michaelson, who looked away, back at the harbor. "You seem to have a case of the jitters, dear. It's natural. I see it in all you first-timers, especially Americans. Listen, I've lived in Israel for six months, so I'm something of an expert now, and I can tell you we're far safer here than in the States. Street crime's practically unheard of. Death by tourism? Extremely rare."

Mrs. Michaelson preferred not to dwell on morbid subjects

like death. Someday she would die but, thankfully, when it happened, she wouldn't be around to know about it.

"If we change how we live, then the terrorists win," Sherry said with a firm nod. "You're far more likely to die in a horrible car crash at home than by a bomb in an Israeli marketplace, but do you stop driving? No. You minimize the risk by wearing a seat belt, which, thanks to Ralph Nader, is now standard in all vehicles. Rabbi Rick and I have decided to vote for Nader in November, but he'd never tell you that, because my son makes it a point to stay out of American political debates. Can I ask why you're holding that wineglass?"

"To calm my nerves" would have been the honest answer. At dinner, Mrs. Michaelson had slipped it into her purse when her son wasn't looking, in case one of the waiters forgot her warnings and filled the glass by accident. She'd imagined the resulting scene: Jeremy grabbing the glass of wine in a fit of weakness, downing it in a single greedy gulp, and then falling to the floor, where he'd lie twitching like an epileptic.

But how to explain all that to Sherry Sherman, who said, "Oh, I see it's a sore subject. I never pry," and padded away.

———

For two weeks, their troika of air-conditioned buses trekked up and down the Holy Land, from the snows of Mount Hermon (no snow in summer) to the sandy wastes of the Negev (hot, poisonous winds, and dreary scenery).

Mrs. Michaelson applauded for an orchestra of Russian immigrants playing Gershwin at a kibbutz in the Galilee, though she didn't really like Gershwin. Too showy.

She ate pita pounded thin and then toasted over an open fire by Bedouins in a desert camp in the Negev.

"Good?" they asked.

"Good, good!" she reassured them.

She watched Mr. Michaelson, who'd mysteriously dropped the title "Doctor" when he got sick, rape the Holy Land of its souvenirs: heart-shaped blue-glass eyes, inflatable camels, Dead Sea mud masks, a book of Golda Meir's favorite falafel recipes, an antique Roman coin that came with a certificate of authenticity.

She received a welcome kit with a miniature cake and an airline-size bottle of kosher red wine (she confiscated Jeremy's bottle while he was in the shower), a *Millennium Marathon Daily Bulletin* photocopied on goldenrod paper, and a plastic bottle of FROM SAND TO LAND sand, which Jeremy dumped into her glass of wine one night at dinner to prove he wasn't the least bit tempted to steal a sip.

She pressed flesh with the mayors of Tel Aviv, Rishon Le-Tzion, and Eilat, where their hotel offered free samples of peppermint foot lotion, which she used to massage her bunions.

She witnessed a phalanx of ten women dressed all in black standing by the side of the highway near the Megiddo junction. Perfectly silent and still, the Women in Black carried signs in Hebrew, English, and Arabic calling for the end of the "occupation."

She quickly learned the two ways to say "No thanks, I'm stuffed" in Hebrew, a matter of life and death in a country where tourists were apt to be pelted with unwanted extra helpings. The first expression meant "I've had enough to eat." The other, which wasn't particularly nice, meant "I'm so full I'm going to explode like an Arab."

She clipped a photo of Ehud Barak from the *International Herald Tribune*, because he looked exactly like her father when he'd been Barak's age. Back then, her father woke up at six A.M. to work at his grocery stand, then came home late, his hands chafed raw from washing vegetables in ice water. She loved him, but she used to hate touching his hands.

She posed for a picture beside a camel tied to a parking meter and invited Jeremy, standing a few feet away from everyone as usual with one of his cigarettes, to pose too. And, just for the picture, could he take out the safety pin he'd seen fit to stick through his nose? (There was nothing they could do about the green stripes in his hair, though by pretending to pat him on the head, she often managed to smooth out the sharp edges of his "faux Mohawk," a pyramid of hair cemented with gel.)

It wasn't a safety pin.

"It looks like a safety pin," Mrs. Michaelson said. "What's the difference?"

Jeremy pulled at the metal, stretching out his nostril. "*This* is sterilized. Also, for your information, camels aren't the least bit biblical. They weren't domesticated until six hundred years after Abraham, Isaac, and Jacob."

At times like this she saw some of her own awkwardness in him, and she couldn't help laughing.

"Why do I open my mouth?" he said. "You never listen to me anyway."

So Mrs. Michaelson stood alone by the unbiblical camel, blinked away the beads of perspiration dripping into her eyes, and claimed to be enjoying herself. She recalled the dignity of the Women in Black silently protesting near Megiddo and imagined that by taking the picture she, too, was staging a silent protest.

As soon as the camera flashed, several charming Bedouin boys jumped down from the olive trees and came running at them, shouting, "Money! Money!"

Mostly she sweated. Miserably. They all sweated. Everywhere the Michiganders traveled, guides and drivers and souvenir hawkers told them how unlucky they were to visit Israel during a *sharav* (Hebrew) or a *hamsin* (Arabic), a blistering heat wave. These *hamsin*s (most Israelis preferred the Arabic word) scalded the Levant every summer, but there hadn't been one this bad in a while.

"We didn't have one so bad for maybe fifty years, giving or taking," said Baruch, their Israeli driver, as they churned along Highway 1 from Tel Aviv to Jerusalem. She preferred Baruch to Igor, who stank of dill. Beside her snored Mr. Michaelson, leaking threads of drool from the corners of his mouth. She was so glad to see him enjoy a good sleep, she didn't care how he looked. Jeremy sat four rows behind them and pushed up his hair. He'd caused a sensation that morning by pinning his name tag to the zipper of his camouflage cutoffs.

"The last time we had such a *hamsin*, it was a few weeks after our War for Independence," said Baruch, his shirt unbuttoned down to his navel. He was always trying to impress her by careening around the edges of sheer cliffs or aiming their bus at fruit stands in picturesque stone alleys. "I was a boy, but I still remember everywhere there was shooting and crazy men with guns in their hands."

"Terrifying," she said as if she cared, but she'd heard so many *hamsin* stories by then, they blended together. She was surprised there was no commemorative T-shirt.

"That's only the start, my dear Shoshana." Baruch always called her Shoshana, Hebrew for Rose, though it wasn't her name. "In a *hamsin*, a man can get all turned around. Normal becomes crazy and crazy becomes normal."

Mrs. Michaelson had dreamed of exactly that kind of transformation for her son when she'd signed them up to visit Israel. No luck so far, and now they had only five days left before they returned home. She felt ashamed when she thought of how naïvely she'd pushed them all to come, and at such expense.

Their bus grunted uphill, slouching beneath a heraldic banner across Highway 1: Peugeot welcomed them to Jerusalem, Mrs. Michaelson's final, though perhaps best, hope. If Jeremy was going to find himself, where could be more fitting than the capital of the Jews' home turf?

———

Almost fifteen years earlier, Mrs. Michaelson had transferred her two boys to Jewish Day School after an economically and educationally challenged African American boy had punched Jeremy's older brother, Robert, in the jaw at recess. Robert went about religion in the same methodical, businesslike way he went about everything. Jeremy, however, decided at the tender age of six that he wanted to become a prophet. He'd dress up in a white beard and black robe and quote passages from his *Children's Bible* to point out the family's sins. For example, they washed milk and meat dishes in the same sink, and ate swordfish, which in infancy had scales like a kosher fish should but then lost its scales in adulthood. He began wearing a yarmulke to meals and then all the time. After his bar mitzvah, he attended an Orthodox shul and wore a wrinkled cotton shirt with fringes under his clothes. One Rosh Hashanah, he refused to ride in their Buick to her brother's house for dinner, because operating any type of machinery wasn't allowed during the High Holidays. There Mrs. Michaelson drew the line, calling on a higher authority:

"My mother, may she rest in peace, used to ride in this very car on Rosh Hashanah, and so will you."

But then in high school Jeremy slipped off track, very far off track, and you didn't have to be a prophet to figure that one out.

He ditched the Orthodox synagogue and the yarmulke. He ate cheeseburgers and then pepperoni pizza. On weekends, strange cars blasting shrieks and yowls on their stereos dropped him off on the Michaelsons' porch in the middle of the night. The clothes he wore became increasingly tattered and reeked of smoke.

The University of Michigan had been good enough for Robert, but Jeremy chose to attend NYU, where he'd been dropping classes and switching majors for five years now, with no degree in sight, and barely enough credits to qualify as a junior. After his first year, he came home with spiked hair. The next year, a hole appeared in his ear. Then came green hair and then another hole in his ear and then the hole in his nose.

He lectured her and Mr. Michaelson about migrant workers and animal rights. He boycotted Coke because they supported slavery in Africa. He became a vegetarian, though he occasionally indulged in bacon cheeseburgers. He said he was gay, like Robert, only Robert hadn't seen the need to carve a hole in his nose to become gay.

Two gay sons. How had she managed it?

So it hadn't been her first inkling of trouble when Jeremy's roommate called them in March, crying hysterically, "I never saw anyone passed out like that in my whole life!"

"It was a mistake, not an overdose," Jeremy informed her and Mr. Michaelson after the Catastrophe. They'd flown in from Michigan to pick him up from the hospital. In his apartment, he changed into a Che Guevara T-shirt that highlighted the red in his plaid boxers. Spread across his couch like a Roman emperor, Jeremy propped up his feet on the edge of his coffee table, sprinkled with stale fries from McDonald's, hard as pencils.

Mrs. Michaelson poked in the refrigerator and found a plastic tub of rancid hummus and an empty bottle of Estonian vodka with a bright orange sticker: 2 for $5! Then she stood in the middle of his living room and examined his bottle of Xanax. There was nowhere to sit except the couch, but Jeremy didn't offer to make room. He leafed through a book called *Anti-Gay*, with a pink target on the cover.

"This explains everything!" she said, and held up the bottle. "Your pharmacist made the mistake, not you. This prescription is made out to Christine Moore."

"You're not listening," he said, waving his long white hand. She marveled at how beautifully he kept his nails trimmed. Perfect, shining arcs. You could use them to sketch curves in a geometry class. "My shrink refused to renew my prescription unless I slept with him, so a friend gave me her extras to tide me over, for emergencies. I didn't realize how many I was taking, or that I wasn't supposed to mix them with alcohol."

Mr. Michaelson came back in from the bathroom with a roll of toilet paper, which he was using for tissues.

"Emergencies," she repeated, and looked to her husband, as if to say, "You handle him, Mr. Trained Expert Analyst. I just keep the books around here." When Mr. Michaelson had first gone into practice, he never seemed to earn anything, even though he'd collected a full weekly roster of appointments. Then she stopped by his office and examined the shameful state of his accounts. From that point on, she took charge of billing. Mr. Michaelson and his patients called her the Enforcer. She didn't care if they joked together behind her back (well, perhaps she did care a little), as long as they paid.

"Emergencies," Mr. Michaelson repeated.

Jeremy moved his legs to make room for Good Old Dad, who slapped his knee affectionately.

"If we promise to find this wayward boy a new therapist,"

said Mr. Michaelson, "a highly qualified *female* therapist, I'm sure he won't do anything like this again, will you, pal?"

"Of course not, Dadums," Jeremy said, like it was all a big joke she didn't get.

"Good boy." Head pat. A couple of quick shoulder squeezes.

Mrs. Michaelson was highly dissatisfied, and in April, two weeks past the deadline, she registered the three of them for the Millennium Marathon 2000. (Robert said that associates hoping to make junior partner in important law firms couldn't take three weeks of vacation simply because their mothers asked them to.) "I understand I'm a bit late," she told Rabbi Adler's secretary over a mug of soapy tea in the synagogue office, "but this is an emergency."

Why not Israel? Mrs. Michaelson and her husband (though mostly Mrs. Michaelson) had tried everything else: therapy, Toughlove, unconditional love, threats she never intended to fulfill, reasoned argument, spiritual counseling, heart-to-heart phone calls with Robert. No luck. Then she read a story in the *Detroit Jewish News* (to which she held a lifetime subscription) about young people who'd found themselves while on "Missions to Israel." She was inspired by the testimony of a twenty-two-year-old former anorexic and now University of Michigan graduate, Abby Finkel, climbing Masada for the first time:

One boy was praying. That was what his experience meant for him. One girl listened to Simon and Garfunkel on her Walkman and that was her experience. I just sat with my friend and we looked at each other and started crying. I'm not sure why. It was just so beautiful, I couldn't believe it.

Exactly, thought Mrs. Michaelson. These spontaneous outbursts of piety occurred as a result of a sensory overload, a natural high from all the deep whiffs of holy air and hot sand. After walking in the footsteps of his forefathers, her son would shed a tear or two, get a vague sense of his place in the universe, and then finish his bachelor's degree.

The word "Mission" reminded her of Audrey Hepburn giving up her life to kiss black babies in Africa in *The Nun's Story*. She was surprised to learn the Jewish version of the "Mission" required an almost similar level of commitment, what with all the meetings, the prayer services, the lectures, the private tours, and especially the voluntary donations she was expected to contribute. She also hadn't expected Missions to come in such a bewildering variety of flavors. There were Missions for teens, singles, humanists, families, even atheists (her husband's choice). Missions to end hunger, violence, homelessness, and deforestation. The Millennium Marathon 2000 appealed to her because it emphasized history over religious brainwashing. She wanted Jeremy to be a Jew, but his thoughts on God were his own business.

Mrs. Michaelson wiped away the fog on the bathroom mirror and let out a lazy sigh. " 'You are old, Father William,' " she quoted to herself, and pulled out her cheeks, lit up ghostly white by one of the Hilton's fluorescent bulbs. Israelis preferred cold harsh lighting, which exaggerated the few tiny folds in her brown skin, still soft after more than half a century. Her secret was simple: plain old Dial soap. And good genes. Her mother had passed away at ninety-three with barely a wrinkle.

Oddly, she sometimes imagined that her features weren't yet fully formed.

Mrs. Michaelson's digital watch, a travel present from Robert, beeped to announce the hour. It was still set to Michigan time, because she hadn't figured out how to change it. "9:00 AM" "9:00 AM," it flashed, which really meant "4:00 PM."

Robert, gay like Jeremy but not difficult, lived with a nice young Chinese man named Huang, who was very quiet and made a tasty puttanesca sauce. She'd never heard of puttanesca before.

"It means 'hole,' " Huang said, and at first she thought maybe he meant hell.

"Oh, because it's so spicy," she said, not meaning to shout, but she always felt as if Huang was a bit deaf because his English was so poor. "Spicy as hell!"

" 'Whore,' not 'hell,' " Robert explained, sounding annoyed. Like his mother, he was easily exasperated when things failed to run smoothly. "It's a sauce whores used to whip up for their johns in Italy."

So in Jerusalem it was four P.M., but what did "4:00 PM" mean? It meant they still had a few hours of Free Time before their reception at the Israel Museum. They would hear an address by Shimon Peres, famed dove and perennial losing candidate for prime minister until the Labor Party had dug up Barak. During the bus ride from Tel Aviv, Sherry Sherman had confided to Mrs. Michaelson that many Michiganders were butchering the pronunciation of Peres's name by putting the accent on the "Rez" and not the "Pear," as if he were Hispanic and not a Polish Jew. "I don't like to embarrass anyone by correcting him or her," Sherry had said loud enough for everyone on the bus to hear, "but someone ought to spread the word by this evening, for the sake of Mr. Peres's dignity."

Mrs. Michaelson left the bathroom and peeked in Jeremy's room, where her husband and son were laughing together like old friends. She wondered what the joke was, though she probably wouldn't have understood even if she'd heard; she never got their sense of humor.

Jeremy wore a purple tank top with POOT! printed in silver and was trying to bounce on his queen-size bed, but even with his shoes off, he was too tall to bounce. His dark head kept bumping against the ceiling.

Her husband sat in a padded chair with a biography of Jackie O on his chest. He lifted his I ♥ TEL AVIV baseball cap with his finger and beamed at her. His nose was streaked with sun cream; since getting sick, he'd been obsessed with protecting his skin.

Mrs. Michaelson clapped twice. "David, look at him! Why don't you say something?" she pleaded. "Down, Jeremy! Are you trying out for the circus? You know, if you break that bed, you're paying for it."

"You're no fun, Helen," Jeremy complained. " 'Life's a banquet and most poor suckers are starving to death!' " (Her favorite movie was *Auntie Mame* and he liked to quote it out of context to torment her.) " 'Live! Live! Live!' " Still, he stopped bouncing and sat down properly. Apart from the mussed bedcovers, his room was in perfect order, right down to his shirts and underwear, folded neatly inside his chest of drawers. Mrs. Michaelson knew because she'd checked the drawers earlier for contraband and found nothing out of the ordinary except the latest copy of *Martha Stewart Living* and a note in Jeremy's frantic scrawl: *"To Helen: I know what you've been doing this summer!"*

They waited for a bit of wisdom from her. She felt as if she were suffocating.

"So what do you feel like doing?" she asked out of desperation.

"Why don't we take a break from being tourists for one afternoon and see something real?" Jeremy said.

"Could you be more specific?" asked Mr. Michaelson.

"I don't know. How about a nice opium den?"

"What about the Wall?" said Mrs. Michaelson, cutting off this dangerous line of conversation. Jeremy groaned, protesting that the Wall was a reconstruction from Roman times that had no actual religious significance, but she proclaimed with a grand wave of her hand: "The Wall it is. Does everyone have his water bottle?"

They sought guidance at the front desk, where the help, clad in green polyester, tripped over one another to answer phones that buzzed instead of ringing. A clerk with a British accent tried to mediate between two bickering families who'd been promised the same room, while the latest Mission-load of tourists flooded the lobby. African and Romanian bellhops argued in English over the right to cart their luggage onto brass trolleys.

As Mrs. Michaelson rapped on the front desk, her husband calmly fanned himself with a brochure about the Holocaust memorial at Yad Vashem. Jeremy studied the menu of the hotel restaurant, salivating over the wine list, no doubt. Thankfully, he'd changed his safety pin for a subtle diamond stud, perhaps in honor of the Wall.

She rapped on the desk again, her gold bracelet clanking against the marbleized countertop. "Can we get some help?" she inquired in an impossibly high voice. One of the boys stared dumbfounded at his computer screen and typed for dear life. His shirt was too tight, and the fat knot of his green polyester tie had slipped a good three inches below his open collar. A tuft of chest hair had sprung up through the gap.

Mrs. Michaelson reminded the boy they weren't paying 250

smackers a night to be ignored. Could They Get Some Decent Service Around Here?

"That sounds expensive," said Mrs. Michaelson when he recommended a taxi. "Is there a bus?" But it was too far for the bus, especially in such heat. So the three Michaelsons jammed themselves into the back of a white taxi. As they sped out of the gravel driveway, she glanced back toward their hotel, a tower of cement and glass that stuck out like a middle finger in a field of lumpy dried earth, bulldozers, and cranes.

The taxi was a Mercedes, like most taxis in Israel. Their driver, who had a velvet yarmulke and a stringy black beard, sucked the meat out of a smoked fish with the skin still on. A plastic dog on the dashboard bobbed its loose head at the traffic. When the driver slammed on the brake, the dog's head shot forward into the windshield.

"How do you like this weather we're having?" the driver said in a Brooklyn accent. He reached for the plastic head and set it back onto the dog's neck.

The CB radio up front crackled so frantically in Hebrew, it sounded like Arabic. The A/C was broken, so they rolled down all the windows. At least while they were moving, gusts of warm air relieved the heat that greased their foreheads and the backs of their thighs. Mrs. Michaelson let her elbow hang lazily over the open window and stared at the furry curve of a brown hill in the distance, like the back of a camel. At times like these, her heart sped up like a girl's and she felt especially sensitive to the romance of a trip to Asia. She should have traveled more. Why hadn't she?

The taxi screeched to a stop at a red light, and the dog's head hit the windshield again. Mr. Michaelson blew his nose like a French horn. "I've got more Kleenex in my purse," Mrs. Michaelson reminded him. She also had three different kinds of over-the-counter pain relievers, orange bottles of prescription pills that rattled like castanets, wrinkled tubes of ointment, foil packets of moist towelettes, and a bottle of suntan lotion. Her husband's illness had transformed her into a walking medicine chest.

On the side of the road, young women in baseball caps and long denim shirts screamed out slogans under a white banner and showered passersby with leaflets. Their long-sleeved shirts were printed with the same Hebrew words as the banner.

The cabdriver tossed the skin of his fish into the road and honked at the girls, whose faces were as white as their flyers.

"What does it say?" Mrs. Michaelson asked, leaning forward to make out the banner. "Jeremy, help us out here with your expertise."

"I don't remember my Hebrew anymore," Jeremy said. He sat wedged on the hump between his parents, even though he was tallest. His thin, sharp knees poked into the vinyl seats up front. "My new shrink wants me to let go of the past."

What "past" could a twenty-two-year-old possibly have, except for the abuses she'd committed, since her husband, being an analyst himself, was too innocent to blame? Oh, that new female therapist of his with the short skirts and the sexy smoker's voice—she and Jeremy were in league against mothers; that much was clear.

Fine, Mrs. Michaelson thought. I'll figure it out myself. She stared again at the Hebrew letters to bring them into focus. "B-R-K. Barak. Something about Barak."

Jeremy finally spoke up. "The sign says, 'Barak is losing the State!' "

The light changed. Their car lunged forward.

"You're cutting off the circulation in my leg," Jeremy complained.

"What do you want me to do?" asked Mrs. Michaelson. "Jump out?"

"That'd be a start."

Now they were stuck again, behind a sluggish Mercedes truck spewing hot clouds of poisonous gas that smelled like tar and made them gasp for air. Suddenly they lurched to the left, passing a tour bus, a compact car with a blue Palestinian license plate, and a moped, all competing for the same lane.

The cars on the road were mostly small, white, Japanese, and covered in dust. Their licenses were narrow yellow rectangles surrounded by bumper stickers: "Stay back!"; "Peace Now!"; "The nation WITH the Golan" (which made a pun in Hebrew); "Shalom, Haver," or "Good-bye, Friend," a tribute to the slain Yitzhak Rabin.

"Shortcut," said their driver, holding the dog's head in place as he turned sharply at a restaurant called Taco Taco Tex-Mex. Across the street was a modern sculpture garden with a giant revolving metal screw and water running over it. The sidewalks were crowded with shoppers stocking up before the stores closed at nightfall for Shabbat.

The driver pointed out an old prison from the time of the British Mandate, now a museum of the Jewish resistance. Menachem Begin had done time there. "What do you Americans think of this Camp David?" said the taxi driver. "Can Barak get us out of this mess?"

"No opinion," Mr. Michaelson replied with a calm, contented smile.

"Americans never have opinions," the driver replied. "Israelis, on the other hand, are like the desert fruit sabra. You know what it is, a sabra?"

Mrs. Michaelson knew. She'd heard the sabra story so many

times she could tell it herself, but that never stopped Israelis from telling it.

"A sabra, it's the fruit of a cactus. Outside it's all thorns. But inside it's soft and sweet. Americans, they're all soft, like rotten plums. That's why I had to move." He turned again, and just when Mrs. Michaelson was thinking their ride would never end, the Old City walls appeared dead ahead, shorter than she'd imagined, dwarfed by two mid-size cranes. The moon hung above it all, visible in the pale blue afternoon sky.

So this was the Jerusalem she'd heard about for so long: squat, brown, and dirty.

"Wasn't that a quick ride?" remarked Mrs. Michaelson, thinking, *Someone else please speak.* She hated chitchat but felt obliged to cut into all silences with something, anything. Even as a girl, she'd never known how to talk to people. Faced with the choice of her parents' Yiddish or her schoolmates' English, Mrs. Michaelson had chosen to remain silent until age six. Even as a teenager, she was often flummoxed by new slang idioms and had to ask her older brothers for translations.

As the road curved around the Old City walls, the landscape on their right fell sharply into a deep green basin scattered with white rocks. "I'm surprised the grass doesn't burn in this heat," she said, and tapped the driver's shoulder. "Do you know the name of that pretty green valley?"

"Hell," said the driver without turning his head.

"Don't bother him, Mom," Jeremy said. So he was capable of calling her Mom after all.

But the taxi driver didn't seem a bit bothered. "This valley, it's where the geographical position of hell is supposed to be," he explained cheerfully. "The archaeologists figured it out from the Torah. When the children of Israel cleaned all the idols from their Temple, they dumped them into this valley. And like magic, they disappeared. Someday, that's where we'll throw the Dome of the Rock, too."

He swerved to avoid a backpacker crossing the road. Two Gypsy women languished noisily on the curb, by the backpacker's feet.

"Oh," said Mrs. Michaelson with what she hoped sounded like a laugh. She supposed she should have thanked him for the story, but she didn't.

———

The headline in Saturday's *International Herald Tribune:*

CAN BARAK SURVIVE?
ON EVE OF CAMP DAVID II, EMBATTLED PM ASKS
KNESSET TO CHOOSE BETWEEN WAR AND PEACE

The headline of the weekend edition of the *Millennium Marathon Daily Bulletin* (photocopied on blue paper instead of the usual goldenrod):

SHABBAT! COMMANDMENT OR OPPORTUNITIES?

Mrs. Michaelson had become so used to reading about the world in headlines, she'd thought up a couple of her own:

TOURISTS OVERCHARGED FOR TAXI RIDE TO WALL
EXTRA 14 SHEKELS VIEWED AS
"REDISTRIBUTION OF WEALTH"

DETAILED WEATHER FORECAST
SAVE YOURSELF THE TROUBLE OF STRAINING YOUR EYES
IT'S HOT TODAY AND IT'LL BE HOTTER TOMORROW

She bought a bottle of water and joined her husband and son among the tourists pressing against the metal detectors in the hope of getting to get to the Wall before sunset. Only after taking a deep, cool drink of water did she notice the gaudy pink label: JERICHO WATER, FROM PALESTINE. Rabbi Sherman had warned them against Jericho Water, because the proceeds lined the pockets of Yasir Arafat, who was pretty much the same thing as evil. However, Aliza, their rabbinic intern, had warned them to avoid the Waters of Paradise brand, because it was owned by extremist settlers from the Golan Heights, which Israel was supposed to trade to Syria for peace.

The only solution was to buy your water from somewhere neutral. But where would that be? France?

It was too late to take the water back, so she offered Jeremy some. He gulped down half the bottle before choking and spluttering all over their neighbors in line. "Behave," she said, slapping his back, hard.

The tourists plucked uselessly at their sweat-stained shirts and blouses as they waited to get closer to the inspection tables. A pink-faced Orthodox man in a pinstriped suit shook a coffee can of change at Mrs. Michaelson, who quickly turned her head. Jeremy, however, pulled the man over to contribute a few shekels. In return, the man tied a length of red thread around Jeremy's wrist to ward off the evil eye.

"It says in the Talmud, poverty reflects on Israel like a red ribbon on a white horse," the man said in an Eastern European accent before scurrying away.

"What a perfectly adorable accessory," Jeremy said, modeling the bracelet with an exaggeratedly limp wrist.

Suddenly the olive-clad guards hurried the Michaelsons and all the other Jews through the metal detectors. Jeremy was fiddling with the diamond stud in his nose to throw it into a basket with their loose change, but a guard said, no, the machine didn't pick up nose rings. On the other side, a bald man in glasses said he was going to sue the Israeli government for incompetence if the X-rays damaged one frame of his Masada photos. "You pushed me through!" he cried. "I didn't have a chance to explain!"

The tourists reunited in little pools beside a fleet of white police vans. A group of Israeli teens lay stretched out on the slippery pink Jerusalem stone as if it were a beach in Tel Aviv and jerked their heads in time with their portable CD players. The boys wore basketball jerseys while the girls wore the shortest of short shorts to show off their legs. A frizzy redhead with a scuffed rifle stood watch over them.

The rifle made Mrs. Michaelson nervous, though she knew the law required all tour guides to carry guns, even the ones working for the Millennium Marathon. Occasionally, the Michiganders borrowed their guides' sidepieces as photo props and pretended to shoot one another. Mrs. Michaelson couldn't look. Just the idea that she might brush against a gun was enough to make her feel a real bullet rip through skin, peel back fat and cartilage so the blood spurted out. How could anyone stand to pull the trigger? She imagined it as cold, probably very stiff, and she hoped it was a difficult thing to pull.

Hemmed in by the tightly packed stone buildings of the Old City, the glowing pink plaza was an oasis of light, space, and air rushing up to the craggy limestone Wall, a high orange-gold cliff crowned by a pine grove and a pair of domes. At the top of the Wall, the smaller stones were crowded together like eggs in a nest. Straggly green brush drooped like whiskers out of the middle layers, while at the bottom, worshippers in black huddled against the massive golden blocks, each one as wide as a truck.

"You see so many pictures of the Wall," said Mr. Michaelson. "When you see the real thing, it looks like another picture." He pointed at the domes above, the big one the color of
brass, the smaller a dull silver. "You think they ever throw rocks
down at us?"

"They wouldn't dare," said Mrs. Michaelson with a wary
glance upward.

They were forced to split up by sex at a black chain-link
fence capped with small five-pronged menorahs. Men without
head coverings got cardboard yarmulkes. Women got nothing.
A cluster of young Orthodox maidens chatted excitedly next to
the washing basin by the entrance, where a guard inspected
them to make sure they were properly dressed. A line of white
screens cut off the women's space from the men's, which Mrs.
Michaelson couldn't help noticing was two thirds larger. Was a
man's devotion worth two thirds more than a woman's? Instead
of protesting, the women in hats stood on tiptoe along the edge
of the screens to watch the men move their lips and rock on
their toes with their eyes closed. Mrs. Michaelson stood on tiptoe and looked, too.

The men in cardboard yarmulkes and baseball caps clasped
their hands behind their backs and tried to look pious. The men
in black velvet hats squeezed between the tourists to set out
plastic chairs and black books for the Sabbath prayers.

Mrs. Michaelson ran her fingers over the pink and white notes
crumpled up like wads of chewing gum and stuffed into the
cracks in the Wall. Up close, the stones were striated in a rainbow of desert tones: white, gray, yellow, dark brown, and rust.
She took out a pen and her small notepad for making lists and
imagined the note she might have written. *Dear God, please let*

my son know You are real so he won't die. That sounded silly. She'd never been good with words.

A woman threw herself against the Wall and cried. This is all very moving, Mrs. Michaelson told herself, but she was thinking about her aching bunions. Impatient to feel inspired, she kissed the Wall, caressed the coarse stone blocks. She felt no God there, but then she'd never felt Him anywhere else, either, not even in her heart. Did He exist, then? Of course He did. It didn't matter that you couldn't pick Him out of a lineup.

So Mrs. Michaelson turned around and left. As soon as she was past the chains dividing the sacred and profane spaces of the plaza, she tore off the damp cotton scarf covering her hair and balled it up in her aching fist. Mrs. Michaelson kept a scarf in her purse at all times. There were so many holy places in this country; you never knew when you'd need to make a show of modesty that you didn't feel.

She'd read the arguments of prophets and great thinkers like Rashi and Maimonides, but they'd made little impression on her, because they were only words printed in books, black ink marks meant to stand in for life. In regard to theological questions, she'd always deferred to the wisdom of her parents, who were unarguably the real thing. They'd come from the Old Country, the land of pogroms and goose fat. Her father had studied at a genuine *cheder*, where he'd been whipped for forgetting his lessons and rewarded with spoonfuls of honey for remembering them. Her mother was the daughter of a famed Polish rabbi who'd been mowed down by Nazis. Their shtetl was the kind of place the Orthodox, these funny trolls in black hats, labored to imitate.

Her parents, however, had adapted to modern times. They joined a synagogue where men and women wore modern clothes and sat together. Her older brothers helped their father in his grocery store after school instead of going to Hebrew lessons, until the year before their bar mitzvahs, when her parents hired a private tutor. The tutor didn't wear his yarmulke outside of synagogue. Instead, he wore purple and maroon ties that matched his handkerchief and patterned socks.

Girls didn't have bat mitzvahs in those days, so Mrs. Michaelson got her Jewish education in the kitchen, where her mother separated milk and kosher meat and kept Passover dishes in the cupboard over the icebox. When her mother became too old to host the seders, Mrs. Michaelson took over, slicing hard-boiled eggs in bowls of salted water and doling out gefilte fish onto a tray of potatoes simmered in the oily water left over from the fish. Now that her mother had passed into the next world, Mrs. Michaelson continued to stuff the fish heads with flour, celery, and onions just as her mother had shown her, though no one ate them anymore except her older brothers.

The Orthodox wouldn't find any of this precious information in their Talmud, or even the Torah. You had to live it to know it.

———

Mrs. Michaelson, who was supposed to have met her husband and son five minutes ago, cut swiftly through the crowds now filling the plaza. Where had all this time escaped to, these minutes that lapsed while she stood there dreaming? She was getting worse with age, constantly drifting because of an image, a smell, a phrase of music. One minute she was packing sandwiches in brown bags for an eccentric little boy in a yarmulke to take to school and the next that same boy was passed out in some hospital going through an actual OD. Like on *Law & Order*.

She finally made it to their designated meeting point, a

stone bench at the back of the Wall plaza, but there was no sign of Jeremy or her husband.

"After I rushed all the way back here," she complained aloud, out of habit, then looked around to make sure no one had noticed her talking to herself.

Where were they? She couldn't trust either of those boys with the tiniest responsibility.

The air was warm and sticky; Mrs. Michaelson felt as if she were breathing through gauze. She folded up her free map of Jerusalem, a gift from Stern's Jewelry, and fanned herself. Now, there was a new way to divide things, she thought. Just fold up the map and voilà—new borders!

Finally, Mr. Michaelson came limping over, sucking on a half-liter bottle of water. He dribbled a bit to cool his chin and neck, and his back was hunched over like an old man's. His face had such a strange, haunted expression; he looked as if he had become an old man since the last time she'd seen him.

"Where's Jeremy?" she asked as her husband sank down next to her and took off his cap, soaked at the rim. His fingers were yellow when they should have been high pink from the sun. He tended to burn, while she turned a handsome brown. I shouldn't have brought him here, she thought. This trip's been too much for him.

"Not coming," he said, breathing through his mouth. "Made a friend."

"He made a friend? What friend?"

"A rabbi." He took another breath, then added, "With a hat."

"A rabbi?" she repeated, knocking over her purse. "Don't you know these so-called rabbis look for lost boys and trap them? Sandy Rothstein's son, the pothead, he met a rabbi here and now he lives in some compound outside Jerusalem and studies with his guru all day. He has two kids, with another on the way." She picked up her purse and dusted it off. "Sandy didn't say so, but I get the sense she sends them money."

"Sandy always exaggerates," Mr. Michaelson said. "Jeremy can take care of himself."

"You're only saying that because you're too tired to go after him."

He coughed. "Well, I am tired. And dizzy. I've done too much today."

His motto for the whole darn trip, she thought. What a mistake this vacation had been. And now, after all her caution, Jeremy was lost. She thought about going after Jeremy herself, but she was tired too.

Two gay sons. How had she deserved this?

The shadows lengthened over the plaza, which was slowly cooling after the day's grilling. Her husband touched her elbow and she let him. There was no point in getting angry. They stared at the Wall until he started coughing again and spitting up mucus into a handkerchief. That hack, hack, hack of those pounding coughs echoing from deep within his chest frightened her. A young soldier stared at them as he picked his teeth.

Guns and more guns, and all this heat—that's how she'd remember Israel.

"Well, we made it," she said when her husband finished coughing.

He looked at her as if she were a child. "Do you really think so?"

"Of course! There's only four and a half days left."

"That wasn't what I meant." Mr. Michaelson wiped his hands on his shorts and cleared his throat. "So, has this experience been a meaningful one for you?" His voice cracked. "I mean, spiritually?" She could tell he didn't mean it as a joke, though sometimes even when he meant to be serious he came off as if he were joking.

Mrs. Michaelson felt at a loss, having to speak to him from her heart. "Yeeeaaah," she said slowly, forcing out the word. "But I felt more moved looking at all those beautiful paintings in Tzfat." She couldn't think of the words, so she moved her hands as if she could pull the meaning out of the stifling air. "It was so . . . It was very quiet up there in the hills. And all those artists."

His cheeks looked pale and ashy, and the rash under his right eye was inflamed. Could he tell she was worried about him? To throw him off the path, she said in a satisfied voice, as if she'd just seen a good movie, "This whole trip was a moving experience I'll always remember."

"You know, I don't think you were ever infatuated with me," he said suddenly. "We never had that kind of feeling for each other."

Mrs. Michaelson looked at him as if he were a stranger. "What do you mean?"

"I'm just making an observation."

"Well, I'm not sure what I'm supposed to say to that."

"You don't have to say anything," he said. She felt she ought to speak anyway, but she wasn't up to making the effort. Finally he stood up and reached for her hand, but only because he needed her help to keep his balance.

two

HAVE YOU EVER HEARD HOW THE WESTERN WALL WAS BUILT?
From *Jewish Heroes for Children*

In the days of Zerubbabel, King Cyrus of Persia permitted the Jews to return to Jerusalem and rebuild their Temple.

The Northern Wall was paid for by Cyrus himself.

The Southern Wall was paid for by the priests, who stood in their rich apparel with trumpets and cymbals and gave thanks.

The Eastern Wall was paid for by the wealthiest Jews of the Persian Empire, who collected 61,000 gold drachmas and 5,000 minas of silver to trade with the people of Sidon and Tyre for cedar logs from Lebanon.

The Western Wall was left for the women and the old men, the ignorant and the poor, the children and the impure, all with nothing to offer but their unskilled hands. These castoffs gathered at the base of the Temple Mount and began to pile stones, one atop another. The other Jews mocked their meager handiwork. "Whatever they build, if even a fox goes up on it, it will fall into rubbish," they laughed.

Several centuries later, when Titus and his Roman legions attacked the Second Temple, angels descended from on high and spread their wings over **the Western Wall**. It alone was preserved from destruction, as foretold by King David in a verse from Psalms: "The stone the builders overlooked became the cornerstone."

Ah, love!

Jeremy didn't know where it came from, this overwhelming thirst to feel love and be loved, but he suspected it had to do with some mistake his parents had made.

At the men's section of the Wall, he'd been cut off from his mother and by default had ended up in the custody of his father, who at that moment was attempting to solve Jeremy like a riddle: "But *why* do you keep egging her on?"

Jeremy wasn't sure why. He'd been complaining for the past three weeks that he couldn't wait to get away from his mother and her spying. Now that he had, he felt lost, even sorry. "Because she doesn't know how to talk to people," he said.

Waiting to touch the Wall, they stood behind a funny old man in a black hat and robe who prayed with his arms spread out like wings. Next to him, a Japanese tourist with a black nylon yarmulke sliding over one ear grinned and flashed the thumbs-up sign for a camera.

Jeremy wore an Adidas baseball cap instead of a yarmulke. When they'd landed in Rome, the cap had been blue, but now, three weeks later, the sun had bleached it pink.

"She doesn't know how to talk to people," his father repeated. "Can you be a bit more specific?"

Poor David, Jeremy thought. You're always trying so hard to be friends, when what I need is a father. "Helen's problem is that she isn't honest," he said. "Not that she's dishonest, but she doesn't reveal herself. Even to you. How does she feel about you? Do you know? Was she ever infatuated with you?"

"Infatuated?" repeated Mr. Michaelson as if he were interviewing a client. "Could you talk a bit more about what you mean by that word?"

The funny old Hasid at the Wall finally finished his prayers and turned to leave, but now he didn't look funny or old. He was Jeremy's age and fairly cute. True, his face was slightly lopsided, one of his cheeks higher than the other, but his skin was unusually white and fine for someone who lived in a desert. His nose was firm, his eyes thoughtful, his lips full, fat, and tempting.

The Hasid caught Jeremy's eye and smiled shyly, as if in apology. He likes me, Jeremy thought. In a New York bar, he wouldn't have bothered to make eye contact with me, but here at the Wall, we're equals.

"My therapist says you and Helen aren't in a relationship of equals," Jeremy said as the Hasid dipped into the crowd, his black hat balanced on top of his hair like a boat. Now I've blown my big chance, he thought, not just to bang a Hasid, but also to find love and live a happy, fulfilled life. I might as well end it all here, right?

Recently, as Jeremy had been complaining as usual about his bad luck in love, his brother had quoted a wise old Jewish proverb (was there any other kind, in Robert's universe?): "If you smell bad cheese everywhere you go, check your pockets." As if it were Jeremy's fault that all men were pigs. But just in case Robert was right, Jeremy had taken a temporary vow of celibacy, with his therapist's approval.

"A relationship of equals. Like Robert and Huang?" asked his father, trying to trap Jeremy into saying something nice about Robert and his Chinese sex slave.

"Why don't we change the subject," said Jeremy.

David stepped forward and slapped the Wall like a newborn baby, but Jeremy just stood and stared. In kindergarten he'd drawn pictures of this same wall with pink and yellow crayons. In the second grade, he'd sung an ode to this wall in Hebrew with his Torah class on Israel Independence Day. In fifth grade, he'd won an Israel bond in a trivia contest for naming the exact date when Israel had captured the Wall from the Jordanians in the 1967 war. But until now, he'd never wondered why the Wall had been built in the first place. Whom, exactly, had the Jews been trying to keep out, and why? Jeremy didn't believe in dividing one people from another except at concerts, when you paid extra to be on the main floor instead of the balconies, so you could get thrown around in a mosh pit by hot, rough men with big muscles.

"My parents never took me on vacation," said David. "The only vacation I ever went on was when we visited my uncle at Slippery Rock Beach."

Where you went fishing in Lake St. Clair and dipped your dog's tail in a can of paint. Yes, I know, thought Jeremy, finishing the story in his head while smiling for poor David, who enjoyed telling it again until he suddenly began coughing his guts out. "All this dust," he spluttered as Jeremy offered him Helen's bottle of Jericho Water and massaged his back. "But I still don't understand," he said after irrigating his throat, "what you meant before by 'infatuated.' "

More therapy talk. Keep repeating whatever your patient says until he trips over his words and reveals his hidden depths, until he falls under a hypnotic spell and tells you, no, he really didn't mean to kill himself, it was just a mistake, a bad night, a little too much fun . . . until he grabs you by the throat and throttles you to death. Poor David. He meant well, but after all those years of listening to nuts, he'd become one himself.

Glancing over his shoulder, Jeremy spotted the cute Hasid again, only a few feet away and talking with a young man wearing a rifle strapped over his shoulder like a purse. As he watched them, Jeremy felt a light stirring above his ribs. He yearned to tell the Hasid how much he admired him, how much they could mean to each other if they met once or twice for coffee. A few evenings later, they could have dinner, after that maybe see a movie, and then and only then go to bed.

"Listen, I want to go check something," said Jeremy. "Will you be okay here?"

"Sure, sure," said Mr. Michaelson, smothering a cough.

"I'll be right back," Jeremy promised, and darted after the Hasid, who'd exchanged good-byes with his friend and was already losing himself in the crowd of black hats, where it was so difficult to tell them apart.

Chasing, always chasing, Jeremy thought as he picked his way between the true believers. I should be kissing that Wall right now and praying for my life, but instead I'll be chasing men until I die. (Which meant the sooner he died, the sooner this nightmare would end. Oh, very funny. You win the People's Choice Award for Black Comedy.) At home, he did his chasing in a bar called the Cock, popular with young men who believed gay culture was a capitalist fraud. They advertised their disdain by wearing outlandish outfits: plaid pants, ripped T-shirts with chains of safety pins, glittering Mardi Gras beads, green stripes painted in faux Mohawks. Generally Jeremy preferred to stalk the back room, where men undid their belts and zippers for anyone willing to play. He held out hope of meeting a prince who'd whisk him off to Vermont to build a comfy log cabin with solar and wind power, where they'd wear wool sweaters, live off the grid, and plant a self-sustaining farm. Or maybe he'd meet a Jewish brain surgeon with whom he'd waltz, arm in arm, into his cousins' weddings to show the world (his mother's world) that it was really true you could OD and still turn out as a success.

Sometimes he tried making conversation with the strangers who unzipped his pants in the back rooms, offered to buy them coffee. Few of these men expressed much interest in coffee, so he gave up on conversation and went back to playing as if he were out for vengeance. One night he blacked out in the back room, and when the lights came on, he found himself on the floor without a shirt, his pants around his ankles. "What is it?" he blurted out as the bartender kicked him awake. "Am I in heaven yet?"

To be fair, if Jeremy had met himself in the Cock, he wouldn't have gone out with himself for coffee, either. He had ugly feet—the wrong shape, and too narrow, like the rest of his body. His eyelashes were curled, his ears were creased, and he had a brown spot on his neck as well as three hairs growing on the back of his left hand. Then there was his nose, his greatest liability and asset. Blocky, thick, and proud, it carved a path all its own, a crooked Jewish path that earned him compliments like "You're a Jew, right? I guessed from the nose."

"I don't believe there is such a thing as a Jew or a Christian," Jeremy would say. "I'm just me." But sometimes he played along for handsome Nordic types with a Jew fetish, like Alex, the last man he'd had sex with before the accident. Alex was a construction worker who stripped in New Jersey on weeknights. They'd met in the back room of the Cock on the night Jeremy almost died; after a bit of fumbling around, they'd retired to Alex's apartment, where Alex showed off his private Judaica collection: silver menorahs, Torah pointers, and kiddush cups, wooden dreidels, a set of tefillin in a blue velvet pouch, even a small Torah. Alex loved all these things but didn't know what they meant, which was why Jeremy was so useful.

"How would you write my name in Hebrew?" Alex asked, and pushed away Jeremy's head, eagerly burrowing against his armpit for comfort.

Jeremy sat up and tucked in his shirt. " 'Alex' doesn't exist in Hebrew."

"Wait," said Alex, opening his pants. "I'm uncut. Ever seen one of these, Jew?"

I should storm out in a huff, Jeremy thought. Instead he sucked on the dick as if it were a pacifier. Later, at home, he watched *Moonstruck* and chewed giant scoops of ice cream sprinkled with M&M's, Xanax, and vodka. (None of his friends knew he owned *Moonstruck* or any other form of entertainment connected with Cher.) It was only two-thirty, still plenty of time to go out and try for someone else, but Jeremy didn't have the strength. He was too ugly, too fundamentally unlovable. He had the wrong kind of feet and eyelashes.

His roommate, an exchange student from Latvia who'd been assigned to him by the NYU housing office, found him passed out in front of a quivering blue screen.

What happened next he remembered mostly as a series of hands: Clumsy hands pinching his nose and pumping his chest. Firm hands anchored under his armpits and around his ankles. Smooth, rubbery hands cleaning his arm with alcohol and then piercing the skin. Warm, moist hands touching his forehead while a voice murmured, "Sleep now." His doctor's hands: gnarled, covered in wisps of hair. The hands of the detective who'd been kind enough to declare his overdose unintentional because suicide was a crime in New York State, smooth on top and cracked along the palms.

Jeremy's first reaction upon learning he'd overdosed was "Wow, just like Liza!" But even to himself, his wisecracks didn't seem as funny as they used to be. The inside of his chest felt cool and hollow, and he wished his mother would come in her Buick to pick him up, the way she used to when he puked in school. (It was part of the Michaelsons' religion to buy Buicks and not Oldsmobiles, to buy groceries at Farmer Jack, not A & P, and to read the *Detroit Free Press* rather than the *News*.) His mother did come to pick him up, but in a taxi, not a Buick, and then everything went back to awful.

One night he stayed up late watching VH-1 and saw a music video that inspired what he later described to his therapist as an epiphany. In the video, a girl dressed in a bumblebee costume went dancing around her neighborhood looking for friends, but everyone she met laughed at her. Finally the girl walked into a field of yellow flowers and found dozens of people dressed in bumblebee costumes. Overjoyed, the girl ran over and joined the other bumblebees dancing around like lunatics. "That's what I'm trying to figure out," Jeremy told his therapist. "Where are all the other bumblebees?"

Jeremy watched the good-looking Hasid drag a dolly stacked with folding chairs through the crowd of black hats pushing one another in front of the Wall. You were supposed to make a wish, scribble it on a piece of paper, and stick it between the stones so your wish would come true. Like when you blew out candles on a birthday cake. Jeremy didn't have any paper, so he made a silent wish for the Hasid to fall in love with him, to save him from a lifetime of misery and purposelessness. Such lips! Women paid thousands of dollars for lips like the ones this guy was lucky enough to have been born with.

Jeremy lit a cigarette and tilted his head to see around a towering, scrawny rabbi blocking his view. The rabbi, whose black raincoat was draped over his shoulders like a cape, stared down at Jeremy through square brown glasses that magnified his mournful blue eyes. His chapped lips gaped open, but Jeremy couldn't see his teeth, just a pink sliver of tongue in a black hole. He resembled those tacky portraits of Moses in the Jewish calendars that Jeremy's mother got free every year from her kosher butcher.

Jeremy tried to move to the side, but the rabbi held up his hand like a traffic cop. "Sorry, I'm not interested," Jeremy said, because whatever the old guy was offering, he wasn't interested. The rabbi scratched his thin, drawn cheeks, then clutched his black cape of death around his neck as he stopped another boy in a baseball cap. They spoke for a minute and then strolled together to a wooden booth where a fat man with a square brown wedge of beard handed out white booklets and black leather straps of tefillin. Jeremy remembered how those straps used to cut into his skin when he was fifteen and still believed in absurdities like divine justice. The fat man rolled up his sleeves and demonstrated how to wind the straps around his hairy arms. When one of his booklets fell to the ground, he picked it up and touched it to his lips like a napkin.

A white hand landed on Jeremy's shoulder. What luck! It belonged to the handsome Hasid he'd been chasing all this time. "You're Jewish? You want to join a service?" He wasn't that good-looking up close—his left eyebrow had a patch of white in it and he had a mole on his ear—but Jeremy didn't mind. In fact, he'd probably have given up on someone more godlike.

"Okay," Jeremy said happily. "If you really want me to."

Which was how he found himself trapped inside one of the prayer circles popping up everywhere in the men's section, each one spinning around a quaking old rabbi like a private hurricane. Jeremy wore a borrowed prayer shawl of yellowed silk that smelled as though it hadn't been washed in several years. One of the old men handed him the cutest little black book with tiny Hebrew letters and no English. Jeremy mouthed "Watermelon, watermelon," once or twice and occasionally threw in a good stock phrase he remembered from Day School to make a good show of it, something like "*oseh shalom bimromav*" (He who makes peace in His Heavens) or "*b'shanah ha' ba'ah b'yirushalayim!*" (Next year in Jerusalem!).

Jeremy had always liked the Bible, because it was full of losers who were bald or old or stupid or friendless but always seemed to have secret powers. And not because they were smarter or prettier, but because they believed more intensely than most people. He still missed saying "Next year in Jerusalem!" and feeling his heart thump at the thought that it might actually happen. Once, as a third grader, he'd felt so moved he'd covered his head with his prayer shawl during the school's morning service. The stunt earned him the nickname Ortho-Freak.

The school had its own Western Wall to pray next to, made of genuine Jerusalem stone. Unlike the original, it had been decorated in brass plates etched with donors' names. The biggest givers were at the top, and Jeremy used to imagine his and his wife's names up there, out of reach to all but the tallest twelfth graders. In those days, he'd believed that he'd been born to contribute to world history like his namesake, the doom-and-gloom prophet Jeremiah. Or even that other one, the one who'd so famously upset the moneychangers' tables in the Temple.

After services, the janitor would wheel the Holy Ark into a long closet sandwiched between the gym and the art room, which smelled of rubber dodge balls and dried ink. Some smart-ass had dubbed it the Gaza Strip. Boys used to go there to smoke tea leaves rolled in notebook paper before moving on to cigarettes. Jeremy hid there at recess and begged "G-d" to send down His Word, to choose him as His prophet.

No response.

Jeremy's first sexual experience had taken place in the Gaza Strip. A bully named Seth Glazer trapped him there during recess, shoved him against the Holy Ark, and undid Jeremy's zipper.

"Please let me live," Jeremy whimpered, his stomach trembling under Seth's prying fingers. He was sure he was going to be sick until one crazy moment when Seth jerked himself off on the clear plastic tarp veiling the Ark.

"Lick it off," he ordered Jeremy. "Like it's ice cream." And when it was over, Seth threatened to have Jeremy's family murdered if he told anyone. They avoided each other's eyes when they passed in the halls.

The encounter left Jeremy shaking but thrilled, and years later, in a New York hospital bed, he thought of the incident in a romantic light. They'd been gay teenagers together, he realized. If only they'd had some time to get to know each other, they could have become friends and fought off the forces of absolutism, capitalism, militarism, imperialism, racism, tribalism, nationalism, and majoritarianism side by side. After he'd been discharged, Jeremy looked up Seth on the Internet—Seth, who was now a grad student in Spanish at Emory University and had written a paper on Buñuel for some conference. A Spanish-speaking Jew in Atlanta.

Jeremy e-mailed Seth-the-grad-student: "Hey, I thought it'd be nice to hear from you."

No response.

The sinking sun burned a jagged gold line along the crests of the limestone buildings and satellite dishes above the Wall plaza. Down on earth, men in black moved their lips, beat their chests with sprigs of pine, and rocked on their toes. The man next to Jeremy tightened the strap of his rifle after the muzzle kept hitting him in the neck.

Jeremy stepped out of his sandals and massaged his feet against the warm stone. He'd lost his place in the tiny black prayer book, though no one seemed to care what he did. You needed ten Jewish men to start a service, but if the tenth stood there making up grocery lists in his head, it made no difference, as long as he stood there. Only Jeremy wasn't making up grocery lists. He was fanning his stomach with the hem of his POOT! tank top and thinking up lines to use on his Hasid, like "Can I hold your jacket?"

"I can't take off my jacket," the Hasid whispered in an accent that sounded like it wasn't from there. ("There" meant America as well as Israel.)

Jeremy, imagining the Hasid's damp white shirt sticking to his nipples, advised, "You really should think about taking it off. You'll asphyxiate in this heat."

The Hasid shook his head and went on praying. Jeremy tried dropping his book on purpose to see the Hasid bend over, but the other men glared so angrily, he forgot to notice when the Hasid picked up the book and handed it back to him.

"Kiss it," he demanded. Jeremy promptly obeyed, with such zeal that he grazed a forbidden centimeter of Hasidic finger with his lips.

Crowds of men pressed against the edge of their prayer circle like screaming fans rushing the barricades at a movie premiere. Jeremy, afraid of getting trampled, jabbed back at the men with his elbows.

The service reminded him of the Orthodox synagogue he used to attend as a teenager. In those days he still believed in his prophet potential, even if he'd begun to doubt that he had what it took to fulfill the commandment "Be fruitful and multiply." He'd had trouble finding other Jews who cared as deeply for the Law as he did and had chosen this congregation because it was the strictest sect that met close enough for him to walk to on Friday nights.

"Where are your mother and father?" barked the usher.

"They're hypocrites," said Jeremy. "They say they're Jews, but they don't keep all the laws."

"A young man should pray with his parents" was the reply. "Honor thy mother and father." But the old men allowed Jeremy to stand beside them, and he felt happy. Their rudeness was simply a form of initiation, required by the Jewish prohibition against evangelism. If he stuck it out long enough, they'd accept him. And sure enough, after a month of Fridays, the rabbi wished Jeremy Shabbat Shalom.

"Shabbat Shalom!" Jeremy chirped. At last, he'd found his place. He vowed to attend services every week for the rest of his life, to keep all the fasts, to wash, to dress, to eat, to pray as the Torah commanded. To marry a woman.

The rabbi made a funny face, then grabbed his left arm and fell down. Even when his cheeks turned blue, no one dared touch the phone, because it was Shabbat, and finally Jeremy had to call 911. "You're allowed to break the Law to save a life," he explained. But no one appreciated the lesson in Talmud from a fifteen-year-old, least of all the rabbi, who was beginning to revive a little.

"I took an extra nitroglycerine pill, that's all. You wasted your call," he said as the EMT men forced him into their ambulance. "You broke Shabbes for nothing."

Two heavy arms landed on Jeremy's shoulders. The men in his prayer circle formed a human chain like a line of Rockettes and sang, "Ya-di-di-dai!" Their braying voices swirled up to the twin mosques perched above the Wailing Wall.

"This way," Jeremy's Hasid called out, seconds before the chain jerked them along. They snaked through the worshipping Jews like a current through the ocean. Around they went, raising and lowering their arms, kicking and throwing their heads back and singing that meaningless "Ya-di-di-dai!" over and over. Black shoes kicked in every direction and narrowly missed Jeremy's nose once or twice.

"Ya-di-di-dai!" Jeremy crowed at the top of his lungs, and laughed as hard as he ever had in his life.

The Hasid let go of Jeremy's shoulders to hold on to his hat, which was sliding off his hair. Finally he staggered out of line. Jeremy fell out, too, and they collapsed on the stones along the chain fence, both men sweaty and laughing. The sun had sunk behind the ridge of Old City towers, but the air felt every bit as steamy.

"What's your name?" the Hasid asked, his face flushed pink.

"What's your name?" Jeremy panted, deeply in like.

"Gabriel." He pronounced it the feminine way. *Gabrielle.*

"Like the archangel," said Jeremy, and somehow "You remind me of an angel" slipped out before he could think. "Are you really an angel?" he added in an ironic voice to make it sound like a joke. You're self-destructing, he warned himself. Shut up, quick.

The Hasid raised an eyebrow. "You know about archangels? You've studied?"

"Studied what?"

Gabriel ignored the question, as if the answer were obvious. "Maybe you need someplace to stay? A nice Jewish home?" He had good teeth, very bright and straight.

"You mean your place?" Jeremy asked.

"I have no place here," Gabriel said. "I live in a dorm. I am from Mexico."

"I knew you were from somewhere." Such a stupid thing to say! Jeremy almost cried. The Hasid bent over and wiped his face with a handkerchief sewn to the inside of his pocket. "What is that, a magic trick?" Jeremy asked.

"We're not allowed to carry anything in our pockets on Shabbat," said Gabriel. "This way I'm not carrying anything." He stuffed the handkerchief back into his pocket. "Would you like to attend a Shabbat dinner? It's lonely to be Jewish with nowhere to go on Shabbat." Jeremy didn't answer immediately and Gabriel explained, "Shabbat, Shabbat. You understand? The Sabbath?"

"I know what it is." Jeremy imagined a dinner in the Old City, silver cups brimming with sugary kosher wine, the two of them perched on a windowsill over a cobblestone alley, kisses in a cool, quiet evening breeze. Like a movie. "You're really from Mexico?" Jeremy said. "You must be lonely here." Calm down, he thought. You don't need to fill every gap in the conversation with something dumb.

"I have no time to be lonely," Gabriel said in a calm, blank voice, like he was reciting a poem he'd memorized. "We are lonely when we constantly search for earthly pleasure, as in that fun-and-sun resort to the west called Tel Aviv. But earthly pleasures are fleeting by their nature, so we keep looking for more and more until we become depressed. That's why I fill my life with Torah. We must ask God what role do we have to play, and when He tells us, we must be ready to listen."

"I don't believe in God," Jeremy said, hoping God was listening.

"It's no matter," Gabriel replied. "He believes in you."

Jeremy was trying to think of a smart answer when he heard his father calling him from the other side of the black chain fence. "Wait," Jeremy told Gabriel. "I'll be right back."

"Time to go," said Mr. Michaelson, his cheeks flushed red as if they'd been stewed. "Your mother's waiting. We're late." He stared at Jeremy's chest. "I want you to know I was listening to what you said earlier, about your mother and me. I don't want you to think I don't listen to you."

"You've always been a good listener," said Jeremy, wishing his father wouldn't take everything he said so seriously. "Anyway, I'm not coming. I met this guy and we're having Shabbat dinner at his place. It's cool. He's like a rabbi or whatever."

"When are you coming home?" Mr. Michaelson asked.

How the hell should I know? Jeremy thought. "It depends. Just go ahead without me." But his father stood still. "Come on, David. I've been good this whole trip. And, yes, I know you don't believe in terms like 'good' or 'bad,' but you do believe in them anyway."

Before his father could say no (as if he were capable of such a thing), Jeremy ran back to Gabriel and plucked off his black hat, revealing a velvet yarmulke underneath. Nice hair, Jeremy thought. Plush and very dark. "You don't mind if I try this on," said Jeremy, replacing his baseball cap with Gabriel's hat. "How do I look?"

"Give me that," Gabriel said, but he was too slow to catch Jeremy, who ducked into the crowd. Rabbis and praying Jews scowled as he elbowed his way through a prayer circle. "Ya-di-di-dai!" How delightful! How profound! Out of breath from laughing, Jeremy almost tripped over a chain of Orthodox toddlers handcuffed to a laundry line and dressed in identical black vests and cone-shaped white caps. A Catholic priest in a khaki-colored shirt standing at the back explained in a German accent to his friend, "But that isn't how it works. You cannot pray to the Holy Father for fresh cakes."

Oh yes you can, Jeremy thought as he smacked into the giant rabbi clutching his cape-of-death raincoat tightly at the neck.

Gabriel yanked his hat off Jeremy's head. "Here is Rabbi Walzer," he said.

The rabbi's hat threw a shadow over his cheeks, dotted with moles which he kept scratching like pimples.

Jeremy fitted his baseball cap back onto his bare head and pulled his tank top over his hips like a dress. He didn't want to touch Rabbi Walzer, but Gabriel prodded his elbow. The rabbi's hand felt dry and webbed.

"Where are you staying?" asked the rabbi in a hoarse, whispery voice.

"The Hilton."

Rabbi Walzer pressed his long nails into his chapped bottom lip. "Hilton? It's expensive. We have a hostel here in the Old City. Heritage House. It's free. Save yourself a little money."

"He has nowhere to go for Shabbat dinner," said Gabriel. "Can we help him?"

"You think you would like to go for a Shabbat dinner?" asked the rabbi, gaping.

Jeremy looked at Gabriel, who was pinning his hat back onto the back of his hair with his careful, precise fingers. "Yes," said Jeremy.

"It can be arranged."

"How much?"

"Free, free, free. Everything is free, donated by local observant families. They volunteer to host Jewish boys visiting Israel for a Shabbat meal. It's my job to find such boys and then make the connections, like a matchmaker."

"Excuse me, friends," Gabriel said, and walked off.

"I want to go to his house," Jeremy said. Wait! Wait!

The rabbi scratched one of his moles. "It's not a restaurant. We don't take reservations. If you're interested, meet me by the washing fountains at eight-fifteen."

The sky ripened to the color of a plum. A shrill call to prayer from the Al-Aqsa Mosque floated down from the Temple

Mount to the Jews streaming to the Wailing Wall, now floodlit by fluorescent lamps. The air smelled musky, like the sweat of animals. The frenzied singing sounded like war cries, and the dancing looked like wrestling.

An old man with a black eye patch paced along the black chain fence and announced, "Five minutes to Shabbat. Then no more photos."

Jeremy stood on his toes to look for Gabriel and got elbowed in the stomach.

"Watch it!" he said. The departing offender, a teenager in a silver robe, didn't even bother to look back. "I hope you get hit by a terrorist," Jeremy yelled.

"Three minutes to Shabbat!" cried the man with the eye patch.

Jeremy leaned against the black chain fence and held his stomach. I've got to get out of here, he thought, but he had nowhere to go now that Gabriel had fucked him over. He supposed he should go back to the hotel, but he was enjoying his new freedom too much to go back. Still, he was starving. So then, what if he took up the old rabbi's offer of dinner? Maybe they'd send him to the same place as Gabriel.

"It is now Shabbat," announced the old man with the eye patch. "Cameras off!" A grubby-looking photographer in camouflage pants was still surreptitiously clicking away, but the old man put his hand over the lens. "Cameras *off*!"

Why not? Jeremy thought, and picked his way through the pushy crowd to the men's washing fountain, where he splashed his face with warm water. He'd read in his mother's copy of Fodor's about Jerusalem's chilly desert nights, but it was still boiling out and he was dripping as if he'd been dipped in a warm broth. He sniffed under his arms and splashed a little water there as well. It didn't help. I smell like a wet dog, he thought, and I feel like one too. He hoped Gabriel wouldn't notice.

A crowd of clean, cheerful young people, all eager for dinner, had gathered beside the fountain. The girls wore dresses and the boys wore yarmulkes with Jewish stars, Israeli and American flags intertwined, the Nike symbol, and the caption ISRAEL? JUST DO IT! A Brit with a knitted yarmulke bobby-pinned to his dirty-looking ponytail claimed he'd been surviving on these dinners for a year. He opened his backpack and showed off his Tupperware.

While the other Jews exchanged hostel and e-mail addresses, Jeremy fiddled with his nose ring and pretended to admire the Tupperware. A young woman in a flower-print dress asked him where he was from. Embarrassed by the attention, Jeremy didn't answer quickly enough, and she fluttered away to be introduced to someone's brother.

Her rejection means nothing, he told himself. Anyone else would have shrugged it off. His new therapist was now helping him realize the reason he had so much trouble making friends was that his mother had never taught him how to talk to people. How funny that all his life he'd believed the problem was he had nothing to say.

Even though Rabbi Walzer had said to arrive at eight-fifteen, it wasn't until nine that the old man finally showed up, clutching his cape of death and staring in watery-eyed awe at the purple sky. A short, chubby assistant trotted at his side like a toy dog, panting as he tried to keep up with his master's long scissor strides. The pair stopped a few feet ahead of the young people waiting to eat and whispered about them.

"Dave! Dave!" a few of the boys called out, but the shorter man, whose gleaming pink head was shaved smooth, held up his left hand for silence. He stood on tiptoe to match his ear with the rabbi's lips and then erupted with "Feldman!" He pointed to two young men, who came forward and bowed as they received a blue Post-it note. "Hey, there, Scott," he said. "How's your mother feeling? We said a *misheberach* for her tonight. Yonatan, nice to see you again. You tried that kosher frozen yogurt place I told you about last week? Did you order it with the crushed chocolate cookies on top? Do I ever steer you wrong? So listen, boys. We're sending you two to the Feldmans. Don't forget to eat hearty and say thank you. Capish? Enjoy it, guys."

"Schwartz!"

"Weiss!"

"Klein!"

"Gross!"

In this manner, several more young people were disposed of. "Morelli!"

The bald man pointed at Jeremy, just then craning his neck to see if Gabriel happened to be around, as well as a nice young heterosexual couple from South Africa.

"Morelli's not here yet. Listen for when I call out his name," the man told Jeremy, and entrusted him with the Post-it note. "I don't think we've met before. Call me Dave."

Jeremy nodded and stuffed the Post-it into his pocket. He noticed there wasn't a single hair left anywhere on Dave's skull. Even his eyebrows were shaved.

"Everything all right?" Dave asked, looking Jeremy up and down. "School? Family? No problems?"

"Yeah, yeah. Fine."

"Let me give you my card," said Dave. "I can set you up with tours, dinners, services—anything you need to make your stay *ba'aretz* more meaningful." He produced a card with a

rainbow, a telephone number, and DAVE SAPERSTEIN, JEWISH
YOUTH SERVICES, HURVA SQUARE. A hand-drawn map was
printed on the back.

"Do you know this guy called Gabriel?" Jeremy asked.

"Gabriel? Gabriel Levitsky the tennis player from Skokie, or
Gabe Friedman from Toronto? Sorry. Feel free to give me a ring
anytime you need anything, or if you just want to talk. I used to
be a young person myself once. Young and very confused. Now
I'm not so confused, but I still love to talk to young people. I
feed on their energy."

"You *what?*" Jeremy asked, but the nice young couple from
South Africa stepped between them. The man said something and
held out a clean pink hand for Jeremy to shake. He wore an Izod
shirt with a collar, pleated pants (*Pleated!* Jeremy thought in horror), and a knit yarmulke neatly bobby-pinned to a trim haircut.

"I said my name is Tom," repeated the young man.

"Hi, *Tom,*" said Jeremy.

His girlfriend, in a sack-shaped polka-dot dress, was named
Marla. She looked frightened when Jeremy held out his hand.

"I should have explained," said Tom with a smile. "In our tradition, men don't touch women unless they're family or married."

"Sorry," Jeremy said sheepishly, imagining what a lovely
couple they'd make when they got married, probably pouring
tea out of silver pots into china cups painted with delicate pink
roses that you could see through when you held them up to the
light. A husband with underwear and socks to wash and fold
and rub against your nose when you were horny, a husband to
buy you garnets and those ridiculous white roses with the tips
dyed fluorescent pink. A cottage by the sea. Prescriptions for
Valium. And one day they'd be blessed with a soft-skinned baby
who'd stink of milk and talcum, who'd cry himself to sleep in a
room where teddy bears and balloons floated on the ceiling.

What a life they had to look forward to: a prison of cribs, china, and dirty underwear. How horrible, and how desperately he wished it could happen to him.

His new therapist liked to say, "If you don't know what to say to someone, try asking a question." Easy advice, but what if you couldn't think of a question?

After racking his brain for an awkward minute, Jeremy asked, "Where are you staying?"

They were staying in this free hostel for Jews in the Old City. It was called Heritage House. Hadn't Jeremy heard of it?

"You two are from South Africa?" he said, stalling. "Do you miss home much?"

"We are home," Marla said. "All Jews are at home in Jerusalem."

Dave called out: "Morelli! Who has Morelli? Come on, guys. It's Shabbat here. I want to get home for my chicken and potatoes."

"Oh, that's us," said Jeremy, who ran over with his Post-it note.

"Listen, people! That's all we ask you to do around here." Raising his hairless eyebrows and shaking his head, Dave inspected Jeremy's Post-it, then pointed the three young people to their host, a fat unshaven man with his thumbs stuck into the waist of his shiny black pants.

"Only three?" Morelli asked. "I can take more if you want." His aw-shucks American accent reminded Jeremy of John Wayne's.

"I know you can, big fella. This guy's a prince," Dave said, slapping the prince on the shoulder. "No, no, we're good now."

"Thanks for, uh, inviting us over and all that," Jeremy said, pretending he was a polite person. "It's really . . . nice."

"Okey-dokey. Follow me, kids." Morelli swung his weight forward across the stones like a sailor with a wooden leg.

"Give me a call, Jeremy," said Dave, grabbing Jeremy's arm firmly so he couldn't get away. "I mean it. Even if you just want to check out the latest baseball scores on CNN or use the Internet. I'm always around."

"How fucking lovely," said Jeremy, and then jogged to catch up with the others.

Morelli was heaving himself up the steps leading out of the plaza. "We'll be leaving the Old City via the Arab Quarter tonight," he said. "Ever been there after dark?"

"Is it safe?" asked Marla.

"Plenty safe for us. They know better than to bother with Jews."

This speech didn't make Jeremy feel any safer, but he no longer believed that he had control over things like safety. Not since his doctors had told him that it was an honest-to-goodness miracle Jeremy had survived, that the price to pay for monkeying around with prescription meds was nothing short of his life.

And who said miracles didn't happen anymore?

The three "kids" followed Morelli and his curious stumping walk up the steps to the metal detectors. Two soldiers, one man and one woman, stood smoking by the X-ray machine and swatted the air as they talked about their weekend plans. The woman had tickets to the Radiohead concert in the ancient Roman amphitheater at Caesarea.

Inspired by the guards, Jeremy took out a cigarette.

Tom said, "I'm sorry, but it's not allowed to light fires on Shabbat."

"I don't want to light a fire," Jeremy said. "I want to light a cigarette." But he put the cigarette away.

"Are they allowed to operate metal detectors on Shabbat?" Marla said.

Morelli grinned. "We make everyone go through 'em, but

the machines get turned off every Friday night. Then God takes over."

"With a bit of help from the soldiers standing next to the machines," Jeremy said.

"God works through the soldiers," Morelli explained. "Hey, if we weren't God's people, the Arabs would have beaten us long ago, machines or no machines."

They exited the Jewish Quarter through an arch that led to the souk, the covered Arab market. A video camera was mounted to the old stone entrance, grown over with dried ivy. Tom nudged Marla, who turned her engagement ring around so the stone was hidden inside her palm.

The narrow road they were on, named Al-Wad, was a dark canyon lit faintly by tiny lights strung up like Christmas decorations on black wire along the market roof. The stalls sold T-shirts, wooden camels, blue-glass eyes for good luck, and silver five-fingered *hamsa*s dangling from red strings. The smell of honey blew off steaming metal pans of baklava. Dark, slim men danced expertly between boys who pushed wheelbarrows piled high with boxes of vegetables along the stepped cobblestones, which were littered with shredded ice-cream wrappers, urine-stained Arabic newspapers, crushed pita rinds, and empty bottles that rang like an alarm as they rolled between the feet of the Jewish trespassers on parade in their European robes and beards.

"American?" said an Arab boy, bumping into Tom. "Your Wall is that way!"

They were surrounded now by real Palestinians, sulking young men in heavy gold chains and oversize T-shirts printed with the names of American Jewish designers like Calvin Klein and Donna Karan. "Slaves to fashion," Tom said, but Jeremy found them handsome, with their dark brows and high, hollow cheekbones painted in shadows, their heavy necklaces and belt buckles glinting in the dark. They were much better looking than Gabriel, and probably more fun in bed.

Morelli waved to an Arab man he described as "one of my suppliers."

Three of the good-looking young men passed around a joint, and Jeremy stared into their eyes out of habit. Smoking pot in God's capital, Jeremy thought, impressed. He wished they'd offer him a toke.

One of the pot smokers tossed his chin at Jeremy and nudged his angry-looking friends. Jeremy turned away, too late, and heard them hooting. He looked back again, and they whistled and laughed, grabbing their crotches and baring their bright teeth.

Morelli pointed out an Israeli flag hanging from a window above. "That's Arik Sharon's apartment," Morelli said in his sandpapery voice. "He doesn't live there, of course. He just kind of hangs on to it."

Jeremy pretended to listen, but he felt the young men's eyes on his back. He wished their group could go faster, but they were caught in a mob of metal carts, donkeys, and shoppers inching toward the Damascus Gate, a high stone tower built during the time of the Crusaders. The top of the gate was crenellated like the battlement of a medieval castle, while its mouth, an elegantly attenuated arch, resembled the entrance to a Gothic cathedral. Religious Jews, tourists, and Arabs rubbed shoulders as they crammed into the dark, narrow opening. Inside, the rattle of a metal pastry cart echoed against the vaulted stone roof, charred with soot. Stray fingers pushed against Jeremy's pockets and brushed his bare arms. Everywhere he heard voices speaking a strange, nasal language he didn't know or care to learn.

When they finally popped out on the other side, Jeremy spotted Morelli and the South Africans at the top of a well of steps leading to the ring road that bounded the city walls. Arab women swathed in black rested on the steps next to their husbands and groceries while their children practiced aiming rocks at one another.

He'd made it halfway up the steps when the trio of pot smokers skipped ahead of him and blocked his path. They were even sexier in the light. One of them yelled something right in Jeremy's face, and his friends snickered. Jeremy tried to stand straight and look bored, but the boy knocked off his baseball cap. It landed at Jeremy's feet. Go ahead, do your worst, he thought, terrified and fascinated by their bad manners.

"Your hat, motherfucker," said the Arab teenager, pronouncing the word "muzzerfucker."

"Wow, you speak English."

"Wow, you speak English," the boy mimicked, and pushed him to the ground. Jeremy reached for his hat and the boy stepped on his hand.

"That's hot," Jeremy said, his nose a few inches away from the boy's white sock. It's a hazing ritual, he thought, an initiation. If I survive, they'll take me with them.

"What the fuck you say, nigga?"

But then Morelli came over and shooed the boys away with his plump pale hands. They ran away laughing, their terrible, beautiful white teeth set off sharply against their brown skin.

"Are you all right?" Marla asked as Jeremy, still shaking, dusted off his cap.

"Don't worry," said Tom with a smile on his kind face. "We're on your side."

That's just the trouble, Jeremy thought, staring forlornly after the handsome, snickering Arab bullies. I wish they'd let me be on their side.

three

THE OBEDIENT WIFE
A Palestinian Folktale

Two friends, Said and Ali, were comparing their wives.

"I beat my wife once every week to remind her who's in charge," said Ali.

"I never beat my wife," replied Said, "because she satisfies my every need."

Ali suggested an experiment. "Buy three *selahs* of fish and ask your wife to cook them for you and your guests. Before she can ask how you want her to prepare them, leave the house. When you come back, say her fish stinks, no matter how she cooks it. Then you will find a reason to beat her."

Said did just as his friend said. His wife was confused: How was she supposed to prepare the fish? So she cooked it three ways: fried, grilled, and simmered with rice.

When her husband returned with his friend, she immediately left her child on the chamber pot and ran to open the door. Then she brought out the three kinds of fish.

"Grilled?" Said exclaimed. "Grilled is for goats! And what's this, fried? I hate fried. Cooked with rice? What do I look like, an old Jew?" Said threw the plates against the wall. "No, no, this is shit! Why don't you give us shit to eat!" he screamed.

So his wife ran out of the room and brought back the child's chamber pot.

Ali said, "Truly, your wife deserves all the good in the world."

Meanwhile, Said apologized to his wife.

"I'm sure your vermilion would be lovely on a younger gal," Mrs. Michaelson had said while shopping for silk that spring in her favorite fabric store, a small shop off Nine Mile Road in Royal Oak. She prided herself on being able to make a dress for two hundred dollars that would have cost at least a thousand in a boutique.

Mrs. Michaelson wanted cool blues or greens, but the salesman, who dripped with gold and flowery scent, had brought out a bolt of vermilion red.

The red was an altogether different color from the dusty geranium shade she'd expected. This was a hot, thick Gypsy red, rich, like blood mixed in wine. The price per yard was ridiculous, even for such tempting silk that shifted like fire from red to brown to orange and blue under the lights and set off her eyes.

She treated herself to five yards, then shut herself up in her sewing room with a risky new pattern and set to work. A touch of her scissors was enough to split the delicate fabric into flowing planes, which she had to pin to tissue paper before running them through her machine. The silk slithered pleasantly through her fingers; sometimes she simply stroked the fabric for inspiration.

After weeks of measuring, tucking, folding, and inspecting

the results, it finally came time to trim the collar and hem of the finished dress with fine bright threads. She couldn't help grinning over the last few stitches, her spare pins clenched between her teeth.

Several months later, in the Jerusalem Hilton, her sheer, shimmering sleeves, slit along the sides, billowed as she put on her earrings in front of the bathroom mirror. She'd had the earrings made from antique cut-glass buttons, which she'd ordered from a special store in New York. They sparkled under the harsh lighting, and her cheeks lit up with reflected red glory.

Her husband barged into the bathroom without knocking, coughed up a mouthful of mucus into the sink, then gargled a glassful of tap water and kosher salt.

Wondering if her dress wasn't a bit flashy, Mrs. Michaelson considered toning it down with a scarf Jeremy had bought her on the ship. Blue and gold silk. "I can take it back," he'd said, looking embarrassed as she held it by her fingertips.

"No, no, it's beautiful," she told him, and he smiled shyly. This was how a mother and son should be. "You didn't have to spend your money on me," she said.

"It's David's money, not mine," said Jeremy, always a stickler for accuracy. "I don't have any money that isn't his."

Actually, you could argue it was her money. Since Mr. Michaelson had retired, they'd lived off her savvy stock investments. (Her strategy was simple: public utilities, telephones, and General Electric.) But this was hardly the place or time to quibble over details. "Didn't you pick out this scarf yourself?" she asked.

"Well, yeah," he said. "You could say that."

"So it still counts." Really, she thought, taking it out of her drawer while Mr. Michaelson coughed in the bathroom, it was a lovely scarf. The only reason she hadn't put it on before was that she'd never worn a scarf in her life and had no idea of the proper way to tie one. She experimented with a few different styles, but the scarf either came out uneven or else made her look like a Boy Scout. Finally, she stuffed it into her nightstand with Mr. Michaelson's extra meds.

She wondered what had made him accuse her of not being "infatuated" with him, which she pictured as a scene from the novel she was reading for a book club.

A suburb. The end of the twentieth century. A housewife and her husband take a moment to share a kiss. Time quivers like a diving board after a diver has leaped into an Olympic-size pool, then stands still.

That's how a young person writes, she thought, though she was unable to resist the cheap sentiment. A kiss could stop time. Wasn't it pretty to think so?

She'd been infatuated once, back when Eisenhower was finishing his second term and Doris Day was still a movie star. The object of her adoration was a New Yorker named Adam Levine. How exotic that used to sound to her, the way he pronounced the "vine" to rhyme with "ravine." They met in French class at the University of Michigan, while she was still an awkward freshman laboring to pronounce the word *droite*, as in *à droite* or *à la droite*.

"*Dwot!*" he said, smirking at her. "I just pretend the 'r' 's a 'w.' *Dwot!*"

Adam Levine wore natty cardigan sweaters and sculpted his hair with pomade. He listened to Hit Parade songs that she pretended to know. He ate modern foods like casseroles and breaded shrimp. Giving herself to Adam seemed like the modern thing to do, and she had come to college because she was tired of living in the shtetl with her parents. The first time happened in his narrow dorm room, their clothes half on, the bed still made. It began with several marvelous minutes of foreplay, fingers tweaking nipples, a thumb tracing the curve of her belly and occasionally the band of her underwear. The sex itself proved a disappointment, at least physically. "Can I?" he whispered, breaking off the touching of sensitive places that made her shiver. He then began three minutes of ramming and groaning with his eyes shut that made her feel beside the point. The best word she could think of for the experience was "surprising." Still, she liked it the same way she liked smoking, not for the activity itself so much as for the aura it gave her.

They engaged in four worldly bouts of sex before Adam patted her hand over coffee and said quite coolly, as if he hadn't *deflowered* her, "I know this nice fellow you might like. . . ." Palming off unwanted dates on your friends was one of the oldest tricks in the book, and yet, despite all her delusions of modernity, she was stunned by how carelessly he'd done it.

Once the humiliation wore off, she didn't miss Adam so much as his brittle BLT sandwiches, his charming French accent, and the lacy stubble on his chin that he called a goatee. With her eye for color and his knowledge of fine painters like Renoir, they might have made a sophisticated, worldly couple. They'd have joined the Detroit Institute of Arts and the symphony. They'd have exchanged endearments in French.

The "nice fellow" Adam thought she might like, a quiet, wispy young man named Michaelson, took her for malteds on their first date. It turned out he and Adam weren't even friends, only study partners in biochemistry. Michaelson was thin and long, with a kind of beauty that reminded her of the El Greco paintings she'd studied in art history class. At first he was content to sip his vanilla malt beside her in silence. Then he began talking about psychoanalysis and she couldn't shut him up. She didn't want to, because she was fascinated with the idea that her parents were to blame for everything.

Mr. Michaelson never officially asked her to marry him. After their fifth date, he simply talked about "*when* we get married," and it seemed easiest to go along. He was a much more restrained suitor than Adam Levine, except when it came to smoking, which he insisted she give up. (It wasn't much of a sacrifice; she'd never liked the smell of smoke on her clothes.) In turn, she demanded that they keep a kosher kitchen.

His parents lived farther from the Detroit River than hers, in a neighborhood of Jews who'd been in America fifty years instead of thirty. They were kind to her but distant. His mother had her over for dinner and spent the evening describing her various illnesses, which had confounded the best doctors in Detroit. "We ordered a kosher rib roast just for you, dear," she said as the maid brought in a tray of shrimp cocktail served on china plates from Holland. His father, who came in late as well as a bit drunk, kept forgetting her name but smiled a lot.

After Mr. Michaelson finished med school and his training, she realized her fantasy of a home where a wife baked tarts instead of noodle kugel, where parents rewarded their children with positive reinforcement and not a *patch on der tuchus*, where a black maid pulled elastic-lined sheets taut and folded department-store towels evenly so that if Adam Levine should ever come to visit and happen to inspect the linen closet, he'd find everything in order.

But Adam Levine never did inspect the closet. He moved back to New York for med school, and disappeared. And though her resentment of her parents and their ways transformed into an almost religious reverence for their commonsense wisdom as she approached middle age, they never quite forgot her youthful lapse of faith. Now they were gone and she'd ended up with two gay sons and a sick husband who out of the blue alleged she wasn't "infatuated."

She often considered herself a victim of history. It was too bad she'd had her first lover in the wrong decade. If she'd been born even a year later, she'd have begun college in 1960, not 1959. Maybe she could have ended up as a flower child of the rollicking sixties, when she might have applied the same zeal with which she'd kept house to sampling a string of beaux and throwing them away.

Still, her life hadn't been a tragedy, only a bit quiet for someone who had once dreamed of living boldly. And perhaps she'd never have wasted much thought on this question of fulfillment if it hadn't been for her husband's diagnosis.

His lymphoma had a real name, but they called it Jackie O disease, after its most famous victim. Their doctor, who'd been a pre-med with Mr. Michaelson and Adam Levine, assured them that the earliness of Jackie's death was the exception, that the cancer was so slow-growing that most people died with it, not from it.

"What are you talking about?" she said. "Cancer's cancer!"

"But this kind doesn't spread," explained the doctor. "It only grows." Apparently, if you were going to have cancer, you wanted her husband's kind.

Still, she felt devastated and empty, watching her husband shuffle to the car with a helpless smile and say in a defeated voice, "So there's nothing I can do."

"Never mind," said Mrs. Michaelson, suddenly knowing exactly where she was needed. "We'll manage it, that's what we'll do. There's plenty we can do. There are other doctors—lists of doctors with second and third opinions. There are acupuncturists, natural healers, hypnotists." And indeed, she nearly killed him trying them all. She'd even read a fascinating article about magnets, which she'd torn out of the *Detroit Free Press* and left casually on the sideboard beside his Crown Royal. Later, while emptying the garbage can under the sink, she found the article rolled up inside the empty whiskey bottle.

She'd had to give the Michiganders some explanation for Mr. Michaelson's pounding coughs and constant colds. Unwisely, she'd chosen the truth. Once they heard the word "cancer," that was all they heard, and now they kept asking her in hushed tones, "How's he *feeling* today?" Or "Wouldn't he be more comfortable back at the hotel?" Sherry Sherman took a subtler approach. Whenever the Michaelsons were in the vicinity, she abruptly raised her voice and changed the topic of conversation to the amazing progress of medical science, especially in the field of terminal diseases.

Yes, he's dying, Mrs. Michaelson wanted to scream. We are all dying, a bit more every day. What's the point of making an embarrassing fuss? (Though sometimes—for example, when her husband woke up choking in the middle of the night—it was worth quite a bit of fuss.)

Dying or no, there was nothing to do except treat the symptoms. But so many symptoms! Mr. Michaelson's flagging immune system was vulnerable to every fleeting germ or microbe. (What was the difference between a germ and a microbe, anyway?) In the past month he'd suffered from daily nosebleeds, the flu, a cold, shingles (which left behind a nasty rash under his armpits), hay fever, blurry vision and dizzy spells, bouts of constipation followed by diarrhea, jock itch and athlete's foot, even infected toenails. They'd stocked their medicine chest with pills, patches, creams, steroids, mineral baths, vitamins from China. They'd outfitted the passenger seat in the car with a special back-support cushion and loaded the glove compartment with tissues, tablets, and nasal spray. They'd tried diets from Denmark, Tibet, and the Mediterranean. And every month they visited the immunologist for gamma globulin booster shots. Afterward Mr. Michaelson would be too weak to drive himself home, so Mrs. Michaelson had to wait, leafing through old issues of *Good Housekeeping* if she'd forgotten her business magazines. Occasionally she'd peek in on her husband, strapped to an IV alongside the occasional AIDS patient wasting to nothing, all brittle and yellow, the way Jeremy would end up if he wasn't careful, which he wasn't.

So, it was settled. Her husband would die first. She'd always expected it, if not quite so soon, because her family was famous for being long-lived. And then she'd end up alone with no grandchildren to visit her, because she had two gay sons.

Mr. Michaelson's wooden shoe trees hit the back of his closet with a thud. "I'm ready now," he said, and parked himself on the bed. She kneeled before him to tie his shoes. He couldn't bend over far enough to do it himself anymore.

While she worked on his shoes, he stared up at the lightbulb as if it were the sun. His nose was a mess, red all over, with capillaries that had burst into forks under the skin. He looked like an old man, like his father had before he died.

Mr. Michaelson had pinned his name tag on crooked, so she fixed it. Not wanting to ruin her dress, she'd decided to carry her own name tag and flash it if necessary, like a police badge.

Shouldn't she call the police that evening if Jeremy didn't come back? Or was it better to wait until morning, when the higher-ranking detectives came back on duty?

"Where do you think he is?" She sighed.

"Anywhere," said her husband, his eyes fixed on the light-bulb. "Everywhere."

"I meant Jeremy," she explained, wondering whom he'd thought she meant. "Anyway, this dress is new."

"It's nice." Mr. Michaelson wiped his nose. "Looks like it was hard to make."

"After all these years, I could make just about anything, even a wedding dress."

"You won't need to," he said. "This one's nice enough for when you get married again. After all, you can't wear white twice."

His glum moods always stung, though she knew he meant nothing by them. She was still thinking over his words as they rode down in the elevator. He'd been so odd all day. Where had that business about infatuation come from? He must have read it in a book somewhere, perhaps the bit about the kiss from her novel, which she'd stashed in her purse like a good-luck charm:

Time stands still for the burst of suburban passion. Even the garbage collectors and the lawn boys stand still to pay tribute to this brief thrill of intimacy.

That was just silly talk from a book. But the memory of it made the blood rush into her ears as she stared at the distorted reflection of her dress in the elevator doors, the bright red stitches glittering under gold lights.

Her husband looked at his reflection, too, to pluck a hair out of his nose.

Kiss me now, she thought. If he kissed her right at that moment, like the Prince in *Snow White*, then all would be well. But the door opened at the seventh floor and a Filipino bellhop wheeled in the remains of room service on a cart with a green tablecloth.

Her husband was right, and it was a relief to admit it.

I WAS NEVER INFATUATED WITH HIM
IS THAT SUCH A CRIME?

The sun was melting over the hard brown hills as the Michaelsons emerged from the Hilton's revolving door. She wished her parents could have been there to see that sunset. Mrs. Michaelson had promised to take them to Israel, but the time was never right, and then they'd gotten too old.

Julie Solznick stood armed with her clipboard on the blazing white drive and frowned sadly at the sunset, as if she'd just received some upsetting news. In the falling light, the gravel looked hot enough to burn a person's hand.

"We almost gave up on you two sweethearts!" Julie called out, her bitty mouth penciled in brown. She flung herself into their path to guide them the two yards to their bus, her nipples erect through her silk blouse, damp under the armpits. "Name tags, everybody? I hate being a Nazi about them, but it's my job." Mrs. Michaelson flashed her badge. "And how are we all *feeling* this evening?" Julie asked. "Where's your son? The artsy one?"

"Lost," said Mrs. Michaelson, suddenly flooded with such a deep melancholy that she couldn't look at anyone, so she stared at a gash of sand cutting into the hotel's beautiful lawn. The desert constantly crept in wherever it wasn't being pushed away.

"My wife means our son made other plans," Mr. Michaelson said.

"Swinging for Singles at the Mercaz Yerushalyim, right?" Julie said.

Mrs. Michaelson shrugged, ignorant as usual about the business of young Jews in love. Thanks to Robert and Jeremy, she had no need to know these kinds of details: the Schmooze for Jews dinners, the annual Matzoh Ball at the Jewish Center on Christmas Eve, the "TNT" (Twenties aNd Thirtics) Club at Beth Israel, personal ads in the *Jewish News*, Internet dating services like JDate, speed-dating at Adat Shalom the second Sunday of every month. Maybe these things kept couples going when they got sick and old, studying their children as they performed the same rites their parents had gone through, watching the dream again but in full color.

"This way! This way!" yelled Julie, who was always running around and talking very fast in a practiced manner. "*Y'alah*, as we say in Israel. *Y'alah!*"

You're as unhappy as I am, Mrs. Michaelson realized. You hate shepherding us around while we gossip behind your back. You hate being alone among all these big unruly families. But you're too organized to sacrifice your thinking and planning time for chatter that usually leads nowhere. You like everything your own way and you can't stand the thought of sharing responsibilities with some guy who can't tie his own shoes.

She had to marvel at how Julie kept track of them all. When Mrs. Michaelson used to teach fourth grade (old enough to really learn, too young to mouth off), she'd had enough trouble remembering the names of eighteen children. Yet Julie knew by heart the names of all 254 of the Michiganders, as well as their intimate business: the latest victim of Harry Levinthal's heavy-handed passes, how the Kahns had dragged their boy along after he'd gotten engaged to a shvartzeh, and maybe even just exactly how artsy the Michaelsons' artsy son really was.

Cool, confident, and usually slightly manic, Julie Solznick with her button nose and pointed chin was always ready and willing to offer a Baggie, a Kleenex tissue, or a Handi Wipe. Imodium, Ex-Lax, or Ambien? A pen? A Popsicle? A plastic fan that declared your support for the Jewish state *and* opened up into an umbrella? Suntan lotion that doubled as insect repellent? A stopwatch with an annoying habit of going off while the Michiganders reflected upon holy ground? Or, if all else failed, Julie could whip out a candle: blue or pink for male or female birthdays; plain and thick for the beginning of Shabbat, or braided and triple-wicked for the end; and white candles melted into shot glasses to remember victims of the Holocaust with no one else to remember them besides pudgy, sunburned American Jews tramping across Israel in spotless white sneakers.

"JACOB's just there, in back," Julie said. "Oh, there's the Walds, finally!"

Their tour had commissioned three purple-and-gold-striped air-conditioned buses, each marked by a sign in the front window with the name of a Patriarch: ABRAHAM, ISAAC, or JACOB. After a protest, the names of the Matriarchs, "AND SARAH," "AND REBECCA," and "AND LEAH & RACHEL," were added in black marker. The Michaelsons had been assigned to "JACOB AND LEAH & RACHEL," which they boarded after inhaling the fumes of ABRAHAM and ISAAC.

Their driver, Igor, was engrossed in a Russian newspaper spread out over the steering wheel. A collection of blue-glass eyes dangled from his rearview mirror. The air-conditioning set them dancing.

The Michiganders looked crisp and blow-dried, ready for a dock party in their pressed shirts and flowing dresses. Many of them chatted on rented cell phones. A young married couple from Toledo argued in broken Hebrew. Ai-Ping Cohen, a Cantonese woman who'd converted to Judaism, waved to the Michaelsons while sipping Fanta out of a bottle sheathed in a plastic bag. She'd once told Mrs. Michaelson, "Jewish is not so bad. We got dumplings, you got kreplach. Same thing." Sherry Sherman lectured about the merits of Ralph Nader to her newest best friend, the chairwoman of a food drive for needy Russian Jewish musicians who'd immigrated to Detroit. Harry Levinthal winked at Mrs. Michaelson over the head of his wife, who never seemed to notice. With his leopard-print silk shirt and his spiked hair, he looked like a pineapple.

The only adjacent seats still free were split by an aisle. Rabbi Sherman sat on one side, while Aliza the rabbinic intern sat on the other and burrowed through her khaki backpack for her cell phone, which was ringing wildly to the tune of John Lennon's "Give Peace a Chance." Mrs. Michaelson felt sorry for Aliza. Her basics weren't bad: dark, smooth hair (a bit puffy) and great big cryptic black eyes, which unfortunately she hid behind black schoolmarmish glasses that clashed with her doughy white cheeks. But how she dressed! That night, for example, she'd chosen a baggy wrinkled dress sewn out of cheap crepe, the color of a sour pickle. This extraordinary uniform was topped off by a yarmulke embroidered with images of children of all different colors holding hands. Mrs. Michaelson thought women looked ridiculous even in plain yarmulkes.

Aliza was the grandchild of Holocaust survivors who'd been smuggled into Palestine. She'd been born in Israel, but she and her parents had lived in America for ten years, and her English had the faint yet attractive shading of a Hebrew accent. Shortly after Aliza had moved back to the Holy Land to begin rabbinic studies, her fiancé had been killed by a bomb blast on a public bus.

Aliza and the rabbi always sat apart, because they wanted to get to know people.

The rabbi gazed up at Mrs. Michaelson like a forlorn and

very hairy beagle. "Welcome," he said, looking her up and down and patting the seat next to his. His gaze paused on her breasts, and she hunched forward. "What a dress. A real stunner." Maybe he was hinting that her outfit wasn't appropriate. It must be hard for rabbis to be pious so much of the time, she thought. Bunny Lowenstein said the rabbi's wife had left him for a blond ski instructor from Austria. The rabbi had never confirmed the rumor, though he often joked about the easy bachelor's life, about having more time to hear the complaints... *ahem!*—the "concerns" of his congregants. Then his mother, Sherry, would chime in, "It's so cozy, just the two of us. He's still my baby."

The Michiganders weren't fooled by that kind of talk. A single rabbi in possession of a post at a good synagogue must be in want of a wife, and they wondered why no one would have him.

"There's something funny about Rabbi Rick. I bet he's gay," Bunny had said one night at dinner as the waiter poured their kosher wine. She had a reputation for saying shocking things.

"Oh, I doubt it," said Mrs. Michaelson, covering Jeremy's glass with her hand. "He's busy. Rabbis are busy." When Bunny turned away, Mrs. Michaelson made a point of whispering to Jeremy, "And if he was, it's no one's business." A person's sex life wasn't for by-the-way table talk. And yet, since her two boys had come out, Mrs. Michaelson was continually surprised by how often the subject or related matters cropped up, sometimes unavoidably. Even in the most innocent of conversations.

While Mrs. Michaelson took a seat next to the rabbi, Aliza the rabbinic intern invited Mr. Michaelson to join her: "Care to partner with me?" She moved her bag, decorated with a sew-on decal of a coat hanger with a red line through it. "This is a lucky coincidence. We haven't had our chance to heart-to-heart," she added, arching an eyebrow at her mentor, as if to say, "This is how you invite someone to sit next to you."

"Oh, all right," said Mr. Michaelson, quite happy to do anything anyone asked him to, Mrs. Michaelson thought. Sit next to Aliza, allow Jeremy to run off with some stranger to get drunk, date his biochemistry classmate's leftovers? No problem! Why, if he'd been the prime minister of Israel during the War of Independence, he'd have graciously jumped into the sea, and thanked the Arabs for the invitation to swim.

"Now, is it Dr. or Mr. Michaelson?" asked Aliza.

"Mister," he said. "I'm not a doctor anymore. Now I'm the patient."

While Aliza inquired earnestly about how Mr. Michaelson was *feeling* that day, the rabbi launched into one of his sermons for Mrs. Michaelson, who was imagining Jeremy in an Israeli hospital gown. Suddenly the air-conditioning went off and then came on again full force, blasting into Mrs. Michaelson's eyes and making them tear up. She tried to twist off her overhead fan, but it wouldn't budge an inch. Next, she dug into the plastic nozzle with her nails, then attacked it with a pen. Finally, the rabbi leaned over and pushed a button she hadn't seen. His warm sleeve touched her nose, and she inhaled the scent of Israeli detergent, much starchier than the American kind.

Across the aisle, her husband adjusted himself in his seat; if he didn't sit just right, sharp driving pains shot up his spine. Aliza, who'd studied psychology as well as theology at Tel Aviv University, was asking him, "So what have you learned on this trip? And what haven't you learned? Where could you go to seek that knowledge?"

Mr. Michaelson said, "Excuse me," hacked up an embryo of mucus into his tissue, then spat a few times as he scrutinized the result. "I'm sorry," he said, dabbing his mouth. "What was it you wanted to know?"

Mrs. Michaelson offered him more tissues with a smile, as if it were the most natural thing in the world to spit up mucus all day, even in public.

"It wasn't until my third visit that this country made any impression on me at all," said the rabbi, his breath cool and minty from a hard candy clicking between his teeth. He wedged his forearm onto the armrest, which she'd already occupied. Why did men always insist on armrests as their ancestral right? "This was in 'seventy-three, after the Yom Kippur War. The streets in Jerusalem were empty. A ghost town."

"I followed it on the news," said Mrs. Michaelson, digging her elbow more firmly into the armrest. The friction of their arms was a little embarrassing. "It was a miracle that Israel survived. The kind of thing that makes you wonder if there really is a God."

She worried that her comments about God might sound a bit flippant to a rabbi. He dressed simply, in a white yarmulke, dark pants, and a white dress shirt unbuttoned just enough to expose a slender gold chain bedded in a nest of black hair. His Giorgio Armani tortoiseshell glasses seemed rather worldly for a rabbi until she looked closer and realized they were knockoffs: GIORGIO ALFANI. Yes, he was handsome, but in a Jewish way, just as she'd once imagined Robert's . . . "partner" might be. (She liked the word "partner," as if Robert and Huang were business associates who shook hands a lot.)

Where did rabbis meet women? Singles bars? Did they have singles bars in Israel? An image of the rabbi shaking his fanny under a mirror ball flashed in her mind.

"Lift your arm," he said, rolling up his sleeves and showing off his hairy arms. She could hardly refuse a rabbi, so she obeyed. "Let's pretend Israel is this armrest. The Jews said, 'We want it all, but we'll take what we can get.' The Arabs said, 'We want it all,' and they lost it all." He leaned back, taking firm control of the entire armrest.

Mrs. Michaelson stared at his hairy arm occupying the armrest and said, "Still, something has to be done for them. As long as they agree to play by the rules."

"Rules? Do the terrorists play by the rules when they bomb civilians, innocent old people, our daughters and our sons?" He stopped himself. "You have a son," he said with a pitying look. "With a pin in his nose."

She admitted that she had a son. During a tour of artists' studios in Tzfat, she'd introduced Jeremy to Rabbi Sherman and then wandered off. Afterward, she asked Jeremy what they'd talked about, and he said they'd traded gefilte fish recipes.

"These are different times from when we grew up," the rabbi said slowly. "These kids are making all kinds of choices we never even had to consider."

She didn't want to think about the choices her son was considering. "It's so hot," she said, to say something, and pictured Jeremy lying drunk in some Jerusalem gutter. They should have rented cell phones at the airport so that she could call him now.

Julie jogged down the aisle to count them off. "Let's roll," she said as she hopped down, and scampered toward her place on ABRAHAM AND SARAH.

They pulled out of the Hilton driveway and headed up the road toward the big "canyon," as the Israelis called shopping malls. Mrs. Michaelson had heard rumors of a TCBY there.

"Something's troubling you," said Rabbi Sherman, knitting

his coal-black eyebrows as if he really could see what was wrong. She wanted to look away, so she opened her purse and pretended to consult her pocket guidebook.

"Oh no, not Fodor's," groaned the rabbi.

"What's wrong with Fodor's?"

"Nothing, unless you have any desire to get to know the real Israel."

Mrs. Michaelson wasn't sure what he meant. How could some of the country be real and some of it unreal, and how did you decide which was which?

"Put it away, for your own good. There, now. See how well we get along?"

She smiled and looked beyond him, out the window, where the shops they passed were all shuttered and padlocked for Shabbat. A billboard with the kind, crinkled smile of the Santa Claus look-alike Rabbi Menachem Schneerson invited her to get in touch with her Jewish heritage. Below him an advertisement for Sprite glittered green and lush above the dirt and dried brush. The words in the ads were all in Hebrew except for the e-mail addresses, which were in English.

Maybe the rabbi had a point about the real Israel. She'd been in the country for more than two weeks now, but she felt she hadn't really seen it. As if *they* were keeping the real Israel from her.

"And who, pray tell, do you mean by *they*?" she thought aloud, just under her breath. Luckily, the rabbi was too busy talking to notice.

"They" meant the good side. Gossipy old women who kept house for their sons, erect-nippled young women who took time out from husband-searching to guide you onto tour buses and invite you to buy Israel Bonds, rabbis with hairy arms or long beards, corporate sponsors with Jewish CEOs, the entire Israeli government.

Yes, that was it exactly. *They* were hiding whatever it was that lived behind those lit windows. And yet, somewhere, muffled by all these sad stones and grains of sand, by the sounds of ice tinkling in cold cappuccinos and the cameras flashing and the watches ticking their lives away, she sensed a real heart full of life, beating impatiently to be recognized.

Find me, it said. Know my name and all will be well.

"The Israelis are like the sabra fruit," said the rabbi. "On the outside, the sabra is all thorns . . ."

Couldn't the Patriarchs have wandered somewhere more hospitable with their sheep? While fleeing the Nazis, her own Patriarch and Matriarch could have come here, to the original Old Country. But in their usual infinite wisdom, they'd boarded a ship to the New World, and for that she felt very glad, though now it was too late to tell them so.

The rabbi was still talking. His neck and forehead glowed bright red and he was short of breath, but he was still talking. "They teach their kids that if they kill a Jew they'll earn seventy virgins in Paradise. Horny Arab teenagers are being convinced that the way to sex in the puritanical Arab world is the mass murder of Jews. Not Israelis. Jews." Aliza was explaining to Mr. Michaelson about the two kinds of listening: tolerant and reactive listening. The better kind was tolerant listening, which meant extending the great gift of the imagination to make space in the mind for that which was foreign. Mr. Michaelson looked a bit jealous as he watched his wife and the rabbi talking so intently. "Need anything?" she mouthed, holding out her purse, the medicine chest, but he shook his head sadly, as if she hadn't understood what he wanted.

"We are on the front lines of a war," said Rabbi Rick, or Rabbi Sherman, rather.

"Really? A war?" said Mrs. Michaelson, a bit skeptical about the virgins in Paradise. A rabbi should have had a firmer grip on reality. "What about Oslo? I mean, aren't we in modern times?"

The rabbi laughed. "There's no such thing as modern times in the Middle East. Time here flows constantly from the past into the present and the future."

"Then we have to hope Mr. Barak will succeed at Camp David and all this hatred will end." Why did every conversation in this country turn to politics? She couldn't believe people she'd never met had declared war on her. There was plenty of death to go around from natural causes; no one needed to wish for more. Why was this rabbi trying to stir up all these passionate feelings?

"But first he has to get to Camp David," said Rabbi Sherman. "If he loses the no-confidence vote in the Knesset on Monday, Barak and his government go bye-bye."

"Which would be a catastrophe for this country and all Jews, Rabbi Rick," Aliza called out across the aisle. "We're so concerned with protecting Jewish bodies, we forget the coarsening effect that occupation has on Jewish souls."

What a waste, Mrs. Michaelson thought, watching her. This girl ought to be out traveling the world, reading poetry under guava trees in India (like in the novel she'd finished on the boat), riding horses along sun-kissed waters, and meeting dashing men.

"How are you doing?" she asked her husband across the aisle.

"Fine," he said, clutching his head. "But why are you all making so much noise?"

Shimon Peres droned in a comfortable Eastern European accent that reminded Mrs. Michaelson of her father. When she closed her eyes, she could smell tobacco, strong black coffee, and dill and onions on black bread.

Peres never raised his voice. Everything about the man was dignified, intellectual in a quiet way. His hair was brushed in an elegant silver horn over the back of his head. His gestures were slow and graceful. His tie was a puff of pale blue at his throat.

She was too worried about Jeremy to listen to the speech itself, the usual triumph-of-Jewish-ingenuity routine: guns smuggled inside sardine crates, soda bottles dropped from planes on Arab villages to make a loud crash like bombs and frighten ignorant natives. But there was one electric bit when Peres looked directly at her, pointed, and said, "There is no Israel without *you*." Of course, he meant American Jewry as a whole, not her personally, yet for a moment she felt an intense, vital connection with him.

He made eye contact with her again at the smoky reception afterward, sponsored by United Synagogues of America and Seagram's Coolers. All the Israelis puffed away as if the museum were a nightclub. Mr. Michaelson listened to a blonde from Rio and complimented her on her tiny dress, almost skimpy enough to qualify as a bikini. The blonde's parents had fled to Brazil from Germany before World War II. A couple of years back, after being mugged and stripped of all her clothes at gunpoint, she'd fled to Israel for the security. "Awful, awful," Mr. Michaelson repeated, a little loudly after his third rum and Coke. He had a funny look on his face.

"Maybe he's finally feeling infatuated," Mrs. Michaelson said to herself.

There was nothing to eat besides lox and cream cheese on

mini-bagels, offered by Russians in tuxedos. Mrs. Michaelson turned down the mini-bagels because she felt fat in her new dress, and anyway she was sick. Sick of Coke that tasted like syrup, and water served with mint when you didn't ask for it. Sick of worrying about Jeremy and wine. Sick of the hypnotic, comfortable buzz of A/C and searches through hotel drawers and bumping up and down Judean hills in the padded bellies of chartered whales on wheels. Sick of trying to impress people with a dress no one noticed. Sick of death and sick of politics, which were the same thing.

Several MKs (that's what you called members of the Knesset, the Israeli parliament) had shown up, including Yael Dayan, the radical-liberal daughter of the famous eye-patched war hero, Moshe Dayan. Thin, narrow-nosed, straight-backed, she strode through the room like a knife, alone and rigid in a cherry-colored suit. One of the Michiganders asked her a question in Hebrew, and Dayan replied in scornful English. Mrs. Michaelson felt proud of her.

Shimon Peres, his blue tie matched cunningly to the broad pinstripe in his shirt, nodded at Mrs. Michaelson through his circle of admirers, including Rabbi Sherman, who stood right beside him. The rabbi invited her to join them, but Mrs. Michaelson shook her head. She didn't feel at home with creamy-faced ladies stuffed into cocktail dresses like sausage casings. They wrapped their leftover bagels in napkins for later and mugged for snapshots with their awful white teeth streaked with pink shreds of salmon.

Sherry Sherman threw her head back and laughed like she was choking.

I don't know how to enjoy myself with people, Mrs. Michaelson thought. I'm much better at thinking of ways to tear them down, and then hating myself for it later.

The rabbi waved more insistently. She couldn't say no again without being impolite. Yet as she joined the grimacing women around Shimon Peres, she felt inspired to do something really impolite, something her son would have done. So why not be positively wicked? (Because she wasn't brave enough.) Her dying husband seemed rejuvenated after flirting with an exotic blonde from Brazil. Jeremy had escaped and was free to backslide now. There was no reason anymore to work so hard at being perfect. Everything felt like a waste, even the gorgeous dress she'd worked on for so long.

"The extremists on both sides need to hate," Shimon Peres was saying. "That way you have only killed what was less than human to start with."

Her heart beat faster as she listened to his solemn, croaking voice.

"I don't care if he's a hawk or a dove. He's a genius," marveled a creamy-faced admirer. "He truly deserved his Nobel."

"Ralph Nader deserves a Nobel Prize too," Sherry Sherman added. "And he would have gotten one if the corporate interests weren't lined up against him."

But Peres wasn't a genius, thought Mrs. Michaelson sadly. No one here could learn what was so simple.

"What do you think, Mrs. Michaelson?" the rabbi said, determined to embarrass her. His burnished skin glistened like oil in the lights. Why was he so tan? Rabbis were supposed to sit in libraries all day and study ancient scrolls. "We were discussing the issue earlier on the bus, but I'm afraid I didn't give her a chance to fully express herself."

Everyone turned their heads and waited, even Shimon Peres himself. Silence loomed. She had to think of something. "I," she began, because all thoughts began with "I." But I what? More silence. She imagined someone whispering, "That's right.

Two gay sons!" And then she thought of a quote from the Bible, or maybe from a movie: "I believe that if all the mothers of the different countries could meet, there would be no more wars."

PERESY!

HOUSEWIFE MAKES FOOL OF SELF
IN FRONT OF LABOR PARTY LOSER

They waited for her to finish, but she had nothing else to say. The rabbi studied the pattern in the carpet, while the ladies searched desperately for a few words that might revive the conversation she'd killed with her kindergarten philosophy. Shimon Peres whispered to one of his bodyguards, and Mrs. Michaelson turned red. She looked ridiculous in red.

She heard Sherry Sherman's barking laugh nearby. Mr. Michaelson stared rapt at the blonde from Rio, who was showing off her collection of Israeli key chains. Suddenly he grasped his forehead. Mrs. Michaelson opened her purse, but the blonde asked, "You need some aspirin?" and produced a bottle from a tiny black handbag the size of a softball.

"Thank you," Mr. Michaelson said. "You're an angel."

"Well, if that's how he wants to be," Mrs. Michaelson muttered. A Russian waiter offered her champagne, which she gulped down, even though she didn't like champagne.

"Excuse me," she said, cutting through the glittering people to get outside to the terrace, paved with flat white stones. The air was hot and smelled of sulfur. A small crowd of smokers sipped wine under the lights and slapped mosquitoes.

Now, if I could be anything or go anywhere, she thought, I would . . .

She watched a stray cat pin down a lizard by the tail as it tried to run away. Finally the lizard squirmed free and darted off into the shadows. To escape the noise and smoke, she followed it. Several yards ahead, the smooth dome of the Shrine of the Book gleamed white against the blue hills, swollen and silent for the night. Somewhere in those hills was the famous Valley of the Shadow of Death, the geographic position of hell. Maybe the entrance was a tunnel you could walk through to visit old friends now roasting in the flames. That was some people's idea of hell—flames and pitchforks. She saw it as a sterile white waiting room with nothing to read but old copies of *Good Housekeeping,* no noise or limits, and no one to talk to.

There was a full moon that night, so round and bright it looked as if it were about to burst. In fact, it looked like something you could worship. It was the same moon they'd seen that afternoon over the Old City in a brilliant blue sky, but much, much brighter now.

What time was it in the States? What time was it anywhere?

She thought she heard the cat crying and then almost stumbled over Aliza, seated on a low stone wall and sobbing softly next to a wide-leafed, waxy rhododendron. Her hair had gone frizzy in the heat.

Mrs. Michaelson believed the best way to help friends in pain (as opposed to family members in pain) was to leave them alone, so she cleared her throat and said, "Oh, there you are! I was just going inside. Do you need anything?"

"You caught me." Aliza laughed and wiped her eyes with her thumb.

"I didn't mean to catch you. Wouldn't you rather be alone?"

"Please, sit," she said. There was no escape, so Mrs. Michaelson unfolded a napkin, set it on the wall, and sat down. "It's harder for me when I'm places where he used to be." Aliza sighed. "My fiancé believed in peace. He would still believe in it, even now. He wasn't afraid to explore the wound between our two peoples, but he thought both sides should live together, that this was the way of Torah. He used to talk about Jesus. Not as the son of God but as a wise teacher, a rabbi."

"We always have to remember that Jesus was a Jew," Mrs. Michaelson said, brushing the sand off her hands. The wall they were sitting on was fairly dirty.

"Yes," Aliza said patiently, as if Mrs. Michaelson were a child who hadn't been listening. "I believe Jews belong in this land. But there are times when I think, My God, why don't we all just pack it up and move to Canada?"

Mrs. Michaelson waited for the other shoe to drop, but there was no other shoe, only the cicadas singing and the echoes of voices and the soft slow rush of a jet above. I must show her I feel sorry, Mrs. Michaelson thought.

"If only . . ." Mrs. Michaelson mused. "If only the Palestinians would find some leader like Gandhi."

"Peace is everything," Aliza said, her voice sounding old, like a wife's voice. "Nothing is worth all this fighting. No land, no idea, no son. Let them have their West Bank and their Gaza. We don't need it. Only the Orthodox need it, and for that they hold the rest of us hostage."

Mrs. Michaelson, grasping for an adage, said, "Time habituates us to all wounds."

Aliza peered through her black-framed glasses. "How old is your son?"

Mrs. Michaelson had temporarily forgotten she had a son, or even two. She saw him now, out cold in an Israeli hospital bed. "Twenty-two," she said, plucking nervously at her dress to ventilate herself. She was dripping like a sow. "Isn't it hot?" she remarked. "Even at night, this *hamsin* doesn't even cool off one bit."

Yes, yes, the weather. You could always turn any awkward conversation into a weather report.

Aliza excused herself to the ladies' room and left Mrs. Michaelson free to savor the romance of loneliness under a blue-black sky that wasn't hers. She leaned back to take in the vastness of it from where she stood, so much space without end. Free, free, what a relief to finally be free of everyone. A relief, but also lonely. That was her problem. She was tired of loneliness, but there was no one she wanted to be near.

On such a night as this, not long ago, a dashing gentleman had driven her home from a bridge party after Mr. Michaelson left early, stranding her. This man had had such a solid grip on the steering wheel, the car seemed like a part of him. He'd served in Vietnam, a.k.a. Nam.

If I could go anywhere and do anything, she thought, I'd go to Vietnam.

Maybe she hadn't made such a stupid mistake in front of Shimon Peres, about the mothers, because no mother ever rejoiced in the death of her son. Otherwise, how could there be a God?

She heard soft footsteps and turned to see the rabbi coming toward her in his dress loafers, his hand over his eyes like a sentry. "There you are!" he declared, as if he'd created her. "A very inspired idea of yours, to suggest we meet out here."

"But I didn't say a word——" she protested.

"You didn't have to. That's what was so inspired about it," he said. Mrs. Michaelson nodded slowly, aching to get back to her hotel, where she could slink out of her dress and stand naked in front of the A/C. The high polish of the rabbi's loafers twinkled like little stars out of the shadows and she felt an urge to take off his shoes, to see him standing helpless in his socks.

She murmured something about going in to check on her husband, but she couldn't move.

"A moment, please," Rabbi Sherman said, sucking in a bubble of spit. "I just wanted to say, I had no business lecturing you back there on the bus. My own life's a mess, as I'm sure you've heard. We always think Rabbi Knows Best. But history often bears us out in quite the opposite way." He rubbed his forehead and smiled. "Did you know I live with my mother? I mean, that's what a mess I've made of things."

What was it about her that had inspired these people to open up to her tonight? Maybe because she never said anything in reply, they figured she was listening.

He lifted his arm to massage the back of his neck, and she could smell him. His deodorant had failed—how embarrassing! And yet exciting, as if she'd found out one of his secrets. She drank in a deep whiff, as if it were perfume.

"After my wife left, there didn't seem to be any point in keeping a whole house for myself," he said, heaving a deep, theatrical sigh. "Then I heard about a new Conservative congregation starting up in Tel Aviv, and I thought, That's for me. I'll live out my dream and move to Israel. Mother came, too. I'm an only child. I'm all she has, really. Originally I was going to look for my own apartment, but I just stopped looking. Sons and mothers. Well, you know."

No, she didn't know, actually. She listened more carefully.

"Follow your own heart." He paused, and then added, "Helen. Because I suspect you've got more real common sense than any of us."

Looking at him, she was convinced he'd lost his mind, that anything could happen.

"I feel so relaxed talking to you," he said. "You're not like these other women. You're an independent thinker. Don't try to deny it. I see who you really are."

"I've got to . . ." Her bunions ached. Her brain was swimming in her skull. "I'm going back in, Rabbi Sherman. The heat is driving me insane."

"Sometimes this whole tourism business strikes me as a rich comedy," he said, moving closer. "You Americans shelling out all this money to escape your boring lives for a few weeks by coming to visit our boring lives." His lips parted. "Call me Rick."

"My life isn't boring," she said. "My life is very exciting. I have a family, and hobbies, and I travel. And now I have to go." He frowned as if he'd expected something more from her, so she held out her hand and said, "Nice talking to you."

The rabbi stepped forward and cupped her elbow. His rough brown fingers pressed through her sleeve as he kissed her on the mouth. When he let go, she still felt the warmth and pressure of his body in the places where it had touched hers: on her lips, her arms, and the tips of her breasts. She tasted the rum on his breath.

"Follow me," he whispered. As he backed away between the bushes, he stepped on a prickly flowering shrub, snapping a few branches.

Mrs. Michaelson wanted to laugh. So everything this man said in public, none of it mattered. He didn't believe all that bunk about God, an old man with a white beard sitting on a gold throne in the sky. Not really. No more than she did.

She briefly lost her balance. Maybe he only wanted to talk with her in private, where they wouldn't be overheard. Even so, she wasn't supposed to be there. She was supposed to run back to take care of her sick, dying husband, and yet here he was drawing her into the bushes against her will. Well, she wouldn't go on.

But she did. She wanted to feel careless, even happy, for a short while.

And then what? What will you have to go back to after? She paused mid-step.

Her husband would never know the difference. Him with his blonde. She could enjoy herself, too. There was no point in thinking it over. She gave up trying to understand, and stepped between the spruces.

Somewhere an air conditioner rumbled to life, and at first she thought it was a firecracker, or a gunshot. The one time she'd heard a gunshot in real life, at a car race she'd been dragged to, it sounded like a firecracker.

The air smelled like pine sap. He fell on her neck, but she pushed him back against the wall of the museum and touched his sweaty cheek with her tongue. She tasted salt. "Hold me," she said, thinking, Now I've really lost it.

She was only going to let him hold her. A rabbi comforting a congregant in pain; nothing could have been more proper. But then lips and fingers got in the way, and it felt so peaceful to let them wander where they wanted to, to let her body direct her mind instead of the other way around.

He unhooked his pants and yelped "Ouch!" like a boy when she touched him in his underwear. "I mean, no, no, that doesn't hurt," he added quickly. He tried to fumble with the clasp at the back of her neck, but she murmured, "Rabbi Sherman, it's easier if you lift up my dress."

Their kisses didn't stop time. Actually, by Mrs. Michaelson's watch, the whole operation took about ten minutes.

four

TOP TEN SHABBAT DO'S AND DON'T'S

WHAT'S PERMITTED	WHAT'S PROHIBITED
1. Riding in an elevator	1. Pressing an elevator button
2. Hinting to someone to press the button for you	2. Asking someone to press the button
3. Exercising for fun	3. Exercising for health
4. Cracking knuckles	4. Plucking a blade of grass
5. Sleeping through services	5. Lengthening services unnecessarily
6. Driving to visit a friend in the hospital	6. Applying moisturizing creams
7. Using Rollerblades[1]	7. Carrying Rollerblades
8. Setting a VCR to record on Shabbat[2]	8. Setting a washer/dryer to run on Shabbat[3]
9. Adding sugar to tea	9. Adding sugar to hot water and then tea
10. Lugging a fifty-pound sack of potatoes	10. Building the Temple

---

1. Except in a neighborhood where Jews frown on using Rollerblades on Shabbat.
2. The TV must never go on and the broadcast must not involve Jews violating Shabbat.
3. Using a timer for things not generally used with a timer is forbidden, because people might get the wrong idea. Therefore lights and VCRs are okay, but laundry machines, no.

Morelli lived between the ultra-Orthodox districts of Ge'ula ("Redemption") and Me'a She'arim ("One Hundred Gates"). His building, a whitewashed stucco box on stilts, was typical of the Israeli mania for bunkerlike architecture. Next door, a real estate magnate from Florida had built a glatt kosher hotel in the same style and painted it hot pink. Dirgelike prayers floated out of the open windows, which were covered by white iron grilles.

"Satmars." Morelli spat at the bushes outside the hotel. "They think it's blasphemy for us Jews to have a state before the Messiah comes, so they raise money for Arafat and other terrorists. When Israel won the 1967 war, they were all crying, because they wanted the Arabs to win."

Signs posted along the road admonished the Daughters of Israel to dress "modestly," which the Daughters had interpreted as calling for bulky taffeta dresses printed with bold white dots, starflowers, or birds-of-paradise; wide-brimmed hats that sagged under the weight of lumpy satin bows, ostrich feathers, and cameos of Greek goddesses; glossy patent-leather shoes with gold buckles and fat, clumsy heels; and bulky strands of white pearls clanking against gold chains with diamond-tipped Jewish stars. Confident of their modesty, the Daughters of Israel plowed their strollers through crowds of men dressed in broad black hats and shiny robes in black, silver, gold, or brown, or in black-and-white stripes.

"Do the various colors of the robes bear any significance?" Marla shouted, to make herself heard above the noisy families on parade.

"I guess those crazies like to wear their pajamas all the time instead of just at night," Morelli told her. "Or maybe they want to look like zebras."

"Aren't you Orthodox, too?" asked Jeremy, light-headed with hunger. Before his access to alcohol and drugs was cut off, he'd been a picky eater. Now, like the other Michiganders on his Mission, he'd come to expect a snack every few hours: Popsicles in radioactive shades of red and yellow; melon sprinkled with feta crumbs; pita stuffed with crunchy green falafel balls, red cabbage, and, of all things, french fries all topped with soupy tahini.

"Yeah, but I'm not crazy like them," Morelli said as they turned up the walk to his building. Scrawny stray cats prowled in and out of the front door, which had been left open. "You know all those anti-Semitic stereotypes about how Jews are greedy parasites who control all the banks? Well, those guys in the pajamas are living proof that stereotypes are true. You'd need the Jaws of Life to pry a penny out of their pockets."

Morelli stopped in the doorway to hitch up his pants. "So I got good news and bad news," he declared, as if he'd made up the expression. "Good news is the wonderful meal awaiting us. Bad news is we gotta climb all the way up to the eighth floor to get it."

"There's no elevator?" Jeremy asked without thinking. Tom and Marla exchanged knowing looks.

"You ain't allowed to push the button for the elevator on Shabbat," Morelli said. "There's an elevator that stops automatically on every floor, though it takes about half an hour if it ain't there waiting. But who knows? Maybe it'll be waiting for us."

It wasn't.

"Come along, boys, chop-chop," said Marla, already climbing the stairs. "The faster we go, the sooner we eat."

As they marched up the airless stairwell, Jeremy kicked himself for forgetting you couldn't press buttons on Shabbat. Now these people probably thought he was a moron, and he minded. Yes, Jeremy Michaelson minded so much what other people thought of him that he'd pierced his nose to relieve the pressure.

All the doors of the apartments they passed were wide open, and the sounds of dishes clanking and deep voices singing in Hebrew echoed into the hallway. Jeremy smelled roast brisket and chicken simmered with raisins and sweet potatoes, but he was losing his appetite on those stuffy, winding stairs. His mouth tasted like sand.

"It's such a warm atmosphere," said Marla. "It reminds me of my grandmother. She always made a lovely Shabbat meal. I quite miss her. When she passed away, my parents didn't keep up the traditions, which I find a shame. Do you ever feel that way?"

"No," Jeremy said.

Tom was telling Morelli about the new South Africa: "You could be in line at the post office and a black will cut ahead and say, 'It's the new South Africa.' I knew a woman, six months pregnant, who was shot dead next to a grocery for her spare change."

"Let them have their bloody land," Marla said. "I'd be glad to move to Israel."

Once upon a time, Jeremy had also dreamed of "making aliyah," or moving for good to the Land of Milk and Honey. But that was before he'd studied Cornel West, Tony Kushner, and Edward Said. Before he'd slept with an Israeli grad student at NYU who was neglecting his master's thesis in Holocaust studies to avoid going back to "that garbage dump." Before he'd actually been to Israel himself and experienced its McDonald's, Sbarro's, and Ben & Jerry's franchises.

"It's not just the blacks' land. It's ours too," argued Tom. "My great-grandparents are buried in Cape Town."

Pulling himself up the banister hand over hand now, Jeremy made another of his weekly vows to quit smoking. A little boy cradling a pink blanket stood in one of the doorways and watched them climb. He blinked up at Jeremy and then exclaimed in Yiddish, "Mama, *ein goy!*"

"How long have you lived *ba-aretz?*" Marla asked Morelli.

Impressive use of the idiomatic expression "*ba-aretz*" in a sentence, Jeremy thought. Give the girl a gold star.

"We've been in Israel a while now, looking after business interests," said Morelli.

"What sort of business are you involved in, Mr. Morelli?" asked Marla.

"Import-export. A bit of real estate. Occasionally I'll help out a friend with a loan. And I got my fingers in a few investments up north and over the sea." He paused mid-step to catch his breath before attempting the last set of stairs. "I got my start in carpets, back in Iran, which was great till the Shah got the boot. Then I had to hightail it outta there, the wife in tow. She was a native. It was one of them cloak-and-dagger James Bond narrow-escape type of deals. Then we moved to Detroit."

"I'm from New York, but my family lives in the Detroit area," panted Jeremy.

"Rich people live in 'the Detroit area,' " said Morelli, then paused to catch his breath. "When I say Detroit, I mean Detroit."

"I've always wanted to visit America," said Marla. "Is that a nice city, Detroit?"

Morelli's wife waited for them at the top of the stairs, standing just inside her door. Her round orange cheeks were framed by a stiff helmet of bronze hair. She wore a plaid smock that widened like a bell over her fleshy hips before it slumped over a pleated navy skirt. "The most beautiful woman in the world," Morelli said. "Meet my wife."

"Welcome to you!" she said, her voice jittery and pinched. Mrs. Morelli smiled shyly and bowed without looking at the two young men. Jeremy remembered not to offer his hand. "You hungry? You want eat now?" she said. "My husband like his dinner warm."

They entered a tight, dusty living room lit by a naked coil that hung like a halo from the ceiling. The coffee table (faux mahogany) and the couch (white pleather) were buried in news- papers—newspapers folded, piled, stuffed with books, jammed between flattened cushions, draped over the back of the couch like a picnic blanket.

Jeremy marveled at what a complete disaster it was. Martha Stewart herself would have given up hope. He longed for his mother's orderly salon with her tacky gold-striped tea set on the Lucite shelves beside a coffee-table book about Romanian Jews.

An old man with a shriveled red face like a skinned knee sat hunched forward on the couch, his chin in his fist. "Hello, sir," Tom said. No response. "I said hello, friend!" Tom repeated in a louder voice, and waved, but the old man didn't even blink.

"He don't know much English," said Morelli, huffing into the room. "Just smile and wave." He pried off his cracked black dress shoes and kicked them across the floor. Mrs. Morelli ex- tended her cheek, and her husband planted a loud Shabbat kiss on it. "Sorry we're late," he said. "We cut through the Arab Quarter." He translated into Hebrew for the old man on the couch, then asked, "So what do you say for yourself?"

The question was directed to a tall, lanky young man mak- ing faces into a wall-length aquarium in the back hallway. He had a soft, straggly beard and wore the black-and-white uniform of a yeshiva student. His thick shoulder-length hair was parted down the middle of his scalp, as if he were an actor playing Jesus, and his eyes were so blue they looked dyed, though he had an unfortunate tendency to hide them with his squinting.

"You learn anything useful today in that school I pay all that dough to?" Morelli asked, standing on tiptoe to give his son a kiss on the cheek.

"I hope so, D-D-Daddy," he said, squinting at his father's stockinged feet.

Jeremy stared at Morelli Junior's three-quarter profile, outlined in green by the light of the aquarium. Would I have turned out like him if I'd become a prophet instead of a . . . instead of a manic-depressive homo? Knock off the yarmulke, shave the patchy beard and those forelocks tucked behind his pointy ears, rip his shirt open, pierce that Jewish nose, and I'd find myself under that getup.

"Darling, I don't like when you go by Arab Quarter in the night," said Mrs. Morelli as her husband thumped to his chair at the head of the table, the floorboards quivering under his feet. "It's dangerous times now."

"Babe, would you quit running me down in front of company?" said Morelli. Tom and Marla stood beside Morelli and smiled nervously. Jeremy, feeling hungry again, chose a place beside the old man. The table was set with a sheet of white paper, plastic cups, paper plates and napkins, and plastic forks and knives.

"I'm sorry, my darling . . ." Mrs. Morelli said, then barked at her son, who was making kissing noises at a striped fish: "Noam, come to table now."

"Can I help in the kitchen?" Marla asked.

Shaking her head, Mrs. Morelli pulled the white paper tablecloth over her corner to straighten it, then leaned over to check the result.

Noam tapped on the glass of the bubbling aquarium a few times, as if he wanted to be let inside, and then came over and stood next to Tom. "T-T-Tom? Nice to meet you, Tom," Noam said, surrendering his long, slender hand first to Tom. Next he reached across the table to Jeremy, who found the yeshiva student's grip clammy and limp. "I'm No'am. That's pronounced 'no' and then 'am,'" he said, squinting at Jeremy's POOT!

"I wish we could converse in Hebrew, but mine's so rusty. I haven't had much chance to practice here," Marla said. "Israelis speak such perfect English." She wriggled the tips of her fingers at the old Israeli, sitting mute beside Mrs. Morelli.

"You think so?" said Noam in a confused voice, his fingers drumming on the table. "I've only b-b-been here a few months. I was studying in Baltimore, but when Daddy moved here he wanted to keep me close by, so I transferred. I'm thinking about applying for citizenship. It's pretty easy, b-b-because of the Law of Return, but I just turned eighteen and I don't want to serve in the army. I could never k-k-kill anyone."

"You needn't worry. Yeshiva students are exempt from the army," Tom said.

"For now, yes. B-B-Barak wants to change that. I'm afraid he doesn't believe in God." He turned to Jeremy. "I like your shirt."

Jeremy had been daydreaming about love. I love you, he thought, wishing he had someone to say it to, maybe Gabriel, or maybe anyone. I love you, I love you. I love you so much. He craved something to put in his mouth—cigarette, pill, dick, anything.

"I l-l-like your shirt," Noam repeated.

"Oh, sorry," said Jeremy, his stomach growling. "Were you talking to me?"

"Pipe down," Morelli interrupted. "I'm trying to concentrate here." He was swilling seltzer water in shot-size silver kiddush cups to wash them out. Then he filled the cups with an Israeli version of merlot, one splash per customer, and passed them around. Noam slouched behind his chair and mouthed a few words to a stain in the carpet.

Jeremy sniffed his thimbleful of bloody wine, the first alcohol to pass under his nose in weeks, because no matter how often his father had explained the difference, his mother failed to grasp that he was a problem drinker, not an alcoholic. Anyway, it wasn't alcohol that had betrayed him that night. It was the alcohol *with* the pills.

He wondered why dinner was taking so long. I'm giving them ten minutes to feed me, he decided, or else I'm out of here.

"You wanna lead the kiddush?" Morelli asked Jeremy, who hadn't done it in so long he'd forgotten the words. No one offered him a song sheet to refresh his memory, and he was too embarrassed to ask for one.

"I'm not big on rituals," said Jeremy, "but if you want to say it, I don't mind."

"Allow me," said Tom, who immediately pressed his eyes shut and launched into a bloodcurdling vibrato while rocking on the tips of his toes, as if he wanted to meet God halfway. The words ran into each other so quickly that Jeremy lost track of them.

Robert used to lead the Michaelsons in singing that very same blessing on Friday nights. Mrs. Michaelson held the prayer sheet that Jeremy had decorated in school with glued peas and macaroni shells and struggled to follow along. Jeremy always loved her singing voice, so determined but so jarringly off-key. Let me get to know that unvarnished part of you, he'd think as he listened to the broken notes. But at the end of the song, the veil came back down and his mother's labored chatter resumed.

When Robert left for college, Jeremy took over the service for a time, trilling the notes and rocking just the way Tom was now. His mother asked him to cut down on the theatrics because it made her nervous.

"But don't you realize what we're saying?" Jeremy asked. "We're thanking God for a miracle. Wine, grapes, agriculture, sustaining life every day."

"Is that what it means?" she asked. Then he realized she'd had no clue all this time what the words meant, though she'd been repeating them for years.

Israel's the perfect country for her, Jeremy thought as he listened to Tom's shrill chanting. Not one real thing or person here. What was an "Israeli," anyway? Almost everyone he'd met was a transplant, either American or European.

When the song was over, they drained their cups, and Jeremy drained his too. The wine tasted like oil and didn't burn his throat the way he liked.

"Delicious!" Tom exclaimed, smacking his lips.

"Everything's delicious in Israel," Marla reminded him.

"Thank you," said Mrs. Morelli, taking credit for Israel. "Everyone is welcome."

"How's the wine in South Afrikey?" Morelli asked Tom.

But Marla interjected, "Not half as nice as the wine here! Thank you so much for having us, Mr. and Mrs. Morelli. Thank you, everyone, for a lovely Shabbat."

How much more fucking banter before we're allowed to eat? Jeremy thought, cutting parallel lines into the paper tablecloth with his plastic fork.

"Where c-c-can I get a shirt like that?" Noam asked, staring at Jeremy's chest.

"I can take it off for you," Jeremy said, then asked Morelli, "Is there more wine?"

"Sure thing, young fella." Morelli reached for his silver thimble, but Jeremy handed him his plastic cup.

Next came the ritual of handwashing. Mrs. Morelli went to the kitchen, but her husband squeezed between Jeremy's chair and the wall-to-wall bookcase, crammed with newspaper clippings, ragged paperbacks, and hardcovers with crumbling dust jackets. He hugged himself and pushed against one of the shelves with his shoulder. The bookcase swung on a hinge, opening to a back hallway. "A secret door!" Marla cried in delight as a paperback plopped down to the parquet floor. "Like Anne Frank!"

"It's handy sometimes in my line of work," said Morelli.

Marla and the old man followed him through the secret door to the bathroom while Noam and Tom went with Mrs. Morelli. After draining his cup of wine and pouring himself another, Jeremy followed Noam and Tom, tripping over Morelli's shoes on the way.

The tile walls in the narrow kitchen were so thickly caked with caramel-colored grime that they looked as if they could breathe. A sour smell hung in the air, and the sink was piled high with chipped dishes that would have slipped out of your hands if you'd picked one up to wash. Still, someone had made a half-hearted attempt: a couple of dessert plates crusted with streaks of dried brown sauce were drying on a rusty wire rack.

"I'll say the prayer with you," Noam whispered, breathing into Jeremy's ear.

"This is all very charming," Jeremy said, "but you're not going to convert me."

"I'm not trying to c-c-convert you. I'm just trying to help, honestly," Noam protested. "Wait. You're k-k-kidding with me, aren't you?"

"Yes," said Jeremy, because it was simpler.

"Oh, g-g-good. I thought you were really mad at me." Noam laughed a little, then filled a two-handled silver cup with water and began, "Repeat after me . . ."

But Jeremy recalled these words easily. He recited them without any mistakes: *"Baruch ata adonay eloheynu melech ha-olam, asher kidshanu bamitzvotav v'tzivanu al nitilat yadayim."*

Proud of his performance, Jeremy turned to Noam, who, if surprised, certainly didn't show it. "Now you just, like, run the water over your hands three times."

"No soap? Or do the magic words rinse away all bacteria?"

Noam held out a towel. "Here," he said in such a gentle voice that Jeremy wanted to offer him an apology for the dumb joke. "C-c-can I ask you a question?" Noam said. "Does that hurt? I mean, the diamond in your nose?"

"Not as much as the one in my dick," Jeremy lied, and Noam began gagging over the sink. "It's not true," Jeremy said, patting Noam's back. "I'm joking again. Can't you tell?" Teasing Noam made him feel guilty; it was like kicking a puppy. "Actually, you'd look good with an eyebrow ring. Your face is the right shape."

"Oh no," Noam said, his cheeks high red. "That's against Jewish law. The body is, like, totally sacred. We're forbidden to mutilate it in any way."

"Like suicide," Jeremy remembered aloud. "You're supposed to bury suicides in a separate part of the cemetery, because they've mutilated their bodies."

"Let's not talk about such sad subjects on a happy evening like Shabbat," said Noam, running the water over his own hands. "Now that our hands are clean, we aren't allowed to speak until the b-b-blessing over the bread."

"That's easy," Jeremy said, but Noam shook his head and hummed in warning.

Back at the table, the guests hummed and exchanged embarrassed grins like children playing a game. Ooh, we can't talk now, Jeremy thought. We can't stand it! He finished off his cup of wine, which tasted even more putrid than he'd remembered.

Morelli held up two loaves of challah and recited the blessing. He tore the bread into wisps and dipped them into a glass saucer of salt. Jeremy took a bite, and then stuffed the rest into his mouth. In New York, he was used to getting oily focaccia or dry rustic Italian. The sweet, rich challah polished with beaten egg moved softly, slowly down his throat. He'd forgotten how good challah tasted. He was starving for challah.

"Good," he said, like a boy.

"Take more," Morelli said, but the next piece Jeremy got was stale.

Mrs. Morelli set out cut plastic bowls of muddy pink horseradish she called *chrein*, while her husband brought in bottles labeled COKE and SPRITE, though they'd been filled with watered-down juice. "I don't know what we're drinking, but it's all Diet," he said, and patted his stomach. "We don't serve Pepsi products because Pepsi used to support the Arab boycott. I don't know how any good Israeli can drink Pepsi."

"I don't drink Coke either," Tom said. "Their new ads in South Africa are the same as soft porn."

"I'm happy with wine," said Jeremy, reaching across the table for the bottle.

The stale challah was a grim foreshadowing of the rest of the meal: cold, flavorless chicken, rice and peas flaked with too much mint, curdled gefilte fish from a jar, and potato salad lumpy with mayonnaise that tasted like bleach. Jeremy was so hungry he ate it all anyway, almost as greedily as Morelli, who tucked his napkin into his collar and bent over his plate. The old, mute Israeli man silently picked at his food with a fork. Meanwhile Noam, who was carefully explaining to Marla about kosher chickens, watched Jeremy out of the corner of his beautiful blue eyes.

Through it all, Jeremy kept eating, the way, when he was young, he used to stuff his face at family dinners because he was bored and had nothing to say, while Robert, who'd been straight then and engaged to a lawyer's daughter, blathered on about the stock market. Once, Jeremy had been so bored that he'd tried to get drunk on Manischewitz. He filled his glass over and over, and gulped down the sickeningly sweet wine until he couldn't drink any more, but he only felt overstuffed.

Midway through the meal, Jeremy had stuffed himself with so much starchy food he was almost ready to puke. Smothering a burp, he excused himself to the bathroom.

"The toilet paper's already ripped for you," Morelli explained, and pointed down the hall with a chicken bone. "We don't rip toilet paper on Shabbat."

In the bathroom, rows of shriveled black nylon socks hung over the bathtub on metal drying rods, and when Jeremy shut the door, a rod swung out and smacked him in the forehead. His hands were still shaking as he dangled his penis over the toilet. A sign over the tank warned guests to push on the handle while flushing.

"Is one allowed to flush on Shabbat?" he said in an Eastern European accent to the ceiling, gilled with giant flakes of dried white paint that dangled above his head. After a moment's hesitation, he decided in favor of flushing, then climbed into the bathtub to get as close as possible to the open window. "No more wine," he resolved, lighting a cigarette to settle his stomach. He took off his baseball cap and let out a long, guttural froglike burp, which struck him as hilarious.

Suddenly he felt a wave of heat behind his right ear and realized he'd set one of Morelli's black socks on fire. "Shit, shit, shit!" he cried, flinging the burning shreds into the toilet and flushing again.

"Are you all right?" someone asked in a shaky voice that sounded like Noam's.

"Fine, just fine!" Jeremy said brightly. "One more minute."

You fuck-up, he told himself, his eyes welling with fat, sloppy tears as he leered at his ugly reflection. You vile worm. Vile worm, vile worm, he thought over and over, and felt a little better.

"I'm sorry, it's going to be just a bit longer. I think I'm not feeling well," he told the door. After stubbing out his cigarette and flinging it down to the bushes below, he tried to guess which of the spray cans on the toothpaste-crusted shelf over the sink was the Israeli equivalent of Lysol. In the end, he gave up and sprayed them all.

Before he left the bathroom, he stood in the empty tub with his pants unbuttoned and tugged inside his boxers for comfort.

"I couldn't understand a word that Shimon Peres said," Mr. Michaelson muttered as he peeled off his black dress socks. "No wonder he keeps losing elections."

He hadn't looked at her since the reception. Or was she imagining it?

"It was nice of him to take the time to talk to us," Mrs. Michaelson said, speaking on automatic pilot. She picked up the trail of pants, shirt, and now-dirty socks he left behind en route to the bathroom.

"He probably doesn't have much else to do these days besides speak to tourists," said her husband, fumbling around for the bathroom light. "Still, I don't think it matters so very much." He paused in front of the bathroom door and fixed her body with a bewildered stare. "I don't know what matters anymore."

Mr. Michaelson sounded drunk. Or did he suspect? "Why do you keep staring?" she asked.

He took a deep breath, as if he wanted to speak. "Sorry," he said. "I'll get out of your hair now, take a long soak." He disappeared into the bathroom.

Really, she was the one who ought to take a bath. But she wasn't going to think about that now. She began looking for her nightgown, with her husband's dark socks, still wet from his feet, wrapped around her hand like a bandage.

Half an hour later, when it was her turn in the bathroom, she shut the door, sat on the toilet, and closed her eyes. Had it really happened? she wondered. It seemed too easy. Whenever she'd heard of men who cheated on their wives, she had always thought, Why would anyone go to all that trouble?

It wasn't only her fault that she'd followed Rabbi Sherman into the bushes. Hadn't her husband brought this on by taking her for granted, by flirting with another woman in front of her? Anyway, how did she know he hadn't slipped himself? Patients form crushes on their therapists all the time.

"Stop being ridiculous," Mrs. Michaelson told herself. "You're the one who made the mistake, and you'll just have to fix it." There was no point wallowing in shame. It was time to manage her situation. She took off her dress and hung it up. She made a mental note to call the concierge to pick it up later for dry cleaning. She stepped into the shower and scrubbed herself, lathering up good and thick to erase all fingerprints and lingering smells.

From now on, she'd be extra nice to her husband, do all kinds of little favors for him. She began with pecking him on the cheek as she climbed into bed, where he was already snoring away. The snoring would get worse and worse until deep in the night, when he'd wake up choking on his own mucus and clutching his throat.

Back home, Mrs. Michaelson, desperate to get some rest, had ceded him their bed and now occupied the guest room. At first she enjoyed having the mattress to herself, with no danger of a heavy, hairless arm draped unexpectedly across her breasts. But now, if she didn't occupy her mind each night with flurries of lists and numbers and other little projects, her thoughts wandered into morbidity and she'd wake up the next morning feeling withered, close to death.

In Israel, separate beds would have been ridiculous, so she'd learned to sleep with a pillow over her head. That night, however, she couldn't doze off, even when her husband's snoring died down. She watched him lie there, eerily quiet as he cuddled with a souvenir teddy bear from their ship.

Mrs. Michaelson lifted her half of the heavy hotel quilt and tiptoed to the window. Holding back one of the curtains, she winced though the filmy light from the street lamps at the cars in the parking lot and, beyond them, the soft purple fields. Where might her son be in all that mess? She picked up Fodor's, lying on the table, and caressed the cover, as if the answer might lie there.

Her sleeping habits were worse than ever, and it wasn't just because of her husband's snoring. She'd always heard that old people could never sleep through the night, and now it was happening to her. Did that mean she was old? But she felt healthy, which was hard when your husband was sick. It was hard to feel your blood rise because a man's sleeve brushed against yours or because he followed you outside the Israel Museum and practically chased you into the bushes, where Rabbi Sherman had tried to whisper romantic nothings as they touched. Finally a voice flew out of her throat, commanding him: "Shut up!"

She'd made a mistake, but everyone made mistakes. Mistakes weren't sins. This is bad, she thought, but not as bad as killing someone. I can take this back and never do it again. Better to pretend it never happened rather than hurt David's feelings by confessing the truth. Better to make up for it in dignified silence, like the Women in Black.

There were only four days more to survive before they made it home, and in that time she would allow no more of this sweaty, clumsy fumbling. But the rabbi hadn't touched her clumsily. He had expert hands and thick, sturdy arms lined with dense fur, a heart that raced under her probing fingers, blood that pulsed steadily under taut skin. Here was someone who needed her, who was drawn to her out of hunger instead of duty. She wished she hadn't enjoyed it.

"I have to go," she'd said, pulling at her crumpled red dress as she staggered back into the museum, where she bumped right into a member of Peres's security entourage, a tall, square-jawed bull of a man who'd grabbed her forearms with a stern glare. Shimon Peres glanced her way and then went back to his conversation.

Now, there was a gentleman—subtle, silver-haired Shimon Peres, with his courtly manners and a dapper blue tie that matched his handkerchief. He'd never have touched any woman except on the shoulder. Perhaps, after asking permission, he might have politely grazed the tip of a bosom.

Mrs. Michaelson settled into a chair and glanced at her husband, now snoring again. She wheeled the chair around so that her back faced the bed, and then toyed with the strings of her nightgown. Finally they came untied, and her fingers trailed down her empty stomach to the opening that had given life to two others and would now give herself a bit of life, too.

"Please, I can take it. It is no trouble," said Mrs. Morelli while her husband cleared the paper plates, but Morelli wouldn't allow her to move. "See?" she told Marla with a nervous smile, her clear nails piercing the plastic cushion of her seat. "He treat me like I am the queen."

"S-s-sometimes kids fall away from the Community," Noam was saying. The meal seemed to have loosened his tongue. "First you deny it, like anyone when your family member has a problem. It starts with smoking on Shabbes. Then it's listening to l-l-loud rock music or going to movies, which are more like filth than sins, though I admit Jim Carrey is a comic genius. It's been easier for me to cut back on music—I've got it down to U2 and Yanni. Anyway, when I see one of these *frei*, I don't hate him. I feel sad, especially if you think of the parents. I j-j-just hang my head in sadness."

"What did you call them?" Jeremy asked, his voice coming out louder than he'd intended. "Fry-kids?"

"*F-f-frei*," said Noam, suddenly bashful in the spotlight. "It's Yiddish for 'free.' "

"But isn't that good, to be free?"

"Oh, not free in that way," he said as if Jeremy had made a grammar mistake. "They have less faith in God, so they think they're free from God's rules."

"Aren't we?" Jeremy said, deciding to fuck his resolution and reaching for more Israeli merlot.

"You only think you are," said Tom.

"Boys, could you lower your voices?" Marla said, nodding at

the old man snoring over his plate. "Funny he shouldn't speak English. Maybe when he wakes up we could talk to him in Hebrew. Though, as I said earlier, mine really is quite rusty."

"I don't know modern Hebrew, and I'm happy that way," Noam said. "Somehow I don't believe it's right that the same words in the T-T-Torah are coming out of a bus driver or some woman on the street in tight clothing talking about sex."

"How do you get into a yeshiva, anyway?" Jeremy asked. "Is there an application process?"

"Are you interested?" Noam said eagerly, but then his father came in from the kitchen with a tray of watermelon slices.

"Lighten up, guys," said Morelli, setting down the tray in the middle of the table.

Noam probed the melon with his fork and then speared a slice. "But, Daddy, Rabbi Simeon says that if three people have eaten at one table and failed to discuss the Torah, it is as if they had eaten from animal sacrifices to dead spirits."

"And Rabbi Morelli says shut it," Morelli boomed. Noam dropped his slice. "Let's lighten it up in here. Anyone like a joke? I've got some good ones. What's the difference between a lawyer and a tick? Give up? A tick will crawl off you when you're dead. Or how about this one? Which was the last animal to leave Moshe's Ark?"

"The rhinoceros?" Marla guessed.

Morelli grinned. "Moshe didn't have an ark. That was Noah! So which was the last animal to leave Noah's Ark? The elephants, because they had to pack their trunks."

"Clever," Jeremy said as something hit his ankle. It was Noam's foot, delicately rubbing the edge of his sandal. Jeremy looked up, but Noam was staring at his watermelon.

"What do you call a nigger at Harvard?" Morelli asked

while his wife passed around *benchers*, stapled white booklets with the prayers for meals. "A janitor."

"Hey, now," Tom said with an exaggerated clown smile, his voice strained as he tried to corral the conversation back within the boundaries of polite chatter. "We don't say that anymore, remember? Now we say shvartzehs."

"Like that's not just as bad," Jeremy said, glaring at him. "It's the twenty-first century. We don't refer to people by the color of their skin."

The old man yawned and rubbed his red eyelids as he looked around to see who'd dared to disturb his nap. Mrs. Morelli said "Shh!" with a guilty smile, as if she'd caught Jeremy taking an extra helping of watermelon. No one else moved.

"What's the point of all these prayers? Isn't the point of religion to be a better person, not a racist?"

"It ain't racist to make a social observation about culture," Morelli said. "There's certain people in this world, Arabs, shvartzehs, they don't know how to behave, because they live in the ghetto culture. They don't want to work hard and get an education, so they live in ghettos and their kids live in ghettos and they don't have the evolution we had. Until then, they don't belong with decent folks. That's why we're always fighting." He looked at Tom. "You must know how it is."

"What about Egypt?" Jeremy said. "Egypt signed a peace treaty."

Morelli laughed. "Egyptians are different. Everyone knows that."

"Why don't we sing now?" Mrs. Morelli suggested. "Noam, you lead."

"I don't feel like singing," Jeremy said, but Mrs. Morelli drowned him out with "Shir Ha-Ma'alot," a sentimental hymn about Jews in the Diaspora and their dreams of returning to their own land to work the fields and bring home sheaves of grain. This was the Israel Jeremy had learned to love in Day School, the Israel where tanned children in sandals swung from orange trees on collective farms and never picked on one another because everyone was equal. The Israel where the weather was always balmy and the wind fragrant with jasmine. The Israel where the effete, groveling ghetto-dwellers of Eastern Europe became the hardy pioneer farmers of Tel Aviv, Rishon LeTzion, and Petah Tikva. The Israel where donations from American Jews turned sand into land.

Jeremy took a healthy gulp of the kosher wine, then joined in the singing of "Shir Ha-Ma'alot" in spite of himself. The simple words formed pleasing shapes in his mouth, now lubricated with alcohol. How marvelous Hebrew was! He'd learned in school that the entire language had only nine thousand root words. Nine thousand words for all of life and all those blessings, for waking up, for going to bed, even a blessing for going to the bathroom. In Day School, Jeremy used to compose new ones in his head: Thank you, O Lord, for letting me walk down this hall without getting teased; thanks, Lord, for letting me throw up on Softball Day; most humbly do I thank the King of the Universe for Seth Glazer's blue eyes and feathered golden hairs that trickle over his ears. Jeremy's heart welled up with love, for Seth, for Gabriel . . . and maybe now for Noam too.

At the end of the singing, Morelli suddenly lapsed into Hebrew and invited the old man into the living room. Mrs. Morelli ducked into the kitchen. "We've got to make the one A.M. curfew at Heritage House," Tom explained to no one, and followed Mrs. Morelli to thank her for dinner.

Jeremy grabbed the wine bottle by the neck and polished it

off. He was about to toss his *bencher* on the table with the others, but on second thought he stuffed it into his pants to look through later. As he left the apartment, he heard Noam ask, "D-d-does anyone mind if I go for a walk?" and then come running after him. "Hold up," he said, tapping Jeremy's shoulder. "You'll get lost. Let me show you to Jaffa Road at least."

"Okay," he said. They waited until the angels from South Africa finished their thank-yous and good-byes. Then Jeremy galloped down the stairs as loud as he could, to drown out the singing of big happy families settling in for the night. God was in His heaven and all was right with the world.

Outside, the air felt sticky on Jeremy's skin and smelled as if something were burning. He pulled off his baseball hat. His hair was slick with sweat.

"I'm sorry about Daddy," Noam said as they crunched on the gravel outside the building. "There's this awesome *pasuk* in S-S-Sanhedrin . . . I mean, this verse in the Talmud I could have quoted. 'Why was Adam created alone? So no one could say some races are better than others.' "

"That's great," Jeremy told him. "Why didn't you think of it up there?" He lit a cigarette and inhaled the smoke as if it were fresh air.

The South Africans came out of the building, a good two feet of air between them. "You have to understand the Israeli mentality," Tom was saying. "They use humor to blow off steam. Why can't we laugh at our differences?"

"But Morelli isn't even Israeli," Jeremy pointed out.

"Yes he is," said Tom, who was too preoccupied to scold Jeremy about lighting fires on Shabbat. "All Jews are Israeli. It's the same thing. Or at least, it can be."

"Would you like it if you were made fun of for being Jewish?" Marla asked Tom.

"It would depend on the joke, if it was funny or not," he replied.

"Come off it, Tom," she said. "You know it's different."

Noam and Jeremy listened to them argue all the way to Jaffa Road, empty and quiet. The shops were shuttered, the bus stops deserted. "This time of night, on Shabbat, it's kind of weird to be out for a walk. It makes me f-f-feel pretty lonely," Noam said. "I think about all these other guys with their wives and kids at home, and I have no one."

"What about me?" Jeremy said, enjoying the quiet and their sudden intimacy. He wanted to mess up Noam's hair, maybe scratch his beard. "You have me. You're not alone."

"I don't understand."

Jeremy shrugged. "Just ignore me. Sometimes I'm an idiot."

"D-D-Daddy's really not a bad guy, you know. On Shabbat, he shares whatever he has with strangers like you. And he'll do anything for my mother. Whatever she wants—clothes, jewelry—he doesn't even ask the price. He'll get it for her. And once, this Ethiopian Jew wanted to join our synagogue and some of the members weren't so k-k-kosher with it. But Daddy stood by the guy until he was admitted into that synagogue."

"I'm sure he has his good points," said Jeremy, stubbing his toe on a crack in the road. "All human beings do."

Their arms touched briefly, and then they went on walking in silence for another block. Noam looked over his shoulder again at the South Africans, still arguing. "I bet he wouldn't have minded if you'd told him you were g-g-gay."

Jeremy stared straight ahead. "Why do you think I'm gay?" he asked casually.

Noam looked embarrassed. "I hate to tell you, but it's kind of obvious."

"I don't buy into definitions," Jeremy said, wondering

whether the shirt or the pants had tipped Noam off. "I sleep with men. That doesn't make me anything."

"If it makes you feel any better," Noam began, then lowered his voice, "what I said about Jim Carrey was a lie. I don't think he's a comic genius. I just watch his movies because I think he's handsome. Do you get my m-m-meaning?" He raised his eyebrows.

Jeremy froze. "You mean you're a fag?"

"Shh!" Noam said. "You'll get me in trouble."

"Sorry," said Jeremy, more softly. "I just didn't expect . . . I mean, what about Leviticus?"

"That's only, like, one commandment out of six hundred and thirteen. No one could possibly keep them all. Anyway, I'm trying to fight it, but my *yetzer ha-ra*, my evil inclination, it's too strong for me right now. I only hope God c-c-can understand that I can't help it. It's a sin of weakness, not malice."

"I can just see you sinning with the other yeshiva boys." Jeremy snickered. "Gay orgies in the yeshivas of Jerusalem. I guess nowhere's safe these days."

"Of course I don't p-p-participate in orgies," said Noam. "I didn't tell you this so you could laugh at me. I was hoping you could help."

"Sorry, sorry again," Jeremy said, and hiccupped. "Too much wine." I'm being hit on by a yeshiva boy, he thought. Is this for real? "I really am sorry," he said, and tried to think of something nice to say, something neutral, not mocking. "So, uh, where do you meet guys around here? Are there gay bars in Jerusalem?"

"I don't know," Noam said. "I don't go looking for this sort of thing. But I have heard there's this park, it's called Independence Park, and at night, stuff happens."

"What stuff?"

"I don't know. I've never been, except during the day."

"So you want to go?" Jeremy asked. "Is that how you want me to help you?"

"Oh no. I just mentioned it because I thought you might want to know."

"Come on, then. Let's check it out."

"Hullo!" Tom exclaimed behind them. "What's all this?"

Tom was staring at the pedestrian mall on Ben-Yehuda Street, where the cafés throbbed with house music. American tourists searched for postcards, falafel, and ice cream. Israeli teenagers with skateboards clattered across the cement plaza in front of Bank Hapoalim.

One day, thought Jeremy, those kids will join the army to serve as cannon fodder.

"Doesn't the law mandate the closing of all shops at sundown?" Tom said.

"So what do you say about the park?" Jeremy asked Noam. "Are you in or out?"

The South Africans were still staring thunderstruck at Ben-Yehuda Street. Noam stood on the curb and twisted the threads of his ritual undergarment, his tzitzis, around his fingers. "Okay," he said quietly. "I'm in."

five

GARDEN OF GETHSEMANE LESSON PLAN

1. JUDAS KISS PICTURE SHOW AND TELL
Supplies: Family photos of people kissing
Prep: Before Sabbath School, tell children to bring pictures of family
   members kissing.
Instructions: Tell the children to show the pictures and talk about who
   they are. Then ask: When is it appropriate to kiss? (To congratulate
   someone, when someone is happy, when two people love each other
   in a special way.) Who may kiss whom? In this story, Judas chose to
   use a kiss to betray his friend, a big mistake. Judas ended his life by
   hanging himself. Say, "How sad! If only Judas had chosen to put Jesus
   first!"

2. JESUS CHRIST PLANT POKES
Supplies: Popsicle sticks, glue, Magic Markers, pictures of Jesus praying
   in Gethsemane
Prep: Find a garden or yard near your classroom.
Instructions: Have the children color the pictures of Jesus and glue them to
   the Popsicle sticks. Go to the garden and say that Jesus went to the Gar-
   den of Gethsemane to pray. If you were Jesus, where would you pray?
   Ask the children to stick their plant poke in that spot and say a prayer.

3. PRAYERS IN THE DARK

Supplies: None

Prep: None

Instructions: The children stand in a circle holding hands. Turn off the lights. Tell them that Jesus spent a very dark time in the Garden of Gethsemane. What gave Him strength in this dark time? (Answer: Prayer.) Ask the children to pray. Do not force any child to pray. Turn the lights back on quickly before the children have a chance to engage in any inappropriate behavior.

To get to Independence Park from Jaffa Road, you crossed noisy Ben-Yehuda Street, then followed a narrow lane called Yoel Salomon that widened as it dipped downhill. Tour buses found Yoel Salomon a convenient place to unload bored American teenagers looking for somewhere to walk at night. Long sweaty lines of them trudged past Jeremy and Noam on their way back up to Ben-Yehuda.

"Israeli women!" one of the boys woofed, pulling his baseball cap to the side. "Sha-*lom*!"

If his mother had gotten her way, Jeremy would have been visiting their Israel, a safe-exotic parade of camel rides, kosher tacos, and sandwich cookies served with punch in multipurpose rooms where DJs played klezmer music mixed to a house beat. Jeremy could just picture himself and his nerdy friends, their lobster-pink cheeks padded with baby fat, as they peeked shyly across the dance floor at slim, sneering Israeli teenagers, their rough hands callused from kibbutz labor.

Americans had money. Israelis had good bodies and street cred.

Noam paused in mid-speech, as if waiting for the answer to a question, but Jeremy's brain was pulsing badly from too much

Shabbat wine and he hadn't been listening. Luckily, Noam had
only paused to take a breath.

". . . You probably met Rabbi Dave at the Wall. He's short,
really outgoing."

"You mean the bald guy with no eyebrows?" Jeremy said,
then let out a deep, croaking burp. "I have his card."

"He used to have cancer. That's why he's bald. I mean, he's
fine now, but he still shaves his head to remember. He says the
cancer changed his life. That's why he moved to Jerusalem."

It seemed as if everyone had cancer these days.

"Rabbi Dave was the one who told me about Independence
Park. He warned us that every city in Israel has an Independence Park, and they're all cruising places for homosexuals."
Noam broke off for a second as they crossed a line of noisy
teenagers streaming out of a tour bus marked ISRAEL IS
REAL! "He said if we ever walk through here at night and
someone asks us what time it is, we should keep on walking."

"How does he know so much about it?" Jeremy asked, sticking close behind Noam, as if being a tourist were a contagious
disease.

"Lots of guys from America spill their secrets to him,"
Noam said in an awed voice. "He has this way of talking that
makes you want to tell him everything. You see that old Muslim
cemetery?" He pointed to a fence across the road. "Dave said
that's where the really serious action happens and we should
never go there under any circumstances."

Jeremy stared hard at the black fence. The first time he'd
experienced "serious action" had been in a shabby SoHo apartment with felt curtains duct-taped over the windows. He lay on
a mattress on the floor while an elderly (Jeremy guessed he was
about forty) gentleman from the Cock spooned against his back.
Jeremy pretended he was sleeping, even as the man's cold fin-

gers unbuckled Jeremy's belt and slid his pants down, even as the man nestled his erection into the crease in Jeremy's butt and then slipped his penis in, like a pair of pliers prying him open. Jeremy screamed.

"What do you want?" the man whispered in a husky, angry voice. "What do you want?" But Jeremy, usually such a smart-ass, couldn't think of a single thing he wanted, at least nothing specific enough to name. Being a relatively late bloomer sexually, he looked on each new tryst as an education and let his partner make all the demands. The last thing Jeremy wanted to be was an inconvenience to anyone.

What do you want? What do you want?

The only thing Jeremy could think of was "I don't know. A hug?"

Noam stepped suddenly to his left, and Jeremy, still staring at the Muslim cemetery, collided with a tall American teenager with a big chest. The teenager's bold red T-shirt stood out like a traffic light in the dark.

"Dude, are you okay? I'm really sorry. My bad, my bad. I should have looked where I was going. Do you understand English?"

"Are you making fun of me?" Jeremy asked.

"Nooo. Why would you think I was making fun of you?"

As usual, Jeremy had gotten it all wrong. "I don't know why I thought that," Jeremy said, leaning too hard against the side of his left sandal and falling out of it. "Forget you ever met me." He turned to Noam. "Can we get out of here?"

"Follow me." Noam cut between two of the buses and hiked up into the park.

The park itself was a dark triangle of dried brown lawn that sloped roughly uphill over rocks, loose dirt, sand, and cement. "They used to have more trees here, but the neighbors complained because of all the . . . you know, the action, so they cut them down," Noam said as their shoes cracked a path across the dry grass, so brown it looked fried. The only lights shone along a path beside the Sheraton Hotel parking lot next door.

Park, Jeremy thought, humming a little song as he tried to concentrate. This is a park. How did you say "park" in Hebrew? Once upon a time, when he was in Day School, he used to know.

The dark sloping hillside trapped the hot air, which was dry and warm and had a grit to it, as if they were in a desert. Jeremy tried to keep his eyes peeled for rocks and garbage, but he kept tripping anyway. After a minute of climbing, he looked over his shoulder and saw that they were halfway up the hill, with the tour buses and the road far below them. The perilous Muslim cemetery was only a black mass of trees, beyond which he could see the orange glare of the spotlights on the Old City walls.

Then Jeremy remembered the word for "park" was *gan,* which meant, to be exact, "garden." The Garden of Independence. The Park of Eden. But this place doesn't look anything like a park, he thought. More like an Independence Vacant Lot.

"Do you think it's safe here?" Noam asked. "Maybe we shouldn't do this."

"You're nervous, that's all," said Jeremy, watching a muscle man in a camouflage tank top disappear into a small clump of trees. "Come on, let's see a bit more."

"It's nice talking so openly," said Noam as they began walking again. "Rabbi Dave would just say my mind's straying into impure thoughts because I'm not studying enough. Hey, look out."

Jeremy was teetering on the edge of an artificial stream that had dried up in the *hamsin.* Several of the trees along its banks were painted pink. Gay Pride trees, thought Jeremy, hopping over the dried stream. He heard men laughing behind the pink trees, possibly fucking at that very second. If only someone would invite him over, at least to watch.

"Your Rabbi Dave doesn't know anything about it," said Jeremy. "Rabbis care more about two-thousand-year-old laws than about people, which isn't very Jewish in my opinion, especially if you've read your Hillel."

Noam squinted at the men shuffling between the trees. "Don't you feel it's meaningless, the sexual act divorced from reproduction? Like going to the bathroom."

"Exactly," said Jeremy, hiccupping as he lit a new cigarette. "Both are basic needs of human nature. If you try to deny them, they'll come out some other way."

"I wish it was like going to the bathroom. I wish I could relieve myself, get all those thoughts out of my head and then go back to my regular life. Rashi says thoughts are even more difficult to control than the act itself."

"But Maimonides says thoughts are worse. The act is a product of animal instinct, while thoughts are intellectual and spiritual, part of who you are."

"Not bad," Noam said. "You've studied, haven't you?"

"In one of my past lives," Jeremy replied. "I used to study all kinds of things." Poor guy, he thought, still so unspoiled. Maybe I could show him around a bit, tell him where I went wrong, be a kind of gay father to him. Wouldn't that be noble of me?

"My biggest trouble with homosexuality is the consequences," said Noam. "Where does all this man-love get you? Old and alone, with no family."

"You could settle down with another man," said Jeremy, losing his left sandal again. "You could adopt a child, or father one with a lesbian. Some of my best friends are longtime companions. Long longtime. Very longtime."

"Ha-Shem built man to spill his seed, not to settle down," Noam argued. "It takes a woman to force us to stay in a stable relationship. Men are just for . . . you know."

"You mean this?" asked Jeremy, kneading Noam's neck and then his shoulders and then grabbing the back of his pants so quickly that Noam gasped for air. "You're a little slut, aren't you?" Jeremy grinned and toyed with his own zipper.

Shame, shame. Now, what kind of gay father was he being? A horny one, that's what kind.

"S-s-sorry. I'm not ready," said Noam, stepping back. "You want to go home?"

Yes, yes, home. "Home" being the hotel room his parents had paid for. Of course he didn't want to go home. He wanted to stay, to meet gay people in Israel. He wanted to talk to them, to kiss them hello, to ask for their names. He wanted proof that such a thing as a gay person in Israel was possible, because he had this silly hope that the men here might be different from the ones in New York.

"Let's just keep walking," Jeremy said finally. "I'm a tourist, so I might as well see something." He started to fumble in his pocket for another cigarette but then realized he already had one in his mouth.

"I'll try to keep you entertained," Noam said, quickening his pace.

Jeremy glanced down the hill. The tour buses looked even farther away now, as if he were looking down the wrong end of a telescope. Feeling dizzy, sleepy, and silly, he put his hand on Noam's shoulder. "You know, I'd love a back rub," he said.

Noam frowned and shrugged him off. "I hoped you were going to help me, but I guess you've got other things on your mind."

"I am trying to help you." Jeremy reached for Noam again

but missed. "You said you were curious," he added, his head pounding. "Don't you want a chance to try it out?"

"Nice meeting you, Jeremy," Noam said with a mock salute, and took off.

"Come back. I'm sorry," Jeremy called out, but Noam wasn't coming back. His loss, Jeremy thought. So why do I feel like the one who's lost?

He flopped down on a bench and stared into the dark empty park, a perfect black hole. The branches over his head shifted in the warm breeze.

His mother was probably frantic now. Probably yanking her hair out by the fistful, trying to guess where he'd run off to, while his father was probably making all kinds of shambling excuses. Suddenly Jeremy's eyelids felt heavy and warm; he wanted to curl up on his bench and take a nap. "I'm going to be much nicer to them from now on," he decided with a loud yawn.

He took out the *bencher* he'd stolen from the Morellis and opened it at random, hoping for some useful bit of wisdom. No luck. Only a dopey picture of a girl and boy singing gleefully beside a pair of Shabbat candles. He shoved the booklet back into his pocket, took off his baseball cap, and pushed his hair up into its usual faux Mohawk. He kicked around some plastic, the torn packaging for a product called L.A. Party Boy Fun Pack.

Someone shouted in Hebrew from behind one of the bushes. Jeremy hadn't noticed until then how many men were shuffling back and forth all around him, the ends of their cigarettes flickering in the dark like fireflies.

" 'Strangers in the night . . .' " he crooned, then couldn't help giggling.

He couldn't decide which was more astonishing, that there should be gay people in Israel or that they were of the same pathetic mainstream fag variety as the ones back home, all sniffing around for sex in the darkest holes they could find.

And, worst of all, none of them threw Jeremy a second glance.

The Sheraton sign blinked at him above a line of trees, while Morelli's spongy food, soaked in thick red wine, sloshed around inside his intestines. I need something, Jeremy told himself, briefly standing up and then slumping back down. Tylenol, a Xanax. Half an X, just for the rush of warmth. It was warmth he craved instead of this beastly heat.

Who are you? he thought as he tried with no luck to catch the eye of a cute guy striding quickly past his bench. What are you like once you've shot your load and you go home by yourself to watch romantic comedies starring Cher on TV?

Still not one man paid Jeremy the least bit of attention.

He picked up a stray pine branch and began shredding its needles into green confetti. A boy standing by himself a few yards away was looking at him, so Jeremy looked back. The boy had dark clipped curls, a round face, and a gently curved belly like a baby's. His smile was friendly, patient.

You like me? You really like me? It always came as a surprise. Then the boy ruined everything by winking. Oh, very subtle, Jeremy thought. You're winking. Let me guess. That means . . . you want me? You want to fuck me? I dare you to try.

He marched right over to tell the boy to go fuck himself but at the last second lost his nerve; all he managed to squeak out was "Shalom," in a high, mild voice. There, he thought. Let's hear what a big queen you are, which simpering compliments you have to offer as currency for sex.

The boy, who was almost a head shorter than Jeremy, licked his bottom lip and smiled but said nothing. He wore a blue T-shirt that said IT'S EASIER WITH MICROSOFT and he had a faint mustache, as if he couldn't make up his mind whether he wanted to grow one.

"What's the matter, don't you speak English?" Jeremy asked, and laughed.

The boy took out a white card printed in Hebrew. He turned it over and wrote in pencil: "I AM DEEF." Then he crossed out the second "E." and wrote "A."

"That's cool," Jeremy said, temporarily forgetting what the word "deaf" meant. Deaf, deaf, he thought. Like Helen Keller or Beethoven. He didn't know what to say next, so he pointed to the boy and then to himself. "You're deaf. I'm American."

The deaf boy took out a small notepad and wrote his answer: "I KNOW YOU'R AMERICAN. OBVIOUS." Jeremy reached for the knobby half-pencil, but the boy was already writing something else. "I SPEAK ENGLISH, LITTLE. I CAN REED LIPS."

"How did you know I was American?" asked Jeremy, who'd hoped to pass for British: post-punk, with maybe a dash of pre—New Wave. Definitely anticapitalist.

The boy's chubby face twitched with silent laughter. "EASY. YOUR DRESS."

"Oh really?" said Jeremy, failing to understand how a person wearing camouflage cutoffs, a purple tank top with the message POOT! in silver glitter, and a diamond stud in his nose could be mistaken for a stereotypical American tourist. "Where are you from?" he asked, a little annoyed.

"I HAVE ISRAEL PASSPORT, BUT MY PARENTS, NO. AND YOU? YOU ARE JEW?" Jeremy wasn't sure what he was, alone in a shady park with some deaf stranger who could have easily been a terrorist, but the boy wrote, "I LIKE JEWS. JEWS HAVE NICE FEET."

Why did it sound so awful to admit that you were "a Jew"? "Jewish" sounded so much less . . . aggressive. "So what are you?" Jeremy asked, wiping some sweat off his chin with one of his tank top straps.

The boy didn't understand the question.

"What are you?" Jeremy scribbled. "Muslim? Christian?"

"MOTHER IS MUSLIM. FATHER IS CHRISTAIN. I DONT HAVE PATIENT FOR MUSLIM, CHRISTAIN. I AM NOTHING, ZERO. NOT MUSLIM, NOT CHRISTAIN, ONLY ME." He scratched Jeremy's arm lightly, then pinched the skin, pulling some of the hair so it hurt. It felt nice.

"That's just what I think," Jeremy said, his voice jumping an octave. "Jesus, Buddha, Muhammed, all the same. I don't believe in categories. I defy all categories."

An old woman clicked across their path in high heels. She looked about Jeremy's mother's age, though Jeremy's mother preferred flats. He imagined Helen would have looked quite elegant in heels. But then she would have looked elegant in an old sack. She had the kind of natural lordly bearing that gave some people the impression she was stuck-up.

"I LIVE CLOSE TO THIS PARK," the boy wrote when the woman was gone, and pointed across the brown grass. Come, come. He winked again and kissed Jeremy quickly on the mouth. His skin smelled familiar, like Calvin Klein's Eternity.

It had been a while since Jeremy's last kiss. He'd forgotten how good lips tasted as they softly teased your own, as you inhaled a stranger's meaty and unfamiliar breath, as his sweaty hand at the back of your hair pulled you close. This means nothing, he reminded himself. It's just a dance, with steps that fall into place. First, I close my eyes and trace the top of his lip with my tongue. Then I suck his bottom lip and pry his mouth open. I probe around in his warm mouth like a dentist scraping off the plaque. Still, he was falling for the whole damn routine in spite of himself, forgetting his fear until he felt a hand on his pants.

Where's my wallet? No, it's the dick he wants. Stay calm, he told himself as the kid felt him up through his shorts. There's no reason to be so jumpy. He's an outcast, just like you. You love outcasts, remember?

But he's not just like me. Somehow there's a difference. For one thing, he has far more right to be miserable than I do.

Jeremy pushed the boy away and panted, "At least tell me your name first." The boy didn't understand. "Name, name," Jeremy repeated. "Your name."

"GEORGE" was the response.

"George. Nice to meet you, George." George, George, George, he thought, trying to clear the fog in his brain. You said that already, you dumb fuck. Come on, he's deaf, that's all. It's not like he bites. You've read *The Heart Is a Lonely Hunter,* or half of it, but you've seen the movie. Of course there must be other deaf gay people, blind ones too, but this is the first one I've met. He has a sweet face, like a monkey, but a bit sad. My enemy. (Which was scarier? Deaf or Arab?) A noble, downtrodden Palestinian who throws rocks at Israeli soldiers for Western TV cameras. "How old are you, George?" Jeremy asked.

George held up five fingers five times. Jeremy was surprised. He'd thought maybe eighteen, tops.

The boy (but of course he wasn't a boy) took Jeremy's hand and pulled him forward a few steps. Jeremy shook his head and yelped, "Oh!" as George dove in for another kiss, pulled him a few steps more, then covered Jeremy's face with birdlike kisses that landed on his chin, his nose, his eyelashes. Slowly, with each kiss, George dragged Jeremy away, up the looping asphalt path and out of the park.

It was strange to walk with another person and not speak. George pointed to himself and gulped out a sentence that emerged in a series of bursts, his eyes bulging and the veins popping out of his neck. Jeremy smiled, wishing he could understand, but the noises sounded like the grunts cavemen must have made when they'd invented language. (Which had come first? Hebrew or Arabic?)

They left the park and cut through a deserted sandy playground with an Israeli flag planted atop the jungle gym. The streets were clean and quiet; the cars packed tightly along the curb were mostly white and German. Whitewashed single-story homes stood shoulder to shoulder, walled in by decorative iron gates braided and curled into vines. The trimmed hedges grew thick with white ruffled flowers that gave off an overly sweet perfume.

It seemed to Jeremy a nice enough place to live, if you had to live somewhere.

The street crossed one of the city's main thoroughfares: King George Street, which no one ever referred to by its Hebrew name, Rehov Ha-Melech George. A man and a German shepherd carrying a soft Frisbee in its teeth paced beside a glowing advertisement for peach yogurt. Jeremy stopped in front of a cozy-looking used-book store to read a flyer from Barak's One Israel Party in the window. IT'S FORBIDDEN TO REJECT THE FUTURE! was stamped in block Hebrew letters below a photo of a smiling, digitally slimmed Barak. It was the first ad Jeremy had seen for Barak's party, and it looked pitiful against all the exuberant banners for the opposition Likud flapping everywhere.

A few more turns down winding side streets. Then George pointed to a building with a pair of heavy wooden doors, one pinned open by a small pile of bricks. With another of his patented sly winks, he pulled Jeremy into the dark vestibule, so wide that in New York it would have been subdivided into studio apartments. They climbed a sweeping stone stairwell, cool and cavelike. George took the steps two at a time, jogging higher and higher into the shadows. Jeremy trudged behind him, then dragged himself up by pulling the banister, and finally found himself crawling on all fours. Why am I so sluggish? he asked himself. Certainly not because he'd gotten himself drunk on kosher wine. Even if he had polished off half the bottle. Or was it three-quarters?

George stopped at the third floor, slipped off his shoes, and pointed to Jeremy's feet, motioning for him to do likewise. Then he fitted a heavy iron key into a door marked HOTEL HERZL in Gothic script. An orange notice taped below the nameplate offered cheap bus trips to Egypt and Jordan.

Hand in hand, they tiptoed down a dim hallway of closed doors. The floor was carpeted in woven straw mats that slid around under George's thick blue socks and Jeremy's bare feet. I'm sliding! I'm sliding! Jeremy thought, trying not to giggle. The hallway ended at a tiny kitchen with a hot plate, a divided sink, and a mini refrigerator. A streetlamp outside glowed through the lace curtain. It lit up a tissue-thin geological map of Israel with no borders marked except rivers.

George's room was a concrete balcony walled in by yellow plastic screens. He'd covered the screens in children's drawings of buttery suns with devilish grins and rubbery-looking palm trees. A narrow single bed took up most of the cramped space, which was paved in yellow linoleum and had a metal drain in the middle. A plastic shower caddy of creams and lotions from Germany crowned the pasteboard armoire.

George gently shut the glass door to the balcony, covered the panes with a loose brown sheet, then handed Jeremy a pair of red knee-high soccer socks. It was much too hot and stuffy on that balcony for socks, but Jeremy guessed it was some kind of Arabic tradition to put them on, so he did. George smiled and kissed the top of his head.

Through the gaps in the screens, they had a clear view of dozens of balconies across the courtyard. Jeremy perched himself on one elbow and watched as an elderly couple finished a late meal while enjoying their CNN.

"Sorry," George mimed, and pushed the screens farther apart, as if that would have stirred up a breeze. He sat next to Jeremy and wrote, "ITS HOTEL. TOURISTS FROM ALL WORLD, AMERICA, GERMAN, JAMACA. MY REAL HOME IS ARABE VILLAGE SILWAN. HERE I SLEEP WHEN I WORK IN MY WEEK."

"So, uh, what do you do?" Jeremy said, blushing under George's fierce stare. He had a vague fear they were being taped by a hidden camera. "You know, work? Job?"

"I AM TEACHER FOR DEAF CHILDREN SCHOOL."

When Jeremy smiled to show he understood, George leaned in and kissed him on the mouth, a heavy kiss with a pulsing tongue that leaked saliva down both their chins. The force of it pushed Jeremy flat against the mattress. George fell on top of him, his blue toes curling against Jeremy's red ones. The concrete wall didn't quite hide them from the neighbors' view, but shutting the screens wasn't an option in the heat.

Suddenly George sat up and wrote: "I WANT THIS SHOW YOU."

"Sure," Jeremy said. His head didn't feel so bad now. "Show me whatever."

George pulled out a red vinyl photo album from under his pillow, looked at Jeremy for a minute, and then handed it over. "DONT LAUGH ON ME."

The album began with a magazine picture of a sweaty blond soccer player sitting on a bench and massaging his foot inside a green sock. On the next page, another soccer player, this one in a purple uniform, relaxed against a wall with his purple stockinged feet splayed out like fins. As Jeremy turned the page, George began rubbing the fabric of Jeremy's sock with his rough thumb and forefinger. His dry skin crackled against the cotton. With yet another of his lascivious winks, George got down on the floor and began slurping Jeremy's toes through the socks with greedy wet gasps. His tongue darted over the ball and the arch of Jeremy's foot and then lapped at the sweaty cotton. The licking felt slimy yet firm, almost like a massage, but Jeremy couldn't manage to relax. He didn't like being worshipped. It was as if he'd stumbled into someone else's private moment and was in the way.

"Do you have any poppers?" he asked, but George was too busy unzipping his shorts to look at him.

The Israeli couple across the courtyard cleared their dishes while Bill Clinton spoke on TV. We're surrounded, Jeremy realized, by American tourists dreaming of prophets and camels in some Jerusalem fleabag motel, Israelis who make their living ripping off the tourists, and the president of those tourists speaking to the Israelis on CNN. Then I close my eyes and Israel dissolves. I'm not in Israel or America but in this new space that's neither one.

He was beginning to enjoy himself, without poppers or anything. His therapist would have been so proud.

Suddenly George shoved Jeremy's foot against his crotch, made a series of choking noises, and spurted a white stream onto the sock. When he was finished, he climbed back up onto the bed and patted his neck with an old towel.

Their shirts were soaked with sweat, like they'd taken a bath in each other.

This is too much, Jeremy thought as he yanked off the sock, damp with sweat and semen. Get me out. I need a cool drink, a shower, a real hotel with a front desk and breakfast buffet. I need to get clean, and if I stay here, I'll fall asleep. He stripped off the other sock and handed the pair to George, who cradled them against his heart, then reached for Jeremy's zipper.

"No, thanks," Jeremy said, drawing back. "I'm fine, really. That was nice."

George shook his head and smiled. "NO PROBLEM," he wrote and tucked the socks under his pillow. "I THINK YOU HAVE WRONG IDEA WHEN I ASK YOU TO MY HOME. I DON'T SEX DIFFRENT MEN EVERY NIGHT. MAYBE THREE, FOUR IN ONE YEAR. I DON'T GO OFTEN TO LOOK FOR MEN IN PARK."

Yeah, right, Jeremy thought. "So what were you doing there?"

"IT'S CLOSE TO MY WORK. I WALK HOME ACROSS THE PARK."

"At night?"

George shrugged and then winked again. "WHEN YOU FLY HOME?"

Jeremy held up four fingers.

"MONTH?"

"Days."

George's smile drooped. "ITS SHORT TIME. ITS SAD." Then he wrote, "TOMORROW? I NO WORK. WE EAT LUNCH?"

"I don't know," said Jeremy, who only wanted to get home. "Whenever."

George scribbled quickly, "I UNDERSTAND HOW YOU ARE. I MET MEN LIKE YOU BEFORE," and flung the pencil and paper at him with a maudlin expression. He sniffled a few times and wiped his eyes, dewy with real tears. He even pouted.

Great, Jeremy thought. Now I'm an asshole. But there was no point in meeting George for lunch—not for George, not for

Jeremy. In four days, Jeremy would fly home, where a nice big ocean would separate them.

How do I explain that if he thinks he's found love with me, he'll find it again with so many, with more men than he can count? And each time he'll think, This is the one I should spend the rest of my life with, and each time they say good-bye he'll think, That was my last chance at eternal joy.

I promised him nothing. We've barely shared anything more than a foot massage.

Then why deny George what you yourself have been denied so often: a second date? He's not asking you to spend the rest of your life with him.

"Wait," said Jeremy, but George, still pouting, paid no attention, so Jeremy touched his chin. "You don't understand. No for lunch, but yes for dinner."

George's face lit up. "WE MEET IN MY FAVORITE RESTAURANT," he wrote. "AND THEN, WE CAN VISIT MY ROOM ONE MORE TIME."

"Great, great," said Jeremy, already wishing he could take it back as George slid down to the floor and kissed Jeremy's bare feet to say thank you.

six

THE NIGHT JOURNEY OF THE PROPHET[1]

Muhammed, *peace and blessings be upon him,* fell asleep while praying beside the Holy Ka'aba at Mecca. The angel Gabriel, beloved of Allah, appeared and led him to al-Buraq, a white-winged horse that could leap as far as the eye could see in a single bound. Together they traveled on this noble steed to Al-Aqsa, the furthest mosque, in Jerusalem, where Muhammed, *may his name be blessed forever and ever,* prayed to Allah, and Abraham, Moses, and Jesus prayed behind him. And then the Prophet, *who served the All-Seeing One truly until the end of his days,* was asked to choose between two bowls: one containing wine and the other milk. Muhammed, *blessed be he and each of the hairs on his head,* chose milk, and Gabriel said, "You have chosen the true religion." Shortly thereafter, the Holy Prophet, *who revealed the Word to his righteous followers and may all others be damned to the fate they deserve,* received the command to pray five times a day as well as the revelation of the essential beliefs of Islam.

---

1. Though the city of Jerusalem appears nowhere by name in the Holy Koran, the following apocryphal story should enlighten infidels who may not understand why, after Mecca and Medina, Jerusalem is the holiest city of the One True Religion, Islam.

Just before dawn, Mr. Michaelson woke up gasping for air, tangled in a knot of stiff hotel sheets. His back ached from his habit of sleeping propped up against three pillows for better drainage. Somehow he'd knocked his pillows off the bed, and now his sinuses were so blocked up he felt as if the spackled hotel ceiling and the floor were slowly squeezing together, threatening to smother his body like a sandwich.

His elegant wife slept peacefully beside him with a pillow over her head.

Kicking himself free of the covers and sheets, Mr. Michaelson rolled off the mattress. His mouth was dry. His heart banged behind his left breast. As he kneeled on the floor in his stretched-out underwear, he clutched his throat and gulped in desperate mouthfuls of air like a dying horse. Closing his eyes, he saw heavy stone blocks dissolving into a thousand purple stars and spirals.

Gradually he managed to time his breathing to the muffled purr of the air-conditioning. It had been three years since he'd drawn a breath without trouble, and he'd despaired of ever breathing freely again. At least, as long as he continued to live.

But on their arrival in Israel, he'd experienced an alarming bout of good health. Thankfully it proved only temporary. Thankfully, because if he wasn't dying, then who was he and what would he do with all his time? Why had he been wasting these past few years? Would he have to start seeing clients again, listen to other people's problems and forget his own?

A pacifist all his life, Mr. Michaelson had decided that the only way to fight his disease was through careful study. So he'd quit his practice to devote himself full-time to being sick (just like his mother the hypochondriac, who'd died in her sleep at

the age of ninety-one). He listed the different treatments his
doctors prescribed and his responses on a yellow legal pad. He
noted the size of the morsels of mucus he hacked up each
morning, as well as their density, shape, and tint. He calculated
the increasing severity and frequency of his colds, the recur-
rent, mysterious spells of dizziness and numbness, his failing
appetite, his aching knees, his fevers and nosebleeds, and the
rosy blotches bubbling up on his skin.

His doctors called him an easygoing patient. *But I'm terrified! I'm fighting for my life here!* His family congratulated him
on his equanimity. So easy to get along with for someone so sick,
they marveled, so easy to talk to. *But I'm black inside!*

He'd always maintained that he wasn't going to heaven or
hell because they didn't exist, but he hadn't fully given up hope
on the afterlife until now, when he needed one so desperately.
Standing alone in front of that crumbling stone wall, after his
son had indicted Helen of never being infatuated with him,
he'd finally realized that death was also a wall, not a portal.
Death was simply the end of life, and life was nothing but trouble, yet at the same time too scary to let go. No one was "better
off dead." That phrase had to have been coined by a young person, someone with years ahead of him. It was better to stare at
TV in a hospital than to die and leave your body to rot to nothing but bones and rocks. Because if such things as souls did
exist, that was where they resided—not in heaven, but trapped
in bones and dirt and rocks jammed so tightly into that damn
wall they couldn't escape, tighter and tighter until one day the
whole thing would burst, hurling fiery chunks of rock in great
brown clouds over the mountains, across the sea, through windows and skulls.

"I've done too much," he mused, hanging his head over the
bathroom sink to cough up mucus. A monster with baggy jowls

and a bloated, hairless stomach stared back at him from the mirror. Other victims of cancer, like his father and brother, wasted away. He had to get the bloating kind. "Take me home," he whined, craving his leather chair, his TV, his freezer stocked with hot dogs and peppermint ice cream.

His heartbeat slowed to a gentle trot. No mucus came up. He'd had a scare, and that was all. Now he was fine. A bit short of breath, but fine.

In bed, his wife slept peacefully on her side. Her left hip rose and fell through her nightgown in time with each clear inhale and exhale. She'd been a blaze of red last night, too beautiful for him; he'd been stuck all evening trying to make small talk with some Brazilian bimbo. He'd have picked blue, but his wife had a keener eye for fashion, for everything. All the men had foisted their gazes on her, especially that bully Harry Levinthal, so obviously in love. (And, Mr. Michaelson suspected from his wife's recent prickliness, she felt the teeniest bit of something for Levinthal too—the rat, the fink, the louse.) What a sense of triumph he'd felt when they'd boarded their bus to the Israel Museum and, without so much as a glance at Harry-the-leopard-with-his-cockamamie-hairdo, she'd sat demurely beside the rabbi. A model member of the ladies' auxiliary.

So she'd passed last night's test, but each new day brought with it some other indignity to bear: a two-bit Casanova called Marvin complimenting Helen on her eyes; another man, without a name, dancing with her in a ballroom in Haifa; jaunty couples inviting her to lunch, dinner, and a concert on the beach. Everyone wanted to tear her away from him. Wasn't it obvious why he'd never enjoyed being surrounded by what Mrs. Michaelson called "company"? (He called it "the enemy.") Now that he was dying, he was entitled to spend his remaining time in isolation, in comfort, at home.

Still, he had no right to deprive his wife of "the enemy," if that was what she wanted. What could he offer to compete with attention from strange men, healthy men? She deserved everything he could give for taking perfect care of him over thirty-odd years when he ought to have done as much for her. So he'd let her enjoy "company," be the center of attention. He'd test her out one last time. If she flunked, then fine. She deserved a vacation from him.

There was always the possibility, however remote, that she was happy the way things were, but he wasn't about to risk revealing his true feelings to discover hers. The solutions he recommended to others in analysis never seemed to work on his own family. He could never let on how much she meant to him: If she knew, she'd certainly flee.

It was impossible to fall back asleep, so he opened the curtains a crack and, by the dawn's early light, began counting the souvenirs he'd bought.

HUSBAND SHIRKS RESPONSIBILITIES,
HEADS HOME EARLY
SON MOUTHS OFF TO MOM—WHAT ELSE IS NEW?

"Helen," her husband murmured. She sat up immediately, worried it was something serious. He was sitting next to her on the bed and wearing his traveling outfit, a beige cotton sport coat with a polo shirt and brown pants. The curtains were open, and the hot light pouring through the windows felt like bits of glass pasted under her eyelids. "I think we ought to go."

Was that all? "Go on your own if you want," she said, sliding back under the covers. "They serve breakfast late on Saturdays, remember? I'll meet you down there."

But by "go" he meant "leave."

She threw her pillow aside and sat up. "You mean abandon ship?"

Why had she chosen that expression? They weren't on the ship anymore.

"It's an instinct," Mr. Michaelson said. "If you want to stay, go ahead, but I don't feel safe staying in this country one more day, and I don't think you should, either."

"I thought therapists didn't believe in instincts," she said.

"Call it a feeling, then," he said. "You've seen all these stones lying around. Any idiot could just lob one the wrong way, start a world war, and then all the flights would get canceled and we'd be stuck." He rubbed his eyes. "I can't explain it logically, but I sense it in the air. Something evil."

"I thought therapists didn't believe in evil."

"Well . . ." He looked up at the ceiling. "The truth is, I feel sick."

"You don't look sick. You said you've been feeling so much better in Israel."

"I can't help it" was all he'd say. But he could help it. One of the articles she had given him claimed sickness was as much a state of mind as of body. "So, are you coming?" he asked.

Her windpipe twisted itself up at the idea. How could they leave? They'd promised to stay until Tuesday, not Saturday. Leaving now was like going back on her word. Certain people might wonder why she'd done it and get the wrong idea, maybe blame themselves.

"And what about Jeremy?" she said. "Do we even know that he made it back last night from that escapade you let him go on? Did you even check?"

"No," he admitted.

"You might have thought of that earlier," she said calmly,

throwing off her blanket and stepping into her slippers. While he went next door to check on their prodigal son, she said to herself, "You can go, but I'm seeing this through to the end." She crumpled her husband's shirts and pants and punched them into his suitcase with his bears and antique coins. She filled his worn socks with wooden camels and glass eyes. She stuffed his white Jockey shorts, baggy and stained yellow at the crotch, into a ceramic pitcher.

"I kept knocking, but he didn't answer," Mr. Michaelson said when he came back.

She looked up from his underwear. "You're sure he was there?"

"Oh yeah. I heard him snoring." Ordinarily she'd have gone to check for herself, but she had too much on her mind.

Until Mr. Michaelson dialed El Al, she wasn't sure he'd go through with it. It took over an hour to make all the arrangements, which involved a lot of calling and being called back, because everything was closed on Saturday. The next available flight, not until after sundown, connected in Amsterdam. Also, the regular airport shuttle wasn't available. The desk gave him a number for an Arab taxi service that would send someone to pick him up, but only if he was ready to go early that afternoon.

While he was on the phone, she took out another suitcase and began packing some of her things, too. As long as he was going home, he could lighten her load. She emptied her drawers and her closet, all except for a couple of outfit changes and her vermilion dress, which she'd have the hotel press and wrap in plastic so it wouldn't wrinkle too badly on the trip home.

Have some compassion, she told herself. Especially after that business with the rabbi, you hardly have a right to be angry. . . . But her husband had been ducking out on her long before Rabbi Sherman had entered their universe, even before the diagnosis of cancer that wasn't really cancer. For years he'd been fleeing family dinners to catch a ball game, or bar mitzvah parties when the music got too loud, or wedding receptions because he was hungry and couldn't wait out the veggie sushi and mini egg rolls to get to the grilled salmon.

"You could go too," he'd always say, but she refused to compound his rudeness by leaving with him, which left her to beg like some spinster aunt for rides home from her brothers or, that one time, a dashing Vietnam veteran.

After she latched the two suitcases shut with a few savage swipes at the locks, the Michaelsons sat across from each other in padded chairs and waited for the bellhop. "I'm sorry," he said, "but I've got to get home."

"You don't have to keep apologizing." It felt as if they were talking about his death. Sometimes, late at night when she couldn't control her thoughts, she'd imagine that fateful moment, the loneliness of it, and also, she was ashamed to admit, the release.

"You don't need me," he said. "You always take care of yourself. I never had a chance to try."

"Of course I need you," she said, but he was right. No one needed *him.*

They walked single file behind a brass luggage trolley pushed by a blond Russian teenager in a green uniform that was too tight for him. While they waited for the elevator, the boy bent over to tighten a shoelace and she couldn't help noticing the curve of his hindquar— no, his ass. He caught her looking and smirked.

She drew up her spine and raised her head. So he saw me, she thought. Who cares? She was seeing all kinds of things she'd never noticed. The world was rushing into full, brilliant color after all these years of sepia.

"You'll be glad to be rid of me," Mr. Michaelson said with a smile as they sank down to the lobby.

And she did feel a bit glad, until she watched him struggle into the Arab taxi, which reeked of musk. The car sat low to the ground, and Mr. Michaelson bumped his head as he crouched to get into the back. One of the windows was sealed with duct tape, and the windshield was nearly blocked by the cheap stuffed animals resting on the dashboard. As her husband fell into the ripped and patched cushions, Mrs. Michaelson experienced a wave of guilt, the closest feeling to tenderness she could muster that morning. She leaned in and planted a kiss on his pale cheek. "You're not mad at me?" she asked, handing him a Ziploc bag of medicines, ointments, tissues, and wipes from her purse, to take on the plane.

"I'd tell you if I were mad, wouldn't I?" he said, looking pleased. "And even if I was, I'm not now." He craned his neck toward her. "Can I have one more?" The second kiss hit her with a jolt. They felt love for each other *at the same time*—so rare these days, so precious—but too late! No, never too late. She loved her husband and would tell Rabbi Sherman so with confidence should he ever dare to insult her further. "You can change your mind," said her husband. "You could be home tomorrow."

"I wish I could," she said, backing out of the car. "It's only a few more days."

Jeremy didn't appear moved one way or the other by the news. But then his eyes were hidden behind oversized wraparound sunglasses that made him look like a bug, so she couldn't tell what he thought. He was wearing his camouflage cutoffs as his swimsuit. Also, the safety pin was back in his nostril.

It was too hot to sit outside, so mother and son lounged on

green padded chairs by the indoor pool. The warm light streaming through the honey-tinted glass ceiling looked like smoke. They'd chosen chairs far across the pool from a pack of Michiganders who were mostly listless from the heat, though the usual live wires, Bess Waldbaum, Bunny Lowenstein, and Harry Levinthal, chatted like hyenas. Sherry Sherman passed around a bag of oranges grown by an Israeli friend, an organic farmer. "One bite and you'll never go back," she promised. "I can't. Supermarket oranges taste like pesticide."

"You can't taste pesticide," argued Harry Levinthal. His T-shirt was printed with a pair of fighter jets and the message DON'T WORRY, AMERICA: ISRAEL STANDS BEHIND YOU!

"*I* can," Sherry insisted. "It has a tang of ammonia."

Aliza marched around the pool and handed out colored flyers. She wore a black leotard with faded jeans and a button on her chest that said in Hebrew: EHUD BARAK—ONE ISRAEL! There were bags under her eyes, and no makeup to hide them.

"It's an alternative service I'm leading tonight, for hope," she said, giving Jeremy a purple flyer. "Afterward there'll be a speaker from Peace Now. I wanted to provide a safe space to escape all this warmongering rhetoric. Because in spite of everything, we can hope. God expects it of us."

" 'Hope is a thing with feathers,' " Jeremy recited. " 'Hope springs ever eternal.' "

Mrs. Michaelson gave him a dirty look, then asked Aliza in a low voice how she was feeling. "You seemed a bit upset last evening."

"I'm better now," said Aliza, hovering on the edge of Mrs. Michaelson's chair. "I wanted to say thank you for being there last night. Thank you for one of those moments of genuine connection that make this job worthwhile."

"Well, well," said Mrs. Michaelson, not sure how to reply. The standard "You're welcome" seemed more appropriate for a slice of cake than a moment of genuine connection.

"We'll be singing some beautiful Sephardic melodies at the service tonight. I'd love to see you there." Aliza shuffled her flyers against her stomach. "But please don't feel I'm forcing you. I believe if devotion isn't from the heart, it's not worth it."

Jeremy turned his flyer upside down and folded it into an airplane.

"I'm not sure religion would survive if people didn't feel the teeniest bit forced," Mrs. Michaelson said brightly.

"Maybe it wouldn't," was the response. "But maybe then it wouldn't deserve to."

If Mrs. Michaelson had had any intention of going to Aliza's service, there was no chance of it now. "Are you sure you don't want to sit down for a bit longer before you go your way?" she asked.

"No, no." Aliza sighed and suddenly got up, as if offended. "Excuse me."

Poor girl, thought Mrs. Michaelson, and grabbed a tissue to blot her lips, still greasy from her late-morning croissant. You could tell so much about a place from its pastries. In New York, she'd stared in horror at trays of doughy wheels oozing bright jelly filling under plastic wrap. In San Francisco, she'd practically broken her teeth on all the sunflower seeds, pine nuts, and whole grains that stuck in her gums. Here in Israel, every morning you got a hot buttery croissant that flaked apart in your hands and left your fingers and lips burning and slippery for the rest of the day.

Her towel-skirt came loose, so she sealed the Velcro strap to better hide her varicose veins. Then she glanced at the lead story in the *Millennium Marathon Daily Bulletin* or as Jeremy called it, the *Daily Bull.* Despite the absence of a byline, she immediately detected Julie Solznick's aggressive good cheer:

SHABBAT IN ISRAEL

As long as everything's closed, why not do as the Romans do and mark the sanctimonious nature of the day. Buddy up with a new partner and enjoy an afternoon stroll. Start a new tradition and participate in our stimulant rap groups "Let's Talk!" led by Aliza, the rabbinic intern. Reflect up on today's "Inquiry Question": Ask not what Shabbat can do for you but what can you do to make the Day Different than all others.

A waitress in a green polyester vest came by with a tray of fresh orange juice in champagne glasses.

"No, thank you," said Mrs. Michaelson, remembering the outrageous prices on their room service menu. "We're really not thirsty."

The waitress persisted. "It is on offer from the hotel. You must drink quite a lot in a *hamsin,* especially when you are not used to this hot weather. It's complimentary."

"Oh well, then." Mrs. Michaelson took two glasses. "For health reasons."

"I'll have an iced cappuccino with skim," said Jeremy.

The waitress said, "But this, this is not free."

"Who cares? Didn't you know life's a banquet and most poor suckers are starving?" He smiled at his mother. "Charge it to my room."

Those wraparound glasses really did make him look like a bug.

MOTHER QUESTIONS SON ABOUT PREVIOUS
EVENING'S WHEREABOUTS
SON HEDGES, SNOTTILY

"We should have gone, too," said Jeremy. "You didn't even ask my opinion."

"Your father knocked and knocked," Mrs. Michaelson said. "At least you could have given out a shout to let us know you were alive."

"Why did he want to go home all of a sudden?" Jeremy asked, rubbing his long legs together as the waitress came back with his iced coffee. "Did you say something to him? He's afraid of you, you know."

"You're being melodramatic," she said. "Why didn't you answer this morning?"

"Because I was too hungover to talk. And quit spying on me."

"I don't spy," Mrs. Michaelson lied, hoping he was only joking about being hungover. She folded her *Daily Bulletin*. "But if you really were hungover, I'd have to spy to make sure you stayed sober in the future." Silence. "You're not completely cured yet, remember?" Bug-eyed sunglasses. Mouth set in stone. She sucked through her straw at a bit of pulp trapped in melting ice and accidentally made a loud slurping noise. "You make me sound like a real pill," she added, and didn't mean to say anything else, but felt so exasperated that she had to throw in, "Am I really so awful?"

"Nothing happened," Jeremy said. "You've done nothing. I've done nothing. I wasn't even buzzed. I went to a Shabbat dinner that ran late. All I drank was grape juice."

She wished she could see his eyes, because she couldn't tell if he was lying about the grape juice. You could never tell when he was in earnest; his father was the same way. "So how was the dinner? What were the people like?"

"Interesting."

"How exactly were they interesting?"

"If I had to narrow it down to one thing? I'd have to say it was all those hot yeshiva boys lining up to suck my dick. I'm strongly considering going back. Plus, if I start losing my hair like your husband, I could wear a yarmulke to hide the bald spot."

"I can never say anything in the right way for you," she said bitterly. "If I say one wrong word, you go on the attack. I was only asking you to share a little about your life."

"No, you were asking me to prove I really was at that dinner last night," he said. "Why don't you just come out and say so directly?"

But what if it was true that she'd only been trying to make conversation? And in fact, now that she thought about it, her excuse seemed so plausible that she now believed it. The smartest response was to try a laugh, and she forced a small one, though she couldn't resist adding, "Just so you know, they have cults here."

"I wouldn't mind a nice cult. At least it would be a change from Rabbi Rick and his lectures on the virtues of buying Israel Bonds. Ask him what he believes and you get an envelope addressed to the Jewish National Fund. I'm sure he gets a cut of the action."

Mrs. Michaelson didn't feel the least bit nervous discussing Rabbi Sherman now that she'd made up her mind never to allow herself to be alone with him again. "The rabbi can be a tad formulaic, but there's Aliza. She's young. She has lots of energy."

"What about you? What do you believe?"

"What do I believe?" she repeated to stall for time. She had to think quickly, first to decide what she believed, then what she wanted Jeremy to believe, and finally how to blend the two into a helpful proverb. The problem was that beliefs were difficult to pin down with words. She knew Judaism was essentially good, though the how and why continually escaped her. "Well, I believe in the sanctity of life, for one thing."

"I wasn't trying to kill myself," Jeremy said through clenched teeth. "I wasn't trying to kill myself. I wasn't trying to kill myself. Jeremy, were you trying to kill yourself? Why, no! I wasn't trying to kill myself."

Mr. Michaelson always compared a relationship to two people on opposite sides of a room. If you were always crossing to the other person's side, then he never had a chance to come to your side on his own. But what if you waited and waited and still he didn't come to your side? For example, she and Jeremy had been arguing about it for months, but he still refused to concede that no one could swallow thirty-two pills by accident, even in an ice cream sundae doused with vodka.

"That's an unusual T-shirt you have on," she remarked finally.

"Am I wearing a T-shirt?" He stretched out his yellow top and looked down. It had a grinning monkey face with a red X over it.

"What does it mean?" she pressed.

"That's the point. It looks like it's a symbol, but it doesn't mean anything. You wouldn't get it. It's an attack on our consumer culture, like Jack Pierson, and you don't even know who Jack Pierson is."

"I could learn who Jack Pierson is," she said, but he refused to elaborate.

Mrs. Michaelson picked up her *Daily Bulletin* and then put it down. A fat girl ran across the deck, the crotch of her bathing suit bunched between her legs. Down in the water, a white back glowed eerily above the blue tile.

"I've been thinking," she said. "All that time when I was pressuring you to go to dances and see girls, I should have left you alone. I see that now."

"You never pressured me. Don't you remember? When I talked about girls, I was trying to throw you off course, but you never took the bait. You smiled and said what nice friends I had."

"So maybe I already knew." She stirred the straw in her empty glass.

"Or maybe you didn't think I was capable of getting a girl."

Where was her husband to hear all this bile? Sleeping comfortably on some plane after plenty of gin and tonic. Snoring, probably. "This is all new to us," she said. "You have to give us a little understanding, too. It's easy to blame us, but if you're unhappy, blaming us or drinking and drugging away your sorrows won't help. Do something. Try religion, try therapy, or if that doesn't work . . . try pottery." He snorted, but she wanted to cry. "If your father and I are really so hopeless, why haven't you given up on us?"

"I don't know." Jeremy sighed. "I keep hoping you'll figure me out."

Besides, she thought, who else would pay for your monkey shirts and safety pins?

The lifeguard scolded a young Michigander, a blond boy leaning over the deep end of the pool and filling a pink plastic bucket with saltwater. (Why did Israelis yell so often?) She and this boy had played a heated round of peek-a-boo during the bus ride to Masada. If he'd been the one wearing Jeremy's monkey T-shirt, she could have chatted with him for hours and made up a thousand silly stories about flying monkeys, green monkeys, even talking monkeys.

She was much better at making friends with children than with women her own age. She had her brothers' wives if she really needed company, but Rose was always visiting her grandchildren in Virginia, and Phyllis had her own life, too, which included a job as a part-time manager of a cooking-supply store called Kitchen Glamour. (Current grandchildren standings: Rose 3; Phyllis 1; Helen 0.) So Mrs. Michaelson traveled by herself to discount outlet malls and hunted for things she didn't need. Sometimes she'd catch a matinee in an empty movie theater. Or she'd slurp a smoothie in a food court and then stroll quietly through the aisles of the Half-Off Card Store in the hopes that it would soon be someone's birthday or anniversary.

Robert kept saying he and Huang wanted to adopt, and she tried to encourage them, though once she couldn't help confessing, "They still haven't done enough studies on the effect a home like that could have on a child. A child needs a mom and a dad."

"We had a mom and a dad," Robert replied, "and look how we turned out—a failed suicide and a cold fish who, thanks to you, hasn't felt a genuine emotion in years."

If what Robert said was true, then what had she done wrong? Because according to Robin Williams (or was it Tom Hanks?) on *Inside the Actors Studio,* the story of a life was the sum of all the choices a person has made. All was merely cause and effect.

Perhaps she'd been overly cautious with Robert, since he was her first. And as for Jeremy? The only fault she could come up with was that she'd been transfixed by the miniseries *Roots* while she was pregnant.

Was that it? The curse of Kunta Kinte?

"What's *that*?" Jeremy asked, lowering his sunglasses.

Mrs. Michaelson sucked in her breath.

That was Rabbi Sherman stepping onto the pool deck with a scratchy green hotel towel slung over his bare shoulder. He was barefoot, bare-chested, bare of everything except a clunky gold star on a heavy chain around his neck and a tight red-and-white-striped Speedo. The bikini-cut swimsuit said so plainly, in small white capital letters: SPEEDO. His yarmulke dangled from the back of his hair by a clip, like a ponytail.

Her son snorted. "Nice package."

Actually, yes, she thought. It was.

The rabbi's shoulders and triceps were thick. His stomach bulged just a bit around the middle but was still impressive for a man his age, and his legs were packed with muscles she didn't recognize. What struck her most, however, was that every inch of his skin was carpeted with black curls. She'd never seen such a hairy man before. Hair everywhere, like on a gorilla.

He smiled and nodded to the Michiganders, whom he passed without a word, even his mother, who was busy informing everyone about the use of pesticides in Third World agriculture. The package jutted ahead of him, smooth, sleek, and round.

The sun was frying them all under the brown glass, like strips of bacon.

"He likes me," Jeremy said. "He's smiling at me."

But the rabbi was smiling at *her*, at Mrs. Michaelson of the varicose veins cleverly hidden inside a towel skirt, of the bunions, the pockets of flab tucked into her swimsuit, the sagging cheeks shaded by a straw hat with a pink ribbon, and the light layer of pink foundation over a few brown liver spots on her shoulders. The whole damn mess.

He planted his broad feet between their deck chairs. His black curly hair, streaked with dancing silver threads, was slicked back with dried gel that made it look wet. She wished he'd go away, because she couldn't stop looking at him.

"Hello again," Rabbi Sherman said, folding his arms and flexing his triceps.

Where did a rabbi find time to develop such handsome muscles?

"Is this your date?" the rabbi asked, patting Jeremy's faux Mohawk and provoking an ugly grimace. He looked up at the glass ceiling and locked his hands behind his head; Mrs. Michaelson felt a sermon coming on. "It's one of Judaism's most delicious ironies that the day of rest for everyone else is the rabbi's busiest hour," he said. "The Talmud actually addresses this dilemma. Is a rabbi allowed to work on Shabbat? The sages conclude that, yes, it's okay for him to do synagogue-related work, because you are allowed to break any of the Torah's rules to save a life, al pikuach nefesh. And in this case, he's saving the spiritual lives of his congregation."

"Perhaps you've heard that the Talmud also says silence is good for the wise and even better for fools," Jeremy said pleasantly.

The rabbi smiled. "I bet you'd enjoy Aliza's alternative service." He looked meaningfully at Mrs. Michaelson. "All the chairs seem to be taken."

"I see a few on the other side of the pool," she said, her ears on fire.

"I'm going," Jeremy said, standing up. "You may have my chair, Rabbi Rick."

"You don't have to do that," Mrs. Michaelson said, but instead of behaving like a rabbi and refusing politely to break up a family, Rabbi Sherman said, "That sounds terrific!"

Everyone must be watching us, she thought as her son and the rabbi switched places. Everyone must be making comments.

"Helen," the rabbi said after Jeremy left. He inched his deck chair closer to hers. "I understand if today you regret how forward you were with me last night. I'm your rabbi."

"Not really," she said automatically, meaning he wasn't really her rabbi. Rabbi Adler back in Michigan was her rabbi.

"I see." Rabbi Sherman cleared his throat and then lowered his voice. "Forgive me, Helen, but I must be frank. Are we going to continue seeing so much of each other?"

She stared at his firm furry legs, long healthy lines pointing to the soft package cradled between his thighs. SPEEDO. "How can you joke about it?" she said, but the way he looked at her made it clear he wasn't joking. Was he real? She didn't mean "sincere," she meant "real." The hairiness, the oily fawning, the muscles, and the babble. She had to make him go away.

Somehow, he'd begun a new sermon. ". . . you know, I have this funny habit of comparing our bodies to a stopwatch. We need to take good care of our bodies, to give ourselves the longest possible time to perfect our souls."

It was time for Mrs. Michaelson to contribute to the conversation. "Do you do laps?" she asked.

He grinned. "I do laps," he said. "In fact, I used to be on the team in high school. Every morning I got up at six-thirty to practice. I'd shave my whole body before our meets. I was as bristly as a porcupine during our season."

She looked away. "You shouldn't stare at me like that."

"Like what?"

"Like you're . . . infatuated. It's a very crowded pool."

"But I am infatuated, Helen. If it was your plan to trap me last night, you've succeeded brilliantly." He wore a peculiar, goofy expression that made him look like a raving dog. She half expected him to foam at the mouth.

"Of course that wasn't my plan!"

He shrugged. "We'll agree to disagree," he said. "Helen, Helen, Helen." Why did he have to talk so much? "Do you know how good-looking you are?" he said.

Mrs. Michaelson was always surprised when men said she was good-looking. She didn't really believe them, because they never said "pretty" or "beautiful." They always said "handsome" or "good-looking" or "striking."

"Last night on the bus, before you came on and made your move, I was in the depths." She opened her mouth to object, but he held up his hand and went on talking. "I said, 'God, I don't believe in the literal meaning of signs and wonders, but I'm calling on you now. If I'm going to be alone for the rest of my life, fine. I'll resign myself. But if I'm going to have love, show me some sign as soon as you can.' Then you came, looking like a million . . ." He whistled. "Do you know why my wife left me?"

"I'm sure it isn't my business," she said, imagining that she could comfort him by stroking his hair, untangling it in her fingers.

"She said I was too wrapped up in my own thoughts. I didn't notice if she was there or not. So she said. Of course she'd never had a deep thought in her life. I only married her because I was blinded by her beauty. My mother always said I needed to be with someone more mature."

Mrs. Michaelson bristled at "mature." "Do you realize just how old I am?"

"No," admitted the rabbi. He quickly squeezed her hand, then let it go before anyone could notice. "How old are you?"

He became real so suddenly it scared her. "Fifty-seven," she said, subtracting a year, because she'd only turned fifty-eight in June. "And I'm married. That's one of the Ten Commandments."

"Yes, if you want to be literal about them," he said, batting his lovely curled eyelashes. "But Rabbi Hillel said the law wasn't there to be interpreted literally. It's there to improve our lives. Don't you see, Helen? We love each other, which is as good as being married, I say. Better, actually, judging from what I've seen of you and your husband."

"You know nothing about us. You don't even know who I am," she said.

He rolled over onto his side to face her. His eyes had that compassionate look in them, as if she'd just told him she couldn't afford to donate to the Jewish National Fund at the five-hundred-dollar level. "In fact, one could argue that staying with your husband is the true act of adultery because he doesn't minister to your spiritual needs."

"Just stop it!" she hissed as her towel opened slightly, showing a bit of white leg and those awful veins.

"Should I go away, then?"

Yes! What are you, a moron? Leave me alone! But she said, "You don't have to do that, but we ought to talk about something else." Like what? Then she thought of something she wanted to ask, something she'd never asked her own rabbi, because she'd been too ashamed. With this one, shame was out of the question. "Maybe I could get your opinion on a bit of theology," she said.

"Go on," he said, absentmindedly snapping the elastic strap of his SPEEDO.

"I've always wondered . . ." Mrs. Michaelson hesitated. "Which is to say, what is Judaism's stance on . . . I mean, does it disapprove of homosexuality?"

"We're talking about your son, no?"

She nodded quickly and fixed her towel-skirt.

He lifted a finger and launched into a history of a central paradox inherent in two of Judaism's core values: the perpetuation of the Chosen People balanced against the stipulation that every human being is created in G-d's image.

"So what's the right answer?" Mrs. Michaelson said impatiently. She much preferred him touching her gently in the dark.

"Okay, here's one interpretation. The laws in this area were devised in a time when we understood homosexuality as a behavior. Today we believe it's something so ingrained into the fiber of a person that it isn't subject to change, which means a gay person shouldn't be punished for being how God essentially wired him. But if a gay could change, it would be forbidden for him not to."

His explanation struck her as a cop-out. Either homosexuality was good or bad, like murder. You didn't say a person was wired for murder and couldn't change. It was wrong, wrong, wrong. That was the kind of certainty she'd counted on from religion, from marriage, from her husband, her house, and her children, and they'd all failed her. "The rabbis seem as confused as I am," Mrs. Michaelson said.

"We are," he agreed. "What's wrong with being confused? It's better than pretending you know all the answers." He leaned over as if to kiss her again. Her lips trembled and she was prepared to scream, even near such a crowded pool, though she wasn't sure she'd be able to push him away. He had very insistent lips. But he was only reaching for her novel. "*A Galaxy Far, Far Away*, by Arthur Solomon," he said, turning it over. " 'Another triumph from the author of *Charlotte's Summer* and

Fire in My Heart. A story of life, love, death, hope, renewal, and a woman's courage.' " He opened the book to the first page. "At least it's better than that dreadful Fodor's."

Fodor's reminded her of her responsibilities. "Last night we made a mistake," she said. "Promise me we won't make that mistake again."

The rabbi held up his right hand. "I promise." He set her book on the cement, then jumped up from his chair and dove into the pool. She watched him do a few laps.

"Oh, go away," she whispered, and picked up *A Galaxy Far, Far Away,* which she was almost halfway through. But then she put it down again.

Rabbi Sherman pulled himself out of the water, sleek as a seal. He shook himself off and splattered her feet. In her life, she'd never had the opportunity to touch a swimmer, water raining down his skin as he pulled himself up the ladder, his broad wet feet leaving dark marks on the cement.

After wrapping himself in his towel, the rabbi went over to say hello to the other Michiganders. She waited until he had his back to her. Then she packed up her things and left before he could talk to her again. Unfortunately, he came running up behind her in the corridor.

She made a funny comment about his shaggy wet hair, which she still longed to unravel. The elevator came, and he touched the small of her back as if to guide her inside. When the doors closed, he punched the *Stop* button and insulted her again, on the mouth. "No," she cried, stopping to catch her breath. "You promised."

"As Prime Minister Eshkol said during the Six-Day War, I promised, but I didn't promise to fulfill the promise."

He kissed her again. This time she said, "At least not on the lips."

So he kissed her neck. There were no more complaints.

In the middle of their embrace, he dropped to his knees. She wondered what he was doing until his tongue found its way between her thighs and then she stopped thinking and simply felt. "Oh God," she kept saying, as if it were His doing, and then she heard a voice from somewhere above, a scratchy voice, first in Hebrew and then in English. The voice wanted to know if everything was okay.

Still on his knees, the rabbi grabbed the phone below the control panel as if he stopped elevators every day for romantic moments. "Sorry," he said. "Sick passenger."

"This really has to be the end," she said, playing with his hair one last time before he stood up. Then they pulled out the *Stop* button and continued their ride.

——

George sat with his notebook at one of the red tables in his favorite restaurant, the Sbarro's on the corner of King George and Jaffa Road. The restaurant was managed by a family friend (Arab) and it was kosher.

Until Jeremy sat down at the table, he wasn't sure whether he'd dreamed up the night before or it had really happened. Even George's hair was a different color than Jeremy had remembered. Light brown instead of black.

"JUST LIKE AMERICA?"

Yes, Jeremy assured him as they stood in line and with their orange trays, this Sbarro's was just like in America.

So what was authentically Israeli? Jeremy made a list in his head:

1. The women have nails like drag queens.
2. Lime is more common than lemon.

3. Pants are always stretch and no one wears socks—except George.
4. Mint in everything.
5. Arabic here is like Spanish in the States.

The girl at the counter addressed George in Hebrew and then, when he didn't respond, in English. After he handed her his card, she apologized in Hebrew and asked what he wanted. He pointed it out to her.

Jeremy was excited to see beer on the menu until he realized it was *bira shchora*, or "black beer," which was nonalcoholic. He ordered a slice of pizza and a Diet Coke.

"YOU DONT NEED DIET," George wrote.

"It's not that. I'm a NutraSweet addict. It's my mother's fault, like everything else that's wrong with me. She raised us on diet soda."

A pair of Orthodox Jews in black coats stared at Jeremy as he carried his tray back to the table. "I DONT LIKE BLACK JEWS," George wrote when they sat down. "EVRY DAY I READ IN NEWSPAPER HOW THEY MAKE TROUBLES. THEY DONT DO NOTHING, NOT EVEN GO IN ARMY. JUST MAKE MORE SETTELMINTS AND TROUBLES. IF GOVERMENT DON'T GIVE THEM WHAT THEY WANT, THEY SAY THEY CANCEL GOVERMENT AND NEW ELECTIONS. NORMAL JEWS LIKE YOU OKAY, BUT THESE BLACKS NO GOOD."

"I guess," said Jeremy, who kept forgetting that George wasn't a boy. He only looked like a boy.

The familiar aroma of industrial-strength tomato sauce and processed cheese melting under iron-hot lamps comforted him. He took a bite of pizza and felt George's foot pressing his calf.

Jeremy grabbed the pencil and wrote, "Have you ever had a Jewish boyfriend?"

"WHAT YOU THINK? I LIVE IN ISRAEL. I MUST HAVE SOMETIMES. ONE WAS AMERICAN LIKE YOU. VERY BEATIFUL." George rubbed his chin, pulling at an imaginary beard. "HE WAS JEW. VERY BIG JEW. NO LIKE YOU."

Jeremy blushed. "You mean he was Orthodox?"

George nodded frantically. "SO BEATIFUL MAN!"

"Orthodox how? Like, all the way Orthodox? Even with the sidelocks?" George didn't understand, so Jeremy made circles around his ears.

"YES, YES! HE TIED THEM UP TOP OF HIS HEAD. AND ONE TIME I MADE BOYFRIEND WITH ISRAELI SOLDIER. WE WAS TOGETHER 6 MONTHS. THEN HE MUST GO BACK TO ARMY. I LOVED HIM. NICE BOD. I THINK SOMETIMES I WISH I CAN BE IN ARMY WITH HIM."

"So what am I, chopped liver?" George didn't get the wise-crack, so Jeremy took another bite of pizza. They could at least have sprinkled some Middle Eastern spices on top of the cheese. Still, he couldn't help loving it—so plain and rich, so American. He devoured the slice in a minute and then went and ordered another.

When he came back to the table, George was playing with Jeremy's pack of cigarettes. "WHY YOU SMOKE? BAD FOR HEART."

"I know. I'm trying to quit."

George flung the cigarettes across the table and pointed to Jeremy's nose ring. "YOU DON'T NEED THIS UGLY. WHY YOU HAVE? YOU ANGRY?"

"Yes, I am angry," Jeremy said, swallowing a mouthful of pizza. "No, not exactly angry. See, when you grow up, you learn you're supposed to say please and thank you and take in your neighbors' mail if they go on vacation. Then you get older and you realize these same friendly people who send you birthday cards with a generous check inside are also capable of rape and murder with big polite smiles on their faces." He wagged a pizza crust. "They'll buy you a new sweater for Hanukkah, but they don't care if the company that makes the sweater exploits child labor in a border town in Mexico. They study books on psychology to learn how to talk to their kids and then scream at some underpaid illegal alien because she forgot to wipe the shit streaks off their toilets. They don't see that we're all connected. This is a war we're in, between the powerful and the powerless. It isn't possible to be neutral, even if you smile when you tip your housekeeper at Christmas. Understand?"

"SO-SO. I UNDERSTAND YOU DON'T LIKE HIGH SOCI-ETY."

"Sort of. And once you see how phony everything is, no one wants to be around you anymore. If I disappeared off the face of the planet, no one would care. I almost died a few months ago and no one gave a shit." He paused. "That's not true. My mother gave a shit, but only because she was worried that it was her fault. She thought I was trying to kill myself." He snorted. "Maybe I *was* trying to kill myself."

"HOW KILL?" wrote George. Jeremy didn't understand. "GUN? KNIFE?"

"Pills. Pills and vodka."

George laughed his silent laugh. "THAT MEAN YOU DONT REALLY WANT KILL YOURSELF. I STUDY PSYCHOLOGIA IN UNIVERSITY. IF YOU REALLY WANT DIE, YOU TAKE GUN."

"How would you know anything about it? You weren't there."

George kept laughing. "I TOO THINK I WANT KILL MY-SELF WHEN I AM SAD BUT I NEVER DO BECAUS ITS OUR

RESPONSIBILITY TO LIVE UNTIL ALLAH CALLS US. MAYBE WE DONT LIKE, BUT ITS OUR JOB. NOW TAKE THIS UGLY PIN OUT YOUR NOSE."

He reached over to finger the safety pin, and then gently traced the ridge of Jeremy's nose, as if he were blind and seeing his face by touch. The Hasidic Jews were watching. "Touch me here," Jeremy said, plunging George's fingers down to his nipple. George grabbed the tender skin and squeezed. The Hasidim covered their eyes.

George let go of the nipple and wrote, "WHY YOU COME TO ISRAEL?"

"My mother's idea," Jeremy wrote. "I didn't want to come."

"YOU MAYBE COME BACK AGAIN?"

"I'd like to say yes, but I have to be honest. I really don't know right now."

Sliding his foot up Jeremy's leg, George wrote, "I KNOW," and winked. "YOU WILL COME BACK AGAIN. MANY BEATIFUL SITES YOU CAN VISIT. YOU KNOW THE SILWAN, WHAT IT IS?"

Jeremy shook his head.

"THE SILWAN, THIS MY HOME. BEATIFUL VILLAGE BY OLD CITY. PEOPLE OF ALL WORLD VISIT ARCHEOLOGE SITE OF KING DAVID. SILWAN IS REAL JERUSALEM. MORE OLD THAN OLD CITY." He underlined "IS REAL JERUSALEM" several times. "I SHOW YOU THE SILWAN. OK?"

"Sure." He wasn't hungry anymore and was going to throw away the rest of his pizza, but George grabbed his wrist. Wasting food was a "SYN." He brought Jeremy a box to take it away, and then showed him his notepad: "I WANT TO SEX YOU."

Outside, George pushed Jeremy against a leaning palm and kissed him on the mouth. He pointed to Jeremy and then hugged himself, like he meant "Because of you I love myself." Standing on tiptoe, he kissed Jeremy's nose. Then he clamped his teeth on the metal safety pin and tugged.

"Ow!" Jeremy yowled. "You're deranged, you know that?"

But George didn't know what "deranged" meant.

"Anyway, it's a compliment." He let George kiss him some more. The bark of the palm tree stuck to his shirt as the wide fronds above them whispered, "Shh, shh, this is secret!" But George began moaning. The noises he made might have sounded romantic from a person who could talk, but from a deaf guy they sounded ugly and primal and exciting. Jeremy dug his nails into George's neck.

Suddenly, George pulled away and took out his notepad. "WE GO HOME," George scribbled. "Okay?" he mouthed with a deep groan.

Jeremy was so turned on he'd have said yes to a hanging. George ran into the street and hailed a cab. He wrote down the directions and passed them up to the driver.

In the cab, Jeremy rested his head against the warm vinyl seat and closed his eyes. A few minutes later, he looked up and was surprised to see their car heading eastward and the orange spotlights on the Old City walls disappearing behind them. "Where are you taking me?" Jeremy asked, but George closed his eyes, as if he wanted to sleep.

This is a bad movie, Jeremy thought, looking over his shoulder as they headed even further east, toward the West Bank, Jordan, Iraq. I'm being kidnapped by terrorists for ransom. I guess I'm just destined to die young. He wanted to tell the driver to stop, but the driver looked like an Arab, too.

Something hard hit his shoulder. It was George's head.

So what next? In a movie, the terrorists would ambush their taxi and drag the unsuspecting American, blindfolded, into their jeeps and up into the mountains. But this wasn't a movie, and how could such a little boy as George hurt anyone? Jeremy squeezed George's small chubby body, so easy to fold into his arms. He squeezed again, as tightly as he could, as if he could squeeze out the air and then the skin between them. I love . . . he thought, not quite ready to supply the object to complete the sentence.

Their taxi dipped into a warren of cement houses clinging to one of the silvery rocky valleys around Jerusalem. Jeremy's stomach lurched left, then right, as the car zigzagged through ever narrower alleys before it stopped suddenly in front of a small house.

Jeremy left his pizza behind as he got out, but George grabbed the box, then led him by the hand up a set of crumbled steps into the house as the taxi sped away, its tires squealing. The front door had been left unlocked, and they took off their shoes before going in.

The dim, sunken living room had what Jeremy imagined as an Arabic smell: something like a mix of cinnamon, oil, and hot pepper. They stepped on a thick rug that felt soft and synthetic under Jeremy's toes. He couldn't make out any furniture except pillows on the floor and the glint of a dark TV screen.

Feeling his way along the chalky plaster walls, Jeremy followed George down a tight hallway paved with tile. One of the narrow doors opened into his cramped bedroom, which would have been a walk-in closet back in Michigan. The walls were decorated with pictures of soccer players. A keyboard, two fax machines, and a printer wrapped in black wires were stacked in the corner. "I WANT APPLE IMAC BUT NO MONEY," George wrote.

Jeremy set down his Sbarro's take-out box on a stack of spiral-bound software manuals. "Do your parents know you're gay?" he asked.

"I'M NO GAY. I'M BISEXUAL."

Jeremy couldn't help snorting. "Well, do they know you're bisexual?"

"FATHER NO SAY. BUT HE KNOW. MOTHER KNOW."

"And she doesn't care?"

"YES CARE, BUT SHE WANT I AM HAPPY. MY BOY-FRIEND, ISRAELI SOLDIER, HE STAY IN THIS HOUSE IN SILWAN, IN MY BED."

"And they knew he was your boyfriend?"

"ALL. THEY KNEW ALL."

He began fiddling with a lamp, but Jeremy grabbed George from behind and dragged him down onto the low mattress. It had a valley in the middle and was wrapped in cool, clean Snoopy sheets. Jeremy gnawed on George's neck, attacked the salty skin with darting stabs of his tongue. He molded George's moist curls against his forehead. "I hope you like it rough," he whispered against George's useless ear. Anyway, Jeremy thought, if he can't understand the words, he can feel my breath heating up his neck.

This guy really is an Arab, or isn't he?

When they fell on the bed, George grabbed a pair of socks under his pillow, but Jeremy shoved them away. "Fuck the socks," he said, and stripped George's feet bare.

They couldn't get naked fast enough. George hummed as Jeremy pulled down his jeans. He wore a bathing suit instead of underwear.

"Is this okay?" asked Jeremy, but George's eyes were shut so he couldn't see or hear. Jeremy touched him again, and George grunted with his lips clenched tight and his cheeks beet-red as if he were being strangled. To keep him from waking the whole house, Jeremy sat up and shoved his penis into George's mouth.

George began moaning again, more softly now, and Jeremy wondered if the kid was even aware that he moaned. Was it something one of his old boyfriends taught him, that moaning was part of sex, what hearing people liked?

Have I conquered him? Jeremy thought. Have I absorbed the whole of his being?

Suddenly George let go and, with saliva dripping down his chin, looked up at Jeremy as if for some sign of approval. "It's good, it's good," Jeremy said, pressing the kid's head closer to his body. This is a good reason to be alive, he thought. This, Marlboro Lights, and Captain Morgan mixed with Diet Coke. He tapped George's shoulder as he was about to come, but George wouldn't let go. Jeremy drew back, but when the explosion came, George lunged for the erection and managed to swallow a jet or two before Jeremy pushed him off and splashed white all over the sheets.

"Don't you know that's dangerous?" asked Jeremy, quickly drying himself with the Snoopy pillowcase. "You know AIDS? Do you want to die?" George seemed content to dab the cum off his face with the edge of the bedsheet, very ladylike, but Jeremy wiped his cheeks roughly with the pillowcase before cleaning his chest.

George turned on a small brass lamp and slid his fingers between Jeremy's nipples. For a while, they lay with their pants around their ankles. "HERE IS PEACE," George wrote. "I WANT TO GO TO ALJASKA. I HEAR IS VERY PEACE."

"Okay," Jeremy said, and kissed his cheek. "We'll go to Alaska." At least it was cooler in Alaska.

George rocked with silent, choking laughter. He switched off the light and flung his head onto his pillow. Jeremy felt safe beside him in the dark, in a strange place he didn't know how to escape from, where no one could find him. It was easy, with George's head turned so that he couldn't see, for Jeremy to finish the sentence "I love" with the object "you."

seven

A BRIEF SEVERAL-THOUSAND-YEAR HISTORY
OF NOTHING VERY IMPORTANT

Come hear the story of the Jews who shooed away the Jordanians
Who divided the city abandoned by the British
Who, under General Allenby, blasted out the Ottomans
Who slit the throats of the Mamluks
Who dismembered the followers of Saladin and his Egyptians
Who decimated the Crusaders
Who massacred forty thousand of the city's Muslims
Who disemboweled the Byzantines
Who inherited the Holy City from the Romans
Who skinned the Jews alive with metal combs to punish their
    bands of Zealot guerrillas
Who, years before, led by the Hasmonean dynasty, slew the armies
    of the Greeks
Who hacked up the Persians
Who destroyed the Babylonians
Who pushed back the Assyrians
Who permitted the Jews to restore the rule of the family of King David
Who wiped out the Jebusites
Who founded G-d's holy capital of peace.
(But who the hell are the Jebusites?)

Just before sunrise, the town muezzin called all believers to mosque over a loudspeaker made in Japan. The old man's piercing voice woke Jeremy from a fitful sleep, though George snored right through it.

The hot, cramped room glowed brown in the morning light. Jeremy stared at the rough walls and tried to remember where he was. His bladder was teeming with urine, but he was afraid to venture into the hallway. ("Hi there! I'm the American fucking your son. Now where might your bathroom be?") He closed his eyes for what seemed like a minute. When he opened them, George was gone and the sun, having found a crack between the houses, lit up the room like a hospital ward.

One thing was clear: Jeremy needed a toilet soon, or at least an empty bottle. Rubbing his eyes, he dragged himself to his feet and peeked into the hall.

Someone was taking a shower in the bathroom, but luckily the toilet was in a separate, stinking closet. The water tank was decorated with a cartoon of an African boy holding a strip of smudged toilet paper and staring in horror at a patch of white on his ass.

Jeremy relieved himself with a deep moan and then flushed, summoning a brief but thunderous flash flood. He caught a glimpse of his face in a hand mirror mounted on one of the pipes. His forehead was pink and moist, his lips were dry, and the piercing in his nose throbbed red around his safety pin. As he probed the side of his swollen nostril with his fingertip, sparks of pain shot up his nose into his skull. He touched the nostril again and kept touching it until he got used to the pain. Then he scratched off a flake of dried pus that had crusted over the piercing. Thin rivulets of blood bubbled out of the hole; it was all he could do not to scream as he slid the metal pin out of his nose. Shuddering at his ugliness, Jeremy clipped the pin to a belt loop and threw his head back to stop the bleeding, banging his skull against the water tank in the process.

The nostril still twinged a bit as he stepped out of the toilet-closet, though the bleeding had slowed. He crept down a narrow hall decorated with photos of dark-skinned teenagers in Levi's posing around an old man in a white headdress.

In the kitchen, a woman wearing a brown robe and pink scarf pinned tightly around her face kneeled on a bathmat and kissed the floor. Jeremy waited in the doorway and dabbed his nose. He found the kitchen disappointingly modern, with a white gas range instead of a fire pit, a white sink with white plastic faucet handles instead of a well, and a white dishwasher.

The woman finished her prayers, stepped into a pair of slippers, and began mincing cloves of garlic in her white food processor.

"Good morning," Jeremy said with a wide smile that showed all of his teeth.

The woman jerked her head around and spoke sharply in Arabic.

"You don't speak English, do you?" Jeremy asked, his monkey smile frozen under his chapped, sunburned nose, which was still oozing blood and pus. "English?"

She shook her head while massaging her heart and breathing slowly, deeply.

"*Salam alekem,*" he said, which was all the Arabic he knew.

"*Alekem salam.*" Motioning to the kitchen table, the woman continued preparing breakfast, her brown robe trailing across the mismatched white-and-gray tile floor. Jeremy sat down in a plastic chair. He and the woman ignored each other politely for several minutes.

Enter George stage left, his curls still wet from the shower. He wore a T-shirt that said GOT MILK?, Snoopy boxers, and a wide morning-after grin. His mother spoke in Arabic and he replied in precise, modulated hand gestures that looked like a private language they'd worked out themselves. Jeremy looked on in silence as if he were the deaf-mute.

Together George and his mother set out glasses of hot tea with fresh mint, warm pita, hummus, tabouleh, and a mashed bean dip soaked in oil. They served Jeremy scoops of hummus with a silver spoon, then used strips of pita to dish out their own portions.

"Delicious," Jeremy said, gulping down some hummus. "Tell her."

George tried his best to convey the message to his mother, who stood next to the sink while she ate. She shrugged and licked her fingers, cleaning them delicately with her tongue as if they were someone else's fingers.

"Does she know who I am?" he mouthed as George noisily chewed his pita.

"SHE KNOW WHAT SHE WANT TO KNOW. I SAY HER YOU ARE MY ENGLISH TEACHER," George wrote, and then reached under the table for Jeremy's penis while his mother's back was turned. "I WANT MORE."

George's mother brought over a Coca-Cola bottle filled with olive oil, then stood beside Jeremy as he ate. "*Parlez-vous français?*" she asked, her eyes fixed on his.

Jeremy shook his head. "Just English," he said. "And some Hebrew. *Ivrit.*"

"I speak Hebrew," she said in Hebrew. "Little."

"Me too!" Jeremy said with another monkey grin. "We can speak together."

She stared curiously at the wound in his nostril, which he

quickly dabbed with a napkin. "You are Jewish, yes?" she asked him in Hebrew. "I have met many of my son's international friends. He is good student, good boy, very good. He works and brings home money. His brothers are stupid donkeys. They prefer to complain about politics than to work, but this one, he is smart. It is not too hot for you in this weather?"

"Really, it's okay. And this food is very excellent," Jeremy said.

"I try to make it not so spicy, because Jews have different stomachs than we do. Also Chinese and blacks, even Christians. If I go to a restaurant and the owner is a Christian, I will not eat there, because what is delicacy for one man is poison for another. Even when I first met my husband, who is Christian, I would not eat if he made the food. Thank God, Christians can eat Muslim food. All the world can eat Muslim food. It's the cleanest, safest in the world. Tell me, is it true that in America no one believes in God?"

"Yes, it's true," Jeremy said. "Especially the ones who say they believe."

George served Jeremy another dab of hummus with the silver spoon.

"Why you aren't married?" she said, pointing to his ring finger.

Surprised at the question, Jeremy pointed out, "Your son isn't married."

"He doesn't need no wife. But you, you should get married. Marriage, it's best medicine for a young man. It's written in the Koran."

An awkward silence passed. Jeremy said, "You have a beautiful home."

"You like it?" she said, picking a flake of parsley out of the gap in her front teeth. "It's nothing. Before 'sixty-seven, we lived in the Old City in a beautiful house made of stone. It was a paradise up there. Then the Israelis came with the war and they say to us we got one month to leave our house. We got no money, no nothing. Just go, go, they say us."

"They didn't give you any money?" Jeremy asked.

"Nothing. Just get out, like dogs."

"They were supposed to give you money. I learned about it in school." He remembered this point very clearly from seventh grade. The Jews were different from all other conquerors in history; they reimbursed their vanquished properly.

"Not one lira," insisted George's mother. "The Jews kicked us off the mountain and pushed us into this miserable valley, where it's always too hot. You know they have a nuclear power plant and it changes the weather so it's bad for the Palestinians and good for the Jews. Really. The scientists made proof of these things."

"I'm sorry," said Jeremy, who as a Jew felt directly responsible for her plight. "That's very bad to lose your home," he said. "I believe in peace." Even if she was stretching the truth a bit, she had his sympathies.

"Peace?" she said, gripping the back of George's chair, her worn brown knuckles hard as walnuts. "It's no more peace. Now it's a bad time to be a mother. I have three sons. And this one, but he don't count. He don't get married. He don't fight."

George waved his hands. He tried to groan out a couple of words.

"Why can't they share Jerusalem?" Jeremy forced a laugh. "They have to learn to share, like in kindergarten."

George's mother pulled her scarf tight around her sharp yellow face. "Who cares about Jerusalem? Jerusalem, it's the past. I want to know about future. Jobs, money for the family. When you are Arab in Israel, you have nothing." She pointed to her-self and her son. "We nigger," she said in English.

"NO POLITICS," George wrote on his message pad and un-derlined "NO."

"We don't say 'nigger,' " Jeremy said in Hebrew. "We say 'African American.' "

She shrugged, then switched back to Hebrew. "Schools in Israel are not open for Arabs. And even if he gets U.S. university education, when he comes back he cannot get jobs. The Jews say he don't speak good Hebrew or he was not in army or he smell bad. They say anything. But some Jew from America who don't speak one word of Hebrew, they say okay, you have your Law of Return. Where is our Law of Return? The Jews, they always have to live better than us. We go to grocery and the date on the yogurt it's too old. Why they keep the good yogurt? When my son goes to work, I tell him to bring yogurt from Israel. We see how they live. Believe me. We are not blind."

Not blind, Jeremy thought, just deaf. "But your son has a job in Israel," he said.

"NO POLITICS." George circled the message in English, then wrote it underneath in Arabic.

She covered George's eyes and kissed the top of his head. "He is different. They like to help him. Every day his father wake up at five o'clock and comes home late in the night. My son teaches half-day in Israeli school and gets more money than his father."

George pushed his mother's hands away and started arguing with her in their private sign language. His mother burst into loud sobs and scolded him in Arabic. In response, George waved his arms and wiggled his fingers wildly. Finally, she wiped her eyes with the corner of her sleeve. When Jeremy tried to take the plates to the sink, she frowned and grabbed them from his hands like he'd insulted her.

Come on, George said with his hands, but Jeremy hung back. I want to help, Jeremy thought. It's the least I can do. No, George said with his hands. Come on. Now.

They retreated to the bedroom. George hung a heavy red-and-blue Bedouin blanket over the window, though a few shafts of white shot through the seams. The shade comforted Jeremy, especially after sitting in the hot, glaring white kitchen for so long. He watched George pull on a pair of blue soccer socks with red stripes, then step into a pair of "L.A.–U.S.A." jeans that outlined the curve of his butt. "Hold me, would you?" said Jeremy, tugging at George's waistband. George grinned and fell on top of him.

"LAST NIGHT WE DID A GOOD THING," George wrote as Jeremy kissed the bulge in his jeans. "WHY YOU IN HOTEL? YOU CAN STAY IN MY HOME. NEXT TIME IN ISRAEL, YOU MY GUEST. YOU PAY ONLY FOR PLANE TICKET."

"Okay, okay," Jeremy laughed as George kissed him on the mouth, sucking his breath as if he needed the carbon dioxide to stay alive. "I should probably go," Jeremy whispered. He held George's face still to get his attention. "I'm sure my mother's sick worrying."

"I TAKE YOU TO YOUR MOTHER, NO PROBLEM. WHERE SHE LIVE?"

"They must have left the hotel by now," said Jeremy, calculating a schedule in his head. "We're supposed to visit the Wall today. You know the Western Wall?"

"I KNOW. I KNOW. IS TWO STEPS FROM HERE. I TAKE YOU. YOU MEET MY MOTHER, NOW I MEET YOUR MOTHER."

"Yes, I want you to meet her sometime. But don't you have to work?"

"TODAY I GO TO WORK WHEN I WANT BECAUSE TODAY YOU ARE HERE." George kissed Jeremy on the cheek, then jumped up and held out his chubby hand, his fingers waving. Come, come with me.

On their way out, George's mother handed her son a brown bag with his lunch. "Bye-bye," she said in English to Jeremy, and dropped two dusty Tootsie Rolls into his palm. She had an expectant look in her eyes, red at the rims and so dark they seemed to lack pupils. "Do something for me," she said in Hebrew. "Don't hurt him, please."

"No, no," Jeremy said. "I care about him."

She didn't seem to hear his answer.

Outside, a scrawny black dog, its ribs visible through its hide, barked in warning. "I don't like animals," said George's mother. "They bring disease into the home." George grabbed a deflated basketball lying in the yard and aimed it at the dog, who trotted away, whimpering, into the alley.

Jeremy felt surprisingly alert, even though he still hadn't had his morning cigarette. Maybe I'll try to hold out a bit longer, he thought. Just as an experiment.

They followed the dirt road uphill as it snaked between a jumble of cement apartment buildings, wizened trees, and torn fences. The air smelled sour, as if something had recently died nearby. The men they passed shuffled grudgingly in the middle of the road, while the women moved quickly along the sides of the buildings and kept their eyes down. Jeremy stayed slightly behind George and tried to keep his eyes down, too, but he couldn't help staring when they passed a vacant lot piled high with heaps of open trash that roasted in the sun and stank of feces.

I'm in enemy territory, Jeremy thought, remembering a poem he'd been forced to learn in the eighth grade, about Arabic laundry hanging out to dry.

On a roof in the Old City
laundry hanging in the late afternoon sunlight:

Jeremy had gotten an A for memorizing those lines and the rest of the poem, written by—he'd forgotten who, exactly. And now he was living the life he'd memorized.

the white sheet of a woman who is my enemy
the towel of a man who is my enemy,
to wipe off the sweat of his brow.

George put his finger over Jeremy's mouth. "NOW DON'T SPEAK."

The road bent to the right and cut through a crowded market. Fat women inspected live chickens in cages and bins of mealy-looking fruit. An old man sitting on a used crate held up a wooden tree hung with stringy loaves of bread coated in a dark green spice that smelled like mud. Rows of bloody lamb shanks swung from rust-streaked chains, attracting swarms of flies; Jeremy had to cover his nose and breathe through his mouth. Outside the butcher shop, a donkey hitched to a cart of apricots stepped sideways and let out a stream of bubbling piss. Calmly lifting their robes, shoppers in sandals stepped over the running urine to visit a stand with pirated DVDs. Two women in head scarves fighting over a copy of *Lethal Weapon 4* suddenly scurried into the butcher shop to make way for a shiny red convertible. The driver, a young woman with long black hair, thin arms, and rhinestone-studded sunglasses, pressed her horn and began screaming as if she were on her way to a hospital.

Jeremy felt his heart race as he thought of the shining limestone city up the hill scrubbed pink for spoiled American tourists, fat, rotten capitalists feasting off the fruit of the land like those engorged flies sucking on the lamb carcasses. And down here in this valley, just a few yards from the Wall, these poor innocent villagers scratched for their survival in a festering garbage dump.

He felt angry, then exhilarated with indignation, then miserable. It was as he'd always suspected: There was no way to live innocently anymore.

Maybe you should meet my mother after all, he thought, staring at George. Or maybe my mother should meet you.

At the end of the market, the road widened and shot up steeply toward the ridge of Silwan Valley, where the Israeli Egged buses stopped. George pointed to a fenced-in yard with a sign in English and Hebrew: NATIONAL ARCHAEOLOGICAL PARK OF THE CITY OF DAVID.

———

Mrs. Michaelson arrived at breakfast fifteen minutes before the dining room opened. The rabbi had promised to meet her there. His exact words had been "I told my mom I'd have dinner with her tonight, so I guess I'll see you at breakfast."

As she waited behind the green velvet rope, Mrs. Michaelson felt a new spirit beating inside her, flapping slowly within her chest, then unfolding its wings.

"See you at breakfast, I guess." He'd said it warmly, as if he'd really wanted to see her at breakfast.

A waitress named Natasha waved her in from the other side

of the velvet rope. "Are you sure?" Mrs. Michaelson said. "I know I'm early. I hate to put you to any trouble." But Natasha told her, "Come, come. It's ah-kay."

So Mrs. Michaelson stood by herself with an empty plate and contemplated the usual morning riot that was breakfast: rainbow-colored salads, watermelon boats of cubed fruit, smoked fish marinating in cream, thick white squares of cream cheese, and oily sauces to butter your rolls. Even though he was supposed to watch his diet, Mr. Michaelson used to fill his plate at buffet after buffet from Haifa to Eilat to Tel Aviv. She smiled as she pictured him bending over to sniff the herring.

At first, Mrs. Michaelson had enjoyed the bounty, too, but now the smell from the rich food made her stomach turn. Hadn't anyone in Israel ever heard of rye toast with a poached egg? Or a single table with only the newspaper for company?

"See you at breakfast, I guess," the rabbi had said. Why "guess"? Didn't he know it? Her husband would have chalked up "guess" as evidence of a fear of intimacy. But then, her husband was biased.

Mrs. Michaelson finally settled on a croissant with a pat of butter. And three cucumber slices for health reasons. She sat at a table with a view of the door, and as she bit into a cucumber, a strange man appeared across from her. He said and ate nothing, only smiled, then suddenly reappeared on her left, though she hadn't heard him move.

As she looked more closely at him, she almost fell out of her chair. The truth seemed impossible, but the evidence was there in front of her. She looked again to be sure. There he was, tanner and slimmer than he'd been in weeks, even years.

"Dear? Are you all right?" asked Mr. Michaelson.

She blinked hard and looked again. He was still sitting there; it was no dream. And yet this was not her husband, at least not as he'd left her the day before. This man was healthy, trim, and happy. This man had pretty pink skin instead of dark circles around his eyes.

"Dear?" he repeated.

The man in front of her was waiting for an answer that she felt incapable of providing, or more like unqualified to provide. She took another bite of cucumber, but he didn't disappear. What would he do if she said something back to him?

"I'm fine," she said, swallowing, then lowering her voice. "Only you startled me by appearing so suddenly." Mr. Michaelson nodded as if he understood. "Are you . . ." Mrs. Michaelson wasn't sure how to put the question. "Are you going to start visiting me regularly this way?"

"I'm your husband," he said, speaking with unusual vigor. "Don't I have as much right to court you as your boyfriends?"

"I suppose so," she admitted, her hand shaking as she lifted her cup of Nescafé, which was what you got when you asked for coffee in Israel. "So you knew?"

"You can't keep secrets from a therapist, especially one you've lived with for thirty years."

Her husband wasn't usually so blunt. She liked it. "I wish you'd talk like this to me more often," she said.

"Excuse me, lady." A Filipino waitress named Maria wheeled over a cart of newspapers in English, German, Italian, and Japanese. Blushing, Mrs. Michaelson took a USA Today and hid behind the Life section. Her husband sat in silence while she nursed her Nescafé and blew her nose. (Ever since she'd turned forty, eating made her nose run.) Occasionally she glanced over her paper to watch him stare sternly ahead like a soldier.

More Michiganders trickled into the dining room. A pair of ladies sat down at her table (one of them in the chair where Mr.

Michaelson, who dissolved as mysteriously as he'd appeared, had been sitting) and blocked her view of the door. She quickly stood up. "I'm not leaving," she explained, "just going for coffee."

At the buffet she ran into Aliza with a plastic to-go container heaped high with pita, cucumbers, peppers coated in oil, and bright pink yogurt that looked like laundry detergent. "Helen, you look worried!" said Aliza, her mouth crammed with celery.

"I do? That's nice. Have you seen Rabbi Sherman?"

"Still upstairs," Aliza said, swallowing. "I don't think he'll be coming with us today. But where's Mr. Michaelson? How is he *feeling*?"

"He went home early," said Mrs. Michaelson, not sure she'd heard Aliza right. Not coming? Some nerve! The rabbi had clearly promised: "See you at breakfast."

"I'm sorry to hear that," said Aliza. "I felt I was just getting to know him."

"Me too," said Mrs. Michaelson automatically. How could Rabbi Sherman have lied this way? Mrs. Michaelson was a woman of her word, who kept appointments with the precision of a Swiss watch, who honored a casual promise like "See you soon" as she would a solemn oath. She didn't believe in getting held up in traffic or missing a lunch date because of mysterious overnight illnesses. She arrived early at parties, airports, and restaurants to wait for friends and family members who were congenitally late. Before leaving for Israel, she'd turned off her answering machine so people wouldn't think she'd neglected to get back to them. She'd paid all the bills in advance, asked the post office to hold the mail, set up a schedule for Robert and her sisters-in-law to take turns watering the plants and starting up

their cars. Mr. Michaelson was the same way, and the failure of
the rest of humanity to respect their commitments struck her
as one of life's profound mysteries.

Even on the day her mother had died, Mrs. Michaelson had
kept a dental appointment scheduled months before. Dr. Keller's
time was valuable; she often had to wait months to get in to see
him. And no matter what had happened, she still needed her
teeth cleaned. Wasn't that what Judaism taught? Hide the body
under the ground as soon as possible and move on.

Unlike her father, who'd passed away amid the drama of a
heart attack, her mother had simply died of old age, without
any warning signs. They'd gone over to her apartment that
bright summer morning, and Jeremy (then only eleven) said,
"She looks like she's not breathing." Mrs. Michaelson smiled
because the idea was so absurd, but then her husband felt her
mother's cold lifeless wrist and shook his head.

How could she have just stopped breathing? Whose fault
was it?

Compared with the misery of sitting on her mother's tea-
stained couch with her brothers and making funeral plans, Dr.
Keller's sterile metal drill and cold white basin felt comforting.
Everything went along fine until the hygienist hit a nerve in
her gums and Mrs. Michaelson began sobbing violently and
couldn't stop. The hygienist panicked and called in the dentist.
Mrs. Michaelson confessed everything.

"Why ever did you come?" Dr. Keller asked, offering her a
cup of water that tasted like fluoride. "Go home," said the doctor. "We'll finish another time."

"Actually"—she sniffed and dabbed her eyes with her plastic bib—"I'd like you to finish if you don't mind."

So they did, and she felt very virtuous for the rest of her visit.
She paid her bill, prompt as ever, and then walked to her Buick

with her head bowed. For a while she sat in front of her steering wheel and practiced breathing. "How could she just stop breathing?" she asked, rocking herself in the driver's seat. "Without a fight?"

———

Mrs. Michaelson couldn't wait any longer for Rabbi Sherman to appear at breakfast, so she boarded JACOB AND LEAH & RACHEL, but the rabbi wasn't there either. Baruch was their driver that morning.

"Hello, Shoshana," he boomed. She didn't bother reminding him that "Shoshana" wasn't her name. "No husband today? Hey, when I finish driving this afternoon, you and me, let's go to Geneva, okay?"

"Fine," she said, keeping her eye out for the rabbi as she walked down the aisle. She almost didn't hear Sherry Sherman calling: "Earth to Helen! Come in, Helen!"

"Oh, sorry," said Mrs. Michaelson, shaking her head and clutching the back of a seat for support. "Yes, good morning. What is it we're seeing today?"

"The Kotel!" Sherry said, but Mrs. Michaelson didn't understand. "That's how we call the Wall in Israel. No one says 'the Wall.' It's Kotel. HaKotel, to be precise."

"I've seen that already," said Mrs. Michaelson, backing away.

"But we've got a private tour of the tunnels underneath. Sit, sit. There's no one next to me. Care for the *Times*? I print it off the Internet. Oh, Helen, you forgot your name tag. No, don't run up to your room. It's too late. Anyway, we all ought to know who you are by now. So, I heard your husband left us. I hope he's feeling all right."

Sherry's silences were so unnerving they compelled answers, even from Mrs. Michaelson, who'd decided not to comment when asked about her husband. "He's feeling fine. It was business," she said.

"Business? But isn't he retired?"

"Yes, he is. Partially."

"And your son?" said Sherry, still not satisfied. "Don't tell me he went back, too."

"No, no. He's . . ." Mrs. Michaelson hadn't seen him since the pool. After getting off the elevator, she'd fallen into a deep slumber for the rest of the afternoon, only waking up briefly in the middle of the night to nibble on saltines. "Asleep, I guess."

"You guess? Don't you know?" Sherry cackled to herself. "Call me a Jewish mother, I've got to know what my kid is up to at all times." She tossed a printed-out *New York Times* article on Barak and the upcoming Knesset showdown at Mrs. Michaelson's lap. "That's how I look at the Palestinians, like a mother with a child who's acting out. Maybe you want to give the kid a good smack on the tush, but you have to remember, children act out because they don't know any better. And it isn't just the words you use. You have to show them by your actions how to be adults, because the behavior they see is what they'll learn from you. That's discipline."

"There is no discipline anymore," said Mrs. Michaelson, wishing her husband were there so she could sit next to him. "They grow up like wild animals."

"You really think so? Me, I'm not so sure."

"How about the rabbi when he was a boy?" Mrs. Michaelson asked suddenly. "Let's say he made a promise to do something. Would he usually come through?"

"Absolutely. I'd have gone nuts otherwise."

"But I do go nuts!" She'd raised her voice without realizing.

Several Michiganders turned around to see what the trouble was.

Sherry looked satisfied, as if she'd solved the last clue in a crossword puzzle that had been vexing her all morning. "You sound stressed, Helen, like your life needs a bit of shaking up. That's the real reason you came on this trip, isn't it?"

Far from it, thought Mrs. Michaelson, feeling small next to the mother of her boyfriend, with whom she had nothing in common except the son, and that was the one subject she couldn't talk about. We ought to be friends, but we're not. And now my life needs to be shaken up? What am I, a mixed drink? "What do you mean?" asked Mrs. Michaelson.

"I was just kidding with you. Can't you tell?"

That was the problem—she could never tell.

Behind her, two men were playing Jewish Geography. ("Potomac? No way. My son-in-law lives in Potomac! How about Delaware? Know anybody in Delaware?" "I met a Friedman from Delaware once. What about Philadelphia?") Their wives, just behind them, leaned their heads together and whispered to each other. It gave Mrs. Michaelson the heebie-jeebies, the way these people were so eager to share their lives with strangers who happened to sit next to them on a bus.

Julie Solznick sprinted between their seats and tapped her pen at each of their heads as if it were a magic wand, but no one turned into a frog or a prince.

Where in heck was Rabbi Sherman? Didn't he realize how soon she was going back home, how limited their time together was? Mrs. Michaelson turned her head to look for him so many times, her brain was swimming.

The doors to the bus sighed shut. Still no rabbi. And now they were moving. Too late, even if he did come running out of the hotel at the last minute. But he didn't. She lay back against the headrest. The plush fibers of the seat against her cheek felt like a caress. Her life reminded her of the novel in her purse:

> Rabbi Sherman represented all the passionate yearnings she'd repressed for thirty-seven years. . . .

But that wasn't it. So why was she attracted to him?

She liked that he had his own opinions, which she didn't have to select for him and enforce afterward. Also, his life never seemed boring, and she hated being bored. It reminded her of death. But then sometimes it seemed as if boredom and emptiness were all that life was. And the passionate yearnings weren't what she'd been repressing at all. Rather, they were only a means to fight off boredom and emptiness, which alarmed her more in Israel than at home, because in Israel she'd paid good money not to be bored.

After a fifteen-minute ride, their bus spat them out beside the Wall, where Julie Solznick divvied them into tour groups. Why do we bother? Mrs. Michaelson wondered. What do they want us to learn? Couldn't they just tell us now so we can go home?

She stood apart from the group and rubbed a water bottle against her cheek. Each day it seemed as if this awful weather couldn't possibly get any hotter, but it always did.

Then Jeremy popped up beside her, sans nose ring. "Where have you been all this time?" she tried to ask, but he ignored her and began rattling off another list of grievances.

"Fine, fine," she said, examining her angry son, clear-eyed and full of righteous energy. Anger was good. Anger meant you cared about something. It gave you a way to organize your thoughts, gave you something to do with your time. So he didn't

need her, just as her husband didn't need her, just as she didn't
need that perfidious rabbi. That's right, she thought. Even if he
fell down before her on both knees, she'd refuse him now. Still,
she wanted to see him again, simply to confirm that their relationship really had existed and she wasn't crazy.

Something poked her arm.

"Are you listening to me, Mom?"

"Yes, I'm listening."

"Religion's fine in the abstract, but in practice, it's just another tool people use to divide themselves from each other." Jeremy sounded angry and sure, the way he had when he'd been a
child prophet.

"I see," she said, wincing in the sunlight. Maybe by his absence Rabbi Sherman was trying to send a message that they
ought to call things off. He was right, of course, but she'd have
liked one final meeting to wind things up neatly.

Jeremy was still talking: ". . . and so that's where I spent the
night."

"Sorry," she said, staring at his rumpled clothes. "You slept
where?"

He spoke louder, as if she were old. "In a Palestinian village,
with my boyfriend, George, who is Palestinian." And then she
noticed the young man shifting his feet behind Jeremy and
smiling shyly. He was short, with fat round cheeks, brown curls,
and a deep suntan. Sherry Sherman was pointing him out to a
couple of the wives. "He's deaf," said Jeremy as the young man
began scribbling furiously on a notepad. "He doesn't speak, but
he can read lips, even in English. One minute, George."

But George stepped forward and presented her with a note:
"I'AM HONER TO MEET YOU. I WISH TO OFER YOU A
TUR OF HISTORICL VILIGE OF SILWAN."

Mrs. Michaelson felt sorry for this obviously confused boy.

"What could have possessed you to bring him here, now?" she asked Jeremy as George wrote something else on his notepad.

"He has as much right to stand here as we do," Jeremy said. "His parents had a house here, but they were evicted, driven out by the Israeli army to make room for this beautiful plaza, and it's our fault—mine, yours, and all our tourist dollars."

"Oh, there you are!" said Julie Solznick. "Let me find you a yarmulke. And I don't believe I know your friend. Does he need a yarmulke, or . . . ?"

"Even if that's true . . ." began Mrs. Michaelson, laughing because she was nervous.

"His family told me so. It is true."

She didn't believe him. It just didn't sound Jewish. Since when did you hear of a Jewish terrorist or a Jewish trailer-park serial killer or a Jewish vandal who sprayed graffiti all over? Jews didn't do those things. They invented brilliant theories of physics, led symphonies, guided record-growth economies to soft landings.

The other Michiganders were watching them and whispering. Mrs. Michaelson pulled Jeremy aside and said in a lower voice, "So he's really a Palestinian? I still don't get why you brought him here. What did you expect us to do?"

"To confront the reality you've avoided this entire trip," he said, as if the answer were obvious.

"By making a spectacle of this boy in front of everyone? Did you think we were going to hold a civilized debate on Middle East politics next to the Western Wall?"

"I wish I could talk to him, but my Hebrew's only *kacha-kacha*," said Julie.

"Let me try," said Harry Levinthal. "*Shalom! Ata im-haverim. Ma ha-shem?* I've just told him he's with friends. What's his name?"

"Does he want water? Or grapes?" said one of the wives, holding out a Baggie.

George put his finger on his lips and produced his card, written in Hebrew.

"What's it say?" asked Julie.

"It's too difficult," Harry said. "I can't make it out."

"It's not like I had some plan," Jeremy said to Mrs. Michaelson. "It just evolved. I met his mother this morning, and then when I said I was going to find you, he wanted to come. Should I have said, 'Sorry, I enjoyed meeting your mother and I'd be glad to introduce you to mine, but you're not good enough'?"

And then it became entirely clear to her why George appealed to Jeremy, who was always looking for a savior, a new hobby or cause. George couldn't have been more perfect for him. Their liaison had the potential to last as long as two whole weeks.

"You know I don't treat anyone that way," she said. "You can accuse me of plenty of crimes, and you have, but one thing I've never been guilty of is snobbishness. Am I right?" He didn't answer, which was his way of admitting she was right. "Of course I'd be glad to get to know your friend at a different time, if that's what you really want, but not now, not in this place. See," she said as the Michiganders began closing in on George, who looked bewildered and scared. This kid thinks Jeremy really loves him, she thought. But he's not a toy you can take back to the store when you're tired of playing with it. "How do you think he feels here?"

Jeremy shrugged.

"If you're really interested in getting acquainted and not making a big scene, I suggest you two quietly make your exit and then head to the hotel for lunch. You can charge it to the room, and wait for me there. As soon as I can get away without causing a stir, I will, and then we can all sit and talk. By the way, what happened to your nose?"

"It's infected. I'm going to put some ointment on it."

"You should. It looks awful."

Now Rabbi Sherman came jogging up the road while holding his yarmulke to his head. He was accompanied by a funny little bald man in a shrunken gray suit who began shaking hands with everyone. The bald man's fat wet cheeks reminded Mrs. Michaelson of a Buddha. "Call me Dave," he announced, moving stiffly in his tight suit. She was surprised that he had no eyebrows. "Dave, Dave, that's right."

Then something awful happened. Dave reached for George's hand.

"Hi, there," said Dave, pumping George's hand over and over. His thick neck pressed against his damp collar, fastened tightly at his Adam's apple. "And what's your name? *Shem mish-pachah?*" When there was no response, Dave continued, "Cat got your tongue? Let me check my list here."

He began shuffling some papers in a manila folder, but someone handed him George's card.

At that moment Julie Solznick reappeared with a wrinkled cardboard box and aimed a nylon yarmulke at Jeremy's head. It slid off his hair and fell down his back onto the pavement. Julie picked up the yarmulke and fixed it to Jeremy's hair with a bobby pin.

George looked as if he was going to cry. "He's deaf," Jeremy said, stepping forward.

"I know you, right?" Dave said. "Shabbat dinner. Yeah, I sent you to the Morellis'. Don't you worry about your friend. We have access to sign-language interpreters." He began pressing a few buttons on his cell phone. "I wish you'd mentioned he was in your group before," he chided the rabbi. "Of course I'll get you your interpreter, but I may have to pull a few strings."

"He's not on our Mission," the rabbi explained. "I've never seen him before."

Mrs. Michaelson wished everything would slow down. She wanted to speak, but when she caught the rabbi's glare, she stiffened.

"So he's Israeli?" said Dave. "Even better. Most of them couldn't give a damn about their history. If it weren't for the Americans, the Western Wall would still be the garbage dump it was when the Arabs were in control."

"Another yarmulke coming right up!" Julie said, and dug through her brown box.

George ripped a note off his pad and waved it in Jeremy's face: "WE GO?"

"He has an Israeli passport, but he's not Jewish," Jeremy told Dave.

George shook his paper again. "WE GO?"

Jeremy pushed the paper away. "Right here where we're standing," he announced in a loud stage voice so that everyone around them could hear, even tourists who weren't Michiganders, "this used to be a neighborhood with homes and families and children. Then in 1967, they were all kicked out to live in a slum down the hill from this wall. That's where we ought to be going on a tour."

The Michiganders stood by quietly. Julie Solznick's arm remained frozen in her yarmulke box. Dave folded up his cell phone. A policeman strolled over.

"If he has an Israeli passport, he's an Israeli Arab," said Sherry Sherman. "My understanding is that's not the same thing as a Palestinian. Not at all."

"There's no such thing as a Palestinian," said Dave. "Never in the history of humanity has there been a country called Palestine, not even a territory called Palestine. It isn't even an Arab word. It's Roman. There are no Palestinians in Israel, only Arabs."

"Where's the camera?" said one of the Michiganders.

"Let him come along," said another. "He'll see we're not animals and then he'll report back to all his friends."

The rabbi stared at Mrs. Michaelson, who opened her mouth to speak, but she had no words. "Who is this person?" he asked.

She didn't know what to call him. All that came out was "They're friends."

The policeman asked who was in charge. The rabbi and Dave-the-tour-guide both raised their hands.

"The police are trained for these situations," said Julie Solznick.

"A few seconds ago you were going to find him a sign-language interpreter, and now you want to throw him in jail?" said Jeremy.

"We don't need the police," said Harry Levinthal. "We're all adults here."

The rabbi explained to the policeman (and to Mrs. Michaelson) that Americans often made the naïve mistake of believing everything Arabs said. Sherry Sherman explained to the Michiganders that Israeli Arabs were citizens and had the right to vote like anyone else. Dave explained that it wasn't a matter of politics but registration, and he only had Jews from America registered for his tour. He began reading aloud from his list of registered tourists. Julie Solznick took a head count.

"Let's all calm down," Mrs. Michaelson said, trying to shout over all of them. Why was everyone being so disagreeable? She felt as if she were seeing them all for the first time, and she was disappointed at how ugly everyone was.

"Hear, hear! Not a hair on this boy's head shall be harmed," said Sherry Sherman. "Over my dead body." She turned to shield the boy's head, but he was gone.

"He's gone!" exclaimed Julie Solznick. "I just took a head count."

"You scared him away," Jeremy said, looking everywhere.

"He's gone," Julie repeated. "So we can get started. This way, everyone!" She waved a small Israeli flag to get their attention, then headed for the Wall. Everyone followed except the Michaelsons and Dave, who asked Jeremy, "How well do you know this guy? What I'm getting at is, was this bit of commotion his idea?"

"It was my idea," Jeremy said. "Why? What are you insinuating?"

"I wish you'd taken a moment to think this through," Mrs. Michaelson said. "That's your problem—you rush into everything. This whole episode was unnecessary and ridiculous."

"This whole episode was very necessary. I'm going to find my friend now," said Jeremy.

Dave grabbed his arm. "Do you still have my card?" he asked, pressing something small, flat, and bright into Jeremy's hand. "Here, take another. You seem like a smart kid, but if you run into trouble, call." He gave Mrs. Michaelson a card, too. "I've got connections, and I don't hesitate to use them."

"He's probably on his way to work now. He's probably late, that's all," Jeremy said, and ran away, past the metal detectors and up the road toward the New City.

He makes these attachments so quickly, Mrs. Michaelson thought. And then they let him down and he's left with nothing. Eventually he'd grow old alone, like her gay cousin Walter, a gentle man who lived in a studio apartment and for all she knew subsisted on cat food. She invited Walter to the larger family occasions where he could blend in. He always came, in the same shabby brown suit. He'd nibble on cold salmon and asparagus in cream sauce at a corner table with widows and strangers, and she felt happy she'd included him. Later he'd say thank you and climb into his economy car to slide back into his other life, the sad, lonely life, like Rabbi Sherman, still living with his mother, which was fine for now, but then what?

But then what?—those three little words that ruined everything. You were free to make any choices you wanted in your life. The problem was never in the moment, but afterward, when you faced the consequences.

"Be careful!" Dave called after Jeremy. "This isn't America!" He turned to Mrs. Michaelson. "I've seen this happen before, plenty of times. They come to Israel and fall in love with a cause. He'll be back in his room tonight and after a good hot shower, he'll forget the whole thing. Do you believe me?"

"I don't know," said Mrs. Michaelson, watching Jeremy's back disappear.

"Well, you should. I'm an expert on lost boys, especially of the Jewish variety." He winked, and she smiled a little because it felt good to smile. "Are you coming?"

"I guess so." She sighed. "There's something I want to discuss with the rabbi."

Mrs. Michaelson dutifully held her purse open for inspection at the tunnel entrance, but the guard laughed and waved her through without looking. As she closed up her bag, she noticed a bottle of her husband's sleeping pills that she'd forgotten to pack in his carry-on.

Single file, they entered a sandy cavern lit by bowl-shaped silver lamps that hung from the ceiling. A giant black fan mounted above the ticket booth buzzed ferociously, as if it were about to take off. Mrs. Michaelson was glad her husband wasn't with them. His coughing would have reverberated in there like a thunderstorm.

Dave spoke underneath a pair of frosted glass tablets, inscribed with donors' names in gold letters. "If anyone's interested in tasting the incredible joy of an authentic Shabbat dinner with a family this Friday night, let me know," he said.

"They go back on Tuesday," the rabbi explained, looking right at her, sadly.

So he does remember, Mrs. Michaelson thought, aiming her camera at his face. Robert had bought her an expensive new model for the trip, the kind with lenses and buttons and beeping. She'd left it at home and brought her old camera instead, the one her sister-in-law Rose had recommended: "I went into the store and told the guy nothing too fancy. I'm just an old lady who wants to take pictures of her grandkids."

Maybe that's why other women her age didn't get into trouble with younger men. They were too busy taking pictures of their grandkids.

Dave led them down a flight of steps so steep, it might as well have been a ladder. "Everybody in," he called up from the tunnel below, his tinny voice bouncing off the walls. "Don't be shy now."

The air smelled musty, like clay and rotten eggs, though its dampness felt pleasant after the heat outside. Mrs. Michaelson slowly made her way down the steps until finally her shoe hit the slippery floor, marked with hundreds of crisscrossing treads of sandals and hiking boots; the dizzying pattern made her lose her balance for a second. The rabbi appeared suddenly and steadied her elbow. He was a hairy ape and a boor and she couldn't stand his company for more than a minute, but she was glad for his arm just then. "Thanks, Galahad," she said, and immediately wished she hadn't when he blushed and turned away. Her stupid joke had broken their fragile accidental intimacy by calling attention to it.

Sherry Sherman was telling one of the wives a story about a café in Paris: ". . . and the waiter asked if we were Jewish!" she said in a loud voice. "I asked how he knew, and you know what he said?" Sherry pursed her lips. " 'From ze nose.' "

"That's awful!"

"Oh, the French are horrible anti-Semites."

"It's cooler down here," said Mr. Michaelson, popping up again at her elbow. He wore a spotless suit cut from white linen and fanned himself with a panama hat, as if he'd been dressed by a costume designer for one of those Merchant-Ivory movies that only played at the Maple "Theatre" in Birmingham. He seemed to have shed a good ten years since his appearance at breakfast.

I'm so glad to see you, Mrs. Michaelson thought, and it was the most wonderful thing, now he could hear her thoughts when she directed them toward him. She didn't even need to speak.

We didn't make a mistake, did we?

"You are the only woman I ever wanted," he said. "You are the most beautiful woman in the world."

And I am your wife.

Mr. Michaelson smiled, the insouciant, charismatic smile of a man who knows he has an audience. "But watch out on the left," he whispered.

"Huh? Who's that?" Mrs. Michaelson said. She turned around and almost knocked into Rabbi Sherman, who was walking beside her and rapping on the cavern walls with his knuckles. It suddenly occurred to her that he was in dire need of a haircut. "Why didn't you tell me your husband went home?" he said.

"Shh!" she warned. His voice echoed against the rocks.

The rabbi spoke more softly. "We could have had all evening together."

"To fuck?" What was it in him that brought out her ugly side?

He pushed his imitation designer glasses back with his thumb. "To talk, if you want to know."

They ducked to enter the next chamber, a wide domed cavern with blue-lit walls and several rows of benches facing a plastic model of the Temple Mount. Fans stirred up dust in the corners. The rabbi sat in front, by his mother, and Mrs. Michaelson, sitting behind him, couldn't help admiring his neck. She found the backs of men's necks arousing.

Dave pressed a button in the wall, and the overhead lamps dimmed. A blue light illuminated the model of the Temple Mount, accurate to the last brick of the Western Wall, even the tiniest tile of the twin Muslim domes. Mrs. Michaelson heard a soft horn and a deep voice rumbling overhead: "A *link* in the *chain* of *generations.*"

"You have to know how we got here to understand where we are," Dave informed them. "So let's go back to the beginning of this history, the beginning of Jerusalem, when King David conquered the city from the Jebusites and made it his capital."

The model suddenly split in half, retracted, and sank beneath the stage. A miniature First Temple sprang up through the gap. Dave aimed a silver laser pointer at a tower in the center of the temple grounds. "There's your Holy of Holies. If anyone but the High Priest stepped inside, he would have been killed instantly by a holy light."

Mrs. Michaelson listened carefully, so that later she could explain it all to Jeremy. Rabbi Sherman leaned forward as if he wanted to touch the Holy of Holies.

The music rose by a note and the model split in half again. This time the Second Temple came up, rebuilt by Nehemiah, renovated by Herod, destroyed by the evil Titus.

"Could you say a word about Herod's architectural influences?" Sherry asked.

"Not even one, I'm afraid," said Dave. "That's not my area of expertise."

The model split apart again, but nothing came up. Mrs. Michaelson wondered if there had been some mistake, but Dave said, "The Holy Ark, Aaron's rod, the oil, all the holy relics are still up there. That's our stuff, and if the Arabs would allow some archaeologists to dig we could find it again."

"What do the Arabs have against archaeologists?" asked a Michigander.

Dave came over, planted his foot on the bench, and gazed straight into all their eyes. "My friends, they don't want us to find proof that this ground really is the Temple Mount. Because that would mean we were here in this land first."

"But you said King David conquered the city from the Jebusites," argued Mrs. Michaelson, trying to understand. "So, strictly speaking, weren't the Jebusites first?"

Rabbi Sherman turned around and gave her a stern look.

"Good point, young lady," Dave said with a wink. "And since the Jebusites no longer exist, you have to go by the next-oldest continuous presence, which just happens to be us." He glanced at his watch. "The next group is about to come in."

"Wait," said Mrs. Michaelson, speaking once more without raising her hand. "This is just a thought, but . . . couldn't we do without the Temple Mount and our . . . 'stuff'?"

Now both the rabbi and his mother turned around. "What do you mean?" asked Dave.

"I mean, if it was so important to God for us to have the Temple Mount, would He really need our help to keep it?"

"What's your question?" Dave said. "I hear a statement. I don't hear a question."

"I'm just trying to be fair," Mrs. Michaelson explained to the crowd. "My parents were from the old country and they had a principle of peace in the household. In any conflict, they thought it was always better to give in if it made peace."

"Brava!" Sherry Sherman cried out, applauding. "Teach by example. That's what I've said this whole trip. We've got to do whatever's necessary if it makes peace."

"If!" said Dave, his finger raised, "*if* it makes peace, which, as anyone who has dealt with Arabs knows, is a very big if. Now please follow me, ladies and germs."

The rabbi leaped to his feet and followed Dave and a few of the ladies out of the cavern. He ignored Mrs. Michaelson as if she were one of the germs.

On the other side of the auditorium, the rocky ceiling extended above their heads like a brown sky. Dave led them down a wide set of steps to a giant section of exposed Western Wall, lit bright yellow. "This is just as much Western Wall as what's above," he explained, his dress shoes tapping the dirt floor. "Like a tooth below the gum."

They followed a tight passage next to the Wall while above them, blue lights flashed and the deep voice rumbled "A *link* in the *chain* of *generations.*" Just ahead of Mrs. Michaelson, Sherry Sherman lectured about low-fat frozen yogurt and high-fructose corn syrup.

"I finally found out how she ties her scarves," said Bunny Lowenstein.

"Oh, how?" asked her friend. "That's worth the whole trip."

"You take one short end and one long and then you wrap it around, once, twice, and then again. You can do that with long scarves."

Mrs. Michaelson listened with envy to the lovely lilt of their chitchat. There was an art to the way these pros managed it. Mr. Michaelson's mother had been a pro at it. Mrs. Michaelson had always felt a bit awed around her and her bons mots.

The two ladies were talking more softly now and Mrs. Michaelson crept behind them to hear. "What do you think, Helen?" said Bunny, making room for her to catch up.

Surprised they'd included her, Mrs. Michaelson tried her best to look confused and said, "I didn't hear what you were talking about."

"We were talking about Rabbi Rick. You two were chatting earlier. Did he give you that sob story about his wife leaving him? He tells that to everyone. But then last night, I e-mailed with a friend of mine from St. Louis." Mrs. Michaelson didn't quite get what e-mail was, though it had been explained to her on several occasions. Now she just pretended to know so people wouldn't think she was a dunce. "According to her, Rabbi Rick was the most notorious playboy. She said he used to ask for all the gals' numbers after services, sometimes two at a time. He'd date each one once and never call again. By the time they fired him, he'd dated more than half the single women in his congregation. I told you there was something funny about that man."

"Watch your heads," Dave said as they approached a low lintel wrapped in black padding. But Mrs. Michaelson was so engrossed in Bunny's story that she hit her forehead anyway.

The rabbi himself bounded forward immediately, ushered her to the side of the path, and shooed the other Michiganders into the next cavern.

"But—" Bunny started to object.

"Go ahead. Keep it moving," he said, pulling out his handkerchief. "Go on. I'll make sure she's okay. Yes, Mother, you go on too. There's nothing to see. Keep moving ahead. We're on a schedule. That's it."

As soon as the others were gone, he smoothed the brown skin of her forehead with his rough thumbs, brought her mouth to his, and held it there. "Come on," he said, pushing her into a shadowy recess in the rock walls. She didn't close her eyes at first, but then her lips loosened and she felt as if she'd blacked out. Now her arms were moving. Her hands clutched his shoulders. She felt the hair on his skin through his cotton shirt. Did he do this with all his other women?

"There's another group coming soon," she managed to gasp between kisses.

He stuffed his raspy tongue into her left ear, and she felt as if the ceiling might cave in. At any moment a Michigander might come back to see how she was doing and discover them together. Fine! Fine! she thought, the rock wall digging into her back. Let them come! They must have guessed already, or had they? The rabbi's hands were all over her now. They sprang into action at a moment's provocation. He was so unlike Mr. Michaelson, who required extended passionless foreplay to come to life. Despite the awkwardness of his conjugal visits, her husband insisted on them, maintaining that a healthy sex life was important for a good marriage.

"Finally, we're alone," said Rabbi Sherman in a hot whisper against her neck. "When I heard your husband left you, I was reminded of me and my Lisa so long ago."

"What do you mean, my husband left me?"

"Not so loud," he said, letting go of her. "This is new for me, too. I've never been responsible for breaking up a woman and her husband before."

"But he didn't leave me. He left, but he didn't leave me."

He looked at her as if she were naïve. "Answer me honestly. Do you love him?"

The question made her think of that song from *Fiddler on the Roof,* the one when Tevye asked his wife whether she loved him and she said, "I've washed your socks for thirty years." "I do," Mrs. Michaelson said, and then surprised herself by adding, "And you, too," which wasn't true, and pulled him closer by his waistband. "Kiss me again." She wanted him to disgrace her in front of everyone. She'd given up caring about dignity.

The rabbi stepped back. Had she been too bold? It was his fault. He'd transformed her into some kind of slut. "Call me Rick," he said, tucking the front of his shirt back into his pleated khakis. "Don't get me wrong. I'm glad you told him, though I wish you'd consulted me first. It's just that this is all going so fast." He peeked into the cavern. "Come on," he said, kissing her forehead. "We'll talk later."

"Wait," she said. "There's something I need to ask."

"Don't worry, I promise to take care of you forever and ever and all that jazz," he said, kissing her again. "But now we've got to go back. They'll be wondering."

His kisses were rough and left her short of breath. Still, she managed to collect herself and follow him into the next cavern, where a row of Orthodox women in black dresses bowed their heads beside an exposed section of the Wall. They'd pressed their eyes shut and were rocking on their heels while silently moving their lips. Their faces were lit by white candles dripping over stacks of black books.

Mrs. Michaelson bowed her head by the Wall too and held out her hand to touch the stones. One of the women offered her a black book, but she didn't take it. These were holy stones under her fingertips, just the way it said in the glossy brochure she'd received at the tunnel entrance, but she found it impossible to feel holy on command because of the presence of stones. Contrary to the brochure's promises, these stones had failed to inspire in her the chanting of the Levites, the lyre of King David, or the prophecies of Ezra, Nehemiah, or any of the other personages subsumed in the vague category of "sages."

So why not give this place back to the Palestinians? The only ones who seemed to need it were these dour women in black and their husbands up above, whose rules didn't apply to her anyway. The rabbi and I have broken a Ten Commandment, she realized.

How would these women have punished her? As far as Mrs. Michaelson knew, Judaism didn't have a hell. Judaism was about life, not what came after. It was an honor system, a code enforced by people, not God. The ultimate peer pressure religion.

Which meant she was in the clear as long as no one found out.

"There's just something about candles," Sherry Sherman was saying.

"On the ship, we weren't allowed to use candles because they're a fire hazard," said one of the wives. "Instead, they gave us Flashlights of Remembrance."

While the Michiganders drifted into the next chamber, Mrs. Michaelson screwed up her eyes at the praying women. She tried to imagine they looked happy.

"Helen!" Sherry said, clutching Mrs. Michaelson's elbow. "You look awful."

"I need some air, I think," she said, desperate to get out of that horrible cavern. The ceiling looked awfully low. How could they be sure it wouldn't cave in, especially under the weight of all those sandals stomping carelessly above ground?

Mr. Michaelson, appearing again, gave her a nudge. "Now don't you wish you'd gone home with me?" he said.

———

They walked for another twenty minutes and then reached the end of the tunnel, a wide sandy stairway beside a pool of still green water. The ceiling was punched with hexagonal holes from when the Israelis had blasted out the new exit. The Palestinians rioted when they'd tried to open the old exit, a narrow, ancient set of steps from Roman times.

Mrs. Michaelson stared glumly into the smooth green pool. She imagined dipping her bare toe into the scum and stirring it up.

While passing around a coin box for donations, Dave announced, "An armed escort is waiting for us upstairs. We will walk through the Arab Quarter back to the Kotel as one group. There won't be any trouble as long as we stay together."

They slowly climbed back up toward the earth's surface, and the air grew warmer and smelled clean again. At the top, they passed through a metal turnstile and staggered out into the light, where the heat fell on them like a blanket.

Palestinians were perched on stools in front of the shops by the exit. They smoked hand-rolled cigarettes and stared deadpan at the gathering crowd. Lanky teenagers with thin, ropelike arms ran back and forth with rolls of Persian carpets. A woman in a white headscarf sitting on the ground elbowed the curly-headed boy next to her. Immediately they held out their hands and assumed pitiful expressions on their faces. "Please, please," they wailed in unison. None of them looked like terrorists, as far as Mrs. Michaelson could tell.

I'm ready for a nap, she thought, floating in a daze from the heat and the light. Sleep was one of the few things that brought her joy lately.

Soldiers wearing yarmulkes herded them into a group with their machine guns. Dave barked at the soldiers in Hebrew. "Stay together!" he warned the Michiganders. A teenager, Palestinian or perhaps Israeli Arab, sidled up to Mrs. Michaelson and asked if she was enjoying the weather. "Very hot, yes? Very hot. Even for us it's hot." Before she could answer, he'd offered her a basket of wooden camels. The Israeli soldiers had begun to stray ahead, and she drifted after them.

"You were wonderful," Sherry Sherman told Dave.

"Stay together!" Dave barked, waving the Michiganders into a circle. "Where are you going?" he yelled in Hebrew at the soldiers. "Find a buddy!" he yelled in English.

The rabbi moved toward Mrs. Michaelson, but Sherry grabbed his hand.

"I guess we're buddies," one of the women said to Mrs. Michaelson. "I heard your husband had to go home early on business." The woman had ornamented her name tag with leaves and swirls. "What kind of business is he in?"

"The usual kind," Mrs. Michaelson replied, trying to smile.

"Let's move out!" Dave said, waving his arms. "Let's go! Let's go!" The Israeli soldiers snickered at him when he wasn't looking.

A carpet shop they passed was playing a bubbly pop song that one of the young marrieds identified as "Oh God, not Britney!" Most of the other stalls played Arabic music: tambourines and wailing maidens in distress. Teenage boys ran alongside their procession with deliriously patterned carpets, which they unrolled right on the road. "*Madame*, please! Miss, *S'il vous plaît! Bitte schön! Parla italiano? Español?*" they cried with the most beautiful and charming white smiles. They bowed, then jogged ahead and unrolled more carpets stitched with flowers, vines, and snaking tendrils. "We make you good price!"

"You've done nothing wrong," Mr. Michaelson said. "Stop feeling guilty."

"How can you say that after all I did?" she asked, making a mental note to call him when she got back to their hotel.

"Excuse me?" said her buddy.

It was hard to feel innocent when you were marching in the company of soldiers. She felt as if she and the other Americans were soldiers too, every one of them, staking their claim to the city with their money and their feet.

"Look at it this way," said Mr. Michaelson. "If Jews didn't come here and buy souvenirs, where would the Arabs get the money to pay for their beautiful white smiles?"

True enough, thought Mrs. Michaelson. She asked her buddy if she wouldn't mind stopping for a T-shirt.

"I'm so glad you were brave enough to speak up," said her new friend. "I feel so awful, the way they're all begging. Come on, let's buy something."

But Dave herded them on like a sheepdog. He wasn't giving them time to stop, not even for a postcard. "I wouldn't give them any money," he said when Mrs. Michaelson asked. "They give it all to Arafat."

It was one of those statements that felt true, even if it was false. Like "All Arabs are terrorists." Or "The only thing Arabs understand is force." If she'd seen them written down on a piece of paper, she would have easily recognized these statements as ridiculous. But in the solitude of her skull, they seemed too persuasive to refute with such a weak tool as logic.

So who was wrong? Were both sides wrong and both right? That was her husband's kind of thinking, totally useless, like throwing up your hands when your kid carved a hole in his nose with a safety pin. There had to be some kind of answer.

They marched through another alley and then ended up back where they started, on the slippery, cleanly swept floor of the Wall plaza. Mrs. Michaelson was desperate to speak to the rabbi in private. But as soon as they passed the metal detectors, he was surrounded by admirers, petitioners, and amateur Talmudic scholars who practiced medicine and law and were eager to pick a fight with a man who'd lived out their dreams.

eight

A FEW PALESTINIAN FOLK PROVERBS

1. A man who loves does not hate.
2. Your close neighbor is better than your faraway brother.
3. Don't drink from a well and throw a stone into it.
4. A man who digs an evil hole will fall into it.
5. The house is our father's and the strangers came to kick us out.
6. One day, the oppressor will be crushed like garlic.

George would not be found. Jeremy trudged all around the Old City walls, but his new boyfriend seemed to have melted into the stones. All along the way, the high white noon sun blazed in his eyes, and the hummus from breakfast burned a hole in his stomach like cheap whiskey. Tourists filing through the Jaffa Gate gawked at him with pitying and astonished looks on their kind faces.

He continued his search for what seemed like hours, and was in fact, according to his watch, more like fifteen minutes. Finally he gave up and hopped on a public bus running down Jaffa Road. He was hoping for quiet, but the bus was packed with screaming religious-school boys in black velvet yarmulkes on their way home for lunch. Jeremy could easily have become one of them. He already knew many of their rules. But in the end he could never have gone through with it. Going Orthodox would have been too much like giving up.

One of the boys stole his friend's shoe; it sailed over Jeremy's head like a football.

——

Mr. Michaelson phoned from Michigan to report that Robert, Phyllis, and Rose had neglected the plants, the post office had stuffed up their mailbox instead of holding their letters, and the freezer had gone out. Ten pounds of hamburger as well as a brisket had spoiled. "It's a disaster here," he complained. "Like they all did it on purpose."

"Don't be silly," she said. "Who would do it on purpose?"

He laughed. "Who, who, who. You sound like an owl."

His voice sounded different, more shrill. "How are you on food?" she said, retreating to safer ground.

"I bought some hot dogs, and ice cream," he replied, just as she'd imagined he would. He didn't like to order in, because he hated talking to strangers and he'd never cared for servants of any kind, except his own lovely wife. "The best restaurant is here at home," he'd say, as if it were flattery. Maybe he really thought it was flattery. "The price is right, the meals are tasty, and you know the help isn't spitting in your food." (More than once, Mrs. Michaelson had fantasized about spitting on his steak, his veal chops, his meatballs, always tasty, always served piping hot.)

"My brother and Rose said you're welcome by them," Mrs. Michaelson said. "Or she'll bring food over. You don't have to microwave hot dogs. Didn't they call?"

"They might have," he said. "That led me to the other thing I was going to tell you. I changed the phone number. We're unlisted now."

"What? You did not."

"I did. Your friends keep calling at all hours when I'm trying to sleep."

"What friends? I don't have friends."

"Jeanie Saulson, Elaine Max, and Deborah Kahn," he said accusingly.

But Deborah was the volunteer coordinator where she taught her Russians. That was a coworker, not a friend. Elaine was their neighbor across the street, a chatty mother of three children and one dog that trampled Mrs. Michaelson's (now dried-out) azaleas. Elaine was convinced they were all friends because Mrs. Michaelson took in the mail when the Maxes went on vacation, even though Mrs. Michaelson always made it a point to limit their interactions to nonsense she might have shared with the mailman. As for Jeanie, well, there he had her. She and Jeanie had been friendly since high school. They took turns taking each other out to lunch.

Mrs. Michaelson sank back against her chair. "We've had that number sixteen years. You changed it without consulting me?"

"That's why I'm telling you now."

"Did you at least let Robert know?"

Mr. Michaelson said nothing.

"You were going to tell him, weren't you?" she said. "I can't believe you."

"Fine, I'll tell Robert."

"And my brothers." Was there anyone else? She couldn't think. Who else should he tell? Who else mattered in her life? "What is wrong with you?"

"It's quiet here without the phone, and without your feet going pitter-patter all the time," he said.

"Why don't you catch up on some rest," she said, too angry to speak anymore. "I'll let you go now."

"Without your teakettle whistling either," he added, as if he hadn't heard her, but of course he'd heard. Not like years ago when a transatlantic call was an event, expensive and rife with static. Now it was simply a matter of dialing an extra number or two, and the person sounded as if he were in the next room. "You're coming back soon."

She realized he was asking a question.

"Of course we are. It's on the itinerary. Unless you've changed our address, too."

After he gave her their new number, she hung up and stretched across her empty queen-size bed. If she didn't come back home, who would notice? She stared at her wrinkled toes until she dozed off, and then woke up starving for a cheeseburger.

"Don't you know milk and meat it's not kosher?" said the guy from room service.

She settled for a hamburger and wolfed it down, grinding the meat and fries into pulp, followed close behind by the parsley garnish. It was all gone in five minutes and still she felt so ravenous she could have eaten the drapes. What else? She was too embarrassed to call room service again, so she began rummaging through the mostly empty drawers. She found two outfits, a few souvenirs, and a box of chocolate coins.

Mrs. Michaelson ripped the box open and was making substantial progress through the coins when she heard someone knock on her door. The carpet was covered with twisted gold wrappers, which she kicked under her bed. Licking her fingers, muddy with chocolate, she hurried to see who wanted her.

"It's me," Jeremy said. "I'm going out."

"Don't you look nice!" she exclaimed, wedging herself inside the doorway so he couldn't come in. He did look nice, in a pair of crisp white pants and a pale orange shirt that didn't smell of smoke. His hair was washed and combed straight across instead of pushed up, and the dye had almost faded from the sides. Also, his eyes were clear and alert instead of streaked red. If only the hole in his nose weren't glowing like a welt.

"Are you all right?" he asked. "You have a stain on your shirt."

Indeed she did have a stain, a brown Africa-shaped patch above her heart. "I was eating a hamburger," she explained, and her stomach rumbled as she thought of the chocolate, half a box left to finish. "I'll wash this out now. You go have a good time."

"Don't you even want to know where I'm going? You're not worried?"

"Of course. Yes, I am worried. Very. But you're an adult. I can't watch over you for always. Did you make a date with your friend?"

"Not exactly"—he hesitated—"but I know where I can find him. . . ."

"You care about him," she said, impressed. Really, apart from his nose, Jeremy looked better than he had in months. He could be good-looking when he wanted to be, in the same way his father had been at that age.

And then she had her epiphany: Jeremy was cured. The plan had actually worked, just not in the way she'd expected. Well, if it took a deaf Palestinian boyfriend to bring Jeremy back to the world of the living, then bully for deaf Palestinian boyfriends. Her task was complete.

"Even if I didn't like him, I'd care about him," Jeremy said. "He's a real person."

"I'd like to meet this young man properly," said Mrs. Michaelson, twisting the doorknob. "If he's important to you, he's important to me."

Jeremy frowned. "You make it sound so serious."

"Isn't it, though?"

He rolled his eyes.

"So when do I meet him?"

"At least let me ask him first."

"There's no time. We're leaving the day after tomorrow, remember?" Horrible but true. So little time, and she still had all these questions. "Where does he live?"

"No, no, definitely not there." He checked his watch. "There's this tourist attraction where we could meet. It's an archaeological site called the City of David. The real City of David. It's down the hill from the Western Wall. That should be safe. Look it up in Fodor's. We'll meet you there, both of us."

"When?"

"Lunchtime. Noon."

She was about to say she'd check with his father first, but of course she didn't have to. "Fine. Noon at the City of David. Don't be late. How will I find you?"

"It's not big. Just look around. We'll be there. Or I'll be there if he won't come, but I have a feeling he'll want to." Jeremy wrinkled his nose. "I think he's infatuated."

That word again. "Yes, well, he's got himself quite a catch." She thought about touching her son somewhere. A pat on the head? The shoulder? The forearm? Nothing seemed quite appropriate. Her hand levitated in front of her, between them, and then fell without making contact.

"I have to go now," he said.

"See you tomorrow, then. And . . ." Suddenly she reached out and cupped her son's cheek. She saw a little boy in front of her, the one who'd sneaked into her bedroom at age four and smeared her lipstick all over his face, long before turning gay. "Be well."

He looked at her strangely before he left.

In the back of the taxi to Independence Park, Jeremy tried to feel worthy of the love for George his mother had ascribed to him, but he only felt horny. He wanted to look at porn all day and troll for sex in dirty saunas at night and prance around in underwear in a club where they'd pay him to dance on a bar for dirty old men who'd stuff his crotch with dollar bills. And when it was over, he'd cry in a hot bath.

Hormones ruined everything pure. He wished he were brave enough to slash off his dick. Why had his mother been so dramatic about this fling with George? Either she made too much of things or too little, but she always got it wrong. His father, on the other hand, asked too many dumb questions.

The horny feeling still hadn't gone away when the cab-driver dropped Jeremy off on the wrong side of Yoel Salomon Street, next to the Muslim cemetery where Noam Morelli had promised "serious action." It was just before dusk, and the grove of tall, thin-necked trees inside the black fence looked invitingly dark. He imagined all the orgies going on in those shadowy woods, the moaning men with their arms and legs interlocked.

There were no cars on the road, only a few empty tour buses stationed next to the park. No one watched Jeremy jump over the fence.

The cemetery was overgrown with brittle wild grass. His hands shoved deep into his pockets, Jeremy waded through the knee-high weeds until he found a path, a groove of sand that skirted a cement reservoir, now dry. The bottom of the reservoir was covered in dead leaves.

No writhing naked men. The only sounds he heard were his own crunching footsteps broadcasting his arrival. Maybe he was walking into a trap set by bloodthirsty Arab teenagers. Or what if his sandals were disturbing the peaceful rest of homophobic Muslim ghosts, determined to wrest back their cemetery from the faggots? What if he died there? Who'd find him?

He was relieved when he reached the cover of the trees. Their white trunks gleamed like bones in the soft light. A roof of leaves grew thickly overhead, shutting out the sky except for a few bits of powder blue.

His orange shirt and white pants glowed in the shadows like a sign: I WANT TO GET FUCKED! ACTUALLY, MAKE THAT RAPED. AND WHILE YOU'RE AT IT, FEEL FREE TO STEAL ALL MY CASH AND PLASTIC. Turn back now, Jeremy thought, but he wasn't willing to turn back.

The path ahead was covered by dark green ivy dotted with blue star-shaped flowers. Bending down to pick a flower for George, Jeremy noticed a condom stretched inside out and stamped into the dirt. He probed the condom a bit with a stick, and then flung it away, onto a small square pile of rubble. Coming closer to get a better look, Jeremy realized the rubble had once been a headstone. Bristles of grass sprouted like stray hairs out of the gaps in the rock. An oblong slab, cut in half by a lightning-shaped crack, was balanced on top of the ruined base. The slab was carved with Arabic letters but as the stone eroded they were gradually erasing themselves. The jagged writing moved from right to left like Hebrew, though it lacked Hebrew's blocky rigor.

As Jeremy continued down the path, he passed several more dilapidated graves. In America they'd have been antiquities;

here they were practically contemporary art. How many years would it be before the trees and the grass finally crushed these graves into dust and swallowed up the crumbs? He walked on tiptoe, afraid to step the wrong way and trample over someone's old jawbone.

This is the kind of cemetery I'd like to be buried in, he thought. I'll have to leave instructions for next time.

One of the graves up ahead seemed to be moving. First it grew an arm, then a head and torso. As Jeremy crept closer, he made out a face: a gaunt nose, tired cheeks, a long, drooping mustache. The face belonged to a shirtless man slumped against the stones, his fingers tracing a line down his thin chest.

Jeremy rubbed his sweaty hands on his pants and moved even closer. He found himself opening his own zipper slowly, and when he reached the grave, his erect penis was pointing to the man's eyes.

The man fished in his pocket for a foil packet of lubricant, which he tore open between his teeth.

What if your mother could see you now?

Good, I hope she can. Jeremy locked his jaw and prepared for the worst. He was ready for the pain of fucking. He wanted it.

What about George?

He deserted me, remember? Anyway, I never agreed to anything. I belong to no one.

The stranger's cold, crooked forefinger, rough as a Brillo pad, plunged deep into Jeremy's anus. I can't breathe! I can't breathe! Jeremy pressed his stomach with both hands. I want to breathe! I take it all back now. Get me out of here.

"Sorry," Jeremy stammered, pushing the man's arm away.

The man said something in Arabic and tapped his lip with two fingers, but Jeremy was already hopping back to the path with his pants around his ankles and his erection flapping in the open air. How stupid of me to say "Sorry," he thought, hoisting up his pants. Why don't I just paste an ad on my back: I'M A YANKEE DOODLE DANDY.

He zigzagged between the trees without worrying about following the path or kicking up anyone's bones. A stray branch nicked his cheek. I've got to get out, he thought. No one knows I was here, and if I can find my way out no one will, except maybe God. And even if He does know, with all that's going on in Jerusalem, I doubt He'd give a flying fuck.

The forest came to an abrupt end at a field of tall dry grass, on the other side of the reservoir. Two old men sitting on crates tended a small fire ringed by rubble from the graves. A girl with dirty blond hair mowed circles in the grass on her squeaky tricycle, then aimed herself into Jeremy's long legs. "*Yahood! Yahood!*" she cried, which even Jeremy could guess was Arabic for "Kike!"

But how could she have known the truth just by looking at him?

Forcing a grin for the old men, Jeremy turned the girl's handlebars aside and stepped in a patch of mud, the only patch of mud in all Israel that hadn't dried up. (Besides the Dead Sea mud sold in aluminum packs for tourists to smear on their faces.)

Footsteps cracked through the woods behind him. The man with the drooping mustache emerged from the trees, only a few yards away.

Losing his cool completely, Jeremy ran, fists clenched and pumping, feet flying. The rock mounds were everywhere now, laced with dried grass and wildflowers in purple, yellow, and white. One of the mounds stood in the middle of the path. He jumped clean over it.

Jeremy didn't dare look back until he reached the black iron fence, which he hurdled, and then ran in front of a taxi cruising down Yoel Salomon Street. The cab stopped short of his toes, and the driver stepped out to hurl insults. "Sorry!" Jeremy yelled, scrambling across the road into Independence Park. Sorry, sorry, sorry. Sorry I ever set foot in this godforsaken place. He collapsed on the park lawn and buried his face in the grass. A row of red lights spelling SHERATON winked at him over the blue-black trees.

I'm neutral, goddamnit! Why is everyone out to get me? As he brushed his hair with his fingers, he touched nylon. Fuck, he thought, patting his head in horror. All this time he'd had a black yarmulke bobby-pinned to his hair. He pulled it off and stuffed it into his back pocket with his cigarettes and Dave's business card.

Across the street, the shirtless Arab stopped just inside the fence and pantomimed kisses across the road, as if there were no point in leaving the cemetery. Jeremy gave him the finger and then climbed uphill until the cemetery disappeared.

The park was crowded with men, men in sleeveless shirts leaning against the trees, shirtless men lying on their backs and tweaking their nipples, men in T-shirts, men in suits, men holding hands with other men. Jeremy sat on a bench next to a fat Hasid munching on a sandwich while keeping one hand on his bike, propped up beside him. He had a transistor radio and listened to the news, delivered by an Israeli version of Rush Limbaugh.

"Do you have the time?" the Hasid asked in Hebrew.

According to the radio, that traitor Barak was going to get fired by the Knesset before he got the chance to fly to Camp David and carve up Israel like a honey-baked ham with Clinton and Arafat. No Barak, no deal.

"Do you have the time?" the Hasid asked again. Jeremy

shook his head and got up. He hadn't gotten far when a short, plump man with thin silver hair asked him in polite Hebrew for a cigarette. The old man picked through Jeremy's pack of Marlboros with long, sharp nails. Jeremy took out a cigarette too, but only rolled it between his fingers. I'm quitting, he thought. I want to live a long time.

"And could I trouble you for a light?" the man added in English.

"Is it that obvious I'm American?" Jeremy asked, holding out the lighter. He never let anyone hold his lighter, even for a few seconds. Too many times people conveniently forgot to return it and left him craving a cigarette or a joint later with no way to start one up.

The old man covered Jeremy's hand with his own as if to shelter the flame. "You all have such clean white hands," said the man, blowing a plume of smoke out of the corner of his mouth. He looked old enough to be Jeremy's father. "So soft, like you've never done work in your lives." He smiled. "What are you looking for tonight?"

"I don't know." Jeremy didn't want anything. Only to find George, make sure he was okay. To see that he had a good life. And to be his friend again.

"Do you want to go somewhere?" The man opened his belt as if to adjust it a few notches.

"I'm fine here," said Jeremy. The Hasid with the radio waved at them. "What does that guy want?"

"What do you think? They have dicks like any other man."

Jeremy turned away and spotted George at the top of the hill, standing exactly where they'd met two nights before. He yawned and stretched out his arms, and the hem of his T-shirt lifted over his round stomach, revealing a stripe of white underwear. Jeremy often spent several minutes in front of the mirror hitching down his own pants to achieve that same suggestive effect.

"Is it safe to go with Arabs?" Jeremy asked, staring at George.

The old man shrugged. "Whoever you go with, you have to be careful."

"I'm from New York," Jeremy said. "I know all about being careful. But this is different. They're so full of hate."

"Why shouldn't they be?" said the old man with another shrug, the typically Israeli shrug with the arms and eyebrows raised, the nose, eyes, and mouth wrinkled.

George was looking at them.

"Actually, hate, it's not the right word. But I tell you, I have a Palestinian friend, a very educated and reasonable man, and he said to me recently 'I see no alternative but war.' "

George recognized him now, and was seconds away from drawing conclusions. Jeremy held up his finger. One minute, George. Wait for me, please.

"We are in love with our victim mentality," said the old man. "We're so afraid they're going to kill us, we can't think clearly—"

"I've got to go, actually," Jeremy interrupted.

The man took a puff on his cigarette, then blew out a long head of smoke. "I understand. Go have fun, and thanks for the smoke."

Jeremy ran up the hill, but George turned his back, climbed over a low stone wall, and disappeared into a pine grove. This isn't how it looks, Jeremy wished he could yell. Give me a chance to explain. But what could I explain? I didn't do anything wrong.

He banged his shin as he jumped over the wall and into the wood. The trees grew close together, and Jeremy had to cover his eyes and walk sideways through the sharp branches. The sandy floor was carpeted with a loose layer of brown needles and plastic irrigation tubing pinned to the dirt.

George leaned against one of the pines, his knee bent forward like an invitation. His mouth hung open as he fanned himself with his T-shirt. The waistband of his underwear flashed: CALVIN KLEIN, CALVIN KLEIN. The air smelled like gasoline.

"There you are," said Jeremy. Limping a little, he ducked under a thorny branch and bumped gently against George's knee. He could hear George breathing noisily through his mouth. George's breath tasted slightly rancid when they kissed.

Forgive me, Jeremy thought. You're far superior to all other Arabs and faggots. I understand now.

He fingered the raised bumps of stitching on the waistband of George's underwear. It was a relief to let go, to touch and be touched. Jeremy yanked down his own pants without loosening his belt. I feel alive, he thought. I feel blood pumping under my skin. "I like your underwear," Jeremy said, closing his eyes. He forgot where he was or whose body he was rubbing against.

Someone grunted behind them.

"What's that?" Jeremy said, freezing.

A thin old man with a shrunken head and webbed brown neck was spying on them from behind a tree. One of the straps of his dark green overalls hung loose. As Jeremy pulled up his pants, the man slinked toward them and rubbed one of Jeremy's nipples. "What is time?" he said in crude Hebrew as George pushed away his hand. "What is time?" the man repeated over and over, reaching for Jeremy's nipple again.

George grabbed Jeremy by the wrist and pulled him away. They waded through a bed of brambles that scratched their ankles until they reached the stone wall. Jeremy rested there a minute while George scribbled furiously on his notepad:

"CRAZY! CRAZY MAN! I KNOW HIM. HE GOES EVRY-WERE IN JERUSALEM, SCREAMS TO TOURISTS. HE ASKS BUS TO STOP, GOES IN AND GOES OUT AGAIN AND AGAIN. DRIVER MUST PUSH HIM OUT!"

Below them, men cruised back and forth on the black lawn. On the other side of the trees, brass trolleys of luggage rattled their way through the parking lot up to the Sheraton lobby, and Jeremy experienced a sudden craving for room service.

This is hell, he thought, right here on earth, to wander around this park or a bar for the rest of your life because there's nowhere else to go. "Are we safe here?" he asked.

George nodded quickly, then handed him a card. It was an ad for a PARTY! at some club near the police station in the Russian Compound. A pink-cheeked muscle god with fluffy white wings graced the front of the card. He had several arrows stuck in his chest, and the blood dripping from his wounds matched the color of his pouty lips.

"That's what God must look like for gays," Jeremy thought out loud.

George pointed at the card and held up his hands as if to say, "Should we go?"

"Let's not," said Jeremy, and stood up. "Come on, I need some air."

Hand in hand, they strolled up to the limestone terrace at the highest point of the park. The King David Hotel glimmered in the valley. Most of the benches were taken. The old man who'd bummed a cigarette off Jeremy was there; he waved, and Jeremy waved back. A gaggle of teenagers wearing eye shadow and lipstick held court under the trees, while two drag queens in jean jackets and platform shoes paraded back and forth, swinging their mini backpacks like lassos.

Jeremy and George grabbed the last free bench, at the back of the terrace. Nearby, two Arab teenagers lay on the grass with their legs crossed. Jeremy was learning to spot differences between Israelis and Arabs. Arabs had a more pronounced hook in their noses. They never wore shorts, and their clothes were usually baggy, whereas Israelis had a penchant for anything skintight. Also, Arabs had a tendency to shine, with their silk shirts, their gold chains, the pomade in their hair. Even their skin glistened with sweat.

Jeremy thought the chubbier of the two Arabs, the one with a black-and-white-checked scarf around his neck, was better-looking than his friend, who was too scrawny and had long stringy hair tucked behind his ears like a girl's. The two of them were snickering and joking with each other at the tops of their voices.

"Why do you Arabs always make so much noise?" an Israeli yelled at them in Hebrew. "Shut your big mouths or I'll come beat you up!"

"Why you don't come to us?" the chubby Arab replied in English, puckering his lips and blowing kisses.

"No, you come here to us, niggers!" the Israeli yelled back, stepping into the light with his friends. He was black—from Ethiopia, Jeremy guessed. "We're going to beat you up!"

The Arab made a few more kissing noises. "Come here, black and beautiful!" he said, chewing on a thin gold necklace he was wearing.

"Come here and suck this!" said the black man, grabbing his crotch.

George slid closer to Jeremy and kissed the hole that his

nose ring used to fill. "Ow!" Jeremy yelped, and the Arabs and the Israelis stopped bickering to look. "It hurts." He pouted, rubbing the bridge of his nose.

"SORRY. I VERY HAPPY YOU TAKE UGLY RING OUT YOUR NOSE."

Jeremy took the pencil and wrote, "Why did you run away this morning?"

George shrugged.

"Why? Don't you like me? Did I do something wrong?"

George shrugged again, then wrote, "YOUR MOTHER DONT LIKED ME."

"That's not true. She wants to meet you again. She said so."

"ITS NO MATTER. SOON YOU GO HOME AND I NEVER SEE YOU. YOU NEVER RIGHT LETTER, EMAIL. NOTHING."

"That doesn't have to be true," Jeremy said, though he suspected it did. He was too Midwestern—no, too American—to speak the truth when it was unpleasant.

"ITS NO MATTER. TONIGHT I SO HAPPY TO SEE YOU."

"And I'm happy to see you, too. That's why I want to get to know you." Frustrated, Jeremy took up the pencil again. It was hard to have to speak slowly and clearly like to a child. The notes helped some, but not enough. He had trouble expressing himself fully with just a pencil. Still, he wanted to try.

"Stop," Jeremy said as George licked his ear. "That tickles. Now read this."

"I HAVNT PATIENCE FOR IT."

George licked the ear again, but Jeremy held him back and held up their notepad. "What religion are you?" he'd written. George shrugged. "Please," Jeremy said. "I want to know."

With a dramatic huff, George accepted the paper and pencil. "I STUDY IN CATHOLIC SCHOOL WHEN I WAS BOY. CHIL-

DREN LAUHGED AT ME BECAUSE I AM DEAF, BUT THE FATHERS IN THE CATHLIC SCHOOL WAS NICE TO ME. THEY GIVE TO ME VERY VERY GOOD EDUCATION. BUT NOW MAYBE I MUSLIM. OK. YOU HAPPY NOW?"

George tried to kiss him again, and Jeremy, moving away, fell off the bench.

"WHAT WRONG? YOU HAVE BOYFRIEND? YOU HATE ARABES?"

Now I'm a racist, thought Jeremy, picking himself up. Maybe I should offer him a quick hand job, a little affirmative action to help the peace process along. "I told you," he wrote. "I want to get to know you. Not just for sex."

"WHY NO SEX? YOU DONT LIKE ARABES?"

"Of course I like Arabs. But right now I want to get to know who you are."

George kicked a rock, which skidded into the woods. A stray cat sprang out of the leaves with a yowl.

"You can fuck the shit out of any of these guys here. Is that what you want?"

No answer. They sat for a while without writing. I've ruined it now, thought Jeremy. This is exactly what I complain about to my shrink. Fags always run away the minute you try to get honest with them.

"Get back!" shouted a bald Israeli man standing with his fists cocked across from the two Arab teenagers, who'd jumped to their feet. The fatter teenager stomped forward in his bright white high-tops, his shoelaces stylishly untied, while his thin friend tried to pull him back.

"Get out of here!" the bald Israeli man yelled in Hebrew. "Get out of here! Go on!" he yelled, flailing his arms in wide awkward circles. The thinner Arab pulled on his stocky friend, who bumped his pudgy stomach against the Israeli man's pudgy stomach. Jeremy wanted to slip away, but a crowd of men had quickly bunched up behind him, cheering and laughing like they were at a concert.

The drag queens stood at the edge of it all with their arms folded and snapped their gum. "Watch me now!" one of them said, and began to strut, but no one paid attention. "Watch me now!" she said, swinging her backpack.

"Don't bother," said her friend with a sniff. "This audience has no taste."

The fatter Arab tore free of his friend and spat into the bald man's face. "*Itbah al-Yahood!*" he yelled, pronouncing each syllable precisely so that Jeremy had no trouble making out what he'd said. Israelis, on the other hand, were always slurring their words; when they spoke English, it sounded like their mouths were full of matzo ball soup.

The Arab teenagers began chasing the Israeli around the inside of the circle of spectators. One of the Jews had called the police on his cell phone. "Are you laughing because I'm gay?" he screamed in Hebrew. "I'm one of the people standing here. Send a car this way!"

"They're not coming?" asked his friend.

"They're coming, they're coming. The Arabs are beating up the Jews, but the police hesitate because we're gay."

One of the Jews stepped forward between the men. "Stop it already! It's enough! What you want? You want money?" He took out some bills.

The fatter Arab grabbed the bills and flung them over the heads of the crowd.

"This is our park!" said the bald Israeli, still pumping his fists. "Go back to Ramallah if you want to go to a park. Why you have to ruin everything that's beautiful and nice?"

The Arab threw a convincing-looking punch that was obviously calculated to miss the bald Israeli's nose by a few centimeters. Then he lowered his hands, grinned, and aimed a gob of spit into the Israeli's eye. Blinking away the spit, the Israeli continued jogging in place and pumping his fists.

"Come here," the Arab taunted him. "Fight. No? No fight. Coward. No fight."

He and his friend backed away, headed right for Jeremy. The crowd parted to make room, but Jeremy stayed where he was. I'm on your side, he thought. George can tell you. I'm not going to be afraid. I hold out my hand in friendship. He tried to smile, but was so nervous, he merely appeared constipated.

The scrawny Arab yelled something that sounded like "Smock!" and his elbow popped out, knocking the wind out of Jeremy. As the two young men made their escape into the dark heart of the park, the gay men cruising jumped out of their way.

Jeremy staggered backward as if drunk, and George ran over, trying to hold him up by one of his arms. The silver-haired man who'd bummed the cigarette came running too and grabbed Jeremy's other arm. "Everything is okay," Jeremy wanted to say, because it was the only phrase he could remember in Hebrew. But when he tried to talk, nothing came out and he doubled over in pain. He had no voice, no air inside to speak.

"Congratulations," said the old Jew. "You were just called one of the worst insults in Arabic: *Koos emek*. It means 'your mother's genitalia,' except it's not so nice." He looked at George. "Who's your friend?"

"I'm fine," Jeremy managed to gasp, and then grabbed his aching stomach. He wanted to throw up, but his stomach was empty.

The drag queens began prancing again. Another Israeli in a black BODY BODY T-shirt bent over, put his face up to Jeremy's, and asked in English. "Who did this to you?" He pointed to George. "Did he do this to you?"

"Don't you have eyes?" the old man asked. "This one looks nothing like those other boys."

"Home," said Jeremy, sucking in his breath as he tried to stand up and walk. It hurt to breathe.

"The police are coming. You don't want to stay?" asked the man in the BODY BODY shirt. "What's wrong with your Arab friend? Doesn't he speak?"

George pulled on Jeremy's arm.

"Maybe he knows something," said BODY BODY. "Let's ask him."

"Leave him alone already," said the old man.

Jeremy, still bent over, almost in half, managed to take a few steps. The silver-haired Jew and the mute Arab helped him hobble along.

BODY BODY said, "Why won't his friend even answer?"

Two police cars came wailing around the corner and pulled over at the entrance to the park. Their lights flashed over George's dark face and he let go of Jeremy's arm.

"Don't go," Jeremy mouthed. "I'll tell them you helped me. And this man will, too. He saw."

Two men and a woman in uniform got out of the police cars. The silver-haired Jew let go of Jeremy's arm. "Sorry, my wife doesn't know I'm here," he said, and walked away quickly.

"YOU CAN TELEPHONE TO THIS NUMBER," George scribbled. "YOU SAY YOU ARE CALLING FOR AHMED. ITS MY REEL NAME."

Ahmed? thought Jeremy, his hand trembling as he accepted the paper. I love George. Who is Ahmed?

They embraced, George clinging tightly like he meant it. Finally he let go, pointing to Jeremy and crossing his arms. And then Jeremy felt a spiky rush of love, for George, for Ahmed, for whomever. Without thinking twice, he grabbed George again and held him close, rubbed his face in the kid's shirt, smelled his skin. I feel something, he thought, wishing he could laugh. I can really feel now.

"See you later," Jeremy mouthed, and let go for a second time.

George gave a little wave and then backed into the Israeli policewoman, who pulled his arms apart and held them fast behind his back.

"There he is," the man in the BODY BODY shirt said in Hebrew. "That's the one I told you about."

nine

THE FOUNDING OF SILWAN

A Palestinian Folktale

In the seventh century C.E., the **Caliph Omar ibn al-Khatab** traveled to Jerusalem from Saudi Arabia on foot, while his servant rode behind him on a camel. In awe of the Caliph's humility, the **Greeks,** who ruled Jerusalem in those days, offered him a tract of land outside the city walls, which the **Caliph** passed on to the "**Khan Silowna,**" a community of farmers who lived in the local caves. They called their valley **Wadi Hilwe,** or "Beautiful Valley," because in those days it was a lush valley of orchards, where almonds, figs, olives, wild fennel, oranges, and kumquats bloomed.

Years later, the **Wadi Hilwe** was sold by **Muslim** traitors to **Jewish** thieves in league with **Crusader** infidels, who set torches to their fields and raped their wives. The trees were burned to black toothpicks and the streams drained to the last teardrop of moisture. The invaders sprinkled the earth with salt so nothing would grow there again, and the **Wadi Hilwe,** so full of possibility for good, was turned into a **Valley of Hell.**

A few months after her mother's funeral, Mrs. Michaelson volunteered through her local Hadassah chapter to tutor Jewish children from the former Soviet Union in the public schools. I am the daughter of Russian immigrants, she'd tell them, and this is my way of paying back. They'd say, Very nice, and ask for her help with long division.

She went to school every Monday and Wednesday, never missing once, though when she came home Mr. Michaelson never seemed to remember where she'd gone. The sessions gave shape to her week, and she resented holidays and summer vacation as unnecessary interference with her social life. Many of the other wives quit when the school ran out of Russians, but Mrs. Michaelson stayed on to help whoever the teachers gave her, mostly Arabs now. She still called them Russians, though, unlike the Russians, the Arabs turned out to be unfailingly courteous and never cheated. They looked her in the eye, answered her questions politely, in complete sentences, and said thank you when she baked them brownies.

Her latest "Russians," Ibrahim and Vivian, had made excellent progress under her tutelage. Ibrahim could write an entire paragraph in English with no mistakes. And little Vivian, with the dark, lovely face, had received a B+ on her last math quiz.

Robert had told her that she ought to stop tutoring her "Russians" because their families probably saved up money to send overseas to the PLO. That's why he'd given up tipping Arab taxi drivers. But it struck her as ridiculous to connect Vivian and Ibrahim with the Arabs she saw on television. For one thing, Vivian and Ibrahim came from Iraq, not the West Bank or Gaza. They were quiet kids, not the rock-throwing type.

So what about George? Was he the rock-throwing type? Why would anyone want to throw rocks anymore? Hadn't Israel signed a peace deal?

It was all very confusing, because she was too lazy to keep up with the news. She'd trusted the Israelis to run their part of the world without her input. Also, the Atlantic was such a big pond it seemed like a perfectly safe buffer between her and all that hot hatred. Or rather, it had always seemed safe until three weeks ago, when she and her family had crossed it in half a day.

Immediately after knocking on the rabbi's green door, room 307, she was sorry.

Rabbi Sherman appeared before her in a white T-shirt and nylon running pants that slithered when he rubbed his legs together. His feet were bare, his curls were wet, and his hands were hairy and firm. A towel hung over his shoulder like a prayer shawl. She caught a whiff of his shampoo, fruity in an artificial way, like low-fat strawberry ice cream.

"I need to ask you something," she said, "but that's all."

Somehow the door closed behind her, and she wondered if he'd pulled her inside or merely guided her by the elbow. A rabbi would never pull a woman into his room like some Viking, but the pressure of his fingers lingered on her forearm. And she had no husband to return to upstairs, no excuse to pull back.

This was the first time she'd been in his room, which she was glad to see was the same size as Jeremy's single. It showed Rabbi Sherman didn't put on airs.

He'd left the bathroom fan running, and the sound jarred her nerves. The rabbi set her down gently on the couch, next to a pile of folded dress shirts in pastel colors, fresh from the laundry, and a paperback titled *The Psychology of Winning*. He moved the shirts and book onto his dresser and then relaxed on the bed. His hairy feet bobbed over the edge, and he stared at her in pity, or maybe amusement.

"Where's your son? Still running after his Palestinian friend?" he said, staring at her breasts. Instinctively, Mrs. Michaelson folded her arms so there'd be nothing for him to see. Before she could answer his question, he said, "In every age we get blamed

for all the world's evils. Killing Christ, the Plague, ritual murder, on and on. What mystifies me is why Jews buy into the latest version, the 'poor Palestinians.' "

"Don't you think they're poor? What would you do about
them?" she asked, glad to delay asking the question she'd come
there to put to him.

"Nothing. Because there's nothing any of us can do. One day
you Westerners are going to learn that here in the Middle East,
even in the Arab countries, the Palestinians are troublemakers,
pariahs, garbage, bottom feeders. You know, Jordan kicked their
PLO all out into Syria. Syria mowed down some twenty thousand of them in one day and chased the survivors into Lebanon,
where they almost destroyed the whole country before we in-
vaded and chased them to Tunisia. Now we've invited them
back in again, as if they were ready to make peace with us.
Well, what can we expect?"

Some other time Mrs. Michaelson might have been interested in the lecture about politics, but right then she kept hearing Bunny's voice and the dirty word "playboy." She watched
Rabbi Sherman trace the outline of the flowered bedspread and
was tempted to sit there next to him so they could waste the rest
of the evening simply holding hands.

How did he spend his evenings with his other women?

"So what did you come here to ask me about?" he asked coyly.

Mrs. Michaelson, feeling light-headed all of a sudden, made
another effort to focus, despite the noise from that damn bathroom fan. "I was wondering what exactly brought you here to
Israel," she said.

"I told you. After my wife left me, I needed to get away."

"Yes, but wasn't there some other reason? I mean, weren't
there any other women in your life you maybe ran around with?
Not your wife? After your wife?"

"I don't have a girlfriend, if that's what you're asking," said the rabbi, getting up and reaching over the couch to draw the curtains. "You believe we're committing a sin, yes?" he said, toying with the curtain rod, and she had to twist around to face him. "But you see, the real meaning of the word for 'sin' in Hebrew is 'mistake,' and that's exactly what you and your husband have done by staying together so long after you fell out of love. The whole core meaning of Judaism is to seize life, not throw it away on mistakes."

Was that what Judaism meant these days? If so, Mrs. Michaelson preferred the old version: the unknowable, bottled. "That isn't why I came to see you," she said, staring straight ahead, trying to get back on track. "You've been very . . ." She struggled for the word. "Nice." How inadequate! "That is, I will always think of you fondly." That wouldn't do either. "But I'm not sure if we'd make such a great match. I mean, you've probably dated lots of women and I'm . . ." She thought of her old boyfriend Adam Levine. "Inexperienced. So I should go home to my husband." But just then she had a hard time remembering what her husband looked like. She closed her eyes and then she saw him, his flat freckled brow, his large ears, his slow, loping walk.

"Are you sure that's what you should do, or what you're supposed to do?" said the rabbi, sitting beside her.

Someone said, "Shut up, shut up," and she supposed she'd done it. How could she care for such a man, who drove her to such linguistic extremes? But he'd planted her on his couch and she was slowly growing roots there. Somehow with his presence, he was changing her, he with his absurdly long and meaty legs and the inverted swan's curve of his neck, the curve she'd licked in the hotel elevator. He was offering his hips for her to hold, his heady smell to inhale like a drug. It was the smell of underwear, muddy grass, and sheets that needed changing. It was the smell of boy.

"I know my husband has his limitations," she said as Rabbi Sherman rested his arm on the back of the couch, his long fingers grazing the tips of her hair. "I knew that when I met him. It was how he was brought up. I felt sorry for him, lost in his own family like an orphan. But he doesn't know any better. He'd be lost without me."

"Orphans grow up," the rabbi reminded her. She smelled his strawberry shampoo once more. The gray glinted like streaks of rain in his dark wet hair. "Maybe he left you because he wanted a chance to take care of himself."

"He didn't leave me," she shot back, remembering why she'd come.

"Maybe that's true."

"It is true."

"Then you'll have to leave him." He pressed her shoulder and looked at her earnestly, as if she were an entire congregation. "You two don't belong together. But you and me, we're the same. We're in the same prison, because we're different from these other people. We read, we think, we question. Being a rabbi, I'm constantly besieged by single daughters. You must know how it is. And I've given them a chance. Yes, Helen, I admit I've dated a lot of women, if that's the crime you've come here to charge me with. But they're all carbon copies, empty vessels, if you will, filled with the hopes of their parents and their parents' parents. You're the first real woman I've ever had the good fortune to fall in love with, and I don't want to lose you."

He had her all turned around, like a magnet next to a compass. East, west, right, wrong, they were mixed up. "My husband would be shattered," she said.

"If he has any sensitivity at all, I don't believe he'd be very surprised, and if he has no sensitivity, then he doesn't deserve you."

"I've never felt so . . . irresponsible." He reached around her body to draw her closer. "Rick, no," she said. "This is . . ."

"Helen," he said, clutching her fingertips. "You make me feel so unsure of myself, so green." He rubbed her hands between his hands. "All I ask is, don't shut the door if you're not sure. Don't say no because you haven't made up your mind and you think you're being fair to me by not stringing me along."

What were they talking about now? She was too old for these kinds of conversations. "Just hug me, please," she whimpered, and pressed her head against his shirt, which felt hot from his chest as if he had a fever. "If I did go home," she said, "I could always come back next year on another Mission."

"There won't be any Missions like this next year," he said, stroking her hair. "Not for a while. There's going to be a war. Americans don't travel into war zones."

"Barak might win that vote tomorrow," she reminded him.

"Even if he does, he'd have to divide Jerusalem in half for peace, and he can't."

She thought of Jeremy in Silwan, trapped behind enemy lines. "No more politics," she said, putting her fingers on the rabbi's mouth. "Not just now."

"You're right, as always." Rabbi Sherman held her fingers in place, and then began nibbling them while making strange moaning noises. His tongue felt raspy and wonderful and her body felt so heavy, she couldn't move. She could only sink deeper into the pink hotel cushions and let him collapse onto her. "It's going to be okay," he murmured.

It occurred to her to say, "I love you," but she held back, because in the deepest part of herself, the same part she kept from God, what she really meant was "I love this."

"Go to the bed and take your clothes off," he whispered. "I want to look at you."

"Can't we turn the lights out first?" she asked, thinking about her veins.

"But I can't look at you if the lights are out," he reminded her.

"I guess that's true."

So Mrs. Michaelson dutifully took off her clothes and folded them over a chair. She tried to remember the last time her husband had seen her naked. Even during his conjugal visits to the guest room, they usually fumbled in the dark.

When she finished undressing, she lay on the bed, hands quivering at her sides like a patient on the operating table. The folds of flesh on her legs and stomach, the padding on her neck, and the wrinkles all slid backward, ironing themselves out. "So beautiful," the rabbi said, caressing her limp skin, tweaking the tips of her nipples and then kissing them. His lips prickled like shaved ice.

"Now can we turn out the light?" she asked.

"Sure," he said, relaxing beside her. In the dark, he kissed her for a while, then moved down to her breasts and began nibbling and then sucking. He laid his head on her stomach and sucked himself to sleep.

———

Rabbi Sherman slept on his side, facing the wall. She'd looked forward to sleeping next to a man who wouldn't cough all night, but instead of coughing, the rabbi snored like some kind of woodland animal.

She finally fell asleep, and dreamed she was at the Wall again, trying to stick a pink neon Post-it into the stones, but the note wouldn't fit. Then the Wall transformed into a wall of canned tuna, and she was reaching for a coupon dispenser that some idiot had mounted on the top shelf. When she woke up, she forgot she was in Israel until she got out of bed and saw herself naked in the hotel mirror.

Rabbi Sherman was naked too, and except for all that hair, he reminded her of a baby boy. Mrs. Michaelson smothered a laugh. She wished she could lie in bed longer and do nothing, but this wasn't a country where you could do nothing. There was always something you had to do here.

She tiptoed around the bed to check the rabbi's travel alarm, which he'd left on his side of the mattress. It was almost eleven o'clock. Wasn't there something she was supposed to do that day?

"Jeremy!" she said. Of course! They were meeting at noon. And now because of her selfishness, she was going to be late, and there was never any excuse for being late.

"I have to go," she whispered, shaking the rabbi's shoulder and grabbing her pleated shorts off a chair. "I promised I'd meet someone."

The rabbi rolled over to face her. "Who?" he mumbled. "A new boyfriend?"

"I don't have any other boyfriends," she said, which she immediately regretted because her use of "other" implied that he qualified as a boyfriend. "Do you have any other girlfriends?" she dared to add.

"Of course not," he said. "I told you I didn't."

"Anyway, don't you have to get up for work?" she asked, fumbling with her buttons. Her fingers felt stiff.

He wiped his eyes. "I took the day off. I thought we could spend it together."

"I've already made plans. I'm sorry."

He sat up and scratched the mat of fur on his chest. "I'm sorry, too."

"Yes, well, that's very nice of you, but I have to go. I'll be late. I'm late as it is."

"And when you're finished you'll come back?"

She stared at his hand grasping for her wrist. "I'll come back." It was easier to give in.

———

The *Daily Bulletin*, the *Herald Tribune,* and a hot-pink heat advisory waited on her doorstep. The headlines in both newspapers were about Barak. In the *Bulletin*, he extended his greetings to the Millennium Marathon. In the *Tribune* he fought for Knesset votes. She shoved the *Bulletin* and the heat advisory into her pocket, kicked the *Tribune* across her doorstep, and double-locked herself in her room.

"You're not really going to marry that moron," said Mr. Michaelson, in the guest chair with his legs crossed and arms folded. "But if you must, at least try to bear in mind that you can't wear white twice."

"Get lost," she said. "Enough already!"

She splashed her face with cold water, patted on a cloud or two of foundation, and put in her contacts. After a few fruitless attempts to comb out her hair, she tucked it under a straw hat. Her hair was ruined, and maybe her life was ruined too, because she'd been selfish enough to enjoy a night off and forget why she'd come to Israel in the first place. What would Jeremy think? He knew how she valued promptness.

Her drawers were all empty except for her bras and underwear, a pair of socks, two pairs of shorts with tops to match, her bathing suit, and a denim skirt. The rest she'd sent home with her husband. She opened her closet, but there was only a cotton cardigan and her vermilion dress, shrouded in plastic.

Why couldn't the clock stand still so she could think? She

checked her closet again, as if she could will her khaki skirt and cotton blouse out of her husband's suitcase, now in Michigan. Jeremy hated her denim skirt. He said it made her look like an Orthodox housewife, and he was right. She'd planned to leave it behind as an extra tip for the maid. Wearing it to meet George would be an insult, worse than showing up late.

She stood there miserably tweaking her dress inside its plastic sleeve and trying to resign herself to denim. Jeremy had said he'd meet her at noon, less than an hour away now. Noon, noon, she thought, reminding herself. Noon meant Jeremy expected to be taken out to lunch. "Take them somewhere nice," said Mr. Michaelson, pointing at her closet with his aviator sunglasses. "This could be Jeremy's future husband you're meeting. Don't be cheap."

"Go away," she scolded him. "I suppose you'd want me to take them to the King David Hotel."

The other day, they'd closed the streets all around the King David to make way for Madeleine Albright, who'd settled in there. Mrs. Michaelson tried to imagine George and Madeleine Albright crossing paths, passing crib notes over tea and watercress sandwiches.

Now there was the one place in all Israel where she could have gotten away with her vermilion dress. Hobnobbing with the likes of Madeleine Albright. Mrs. Michaelson, who'd been a leader of the Model UN team in high school, used to imagine herself negotiating peace treaties in New York someday. She'd forgotten all her grand diplomatic ambitions. But maybe it was a good thing she hadn't realized them if it meant ending up with a dumpy figure like Madeleine Albright's. Madam Secretary could never have pulled off vermilion.

What an entrance I would make at the King David, thought Mrs. Michaelson, suddenly ripping the plastic sleeve and staring at the silk dress as if for the first time. Yes, it just might work. Her good shoes were gone, but she had sandals, and luckily they were black. She'd take a taxi to the village and back and be careful not to rub up against anything. The dress would be perfectly safe.

The hardest part would be convincing the ever skeptical Jeremy, who was sure to pester her with suspicious questions. She'd have to arrive in a whirlwind like a movie star, swoop down on the two boys with her taxi, and whisk them away before Jeremy had a chance to object. Like Auntie Mame, live, live, live!

She sped into action, fussing around her room and Jeremy's drawers, fumbling between what looked like Israeli gay porno magazines for a pair of ties and a clean shirt for Jeremy so the boys could change in the King David bathroom, the guidebook, where she found the King David's number, the telephone (their La Regence Grill Room was open only for dinner, but something called the King's Garden served lunch), the pots and tubes of paint and powder on her bathroom sink. Her lipstick had disappeared, so she made do with a few dabs of lip balm, which she automatically blotted with a tissue as if it were lipstick.

As she grabbed the Fodor's off the dresser, her Michigander name tag fell into the garbage. Just leave it, she thought, slinging a canvas tote bag over her left shoulder and bending to tighten the buckle of her sandals, but the buckle snapped off. Damn, damn, damn, she thought, but there was no time to fix it, so she put on her white sneakers. The glare of them against the vermilion was blinding. So she'd drop the boys off at the King David to change and then run out and buy another pair. You see how easy and manageable everything was if you had a little imagination?

"Well, I'm ready," she said, as if it were true.

The hush in the carpeted hallway seemed apocalyptic. One of the lights flickered on and off, which didn't help. To steady herself, she thought of her responsibilities: her husband (surviving on hot dogs), her older son (shaking hands with his partner), and her younger son (shaking hands with *his* partner, at the City of David).

In the elevator, she caressed the button for the fourth floor, Rabbi Sherman's floor, and accidentally pressed it in. As the doors opened, she searched for *Door Close*, but someone shouted, "Wait, wait! Here I come!" And then Sherry Sherman appeared in a cherry-red scarf and red plastic sandals. "Good morning, Helen! You overslept too?"

Mrs. Michaelson paused as if she hadn't understood the question. How could this woman have produced Rabbi Sherman? What in the world had she given him of herself?

Sherry squeezed Mrs. Michaelson's hand. "Don't beat yourself up over it. No one ever said it was easy to be a Jew, especially among all these Orthodox nuts in Jerusalem and their reactionary rhetoric. In Tel Aviv, we're totally free of these religious superstitions. Well, you're dressed up today. Are you going to the theater?"

"No," said Mrs. Michaelson, impatiently pressing the lit button for the first floor.

Sherry waited for another explanation that didn't come, then said, "It's lucky we ran into each other. I'm catching up to the group by taxi. Rachel's Tomb is like nothing from here. I'll pay. The Mission reimburses me."

"That's kind of you, but I couldn't say yes."

"Not at all. The Mission reimburses me, I said."

"Tell her to mind her own business and shove off," said Mr. Michaelson.

But Mrs. Michaelson couldn't shove off without giving

Sherry some kind of reason. Anything as long as it didn't involve her son, which might have suggested the true reason. She could say that she didn't trust Israeli taxi drivers, but lying struck her as ridiculous. Maybe she could hide in the bathroom. If she stayed there long enough, Sherry might give up and leave without her.

"Why can't you tell her to shove off?" her husband persisted, switching into therapy mode.

Oh, easy for him to say. It was all right for him to disappear, since he was sick. And Jeremy was a young man, so it made sense he'd want to abandon them. But a middle-aged matron like herself? Setting out alone in Jerusalem? With no friends? When she barely spoke a word of Hebrew?

"Why do you care what any of them think of you?" said Mr. Michaelson. "Do what you want. I give you permission. You have nothing to feel guilty for."

"But I have to go," she thought aloud. "I just told her I would."

"Helen, are you on one of those new hands-free cell phones?" Sherry asked.

"There's no such thing as 'have to,' or 'must,' or 'should,' " Mr. Michaelson said. "There's only what you'd prefer to do or prefer not to."

She much preferred him this way, as she imagined him to be, instead of as who he really was. "How can you still speak to me?" she asked. "Look at how awful I am."

"Maybe your actions are awful, but you aren't awful," he explained as he'd explained to so many other miserable people. "How can you judge a person by her actions when a person commits thousands of actions on any given day? So what you do may be awful, but you, Helen Michaelson, are never awful."

"Who are you talking to?" Sherry asked again.

"You know what I really think," said Mrs. Michaelson, her eyes shining as she turned to Sherry. "Screw Rachel's Tomb. Religion's fine in the abstract, but in practice it's just another tool for people to divide themselves from each other."

"It's a good thing your son can't hear you now."

"Why shouldn't he? It's what I really think." The elevator doors opened and she stepped out without waiting for Sherry to go first.

"Helen," Sherry called out behind her, huffing to keep up. "You're keeping something from me, and I think it has to do with how you're dressed and where you're going. From day one, I've tried to be your friend, but you keep holding out. Now I see why. You're the kind of woman who doesn't make friends with other women. Maybe that's why you prefer the company of men other than your husband. Still, believe me when I say, as your friend, that Israeli men are different from the species we know in America. Be careful. Remember who you are."

Mrs. Michaelson had to laugh. "Now you're making fun of me," she said. "And you're forgetting that I'm married."

"Well, there's the rub, obviously. What do you intend to do, *Mrs.* Michaelson?"

"*Mrs.* Sherman, am I free to go where I want, or not?"

"Obviously, you're free," Sherry said, looking steadily into her eyes. "If you ask me, there's far too much freedom in this world, and far too little responsibility."

It was a beautiful day, but every day in Israel was beautiful, so relentlessly beautiful that it got on a person's nerves. A cloud or two would have gone a long way toward soothing Mrs. Michaelson's severely frayed spirits. But then clouds made her think of the rabbi dripping in a thunderstorm, which only served to get her worked up again. This whole plan's ridiculous, she thought. No, it's not. But she couldn't think of why not.

Wait for me, Jeremy, she thought. I'm on my way.

It was too bad that Sherry Sherman had been so annoyingly perceptive as to see right through all excuses.

"Not a very good start," Mr. Michaelson kidded her, "to be caught lying to a woman who might turn out to be your future mother-in-law."

As if it were possible she might really choose the rabbi as her fiancé. How would she explain him to Jeremy? "I really enjoyed meeting your boyfriend. Now meet mine." He'd never forgive her when he found out, and neither would Robert. But if she went on seeing the rabbi, she couldn't keep him a secret forever. It was wrong to hide the people you loved as if you were ashamed. Her sons would have to understand.

"But of course they'd understand!" she thought out loud, laughing. "They'd have to." They'd understand it all, the lying and shambling, the burden of keeping secrets when you were aching to tell the world you were in love!

A butterfly fluttered across the windshield of her taxi, caught in the midday traffic on Jaffa Road. The sidewalks were clogged too. Bowed women wheeled shopping carts between Africans hawking pirated CDs and videos spread out on straw mats. Steam floated out of a falafel stand where fat men in aprons molded bright green balls of chickpea mush for the lunch rush.

A man ringing a bell wore a large cardboard sign in English around his neck: NO JESUS, NO PEACE. KNOW JESUS, KNOW PEACE.

Back home they'd have finished the renovations at her local Farmer Jack supermarket, where a sign on the door announced they were proud to support the Israeli economy. She'd read in one of her magazines that you spent seven years of your life on the toilet; how many years had she wasted grocery shopping? Though just then, she'd have given her soul to hide behind a fortress of cereal boxes and tuna fish cans.

The cabdriver pulled up next to the metal detectors by the south entrance to the Wall. "But I don't want to go to the Wall. Silwan, I said," she reminded him.

"It's not a place to go alone for a woman alone," he said. "It's an Arab area."

"And where am I supposed to go alone?" she said. "Shopping?" Those Israelis made a fuss over every little thing. No wonder the Palestinians couldn't stand them.

He shrugged. "If you still want to go, it's a few meters' walk on this road."

In Michigan, Mrs. Michaelson would have ordered him to drive those few meters, but over here she didn't know what the customs were, and this man looked dangerous, as if he hadn't shaved in days. It occurred to her that she should have brought the rabbi along to help. No, she thought, I can do this myself. As she searched for her wallet, she wondered how much to tip. Paying taxis had been her husband's job. "*Yala*," said the driver, impatient for his fare, and she was so flustered she counted out exact change without a tip and handed it up front.

Blinded by the brightness when she stepped out of the cab, she felt with her toe for the cement. How far was a meter, anyway? After putting on her sunglasses, she consulted Fodor's and confirmed that Silwan was only a few minutes' walk. The directions were confusing, but she oriented herself by checking them against her map. Directions in guidebooks could be so cryptic, open to interpretation like a page of Talmud. In Rome, for example, "across the Plaza" had meant "behind the Plaza," while "two doors down" meant two doors plus a few more doors that didn't count as official doors according to the people who wrote guidebooks. Really, she was ready to throw the silly thing right into the trash, except that without it she'd have been utterly helpless instead of a little lost.

The downhill road was quiet and, after the New City traffic, refreshingly deserted. The sidewalk petered out, so Mrs. Michaelson continued walking on the shoulder, a bleached dirt track where nothing grew except withered weeds and a tiny flaming red flower. The sun was worse than ever. It wasn't like the sun back home. It did something here.

She tried rolling up her sleeves, but they kept rolling back down. She swished some water around in her mouth, but what she really craved was a swallow of ice cream, a cool kiss of milk at the back of her scratchy throat.

The road took a sharp dive, and the village of Silwan spread out below her feet: corrugated tin roofs, white satellite dishes, and lines of laundry snapping in the hot wind. Across the valley, a bulldozer whined along a brown mountain ridge scarred with yellow tracks. That was probably the dangerous Arab neighborhood her taxi driver had warned her about, an entire valley away. Here where she stood she was perfectly safe.

A wooden sign etched with an arrow and CITY OF DAVID pointed down one of the gravel roads. Careful to stay away from the edge of the road to protect her dress, she followed the arrow downhill, kicking up hot clouds of dust that made her cough. The houses she passed looked empty, with black square holes for windows, and doors sealed shut. No porches or lawn furniture or welcoming pots of geraniums. Still, the area hardly struck her as dangerous. A bit depressing, but not dangerous, and not such a bad place to live if you thought about it. At least it was quiet.

She was joined on the road by an Arab housewife wrapped

up like a mummy dipped in India ink, two sharp eyes peering out of black cloth. What if Jeremy's new mother-in-law dressed that way? "It's just the style here," she thought aloud.

Really, this town wasn't so bad. The life was probably simple, very back to basics. And look, a cat! (Though so thin, it was almost a skeleton.) It pressed its back against the shady side of one of the homes and glared at her.

Oh, thank God, thought Mrs. Michaelson when she saw the City of David site, a wire fence with a small green English, Hebrew, and Arabic sign she almost missed. She didn't understand Hebrew, but she could make out the letters and differentiate them from one another. This Arabic, on the other hand, all ran together like diarrhea.

She tried to push in the park gate, but it stuck. The Arab woman in black stopped walking to watch. "Come on!" Mrs. Michaelson grunted, pounding the stubborn latch with her fist until it gave way.

The gate opened up onto a trim lawn, a healthy shade of green, planted with evenly spaced palm trees. Two screaming Orthodox boys chased each other around picnic tables, while their mothers sat in the shade, their feet up on the benches. The women spoke French in a sexy, breathy accent that Mrs. Michaelson had struggled to imitate in college. Somehow the idea of Orthodox Jews speaking French struck her as a waste.

At the back of the yard, a bored teenager in a chef's hat and green Nathan's Hot Dogs uniform swatted at flies beside a log cabin with a red tile roof. His hot dog cart shimmered in the sun like a mirage. Mrs. Michaelson checked her watch: a quarter past noon. Somewhat late, but she'd made surprisingly good time. It should have taken much longer to walk from Israel to Palestine.

So I'm here, she thought, dusting off a bench and sitting at one of the picnic tables. All I need to do now is wait. The shade felt good, though the smell of hot dogs roasting nauseated her. She comforted herself with the thought that her son would come soon and then she'd send him for a taxi.

And if he doesn't come?

He had to come. She sat there tapping her foot, slowly tapping away several stubborn, shameful seconds, as she wondered where her son could be. The possibilities ran through her mind, ones she usually tried to shut out: namely, drugs and sex. She felt reasonably sure Jeremy didn't have access to drugs, but sex, well, even she'd had her share lately. What did her son do in bed with these men? Not anal sex, she was sure, or she hoped. Once she'd tried it with her husband, but it had been too painful. That's what she imagined when she pictured her son and the anal sex, her own pain. It was too awful. She had to close her mind.

Aren't I selfish? she thought. I try to imagine my son and I see myself.

Her dress caught on a splinter in the bench and she gently tugged herself free. The French Orthodox ladies were staring at her. Maybe they mistook her for one of them because she wore a dress and not shorts like the other American tourists. No, she decided, even next to the Orthodox, I stand out like a vermilion sore. Why had she worn it? Because she didn't want to wear denim? No, no, to apologize, to atone for all her crimes. But instead of dressing up in sackcloth and ashes, she'd marked herself with red silk, in the dress she'd wanted to wear all along. How perfect. Edith Head herself couldn't have picked a more fitting outfit.

Sure that an hour had passed, she checked her watch, but only a few minutes had crawled by. So she mulled over the world of fancy hotels and fancy dresses, lovers and peace treaties, marriages on life support, suicidal sons. None of it mattered then. All that was left was death. Was she the only person who felt this way?

But if Jeremy came, it would all be worth it.

Somehow an hour slowly expired. Still no Jeremy. There was nothing to do but go back to the hotel and then home. But home felt like a death sentence to her now.

Hoping for a miracle, she took a peek inside the cabin, which smelled of hair spray. A young woman in a soldier's uniform relaxed in a padded chair and chatted excitedly into a heavy black telephone. She pulled one of her long, dark curls across her top lip like a mustache.

"Hello," said Mrs. Michaelson, catching a glimpse of her blazing dress in a mirror on the wall. Pay attention to me, she wanted to scream.

After a full minute, the woman put her hand over the mouthpiece of her phone and arched an eyebrow at Mrs. Michaelson.

"You haven't by any chance seen a young man, tall, slim, American? Or another one, short, husky build, and a bit dark in complexion? I believe his name is George."

"No, I didn't. But we have many visitors here."

"This is the City of David park, right?"

Yes, it was.

"Well, then. I guess I've been stood up." It was really the end. Mrs. Michaelson sank into a chair to absorb the full force of the blow. Even if her son hadn't been the one who'd inflicted it, she'd have felt ashamed. When people stood her up, it was as if they were saying her time and, by extension, her self weren't worth anything.

Her trip was almost over and there'd be no more traveling. She'd never come back to Israel; she knew that now. All her dreamy talk with the rabbi had been a lie. Not just because of the war everyone was talking about, but also because at her age travel was becoming an increasingly laborious proposition. You needed pills and lotions, spare glasses, Metamucil, energy, concentration, and above all the desire to leave your own backyard. She was becoming what was known as an old person. True, some old people liked to push themselves, but she'd never been that adventurous even as a young bride. Seeing new countries didn't interest her anymore, because these days all countries were basically the same. She wanted grandchildren to fill her life with their dreams and, short of that, she wanted to be buried beside her parents.

But before she could be buried, she had a long, empty afternoon to get through. The Mission was off who knew where. The rabbi had probably gone to join them, and even if he hadn't, she couldn't face him again. But she couldn't stand the thought of being alone either. She craved distraction—not a newspaper, either, but a movie, an exhibit, something to orient herself. She was not nothing, and she could prove it. She could look at things.

"Tell me," she said to the soldier. "Is this the whole park or is there more?"

"At the bottom of the hill, you have the water tunnel of Hizkiyahu. It's a beautiful experience."

"So you think it's worth a visit, then?" said Mrs. Michaelson. The soldier nodded. "Is it dangerous to go down there alone?" She could hear the young woman's friend still talking on the other end of the line.

"Not at all." The woman handed her a sandy-colored brochure printed in English. "We have this little book to tell you what you are seeing. It's one shekel."

While Mrs. Michaelson looked over the brochure, the woman

scratched the back of her ankle with her machine gun and went back to her phone conversation. The print in the brochure was small and full of phrases like "Hasmonean lodestones" and "Herodian cisterns." The photos were of the usual piles of rocks. Everywhere in Israel you looked at rocks and relied on pamphlets or tour guides to tell you what you were seeing. She wished she were visiting a place like Paris or Venice, where when you looked at something, it was actually there and not a pile of rocks.

Still, this would be her last chance to see Israel. More important, it was something to do.

She waved to get the young soldier to turn her head. "Those two boys I was telling you about, if they happen to come in here, would you mind telling them to wait? I'm just doing a bit of sightseeing."

No answer, but a slight upward roll of the shoulders that might have been a shrug.

"Well, I guess I'll take a brochure," Mrs. Michaelson said and produced the requisite shekel. The young woman broke off talking just long enough to accept her silver coin with a crooked smile. "Sorry to interrupt again, but could I leave my bag here? It's a bit heavy and I'm used to leaving it on our bus."

The woman pointed to a closet.

Mrs. Michaelson removed her guidebook, a bottle of water, and her wallet, then hung the bag on a wooden peg. As she straightened her straw hat in the mirror, she wished she'd brought something to change into, but it was either soldier on as she was or return to the hotel in defeat.

Outside, the Orthodox tourists had gathered around the picnic table and were saying a blessing over Nathan's hot dogs and Coca-Cola. One of the mothers waved.

After a last look around (in case Jeremy and George came

running breathlessly through the gate with excuses), she passed through a little gate behind the hot dog cart and hiked down a sandy path, marked with a sign: "City of David: HERE." Her brochure welcomed her to the oldest part of Jerusalem, the confirmed site of the Jerusalem that Jews read about in the Torah, the city of David, Solomon, and Jeremiah.

So the Old City wasn't really that old, after all. This was the real Old City, in the heart of an Arab village. Then why all the fuss over the other place if it wasn't the one where David had lived? Why had they hidden this Jerusalem from her?

The site had been scooped out of the side of a mountain. She took a short break from hiking to admire a sweeping view of the surrounding hills, striped red and brown, and crowded at their tops with yellow cranes. Chunks of brown rock stood wedged into the dirt like headstones. Olive trees grew sideways and leaned out over the valley. Their branches had twisted themselves up into knots.

"Jeremy!" she called out, just in case, then went on walking.

The path grew steep and she had to waddle a bit to keep her balance. Luckily, there was no one to laugh at her duck walk except for a group of schoolchildren sitting on rocks at the side of the road and drawing in their notebooks. Their teacher pointed to a large wall of rubble with three smaller walls jutting out like a capital E. The brochure claimed these walls had once been a kitchen, but all Mrs. Michaelson saw was rocks. She tried to imagine her own kitchen looking that way someday.

It was so hot that afternoon, Mrs. Michaelson felt as if someone were aiming her travel blow dryer in her face. She took shelter in a small limestone building with a domed roof. A shirtless young man sat by the door and read a hardback in Russian. She asked whether he'd seen Jeremy, but the young man didn't speak English.

She climbed down a spiral staircase in the center of the room to a cool basement chamber that smelled like glue. Light panels on the cavern walls told the story of the City of David excavations. It looked like a big party with chummy archaeologists dressed in seventies fashions. When they weren't staring at shards of pottery, the tender comrades laughed over Popsicles or linked arms around campfires and sang. The women wore hot pants. No doubt they had careers and lovers and, occasionally, disappointments, but even so, theirs were the best kinds of disappointments, their own.

The seventies were a while ago, she realized. How many of these people were dead?

Her family had been happy in the seventies, living in a brick ranch house with a yard full of cottonwood trees. In summer, the seeds blew around like snow.

The basement floor sloped down toward another stairway, sheer and very slippery. It had been tunneled out of the rock and was lit by dim lamps like the ones in the Western Wall tunnels. Mrs. Michaelson grasped the railing tightly and took the stairs one by one. The air was brisk, even a bit chilly, and she shivered in her silk.

She stopped to check Fodor's, which claimed the stairway was actually an old water shaft. But her brochure said the stairway was now, owing to "new developments," known for certain not to be a water shaft. Perhaps it had been a drainage tunnel.

"Jeremy?" she warbled. Her voice echoed down into the muddy hole, bounced off the rocks, and then vanished. She shuddered, then turned on her heel and pulled herself back up the steps, which were painfully steep, and the stone was slick and treacherous. Thank goodness for the thick tread on her gym shoes. One wrong move and you'd break your leg, and then you could be lost for days, without light, water, or air.

At the top of the stairs, she felt as if she'd scaled Masada again, but this time without a cable car. She stepped outside and collapsed in the shade of the doorframe, sucking at her water bottle until she'd drained the last drop. Her diamond watch said it was two o'clock.

The boys were never coming. What a fool she'd been to believe they ever would.

Glancing uphill, she realized how far down she was. She was far too tired to hike back up the way she'd come, unless there was some shortcut, or maybe a little golf cart or a car service. Of course! They had to have some sort of car service at the end of the path for tourists to get back to the top.

But before she could continue to the bottom, she had to wait for the schoolchildren to toddle past in parallel lines. She tried to play peek-a-boo with them, but one of the girls started crying and jabbering in Hebrew. The teacher looked suspiciously at Mrs. Michaelson, then prodded the girl along.

She had always said what she loved about kids was that they were honest.

Mrs. Michaelson kept a few feet behind the school group the rest of the way down the path, which ended in a flat open square of new limestone houses chiseled to look old. The schoolchildren settled down in the middle of the plaza, directly under the sun. They took off their sneakers and drank water.

A circle of old men in flowing white headdresses played backgammon under the awning of a souvenir shop. Their hands shot up theatrically in the air as they rolled the dice, as if they were about to make rabbits disappear. Without the headgear, she wouldn't have been able to tell whether they were Arab or Israeli. Everyone was so dark-skinned here.

One of the old men sold her a liter of water from a refrigerated cart outside the shop. The water came from Jericho, but Mrs. Michaelson didn't care where it came from. It was cold and wet, and she downed several gulps of it to Yasir Arafat's health. She asked the men about the car service, but none of them spoke English.

Her silk dress stuck to her skin, and the sheer sleeves drooped instead of floated. It hardly mattered to her just then if she ruined the dress. In fact, she hated the old thing. What did she need a dress like this for? There were no weddings or bar mitzvahs in her future to wear it to.

Next to the shop was a locked gate barring the mouth of a black cave. The darkness looked inviting, like a cold shower, and she heard water splashing against the bars. That must be the famous water tunnel, she thought. A bony African man with purple-black skin sat just outside the gate and soaked up the sun. His red-and-black Chicago Bulls jersey hung loose from his narrow frame.

She asked whether she could go in, and the African pointed her to a ticket booth with bars over the windows. A pale man with copper curls sat inside, listening to an Israeli radio station at its highest volume. Occasionally, he licked his thumb and turned the page of his tabloid newspaper, mostly ads featuring buxom young women caressing bottles of water.

"Is there a car service to get back to the top?" she shouted over a blaring ad jingle, but he shook his head. "How else can I get back?" she asked. "I can't go back the way I came. It's too hard."

The redhead pointed to the cave.

"Faster than walking back up the hill?"

He turned down his radio a notch. "You can go back up the hill, g'veret, but it's takes longer with all the turns," he said with a thick Hebrew accent. "Also, now it's too hot. You would have to stop every two minutes. In the cave it's in the shade. Then, when you come out, you are maybe five minutes' walk from where you started. And sometimes there are tour buses waiting there and maybe they would give you ride."

She looked at the cave again. Something about it tempted her, like the dark spaces where she used to hide when she was a girl. "What's in there, anyway?" she asked, fanning herself with her straw hat. The man put his hand to his ear, and she repeated her question.

"The water tunnel of Hizkiyahu."

"But what is it? Some kind of archaeological ruin?"

"Nothing," the man said. "It's just very beautiful experience." He peered through the bars at her dress. "You're going to some party?"

Mrs. Michaelson ignored him and looked up the water tunnel in her guidebook. She skimmed the useless description, a flash flood of archaeological jargon that ended on the mysterious, fateful-sounding coda: "Either way will get you wet."

The man turned up his radio. "Please, g'veret, you blocking my view. It's costs six shekels. You want go in or out?"

She stared longingly into the cool, black mouth of the tunnel. Well, then, since it was both a beautiful experience and the quickest way . . . Mrs. Michaelson held up a fifty-shekel note.

"You have nothing smaller?" He sighed as if he'd been crossed in love, shuffled across the sandy floor in his unbuckled sandals, and reflected for a moment before his cash register, a relic from the sixties. After carefully punching in the amount, he picked out the correct change and slid the coins to her through the bars: four ten-shekel pieces and the rest in dull gold agurot coins, a few the size of a contact lens. She'd never seen money that small before, and so much of it at once.

She slid the coins into the change pocket of her wallet. The African pushed himself off his stool to unlock the gate, but the redheaded ticket seller asked her, "G'veret, you have some shoes for the water?"

"Do I need them?" she said, irritated that he hadn't asked before taking her money.

"Of course! The café there sells shoes for water. And did you bring a torch?"

"A torch?" she repeated, and then realized he meant a flashlight. "No, I didn't."

"The café will give you also a candle." Tucking his paper under his armpit, he disappeared into a back room and slammed the door behind him.

Back at the souvenir shop, the old men playing backgammon grinned as if they'd expected her. "Azim!" one of them called out as she went inside.

Sunlight streamed into the shop through a pair of picture windows. Mrs. Michaelson waited beside a case of miniature menorahs and old coins glued to certificates of authenticity. A gold plastic Jesus languished on the wall under a handwritten notice: VISA OKAY BUT DON'T EVEN ASK ABOUT AMEX.

"Hello?" she called out.

A string of bells tinkled in the back of the shop, and then a dark little man with a neat, sharply carved mustache appeared from behind a curtain of plastic beads. He wore a Calvin Klein T-shirt under an embroidered vest, Levi's, and Adidas sandals with black socks.

"I need shoes for the tunnel," she blurted out. "And a light. Quickly, if you can."

"No problem, madam." He performed a deep bow for her, like one of the Three Musketeers. "Speak and it is done. A candle I will give to you as a present, and matches. I have many excellent pairs of sandals for sale." He led her to a tall white cabinet and pulled out a ring of keys. "You will be able to wear these sandals for your entire life."

He seems pleasant, she thought. Too bad more of them weren't like him. "I want the cheapest kind," she said, clutching her wallet so the coins wouldn't jingle.

Azim pouted. "Madam, I only carry top-quality sandals. You can wear them to the beach. You can wear them in the house. They are top-quality."

She reminded herself to be firm. "I'm sure they are, but I never go to the beach."

"You can wear them in the house," he repeated. "The floor of this tunnel is quite irregular. You want top-quality sandals to protect your feet. Fila brand is from Italy. 'Fila' means iron. I studied Latin as a boy." Azim threw his shoulders back. " '*Sic semper tyrannis!*' Not bad for a poor Jerusalem boy like your humble servant." He had a charming smile if you overlooked his teeth, which were brown and unevenly spaced.

"Please, may I see something cheaper?" she asked.

After an offended sniff, Azim made a show of sorting through his keys until he found the right one and unlocked his cabinet. "What size?" he asked curtly. He tossed her a suitable pair wrapped in plastic.

Mrs. Michaelson stepped into the sandals and walked in front of the mirror. She was shocked to see her reflection, her windblown hair grayer than it ought to have been, her skin sunburned, and her dress wrinkled and sweat-stained. As for the flip-flops, well, they were flip-flops, though they looked a bit less ridiculous than gym shoes next to a vermilion dress. "How much?"

"Thirty shekels," he said, polishing the gold cross around his neck with his thumb.

"You're supposed to bargain," Mr. Michaelson whispered. "He'll be offended if you don't." But she wasn't sure how to start. During the trip she'd relied on her husband to charm everyone into reaching his price. He was an expert wheedler.

"Ooh, that's very high!" she said, trying to sound outraged.

"Okay," said Azim. "Twenty-nine."

"I could offer you twenty," she said, counting the coins in her wallet.

"But my cost is twenty-five! I must make back for these shoes what I pay for them. This is not a charity house."

"Twenty-three?" she said doubtfully, and felt she'd given up too fast.

"Twenty-four," he shot back. "And I will give you the matches and candle for free." This didn't seem like much of a bargain, since he'd offered her the candle for free when she'd walked in, but then he snapped, "Two, three shekels. This is a game for you, but it's real money for me and my wife and my son. Do you have a son?"

Yes, she had a son. "Okay," she said, feeling small.

His thin face relaxed into its usual enchanting smile. "You will enjoy the tunnel in your new sandals. Our Savior Jesus Christ cured a blind man in the water. A true miracle."

"I'm not a Christian," she admitted, blushing.

"Don't worry," he said. "You will be. Jesus loves you. I see it in your face. Can I interest you in some authentic antique coins?"

"Actually I'm in a hurry," Mrs. Michaelson said, as if that chatty soldier up in the cabin would keep her promise to tell the boys to wait, if they even bothered to show up. Jeremy had no right to stand her up in this strange land where it was so easy to get lost.

"No pressure. We never pressure anyone here." Azim opened

a drawer behind the register and took out a gnarled gold candle and a box of matches. "Don't get them wet," he advised. "And here is a plastic bag for your shoes, absolutely free of charge."

"Have you been in the tunnel?" she asked, putting her shoes and socks in the bag.

"Never. You are with these children outside? They are your grandchildren?"

"I'm not with anyone," she said proudly. "I'm alone."

"How do I know you are not CIA?" he said, and then laughed. "Only kidding. You are a brave world traveler, no doubt. I myself would like to travel, but I have never left this country."

"You mean Israel?"

Azim smiled politely. "That is how some people call it." She had no answer for that one. "Enjoy the tunnel," he said, guiding her outside. "You wouldn't like to see some of my coins? Something to take home?"

"No, no, no . . ." she said, putting on her hat.

He bowed quickly and waved, as if to apologize for having offended.

The old men and Azim traded remarks in Arabic, then looked at her and laughed. "Don't get the matches wet," he called out as she hurried to the tunnel in her flip-flops.

The redheaded ticket seller pretended he was too busy adjusting his radio to say hello, but the African man said, "Welcome," in a low voice as he unlocked the metal gate. Finally, she was on her way. It was a little adventure, really. She hunched forward and descended into the dark cavern. The steps disappeared into a pool of cold water that came up to her ankles. The water felt wonderful on her hot skin, like a fountain of youth.

" 'Either way you'll get wet,' " she quoted to herself. Well, those guidebook writers had gotten it right for once.

The gate rattled at the top of the steps as the African man locked her inside. She tucked her guidebook into her plastic bag with her shoes and took a step forward. Cold clear water lapped pleasantly at her knees. The floor was every bit as choppy as Azim had promised, and her left foot, the one with the bunion, slid around in its flip-flop and made a soft slurping noise. Determined to keep her matches dry, she grabbed onto the wall to steady herself and continued forward.

The cavern quickly tapered into a long dark tunnel. She needed the candle now and struck her first match. As it burst into flame, the moist cavern walls glistened like polished steel. "So unusual," she marveled, touching the rock. A curl of hot wax nipped her finger, so she held the candle out in front of her instead of straight up. As the bits of melting wax hit the water, they hardened into twirling white spirals.

The walls grew so narrow that her shoulders scraped against both sides and she barely had room to squeeze through. The air smelled funny, like Miracle Whip that had gone bad. Mrs. Michaelson poked into the dark with her candle, but the light projected only a few feet. Beyond that everything was black. She tried to move faster, but her dress ballooned up with water, weighing her down. And her candle flickered wildly with each shaky step.

"Why is this vacation so hard?" she complained to no one, dragging her legs and the soggy dress through the water. She couldn't call this trip a vacation. It was more like a job. Worse than any job, actually.

A drop of water hit her thumb, barely missing the flame.

Her candle had already shrunk by a third, but all she saw ahead of her was darkness, bleak, empty, and terrifying. Each step brought her closer to the same black wall.

If she didn't hurry, her candle would be gone.

Then somewhere up ahead in the darkness, past her candle's reach, she heard a splash. Just one, but definitely not hers. "Who was that?" Mrs. Michaelson whispered. She stopped. First she heard nothing, but then the noise came again. Another splash, this time followed by a high-pitched whine. "Who was that?" she said, louder now, and took another step. The wind? But how could the wind have gotten down there? Then she thought of that sneaky Azim. It's a scam to rob tourists, she realized. They sell you shoes to see how much money you have, and then trap you in the tunnel. They all saw me go in.

"They" being . . . ?

Azim. His friends. Palestinians, Muslims, Arabs, Germans, the anti-Semites in Russia who'd persecuted her ancestors, her own sons, who tortured her with Chinese boyfriends and sterilized safety pins. The invisible forces of evil and chaos that preyed on innocent middle-class families around the world whose only crime was their love of order and good manners.

TOURIST MURDERED IN CAVE
ON EVE OF FLIGHT HOME
MOURNERS INCLUDE SON, HUSBAND, AND RABBI/LOVER

"Come on! Come on!" she scolded herself, crying now. Her legs splashed water everywhere. The plastic bag with her shoes swung from her clenched fingers. Those awful coins jangled in her wallet, heralding her approach like wedding bells.

Her flame bent in half before it went out.

ten

Rabbi Jose ben Gabriel, the famed Kabbalist of Worms, devoted his life to diagramming the various tortures of Hell. An excerpt follows:

CRIME	PUNISHMENT
Neglecting study	Snow
Evildoing	Fire
Failure to say blessing over a meal	Reincarnation as fish and eaten
Idle words	Soul flung via slingshot across the universe until idle words are erased
Gluttony	Force-feeding and vomiting
Lust	Storm
Passion	Lashings
Philandering	Vat of boiling semen
Rebellion against G-d	Eternal darkness

After presenting his findings on Hell to the Rabbinic Council in Frankfurt, Rabbi Jose was promptly excommunicated and condemned to an eternity of bee stings in the world to come, the Council's punishment for blasphemy.

The narrow streets in the Jewish Quarter seemed suspiciously quiet, especially compared with the jarring clatter of Silwan. The sparkling sidewalks were clear of dirt and trash. The buildings, all post-'67 reconstructions chiseled from new limestone, were scrubbed fleshy pink like a baby out of a bath. Their windows had been fitted with freshly painted green shutters and flower boxes.

Jeremy stopped under an awning in Hurva Square to check the hand-drawn map on the back of Dave's business card. Beside him, a heavyset boy in a New York Jets jersey peered hopefully into a refrigerated case of Ben & Jerry's ice cream. The boy kept counting the change in his chubby palm and looking over his shoulder, but no one came to take his money. Still he waited, looking increasingly forlorn until Jeremy said, "Just take an ice cream. You look like you need it. No, don't worry about that," he added as the boy tried to hand him his coins. "It's on me."

The boy left with his carton of Chunky Monkey, and Jeremy, who'd drunk and smoked himself sick the night before in the Hilton's air-conditioned lounge, examined his reflection in the ice cream case. He saw a tired old man with sharp lines and sore skin under his eyes, a red, swollen nose, and bloated cheeks.

That morning, he'd put on a blue shirt with a soft collar and the same white pants he'd had on last night. There hadn't been time to have them dry cleaned. He also wore a blue knit yarmulke (still stiff), a new acquisition from the gift shop in the lobby. His hair was combed flat, with only a faint tint of silvery green dye visible on the sides, if you were looking. And the nose ring was gone.

He looked like a fucking dork. But if his mission worked, it would be worth it.

Jeremy lit a cigarette as he crossed the square, bordered by palm trees, shadowy stone arcades, and parked cars with giant cardboard sunglasses in their windshields. Dave Saperstein's building, a squat cement cube, sat sandwiched between a bank of public phones and a restaurant called Mama's Home Cooking. A cartoon of a beefy Jewish mother swung over the door.

After finishing his cigarette, Jeremy recited his line—"I've come to ask for a favor"—one last time, and entered Dave's building. A laminated sign pointed him up a flight of stairs and down a hall lined with posters and folding tables covered in stacks of leaflets. Apparently, Jeremy could spend a month or why not two at a yeshiva. He could expand his mind, sleep in a free bed, and enjoy a home-cooked Shabbat meal with a local family. He could eat kosher pizza. He could learn more about Judaism and a healthy sex life. He could find himself.

And with Dave's help, he could spring his Palestinian boyfriend from jail.

No, "boyfriend" wasn't the right word. He hadn't had enough time to earn that privilege, though he'd needed only a few seconds to destroy George's future.

The office door was propped open by several copies of *Jewish Heroes for Children*. No sign of Dave. Only two teenage girls who'd wheeled themselves away from their desks and were chatting loudly in English above the whir of three fans that furiously churned air in the corners. A fourth fan, broken, hung its head by the window.

Jeremy patted his new yarmulke to make sure it was in place before he knocked on the doorframe. The first young woman, her hair and ears hidden in a white turban with a faux diamond clasp, wheeled back to her computer and started banging on the keys.

"Welcome, friend. How can I serve you?" asked the other woman, whose long black curls tumbled freely past her shoulders and looked real.

"Is Dave here? He told me I could find him here. It's important."

"Can I bring you a drink?" she asked, studying him with her steady gaze.

At first he thought she meant a good drink, so he said, "I'd better not," in his polite voice, which was a bit rusty. "I just need to talk to Dave. As soon as possible."

"Sure," she said, pulling down her dress to cover her ankles. "My name is Tali. In America I was Teri, but now *Baruch ha-Shem* I am Tali." She nodded, but didn't extend her hand, and Jeremy had learned by now not to offer his. "Dave is at the school, Lev Ha-Torah. I can walk you over and while I look for him, you could sit in on a class."

"I'm anxious to talk to Dave as soon as I can," he said. "It's an emergency."

"You don't look well," she said. "Are you sure you don't want a drink? Or we have a bed in the back where you can lie down."

"That's very nice of you," he said, "but I can't waste much more time."

"I understand," she said, grabbing a slim tan sack slumped on the floor. "You're all right here alone, Rivka?"

"Fine," said her turbaned partner, who'd glued her eyes to her computer screen.

As Tali slipped past Jeremy into the hall, a plain Jewish star on a gold chain bobbed above her breasts, full but small, like a pair of oranges. "You didn't sleep outside last night, did you?

Because if you need somewhere to stay, there's always Heritage House. It's free." She bent over one of the tables in the hall and selected three sheets of paper, one blue and two pink, and then a tiny white booklet. "This you fill out with all your information. And this one's a list of classes at Lev. And this tells you all you need to know about Heritage House."

"Thanks," Jeremy said, stuffing the papers into his pocket as Tali marched downstairs, her penny loafers slapping the carpeted steps. "Do you really think Dave can help me out?" he asked. "I'm in some very serious trouble."

She stopped short at the last step, and Jeremy almost fell backward. "Where did you say you were from?" she asked, holding the door open for him.

He hadn't said, and he wasn't sure how to answer. New York? That was just a playground where he'd skinned his knee once too often. Detroit? A prison. His grandparents' shtetl in Russia where he'd never been? Or Israel, the land of his ancestors? He settled on New York.

Tali took a small black umbrella out of her purse and opened it to ward off the sun. The sidewalk was blocked by two American youth groups battling over the orange Bezek telephones so they could tell their parents they were alive. Brandishing her umbrella gracefully, like a lance, Tali waved the phone card–clutching teenagers aside. "Are you a student?" she asked.

"In a way," Jeremy said, taking out a cigarette. His forehead and the back of his neck were already slimy with sweat. It was a good day to get naked. If only he'd immediately whisked George off to his hotel room the second they'd found each other. Then they could have been lounging in an air-conditioned paradise today, with soft towels, room service, and lots of clean socks, as many as George wanted.

A car alarm began to wail. The sound of sirens sent a flock of American girls screaming into the middle of the square, until they realized what the sound was and burst out laughing.

"Turn here, please," said Tali, directing Jeremy down an alley where a waiter in a tuxedo shirt dumped a bucket of melted ice onto the roots of a palm tree. Jeremy wondered which of the buildings they passed had belonged to George's family. Or perhaps the house had simply been razed. "Is it some specific spiritual quest that has brought you here, or do you just want to learn?" she asked.

Jeremy understood when she said "learn," she meant "learn about Judaism," as if no other kind of education were possible. "To learn," he answered, hoping that might take him to Dave faster.

They squeezed past a crowd of tourists from Japan holding out their crisp New Shekel notes in front of Bonkers Bagels. A few of the tourists wilted under the white umbrellas outside and poked at the balls of falafel tucked into pita pockets.

"Don't you miss the U.S.?" he asked.

"I miss Dial soap and black socks. But there's no place else I'd rather live."

"Why? What's so great about it?"

Tali pointed her umbrella at the reconstructed stone buildings all around them. "It's a feeling you get living among all this history. Everything's so old here, you feel your roots, physically. Either you're open to that feeling or you're not."

But he'd had that feeling once upon a time, and then he'd grown out of it. Did that mean religious people simply hadn't grown out of their childish illusions about God? No, there had to be something more, something he'd missed. These Jews weren't stupid. They could wring ten different meanings out of a transposed vowel in the Talmud. And even George's mother so fervently kissing her kitchen floor to get to heaven, with all her dubious theories about the human digestive tract, she had a solidity any four-star general would have envied. "Explain it, then," he said. "I want to understand."

"Careful," she said, holding him still as a beeping minivan backed into their path. "In America, all I cared about was which meaningless garbage on TV should I watch. But here I think about how to live my life as a righteous woman. And then, what if, God forbid, the entire world decided to exterminate their Jews? Where would you go?"

"That's not going to happen."

"Fine," she said, trotting down a set of steps. "As long as you're sure."

"Anyway, if the world wanted to destroy us, wouldn't it make more sense to spread ourselves out instead of all coming here to make a nice easy target?" asked Jeremy, staring at the sweat stains under her orange-size breasts.

"God forbid," Tali said, and spat twice over each shoulder.

Lev Ha-Torah was in front of them now, a flat-sided limestone garrison with four saplings tied to stakes in front. A brass sculpture of a burning bush had been nailed up next to the door. "Kirk Douglas paid for the courtyard," Tali said, unlatching a short metal gate. "It's pretty, no? Sometimes I come here and just stand." Shutting the gate behind them, she took a deep breath and smiled. "The class is through that glass door."

"You're not coming with me?"

"I have to return to the office." She waited there like a mother seeing her child off on his first day of kindergarten. "Go on. The worst thing that could happen is you might change the rest of your life."

"I want to see Dave now," he insisted.

Tali took a sleek silver cell phone out of her purse. "This is a big school. I could never find him by running down hallways and needlessly exciting myself. I'll have him come meet you in class. It's the easiest way. Don't worry. Now, go on in."

He wasn't sure he liked the idea of class; it smacked of indoctrination. "Do you mind if I finish this cigarette first?" he asked, to stall, but she plucked it out of his mouth.

"No good for you anyway, for health reasons. Go on, my friend." She gave him a feeble little wave, just as George had done before he'd been handcuffed.

Blasts of cool air blew through Jeremy's flattened hair like a shower as he went in. He thought he'd wander on his own to see if he could find Dave himself, but the door opened directly into a classroom, where several young men dozed at their desks. Everything in the room was white except the cornmeal-colored curtains that covered the windows, and the black books stamped in gold on the shelves. There was no chalkboard. The walls were decorated with laminated posters of skateboarders in backward baseball caps putting on prayer shawls or smiling over books of Torah. A computer-printed banner hanging above the empty teacher's desk advised:

> If your enemy assaults you, lead him to school. If he is of stone, he will dissolve. If he is of iron he will melt into fragments. —The school of Rabbi Ishmael

A lovely turn of phrase, Jeremy thought. Here was the Judaism he'd always been attracted to, broad-minded, idealistic, a religion of righteous victims, not conquerors.

A young woman with a black ponytail sat alone in the front row. The rest of the yawning students were men and wore name tag stickers with messages above their names, such as "Prayer is a two-way street" and "Coming out of the Jewish closet." They looked like regular tourists, with their white T-shirts and hiking shorts bulging with enough side pockets to store provisions for a small family. Jeremy noticed several yarmulkes in the latest style like his own: oversize, brightly colored, and easily mistaken for African tribal headgear.

Suddenly feeling shy, Jeremy sat down in back and was copying the proverb about leading your enemies to school when the pen flew out of his hand, stolen by a young man with a new beard. "You don't need that here," he said, suspending the pen over Jeremy's head. "They'll give you all the Xeroxes you want."

"Do you know Dave?" Jeremy asked, grabbing his pen back.

"Sure. Everyone knows Dave."

"Is he here? Or does he have an office?"

"He'll be here. Relax, dude." He sat next to Jeremy. "Call me Amitai. That's what I go by here. I've been here two months now, and I'm keeping an open mind."

Maybe that's my problem, Jeremy thought. I don't have an open mind.

"Hey, did they give you a schedule?" asked Amitai, handing Jeremy a blue flyer with a schedule of classes for July. Today there was "Genesis and the Big Bang," "Contemporary Jewish Issues: Your Questions Answered," "FREE LUNCH prepared by our own CHEF MORDECHAI," "A Taste of Talmud," and, finally, "Faith for Beginners."

"Free lunch," said Amitai, flashing a thumbs-up. "Oh yeah."

He introduced Jeremy to a few of the boys, most of whom were still in college and looked bored and sleepy. One, from Slovakia, was very pretty, with long eyelashes and soft blond hair. "Did you convert?" Jeremy asked, temporarily forgetting George.

"Of course not," he said. "I'm Jewish as you. Why you ask such a question?"

"I don't know," said Jeremy, doodling on the back of his class schedule.

The pretty boy turned to a friend and indignantly repeated the story in his own language. Luckily, Dave himself jogged in, still wearing his shiny gray suit. He pointed and high-fived the students on the way to the teacher's desk like a politician at a rally. That's the instrument of my salvation? Jeremy thought, trying not to lose heart.

"Dr. Schwartz is running late. He just called on his cell," said Dave, hoisting himself onto the edge of the desk. His feet, in black dress shoes with white socks, floated high off the floor. "In the meantime I wanted to let you guys know that after dinner there's a free concert of Jewish folk songs in the ruins of the Burnt House at seven-thirty." He held up a sheaf of green flyers. "And tomorrow, after my tour of Jewish sites in the so-called Muslim Quarter, we're having a movie night with free kosher pizza. It's a very powerful documentary about the Holocaust." He looked at the flyer again and raised his shaved eyebrows. "Free pizza? Wow. All you guys do is eat over here."

Dave jumped down from the desk and passed out flyers. "Hey, Gary, how's your brother doing?" he said to Amitai, and handed him a flyer. Jeremy was trying to get Dave's attention when a wiry man in a pale yellow shirt burst into the room carrying a battered leather briefcase, two bulging shopping bags, and a ream of photocopies wedged under his armpit. "*Mea culpa,*" he panted, bumping into their chairs on his way to the teacher's desk. Both his shoes were untied and a fat, old-fashioned cell phone hung off his belt like a hammer.

"Gentlemen," Dave said with a short wave of his arm, "I give you Dr. Schwartz. This guy's lectured at Harvard, and now you're hearing him for free."

"MIT," said the slender doctor, unloading his papers on the

desk as his digital watch began beeping. Two pairs of glasses sat on his wrinkled forehead: brass-rimmed bifocals and a second pair with dark lenses clipped to the frames aviator-style.

"MIT? Still pretty good," said Dave, dancing down the aisle. Jeremy held up his finger and Dave winked at him.

"Did they tell you I was here?" Jeremy squeaked, his voice breaking unexpectedly so he cleared his throat.

"Of course, of course. You know, you could use a name tag, my friend."

"My name is Jeremy, and I came here to talk to you. Can we go outside?"

Dave crouched beside his desk. "What's the matter, son? You look upset. Or else you haven't slept much lately." He sounded like Jeremy's father in his I-am-a-trained-analyst mode.

"I am upset." The scene in the park, which had been repeating itself all morning, played once more in Jeremy's head. Each time, he felt worse. He leaned forward out of his seat and whispered, "Do you remember yesterday, at the Wall, you said you had some friends in the government who could help a young man in trouble?"

"Say no more," said Dave, clapping Jeremy's shoulder and pushing him back into the chair. "I can take care of you, no problem."

"But you haven't heard what the problem is."

"The only thing is," Dave went on, "today I'm backed up. Could you hang out here for the afternoon and then maybe we could meet tomorrow morning?"

"No. It's got to be today," Jeremy said.

"These damn meetings," said Dave, counting them off on his fingers. "Minister of the Interior, the journalist from Paris . . . I could probably steal away for twenty minutes between the CEO from New Jersey and my afternoon Tunnel tour.

Wait for me here. As soon as I can get away, I'll come and grab you."

"You promise you'll come?"

"Trust me. Lost boys are my specialty," he said with a wink and scurried away, ducking his head as if he were being shot at. Jeremy didn't trust him for a minute, but he wanted to because he had no better option.

"No need for you all to take notes. I'm giving you the info right there," said Dr. Schwartz, passing out his yellowing photocopies. His hands and nails were yellow, too, and the nails needed trimming. Amitai brought the doctor a cup of bug juice, which went down in one gulp.

What does George get to drink? Jeremy wondered. What has he had to eat?

"When I think of evolution . . ." said the doctor, who pronounced it "*evil*-lution." He patted down his pockets in search of his glasses and then, recalling that they were perched on his forehead, slid the bifocals down his nose. "When we're young, all we hear in school is evil-lution," he began again, "so we fight tooth and nail for it. But today, I ask you to keep an open mind. This isn't going to be me trotting out the Lev Ha-Torah party line and telling you what to think. I just present the facts. You decide."

Maybe George is already home, Jeremy thought. They can't hold him based on circumstantial evidence. Anyway, one look at the kid and it's obvious he's innocent.

The doctor squinted at Jeremy's chest, but didn't see a name tag. "You're new, aren't you?" he asked. "And where are you staying in Jerusalem?"

"Heritage House," Jeremy said quickly. Wasn't that the right answer?

"Nice place," said the doctor. "And you can't beat the price."

Amitai gave Jeremy a funny look. "Why haven't I seen you around before?"

Dr. Schwartz explained he wasn't against "*evil*-lution" for religious reasons, but because it was bad science. He whipped through the tissue-thin pages of a brown leather Bible and explained that what King James had translated as "fowl" could actually be interpreted to mean "pterodactyl." He passed around a *Time* magazine article written by "a dear friend" and mended with yellow Scotch tape. He held up one of the two books he'd written. (The grand total was five if you counted the ones he'd co-authored.) He dug into a purple sock and pulled out a red clay model of a trilobite. "I keep it in this sock. It's purple because it belongs to my daughter."

"I wear purple socks sometimes," Jeremy said, writing the words "purple socks" on his paper and crossing them out. Come on, he thought, checking the door again for Dave. There's a life at stake here, though he wasn't sure whether it was George's or his own.

"No crime in that," said Dr. Schwartz. He squeezed a couple of buttons on his digital watch, now beeping once more. "Does any of this prove beyond a shadow of a doubt God set this all in motion? I don't think so. But there are some things scientists, responsible scientists, will tell you they can't explain. And so there may be a God. But don't take my word for it. Check out His track record. Respected archaeologists around the world use the Torah as a map to find ruins of civilizations buried underground. In fact, the Torah has such a perfect track record, I'm beginning to believe God wrote it."

Amitai leaped up and led the students in a round of applause. In spite of himself, Jeremy felt the little hairs on his arms and the back of his neck stand at attention. Only religion had the power to stir him up this way, not his self-invented brand of humanism, not Tony Kushner and Edward Said and Cornel West, not "sexual minoritarianism," not socialism, not even sex itself. All those "isms" seemed merely like ways of denying the truth, which was, as Jeremy had always suspected deep down, that religious people really did hold the copyright on Being Right.

Dr. Schwartz pulled two stacks of books out of his shopping bags. "I happen to have a few extra copies of my books. I get them directly from the publisher at cost and I can pass them on, signed, for ten percent less than what you'd pay in stores."

Amitai was the first in line for a signed book.

I need ... something, Jeremy thought, feeling need itself stretch up from his stomach through his throat like a claw. Where the fuck was Dave? He doodled on a handout for a few minutes, then walked over to the windows to stretch his legs.

Through a gap in the curtains, Jeremy could see a noisy library. Yeshiva students in black and white pounded on lecterns or argued in pairs with thick yellowing books spread open in front of them. Some of the boys climbed aboard rolling ladders and wheeled themselves along the polished wooden bookshelves, which wrapped around the walls and stretched up to the ceiling. Maybe I should join them, Jeremy thought. Better to be a slut or a yeshiva student, one or the other. Everything in between is so pallid.

Tired of waiting, Jeremy was about to make a run for it, to hunt down Dave on his own, but the door was blocked by a burly, frowning stranger, who'd planted himself at the back of the room. He had broad shoulders, a thick belly, and a massive face that gleamed as if it had been burnished with steel wool. His hair and beard were gray and wispy, but his bushy eyebrows, slanted upward, were bright orange. A black velvet yarmulke crowned his bald spot like a mountain peak.

"That's Rabbi Avrum Goldstein," Amitai whispered as Jeremy slinked back into his seat. "The guy sells out auditoriums in LA, New York, Chicago, all across this country," he said, forgetting in his excitement that Israel wasn't "this country." "Just a couple months ago, I was stuck in an office selling real estate. Now I get to hear Rabbi Goldstein every week."

"It seems to me you were better off selling real estate," Jeremy said. "At least then you had a direction."

"No one really knows what direction he's going in," Amitai argued. "The truth is, Jeremy—it is Jeremy, right?—we're all afraid because we have no control over life, so we grasp on to these false certainties like money or real estate, thinking they'll save us. But actually, the answers are right here." He touched his heart and then Jeremy's too.

"What about here?" said Jeremy, pushing Amitai's hand downward, but Amitai yanked the hand away before it could get too far.

"Dude, watch it," he said, turning very red.

Meanwhile, the rabbi marched up to the teacher's desk, where the doctor was still selling books, and let out a thundering cough.

"*Mea culpa. Perdon,*" said Dr. Schwartz, packing up his books and papers and stuffing his trilobite into its purple sock, now twisted inside out. Rabbi Goldstein scooped up what was left of the papers on the desk and dropped them into the cowering doctor's arms. "*Perdon,* Rabbi," said Dr. Schwartz, clutching his papers and briefcase to his chest with his chin as he scuttled out of the room, leaving behind a trail of photocopies, loose coins, and his sunglasses.

The rabbi paused thoughtfully at the desk, as if waiting for the air to clear itself, then pulled out the chair and sat. He looked over the room slowly, his dark eyes evaluating each of their faces.

The only noises Jeremy heard were the hum of the air-conditioning and the female student nervously tapping her long nails on her desk. As the rabbi caught his gaze, Jeremy swore he could hear the old man's gravelly voice admonish him: "I'm looking at your soul, and it's black. You are a cursed harlot."

Finally, Rabbi Goldstein pulled off his gold watch and slapped it down in front of him faceup. He tugged his nose, moved his hand inside his belt, and leaned his chair back on its hind legs. "Ask me anything," he dared them. "Go on." He pointed to Amitai, who'd raised his hand. "Yeah, you. Where are you from?"

"Brooklyn, originally. Then I moved to Boston."

"So they still have a few Jews left in Brooklyn. Is that good or bad? You tell me. Well, what is it you want to know?"

Amitai stood up, gripping the desk as if otherwise he might tip over. "I've done research," he said in a low voice, "and I've turned up a few mentions of a great darkness descending on Avraham, Sh'mot 15:12, and the references to Gehenna, She'ol, and Azazel . . ."

"What's the question? It sounds like you're giving a lecture."

"Okay, okay," Amitai said quickly. "Here's my question. Does Judaism believe in hell, and if so, then where is it?"

Wherever it is, I'm going there, Jeremy thought.

Rabbi Goldstein cocked his head and scratched the inside of his ear with his pinkie. "Is there a hell? Probably not." His chair thudded down on all fours. "At least, if you mean flames and little red guys with pitchforks underground. That's a Greek concept from the New Testament, written by Jews who believed in the false Messiah." The rabbi rocked back in his chair again. "Real Jews look at it this way: The ultimate reward in life is an infinite connection with God. So, conversely, the ultimate punishment is to miss out on that connection. There's your hell."

"So you're saying hell is a metaphor?" Amitai asked.

"Let me finish, young man. Now, you say, Wait a minute, how do you connect with God? God's even more unknowable than your wife. At least women you can give diamond bracelets." Rabbi Goldstein snapped his fingers. "That's why we pray. So God Himself can tell us what He wants. The catch is we can't hear Him if the connection is faulty, like a bad phone line. You see, everything we do strengthens or weakens our connection to God. No sins cut the link entirely except for three." He counted on his fingertips. "One, two, three, no, four. Other than those four, the link is never dead. It may just need to be revived a little."

"So what are the four sins?" Amitai asked.

The rabbi listed them:

1. Murder
2. Idolatry
3. Sexual immorality
4. Violating Shabbat

His ears burning with recognition at number 3, not to mention 2 and 4, Jeremy waved his hand.

"Yeah, you," said the rabbi, "the one taking all the notes."

"What do you mean by sexual immorality?" Jeremy asked, though he felt pretty sure he could guess. "Like Bill Clinton? Is he going to hell?"

"Bill Clinton's going to hell for a lot of reasons," said the rabbi, rubbing his fat, jolly stomach.

Jeremy wasn't satisfied. He wanted to beat the rabbi at his own game, but he lacked the firepower. In fact, the only cogent argument that sprang to mind at that moment was George's urgent I WANT TO SEX YOU. Or George's blithe dismissal of organized religion: I HAVEN'T PATIENT FOR IT.

Still, Jeremy fought on. "What's wrong with sex? Doesn't the Torah say a husband should give sexual pleasure to his wife? It's not only a good deed, it's a responsibility."

"That's right, and any other kind of sex is sexual immorality."

"Like masturbating? Does that send you to hell?"

"It's a good start," replied the rabbi, causing a low rumble of protest in the room. The rabbi raised his voice. "Hey, no one said fulfilling God's law was easy. The body is like a car and the soul is the driver. You have to keep the car in good condition, so it'll take you where you want to go. But the car isn't more important than the driver."

"Then how about homosexuals?" Jeremy said. "They're obligated to give pleasure, but they can't get married, so who are they supposed to give pleasure to? Jewish law is immensely thorough, as well as practical. It wouldn't just neglect homosexuals." The rest of the class glared at him. He was their enemy now, for disturbing their napping, their pleasant Zionist dream.

"Homosexuals must never be ridiculed or harmed, but the sexual practice is explicitly forbidden. Vayikra 18–22," said Rabbi Goldstein.

"So what are they supposed to do? Change?"

The rabbi shrugged. "I don't believe it's really possible they could change."

"Then should they commit suicide? That's against Jewish law."

"I happen to have great compassion for homosexuals," Rabbi Goldstein said sadly. "Unfortunately, I can't change the Torah. That's like saying you want to join a country club but only if you can set your own dues. Hey, maybe the rule seems arbitrary to you, but there's actually a good reason for it. Look at the Romans. Their birthrate decreased due to all the uncontrolled sex they were having. Homosexuality, bestiality, incest—nothing was forbidden. So they ran out of native Romans for their army and had to rely on foreign mercenaries, who were totally faithless, and their empire was ruined."

The pretty boy from Slovakia raised his hand. "Was Jesus Jewish?"

The rabbi replied, "Does the pope wear a yarmulke?"

The students asked about the Torah's position on vegetarianism, feminism, environmentalism, and Rastafarianism. Was Seinfeld Jewish? Would God have voted Democratic? Was it permitted to check e-mail on Shabbat if you had cable Internet access?

Rabbi Goldstein, getting up from his chair and making his way toward a back door, didn't think it was a good idea.

That's why you guys came here? Jeremy thought. Those are your burning spiritual crises? If you're going to ruin your lives by submitting to thousand-year-old rules, at least let it be out of idealism, not because you can't think of anything better.

"And if you dedicate your life to the study of Talmud," said Rabbi Goldstein, gripping the doorknob behind him, "you'll realize a very deep sense of true joy instead of the false transient pleasures of here and now. And now it's time for lunch."

As soon as the word "lunch" escaped his lips, the rabbi threw the door open and, with surprising alacrity, sprinted down a set of stairs. The other students quickly grabbed their bags and scrambled after him. "Come on, dude. You'll miss out on lunch," Amitai called out over his shoulder as he followed the herd.

"I'm supposed to meet someone," said Jeremy. Amitai shrugged, then left.

The room was empty. Jeremy plucked off his brand-new blue yarmulke and rolled it into a ball. The whole notion of joining any group—that's the problem, he thought. What if there were no sides, no religion, no history? But how could anyone escape history?

The first step was to escape your parents. If you could manage it.

Maybe Dave had simply forgotten his promise and was having lunch downstairs with everyone else. Which is where I should be, Jeremy thought. If Dave's not coming, I might as well get my free lunch. He waited one minute more and then went downstairs.

When he got to the cafeteria, his prospects of actually getting any food looked pretty dim. Apparently eating was not on the list of sensuous earthly pleasures to avoid, and the students were taking full advantage of the loophole. Boys in black hats swarmed the buffet, butting at one another's backs with their red plastic trays and grabbing food over one another's shoulders. In the dining area, the students hunched over their plates and crammed heaping forks of fish, salad, and rice into their mouths, sucking the food in with their deft pink tongues. Forks speared fillets of fish from metal trays in the middle of the tables and set them spinning. Warm bug juice splashed over glass rims. Knives and chairs scraped. Bits of corn flew.

Jeremy finally managed to squeeze into a line in front of the metal washing station. A sign above the sink read:

Washing hands is one of the sublime things which stand on the height of the world. —Rabbi Eliezer HaGadol

"Your yarmulke," said one of the real yeshiva students, cutting ahead of Jeremy in line. Jeremy dug the damn thing out of his pocket and put it back on.

By the time he reached the buffet, nothing was left except a heel of bread under a pile of ripped plastic bags, all empty, and two metal vats coated with a shallow layer of loose corn floating in mayonnaise. Jeremy spooned a bit of corn onto the bread and filled his glass from a fountain offering fruit-flavored variations on a watery drink called *Jump!* It tasted awful, like cough syrup for children. At least they could spike this shit with rum, he thought. After two sips, Jeremy threw his cup away half full and shoved the rest of his food into the garbage, along with his tray.

It's all right, he thought, tears filling his eyes. I'm not hungry anyway. But he was starving. There were no words for the empty space expanding in his stomach, pushing up against his chest. He wouldn't have cared, if George had been there to hold him, but George was in jail because the minute Jeremy liked someone, he fucked it up. Someone else hold me, he thought, someone I don't know—any guy—please hold me. Or at least let me have a cigarette. I'm so sick of being addicted, he thought, to nicotine, drugs, alcohol, food, water, sleep, love. It's all the same trap.

Jeremy stumbled out of the cafeteria, his eyes blurry, his head and heart pounding. He almost missed Dave, coming down the stairwell as Jeremy was going up. "I was just on my way to find you," he said, clutching Jeremy by the elbow.

"Sure you were," he said, privately elated at his second chance.

"Young man, I never B.S. a friend." He backed up the steps so that he was looking down at Jeremy. "So what did you do? Overstay your visa? Get caught working illegally? Happens all the time. But the Israeli government wouldn't dare interfere with any of our students, even if they were only taking one or two of our classes. . . . Now, I know you're thinking: School, what a drag. Remember, you don't *have* to do anything. Just come to one or two classes during the day, and then at night you're totally free to come and go as you please. Unlike Heritage House, we have no curfew here. And it's all free."

He handed Jeremy a form asking for his "spiritual orienta-tion." The choices were: Orthodox, Conservative, Reform, Re-constructionist, Humanist, Unsure, and Other.

"Stay a week. Stay a month. Stay as long as you need to find whatever you're looking for. You don't have to decide what that is now—just keep an open mind. If you want, you can fill out your information right here on the stairs and give it back to me."

"What exactly do you do?" Jeremy asked. "Who are you?"

"I believe the question is Who are *you*?" said Dave, looking at Jeremy severely. "Isn't that what you want to figure out?"

"This isn't what I wanted to talk to you about."

"Then what do you want? Speak freely. No one's going to hurt you here."

Jeremy suddenly realized how stupid this idea had been, as if Dave could simply march him straight down to the prison and unlock all the doors before George's mother had noticed her son's absence. "I don't need the help for myself," Jeremy said, then paused while a pair of yeshiva students passed by. Dave stepped aside and saluted the students in Yiddish. "It's for my friend," said Jeremy. "My Palestinian friend who was ar-rested last night for no reason. You met him yesterday at the Wall. Remember? He was totally innocent. We were just walk-ing in this park . . ."

"Which park?"

"Independence Park."

"Aha," said Dave, nodding slowly.

"And there was a fight and they thought he'd started it, but it wasn't true. I was with him the whole time. And he's in jail now and I don't know how to get him out."

"How do you know he's in jail?"

"The police told me before they took him away. So we've got

to get him out. It's all a mix-up. I was with him the whole time, and he didn't do anything."

"Maybe they let him go. Do you know where they took him?"

"I think they called it the Russian Compound."

Dave let out a low whistle and patted Jeremy on the shoulder.

"Why? Is that bad? Can you help him? You said you had some connections."

"Yes I do, but the connections I have that help Americans don't necessarily work for someone like your friend. And that's too bad, because the way you're describing it, it sounds very unfortunate. Though I must admit neither of us is really equipped to know for sure the truth of this particular situation."

"But I do know for sure," said Jeremy. "He's innocent. I was with him." He didn't want to play his ace in the hole, but he had no other cards left. "Would it help if we made a deal? You get George out of jail, and I'll . . . I'll stay here and study in your yeshiva. How about that? Then we both get what we want."

"You seem to think we're all connected," said Dave, "that it's as easy as making a phone call and it's done."

"Hey, I'm a prime catch for you. I'm good at attracting sinners. I could go to Independence Park and catch you a whole net full of sinning homosexuals and bring them back here to get straightened out. Isn't that, like, your wet dream?"

Dave shifted his feet impatiently. "Look, I understand you."

"You understand me?"

"Oh yeah. Your head's spinning. You see something and you're sure you know what it is, because you're judging by what you see in front of you. That's how we're taught to think in America." Dave smiled. "You asked who I am. I'm someone who gives boys the chance to think for themselves—not what their parents think or their rabbi thinks, but what they think. Don't you want to give our program a shot, to find out the facts and make up your own mind, so when you decide about Judaism, you know it's for sure and you aren't just guessing?"

Jeremy wished for the urge to yell and scream and bang his fists, but he only felt tired, and deeply sad. Dave means well and so do I, he thought, but two well-meaning people aren't enough. He added the paper Dave had given him to the collection in his back pocket. "I need some lunch," he said.

"You know there's a free lunch in the cafeteria?"

"It was all gone by the time I got there."

"We have very hungry boys. No such thing as a free lunch, right?" Dave aimed a friendly fake punch at Jeremy's shoulder. "It's all going to work out. If your friend's innocent, he has nothing to worry about. The police have bigger fish to fry, believe me."

Dave headed into the cafeteria, and Jeremy was free. But then he was always free. Freedom was nothing new to him.

So George was going to stay in jail and all Jeremy could do was go home.

He trudged up the rest of the way to the ground floor. A bulletin board at the top of the stairs offered UNUSED HALF OF RETURN TICKET TO NY—ONE WAY. BEST OFFER. There was also: TOO BUSY STUDYING TO DO LAUNDRY? CALL SH'MUL FOR COMPETITIVE RATES. And ASK THE TRAITOR EHUD BARAK WHY HE RELEASES THOUSANDS OF ARAB CRIMINALS WHILE JEWISH SETTLERS SIT IN ISRAELI JAILS. A schedule of yeshiva classes was posted in the middle of the board. Instead of psych, biochem, or Shakespeare, you could take "Halacha 1," "Gemara 1," "To the Source," or "48 Ways to Wisdom." Only forty-eight? Jeremy wondered.

Desperate to get outside, away from Hebrew, God, and eternity, Jeremy ran to the end of the hall and pushed through a pair of glass doors to a balcony with a view of the Wall. Prime real estate. The tourists below looked like figures on a chessboard, while the silver Al-Aqsa Mosque and the copper-colored Dome of the Rock glinted at eye level. He remembered that when he was young, he used to wish the shiny copper dome was the Temple, instead of the crummy old Wall of pathetic old stones bleating, "Help me!"

No, help *me*, Jeremy thought, but there was no one to help him. That was just a childish fantasy. There was nothing to do but go to George's mother and confess, even if she'd already heard. (If she hated Jews now, think how she'd feel once she found out the news.) I'm sorry, George, he thought. I tried.

Now, if he could just find his way out of this place.

A hot breeze blew dust into his nose and throat; he lit a cigarette and inhaled deeply. The only time he'd felt good in this rotten country was when he'd kissed George in that tiny wedge of forest the Sheraton had forgotten to tear up for parking, and now George was gone. It was a relief to inhale death, to stop fighting and let his craving take over.

Two yeshiva students smoking beside Jeremy carried on a heated argument over which would be better for dinner, meatballs or stuffed cabbage. Another student ran across the balcony and yelled into his cell phone: "Sell! Sell! I said sell!"

"What makes you bust out like that in the middle of class?" one of the black hat–black beard types asked a sunburned muscle boy in a basketball jersey and basketball shorts. "Can you, like, share with me how you feel at that moment?"

"I dunno exactly," said the muscle boy, who had a Cockney accent. "I expect it's to do with my childhood."

"We just ask you to keep an open mind, dude," the yeshiva student said.

Jeremy ashed his cigarette over the railing and began looking around for the exit.

The yeshiva student went on in an awed, deadpan voice, like
a surfer describing his favorite wave: "God's actually pretty
cool, you know. Have you checked out the Kabbalah? That
stuff's pretty intense. See, it's all about energy. It's like God just
takes like all these earthly pleasures, sex or whatever, and just
lifts them to the next level, so that the union of a man and a
woman in marriage is like the most mind-blowing experience
ever. Dude, I can hardly wait to get married."

As he edged closer to listen to more, Jeremy was annoyed to
hear someone call his name.

eleven

JEDAIAH EXPLAINS IT ALL

Jedaiah Ben Abraham of Bezares, a mystic who was kicked out of France with all the rest of its Jews in 1306, compares the world to a deep and stormy sea spanned by a thin, fragile bridge of time, suspended between chaos and everlasting joy. On either side of this bridge, as narrow as a single footstep, loom the walls of death and destruction, several miles high. A man's life is as small as a falafel crumb in its shadow. The combined population of a city that has survived for centuries amounts to a ball of snow.

Tell me, asks our good old friend Jedaiah, how do the fields of Sodom and Gomorrah flower now?

T he moaning rippled down the tunnel, surged into a ghostly wail, died down, and then started up again stronger than before.

Frantically smacking the walls, Mrs. Michaelson pulled herself along as well as she could, weighed down by her billowing sleeves and the plastic bag with her shoes, which kept getting caught on the rocks. Her body was good for nothing in this water, this miserable, rotting body that betrayed her in new ways every day. Her hair was falling out. Mysterious brown spots and red bumps erupted on her skin, down her aching back and sagging arms and legs. Bunions popped out of the sides of her feet. And the worst of all, hemorrhoids.

What had people done before Preparation H? What had Abraham, Isaac, and Jacob used against hemorrhoids?

Mrs. Michaelson had no idea where this tunnel led, yet she went on, her chest pounding. The air smelled damp and stale, and every rustle of water sounded like a thunderous flash flood. She kept straining her eyes to bring the murk into focus, but it refused to cohere into shapes she could name. Even though her throat was rough from thirst, she was afraid to drink the icy water splashing up the front of her sodden party dress.

She dipped her free hand into the water, let it stream between her fingers. What the hell had she done with her matches? All she could remember about them was that she was supposed to keep them dry.

The noise grew louder, heaving up and down as the water rushed through her legs. She'd lost track of how long she'd been lost in this ridiculous tunnel. Was it minutes or hours? One year or fifty-nine?

Suddenly she bumped her head on the ceiling, which was closing in on her like a gullet squeezing a morsel of food into its stomach. "I don't care," she thought aloud, and stooped her shoulders. "Swallow me up. It's what I want."

The noise drew nearer. She imagined she could touch it if she reached out her hand. "Give me, give me," the noise seemed to implore. She took another step forward. And then another, and another, until she was right up against the monstrous source of all that crying and moaning. Its hot breath flooded her ear. Its chilling, slimy bulk surrounded her, and now there was nothing in the world but her body and the rocks and that terrifying wailing: flesh, bone, and spirit all battling for the same space. She stretched out her hand to feel for the wall, and something rough and scaly grazed her skin. It grabbed with coiling fingers that dug into her wrist.

The only thing they understand is force, so Mrs. Michaelson made good use of force. *We can't let them win!* Hitting, kicking, scratching, spitting, biting, she flailed her fists and gnashed her teeth. *We won't let them win!* She kicked so hard that she lost one of her flip-flops, so she stabbed the cool water with her naked toes and hit something high and soft like a fat pillow. *We'll fight you to the death!* She found her sandal again and stepped into it. *Stand aside or I'll cut you down!* She wanted to run, but the water, or maybe the monster, kept pulling her back and down. "No!" she screamed, and lunged forward, dragging the water and the enemy and the plastic bag with her sneakers.

She heard a thin, flat scream.

"Leave me alone!"

A woman's voice. My voice, decided Mrs. Michaelson while splashing away with all her strength. She had no hope of escape, but at least she could get a head start on her invisible attacker, wear him out. Her other option was to turn around and mount a proper defense. An instinct told her it was better to run.

She'd always said she wasn't afraid to die. People died all the time—every day. But now she felt the weight of the word. Death, the murderer who had claimed her parents and was knocking on her husband's door, had come for her.

So here it ends, she thought with a shudder, after almost sixty years. I've been a wife and a mother. I've gone to work and to school and I've buried two simple though loving parents. I've donated money to symphonies and made pretty, tasteful dresses. I never smoked or drank to excess. I sent thank-you notes and sympathy cards. I baked coffee cakes and kept them in my freezer in case someone died so I had something to bring for the shiva call. I took in mail for neighbors when they went on vacation. I kept my front lawn trimmed, and filled in the empty spaces around the trees in my yard with annuals. In my own way, I've fought against the forces of darkness all my life, and I shall fight you, spirit. If you want my life, you'll have to wrench it from me.

She collected the soggy folds of her dress and stood still, ready for a good scrap. But the spirit cowered in the shadows like a wounded dog and whimpered, refusing to give chase. So Mrs. Michaelson splashed a bit farther down the tunnel and then paused. Behind her, the noise seemed to grow softer. She froze for a moment to listen. Yes, it really was fading. A little farther, and the noise died down to a whistle that gradually grew faint and then expired. Gone. No more sounds now except the water lapping at Mrs. Michaelson's knees.

A drop of water hit her forehead and trickled down the side of her nose. Feeling crept back into her numb fingers, which she squeezed into a fist. She felt something hard and dry and small lodged in her palm.

How stupid of me, Mrs. Michaelson thought. This whole time I've been holding the box of matches in my hand!

The match burst into life, its high, yellow flame painting the dripping rocks and her silk dress with a warm tawny light. The ceiling was now high enough for her to stand erect once again. Her match went out, so she lit another and then held out her candle, now barely more than a nub. It caught the flame and began rapidly dripping wax that hit the water with sizzles and puffs of smoke.

Had it even been a strange noise she'd heard, or merely an echo of her own voice?

I will not die here, Mrs. Michaelson decided, and slung her

plastic bag over her arm. Her left flip-flop was cutting into her bunion, but she refused to care.

Warm water flowed between her legs. She smelled a fragile breath of fresh air. All at once the flame of her candle danced wildly between her fingers. The cavern walls, suddenly swelling like the belly of a gourd, lightened to a warm brown.

A spark of white glittered in the distance and then expanded into a diamond. The flame of her candle, now barely an inch long, kept nipping at her fingers, so she blew it out.

And now the exit shone a few feet ahead, a craggy curtain of hot light. Could it really be true? She touched her cheeks with her wet-raisin fingers and then heard a high-pitched heavenly chorus calling to her in a language that sounded like Hebrew.

So the world wasn't a howling wilderness. She'd gone through it and come out the other side intact.

Mrs. Michaelson redoubled her pace toward the chorus of angels and the blazing white light, which hit her in the face like a rock. Covering her eyes with her arm, she waded through the white opening. Such a sun! She'd never felt its fire so close, melting over her hair like hot butter, boiling the water running between her legs. Her shredded dress was burning off her skin.

Open your eyes, ninny, Mrs. Michaelson thought, and lowered her arm.

She was standing in a pool of bright green water and marble stumps that had once been pillars. The pool was surrounded by high stone walls, like the bottom of a large well. As her eyes adjusted to the light, she saw a young woman and an elderly couple on a small landing peering down at her.

The younger woman was dressed in a black bikini top, khaki shorts, and a wrinkled safari hat that had a leather band spiked with yellow teeth. She called out to Mrs. Michaelson in Hebrew.

The elderly man, who wore a yarmulke, said in English,

"It's not her," and retired to a bench in the shade. His wife, her hair covered by a floppy-brimmed summer hat, followed him.

"I don't speak Hebrew." Mrs. Michaelson laughed, holding up her shoes in the plastic bag. She felt silly standing there in her sopping silk dress, like a cocktail party refugee caught in a rainstorm.

"I speak English," the woman said in a thick sabra accent, her painted toes hugging the edge of the landing. For some reason, the fat black handgun hanging off her belt didn't bother Mrs. Michaelson just then. She could even imagine herself posing with it in front of the tunnel to take a picture and show people later: "I was here!"

"I'm okay," Mrs. Michaelson said, setting her bag on the stone landing. As she pulled herself out of the water, the Israeli woman gave her a boost. She had rough hands and a strong grip. The muscles around her stomach were chiseled.

"I am Yocheved," the woman said. "Like Moses' mother in Torah. I am a guide."

A guide? Moses' mother? For half a second Mrs. Michaelson wondered if she really had reached the pearly gates, but then she realized Yocheved meant a *tour* guide. "Helen Michaelson. Glad to meet you." She waved to the American couple, but they didn't respond. Maybe they'd just had a fight.

Mrs. Michaelson kicked off her flip-flops and stretched her torn, soggy silk wings. She was finally free of all that water and she felt light, thin, and tall. Even in her bare feet she was almost a foot taller than the squat, muscular Yocheved.

The guide asked whether she was alone.

"All alone," Mrs. Michaelson said, feeling for her hat, which must have disappeared somewhere in the tunnel. "And why not? I suppose now you're going to tell me it's not safe for a woman to be alone anywhere outside of a shopping mall."

"Not at all," said Yocheved. "I am working here alone for one year and nobody bothers me. The Arabs know me now. We say hello to each other, and then everyone goes about his own business. That's how it should be everywhere."

"I agree," said Mrs. Michaelson. She found an empty bottle of Jericho Water in her plastic bag and tossed it into a garbage can three feet away. Bank shot! A steep flight of stairs led to the street, above. All she had to do was climb them, and then she would be free.

How was Jeremy spending his afternoon? she wondered, whistling as she rolled up the hem of her dress to wring it out. The stitching had all shriveled, crumpling the expensive silk. Her torn sleeves drooped at her elbows like soggy feathers. After all that work—such a shame. She'd have to rip the sleeves off now, make an entirely new kind of dress, a patchwork cocktail dress. Like a Gypsy—what a lark! That's what she'd do! She'd swagger into parties with the fringed hem cut off and wrapped around her shoulders like a shawl, and everyone would ask, "Who is that mysterious Gypsy?"

She sank down onto the bench next to the Americans, who stared grimly at the green water. "I feel marvelous," Mrs. Michaelson said, massaging her bare toes against the warm stones. Who cares if anyone noticed her bunions?

Yocheved peered into the cave one last time, then sat down beside Mrs. Michaelson. "We are waiting for one other from our group," she said.

As she felt around in her bag for her socks, Mrs. Michaelson's fingers crawled over her wallet and Fodor's and then landed on something hard, nutlike: the rough brown nub left of her candle. "This was all I had," she said, showing it to Yocheved before dropping it back in her bag. "The guy in the store gave it to me. Azim. Do you know him?"

Shaking her head, Yocheved opened a Swiss Army knife and began sharpening the blade on a strip of leather clenched between her knees.

Mrs. Michaelson unrolled her socks. "What was this place for, anyway?"

"In the days of the Jewish kings, there was a siege around Jerusalem," Yocheved explained. "All the water was in a valley outside and below the walls. But the clever engineers built this secret tunnel in such a way so the water runs uphill into this deep secret well inside the city. Because this water was so important to Jerusalem's survival, some people believed it had mystical properties. The Christians think this is where Jesus cured the blind man."

"So I hear." Mrs. Michaelson accepted Yocheved's canteen, wrapped in an embroidered bag stitched with crosses and squares in red, blue, and orange threads. "Fascinating," she said after taking a deep, long drink. She really was fascinated. Everything seemed brighter now, and louder and clearer.

She handed the canteen to the Americans, but they ignored her.

"Like you, I prefer to travel alone," said Yocheved. "When I finished with the army, I traveled alone all through the world: Europe, New York, India. To places with no McDonald's anywhere. Maybe you heard of Goa?"

"No, I haven't. Who's he?" Even though she'd had few adventures besides the tunnel, Mrs. Michaelson felt every inch Yocheved's equal. They were two explorers who'd bumped into each other in darkest Africa and were trading war stories.

"Goa is a where, not a who," said Yocheved. "It's a city in India."

"Oh, Goa," said Mrs. Michaelson knowingly, though all she knew of India was that it was a good place to get sick.

"Every young Israeli dreams to go to Goa after the army," Yocheved explained. "It's so full of Israelis, all the signs are in Hebrew and the prices are in shekels. Young people go there to sit on the beach, play drums, and smoke hashish. It's a tourist trick."

"Tourist trap," Mrs. Michaelson corrected her in a soft voice.

"My parents were worried about me, what I was gonna do when I come home. My mother, she cried at me all the time. What you gonna do? But now I am a tour guide and in Israel to guide is a very respected profession. You must be educated in all the history of our land, and here we have a lot of history."

"I don't see why your mother was so upset," Mrs. Michaelson said airily. "You weren't hurting anybody."

"Exactly. I think no one needs to make excuses because he wants to enjoy his life," Yocheved insisted. "No one. To be a human being, it's enough of an excuse. To live, it's enough. But it's very hard."

Of course, Mrs. Michaelson thought. It was the kind of wisdom she found in her favorite novels. Only life for its own sake. Every precious hour, every glorious minute.

She wanted to write it on the sky! The universe wasn't a game with walls and sides, right or wrong. The only point was to enjoy life to its fullest. Animals knew it. Babies knew it, but then they grew older and forgot. You ate, you got your exercise, you took long naps, and the rest was unnecessary. Psychiatry and religion created something else and called it "spirituality" to capture it in a box, but spirituality was merely a stab in the dark to keep people civilized. It was all so simple. Why didn't anyone realize?

To finally be herself and just herself. It was no small thing, but would it be enough to sustain her? Only life for its own sake? Making her own distinct print in the sand, though it would last barely long enough for the wind to cover it up again?

Her daydream was interrupted by screeching schoolchildren hitting the green water with their flashlights as they splashed their way out of the mouth of the tunnel. Mrs. Michaelson covered her ears. A rail-thin woman with a blond ponytail chased down the wildest brats and set them on the landing. But no sooner had she pulled one out than another would plunge back in, screaming bloody murder.

A weeping woman with wet stringy hair and an expensive camera hanging from her neck waded out of the tunnel, just behind the children. She wore a white T-shirt that said, in Hebrew "BARAK IS LOSING THE STATE!" over a second white shirt with long sleeves that had been soaked transparent. It stuck to the folds of fat around her stomach.

"Janis!" Yocheved called out, and the American couple stood up and waved.

"Baby!" said Janis's mother, though the woman in the water looked about forty.

"Is she your daughter?" Mrs. Michaelson inquired politely. She stood up too, in sympathy, but the Americans ignored her. Thanks a lot, Mrs. Michaelson thought. Conversations are a two-way street, you know. Why did no one ever meet her halfway? "Did you leave her husband back at the hotel?" she asked, flailing to keep their chatter afloat.

"She's never been married," said the woman in a sour voice.

"Isn't it interesting how the young people are getting married later and later these days?" Mrs. Michaelson replied automatically. What a stupid thing to say, she thought, and coming from me of all people.

Janis stopped short of the landing and refused to climb out of the water despite her parents' coaxing. "You lost me on purpose!" she sobbed, her dripping white head scarf riding down her dark wet curls. Her cheeks, forehead, and bottom lip were covered in jagged red cuts. A trail of dried blood ran down from her nose. What a blubbering mess, thought Mrs. Michaelson, imagining the poor girl stumbling into rocks.

"We told you to stay close, but you kept hanging back," Janis's mother shouted over the shrieking children. "Well, young lady, look where your independence got you."

"My flashlight went out!" Janis wailed. "Didn't you even think to send someone back to check on me? I was attacked in there, by a man."

"It's not possible," Yocheved said. "No man was in there."

Oh dear, thought Mrs. Michaelson, feeling her stomach slide out from under her.

"I was attacked by a man and almost raped, if anyone cares," Janis insisted. "Are you calling me a liar? What kind of guide are you?"

Mrs. Michaelson stared hard at Janis, still sniveling in the water. Could this fatty have been the scaly monster from the tunnel? It just wasn't possible.

"What man?" Yocheved asked. "You see some man here? We were sitting here all the time and no one came out. Only the children and you and this old woman."

Does she mean me? thought Mrs. Michaelson, stepping into her shoes. "Old woman" hurt.

"Maybe he's still in there," Janis said. "Or maybe he has a secret way to get in and out so he can prey on young women alone and afraid."

So I'm "old" and Janis is a *young* woman? thought Mrs. Michaelson. Now, there's a stretch.

A boy paddled up to Janis, tapped her shoulder, and spat out a mouthful of water in a neat arc like a fountain. His friends laughed.

I've made a mistake, Mrs. Michaelson realized, and that's

the same thing as a sin. "If there was a man in there, then why didn't this man prey on me?" she asked, hoping an appeal to the girl's reason might distract her from the truth.

"I'm sorry," Yocheved said to Janis's parents. "People get a little disorientated in there sometimes. Their imaginations go to work."

"I've got scratches all up and down my arms," said Janis, her wet shirts clinging to her lumpy rolls of fat. "See?" She pulled up her sleeves. "These are real."

"Probably from the rocks," said Yocheved as Mrs. Michaelson surveyed her handiwork. Did I do that? she wondered. Was I capable of that? At home she didn't even like to call the exterminator. Her husband took care of hunting the animals, setting traps for mice in the attic, zapping wasps with bug spray. He'd go through a whole can in an afternoon.

"That's enough, Janis," said her mother with her hands on her hips. "Look at you. You're dripping and you're standing in direct sun without a hat. Out of this pool, right now."

Janis flung up her arms. Yocheved and the father pulled, and Janis splashed them all with warm green water. Such violence, thought Mrs. Michaelson as Janis's mother rushed to wrap her daughter's hair in a towel. "In my purse," she told her husband, who dug inside the purse and took out a baseball cap that said THE NEW YORKER. They crowned Janis with it.

"Maybe Janis wants a drink from your canteen, Yocheved," said Mrs. Michaelson, feeling thirsty herself.

Yocheved looked at her strangely. "You did not see her in the tunnel?"

"No, I saw no one. But I couldn't see anything for the longest while, because my candle went out. You're right, though. Your imagination does go to work in there. I imagined I heard someone far behind me, chasing me. Were you chasing me, Janis?"

Janis looked too miserable to speak.

"This never happened before," Yocheved said, and picked up her knife. "I take groups in all the time and it never happens like this. It's always a beautiful experience."

"It's this weather," said Mrs. Michaelson. "No one's himself in it."

A wizened old man with a bent back opened the gate at the top of the stairs and yelled down at the children. The teacher yelled back at him and then at her students, who began splashing to the landing.

Such violence, thought Mrs. Michaelson, staring dumbfounded at all the red faces and open mouths as the children pulled themselves out of the water and rolled over on the stones like toy dogs. Screaming, sobbing, bleeding—it was all giving her a headache. All she wanted was a little peace. A little politeness and a little peace.

Poor Janis was now muffled in two towels and the *New Yorker* baseball cap. Really, her face doesn't look so bad now, Mrs. Michaelson told herself, though it wasn't true. Janis looked awful, as if she'd been attacked by a wild cat. If I have that in me, Mrs. Michaelson wondered, what else can I do?

She shook her head as if waking up from a nap, crumpled her plastic bag in her fist, and said cheerfully, "I guess I'll make my exit." Was Yocheved staring at her suspiciously, or was it just another trick of the imagination, like Janis's rapist? "Nice to meet you," she called out to the girl's parents, the old buzzards. She waved to Janis, who managed a limp wave and even a sheepish smile under her hat and the towels.

The crooked old man waited for Mrs. Michaelson to climb the stairs. When she reached the top, he closed the gate behind them and began babbling in his own language, which didn't sound like Hebrew or Arabic but a hybrid of the two. He pointed to his souvenir shop, a corrugated metal shed at the side of the road.

The shop sold the usual antique coins, wooden camels, cans of holy air (each sealed with a red warning label: CAUTION! DO NOT OPEN OR CONTENTS WILL ESCAPE!), as well as a wicker basket of flaccid chocolate bars. Mrs. Michaelson touched a chocolate bar, and her finger left a dimple in the wrapper. T-shirts in various colors hung from the ceiling and stirred in the breeze from an electric fan. She could choose from I SURVIVED HEZEKIAH'S TUNNEL! in blue and white, TAKE A WALK ON THE WILD SIDE, HEZEKIAH'S TUNNEL, SUMMER 2000 in orange, or HEZEKIAH'S TUNNEL, JUST DO IT! with a Nike swoosh.

Her heart sank as she fingered the T-shirts. So she wasn't an explorer in a far-flung corner of the universe after all. This place was what Yocheved would have called a tourist trick. There was no grain of sand left for her to make a mark where someone else hadn't made a mark first.

You don't care anymore, Mr. Michaelson reminded her. Like Yocheved said: To live, it's enough.

A refrigerated blue barrel of water sat in front of the cash register, the Waters of Paradise brand. She couldn't remember whether Waters of Paradise was good or bad. "How much?" she asked, her stomach growling as she held up a bottle.

Twenty shekels, he said. Five dollars. For such small bottles! She put the bottle back into the barrel and left the shop. "How much you want?" he pleaded, looking hurt. "Tell me your price. Why you don't tell me how much you want to pay?"

But Mrs. Michaelson continued marching up the road. The old man kept calling out for her to name her price.

The hot sun felt pleasant after the tunnel. Her wet silk was almost dry, and she was just starting to calm down when a pair of dark men with eager smiles came running out of a side alley

with T-shirts for sale. I ESCAPED FROM THE TUNNEL! MY PAR-
ENTS WENT TO HEZEKIAH'S TUNNEL AND ALL THEY BROUGHT
ME WAS THIS LOUSY T-SHIRT! HEZEKIAH'S TUNNEL. WATCH
OUT FOR GHOSTS! They had sweatshirts and coffee mugs and
key chains. They had baseball caps and visors. They had
bumper stickers that said MASADA SHALL NOT FALL AGAIN.

She drifted through the men and their T-shirts and hiked up
the gravel road.

Jeremy had probably realized his mistake by now and doubt-
less found some way to blame her for it. If only he'd been more
responsible, she might have had fun with him and his friend at
the King David instead of attacking some poor old maid, whose
bruised face she couldn't get out of her mind. It wasn't me who
did that, she thought. I wasn't myself.

Her shredded sleeves kept tickling her forearms, so she
ripped them off with a satisfying grunt. A black helicopter, the
size of an eagle, ripped through the hot white sky and stirred up
a stinging wind that blew sand in her face. Then it soared away
and all was calm.

Water, she thought, clearing her throat. Where is water?

Four beak-nosed men came out of a house and stared at her
with their black eyes. "Madam, please," one of them called out.
He had a tan so deep that in the States he'd have been black.
"We have antique coins."

"Leave me alone," she mewed, shaking her head and blinking the dust out of her eyes. Two small brown crab-looking
things attacked each other with their claws and scuttled across
the reddish earth. She let out a little scream. The dark men
laughed. Water, she thought. I must find water soon, or I will
die. She turned up one of the narrow side alleys with garbage
and laundry, and then up another road that stank of dung.

"Jeremy?" she called out, just in case.

She would have died to see a HERALD TRIBUNE SOLD HERE sign. And french fries and a two-liter bottle of Diet Coke. But even a two-liter wouldn't have been enough. Whether you ordered one drink or five, you were always thirsty in this country.

Mr. Michaelson was waving to her, trying to shout directions. "No, you're nothing but trouble," she said, running away. "I don't need you."

Her stomach was howling at her now. She tried different roads, turned around unfamiliar corners, though always heading uphill so as not to lose herself.

"Jeremy?"

Water, she thought. Water. She saw more men hanging around on stoops and street corners, arguing over Turkish coffee, smoking cigarettes or puffing on hookahs. How could anyone light a fire in such heat? Anyway, didn't these men have jobs?

Now she'd reached the real Silwan, away from the T-shirts and the tourist tricks. The stucco walls of the houses she passed were marked with Western-style graffiti in black and red paint, pictures of soldiers shooting, children bleeding, a map of Israel in chains, a swastika, a portrait of a black man wearing a Palestinian flag as a bandanna around his forehead and the legend TUPAC LIVES. She wondered which house belonged to Jeremy's boyfriend.

Finally she spotted a small grocery store beside a makeshift dump, a cascade of garbage sliding downhill.

The door was a screen tacked loosely to a chipped wooden frame. Inside, an oily-haired clerk missing the left half of his mustache sat on a stool and read an Arabic newspaper while she strolled between the half-empty shelves.

The heat made her feel slow, stupid. Mrs. Michaelson wrote her name in the dust of one of the shelves and then blew, causing a miniature sandstorm. She stared at jars of olives from

Egypt, biscuits from England, lemon juice in narrow bottles from Greece, and a few lonely boxes of detergent whose brands and origins she didn't recognize.

She was desperate to get back home, where grocery stores were big and bright and stones were stones and not kitchens. The refrigerated case of drinks was in the back. Mrs. Michaelson stared vacantly at her translucent reflection coiled up like a double helix in the glass door. If she moved left or right, her nose expanded like a telescope. If she lowered her chin, her eyes grew to the size of tennis balls.

Minutes crawled as slowly as syrup dripping down a wall. Years could tick away in a place like this. The clerk with his half-mustache didn't care how long she spent gazing into the traces of her reflection.

The bottles of water were all warm, but she grabbed one anyway. The door creaked shut. Step by timid step, she advanced toward the clerk on his stool. Would she never get there? They were expensive steps. Each one cost her several seconds of the rest of her life.

"All the water's warm," she complained in an unfamiliar, raspy voice. The man glared, and she longed for Rabbi Sherman or her husband to raise a fuss for her. Stop whining, she thought. You take care of yourself.

He pointed to the counter and said, "Five shekels."

She set down the coins. The man scratched the few black dots that stood in for the missing half of his mustache, threw the money into a drawer, and returned to his paper.

The sun glared right into her eyes as she left the shop. Mrs. Michaelson sipped her warm water and experienced a painful rush of light-headedness. "Jeremy, Jeremy!" she called out in a panic. But the road was empty except for a few parked cars, and little gnats that scratched her neck and nested in her hair. She tried to wave them off, but they kept buzzing back. Finally, she poured some of the warm water over her head. It streamed down her neck and forehead and into her aching eyes.

She had an idea that if she turned right she'd regain the main road. Instead, she hit a dead end. A bell jingled behind her. She turned around. Two adolescent boys on rusty bikes were blocking the way out of the alley. They looked at her curiously. One of them was tall and thin like her Jeremy.

"You like good beer?" he asked, his voice breaking, which touched her. He had dark shaggy hair that needed brushing and long, wide pants that covered his shoes. She felt a strong urge to fix his cuffs.

"No," said Mrs. Michaelson. Her ragged dress was completely dry now. It was stiff across her chest, and she felt like a slut.

"You like beer?" the boy repeated, and snickered with his friend. He might have been nice-looking if he'd gotten a haircut and a decent pair of pants. What grade were they in? Seventh? Eighth? Old enough for a bar mitzvah, she guessed. Why didn't their mothers tell them to get their act together, young man, immediately? No wonder these people were never going to get their state, even if Israel gave them one.

"I like water right now," she said. "It's so hot."

"You are Jewish?" the second boy asked in a husky voice.

Mrs. Michaelson wasn't sure what she was. Her heart pounded the way it did when she and her husband drove home from downtown Detroit late at night after the symphony. You weren't supposed to show wild animals you were afraid, because they could smell fear. But these weren't wild animals, just teenage boys, and like all teenage boys they were filled with energy and lacking in morals. "What if I were?" she said.

"Bill Clinton is Jewish," said the first boy. His smile reminded her of Jeremy's. Boys are all the same, she thought, united against mothers because mothers are against war. It's written in our DNA. "Hillary is pretty woman," the boy went on. "Why he fuck Monica? Is fat, ugly Jewish girl. Bill Clinton fucks her because he is Jewish."

"You have any shekels?" said his friend. "Give us shekels."

But you never gave charity directly to poor people, because they could use it for drugs and then eventually die of an overdose. You gave money to reputable organizations that dispensed the services to those proven needy. How did you explain all that to two boys with limited English? Think, think!

"I can buy you ice cream," she said. "Do you like ice cream?" That sounded to her like a pretty generous offer, since all boys liked ice cream.

The first boy wheeled his bike directly in front of her. "We don't want ice cream," he said, and she felt as if she were poor Janis. God was paying her back for Janis. Please, she prayed, and thought of the morning when her mother had died, and of her husband grasping her mother's wrist on her deathbed and shaking his head. So she prayed to her mother. Talk to Him for me, she prayed. I don't know the right words. Maybe there were none.

Where was Jeremy now? And, anyway, what good was Jeremy?

Finally, she said, "You look like my son."

"Is he Jewish?" the boy replied.

The savage spirit from the tunnel welled up inside her and she wished she could knock them both to the ground. She longed for the power to truly hurt them, but she was weak. The only thing to do was to speak in a firm voice and walk sensibly to the main road as if this were a civilized place, like Michigan.

"Excuse me," Mrs. Michaelson said, her stomach gurgling with gas. She pushed the wheel of the boy's bike out of her way and stepped around him. Don't look back. She turned out of the alley and walked up the road. Don't turn around now. She saw the main road, maybe twenty feet ahead. And farther on, she saw an ad for Coca-Cola, which she found comforting, and a listless Israeli flag drooping from a flagpole.

Don't look back or you'll turn into a pillar of salt. Or you'll lose Eurydice in the depths of Hades for all eternity. Or the Cossacks will get you. That's what had happened to her father as a young man while he was walking home from the store where he sold groceries. A band of Cossacks jeered at his back, but he went on walking with his head down until finally he couldn't take it anymore and he turned around, which was when they grabbed him and dragged his body behind their horses to the edge of town and then left him for dead in a wheat field . . .

"Give us shekels!" the first boy yelled at her back, but she'd almost reached the main road and he had no power over her there. She heard the whine of a bus somewhere as a spray of hot pebbles hit her on the neck. They probably thought she was a tightfisted Jew, the kind who bent down to pick up a penny. Another volley of pebbles hit her neck. She decided to ignore them, like spitballs in a classroom. When she was a girl, her mother refused to cut her hair, because in the Old Country you didn't cut a girl's hair until she was twelve, and she'd had long, beautiful black hair down to her waist—an alluring target for spitballs. She had tried to ignore the bullies, but they were too much for her. So she cried and begged her stubborn mother for a haircut, to no avail. Finally she screamed, a deep, hurt, angry scream, locked herself in the bathroom, and chopped her hair off herself, with pinking shears. She came out looking like a scarecrow.

After another round of pebble fire, Mrs. Michaelson tugged the back of her dress to brush off the stones and dirt, and then she looked back. The boys were smiling, making catcalls at her in Arabic and jerking air hard-ons in her direction.

"Jews eat shit!" said the taller one, the one who resembled her son. He might have been her son.

"I offered you ice cream, but you didn't want it," she said in a firm voice. She stepped onto the main road and felt a thwack. She stopped and she blinked. She dropped what was left of her warm water, which streamed over the dry earth in crooked rivers.

The boys yelled once more, in Arabic, and then she didn't know where they went.

She took another step, sank to her knees in the middle of the road under a flaming sky and touched the back of her neck. Her head hurt. And her stomach, too. She bit her tongue and tasted copper. Her hand was red.

"I'm going right back to the hotel," she said, staring directly into the sun, even though her mother used to tell her never to look into the sun or she'd go blind. The hot light dripped into her irises, melting them down. She thought of dousing the fire with some of the cool, fresh water from Jericho, the oldest city in the world.

Janis was waving at her now. Or was it Jeremy? Janis/Jeremy called out, "Are you okay?"

Tomorrow she could go home.

Oh God! I've missed Jerusalem! she realized. She'd missed everything that Fodor's said she was supposed to have seen. She raised her hand, but she couldn't block that awful sun, which had transformed her into a bloody monster. Her neck and hands were wet and red, the color of her ruined dress. A lady wasn't supposed to sit down in the road. She heard voices and that was what they were telling her. A lady wasn't supposed to sit in the middle of the road, especially not in the full sun, or in the rain, or in the snow. Not in Israel, not in some Palestinian village, and not in America, either.

Not anywhere.

twelve

THE DESTINY OF THE JEWS AND THEIR ENEMIES
from "Ask a Rabbi," a feature updated daily on the Lev Ha-Torah website

When the wicked Titus sacked the Second Temple, he entered the Holy of Holies, fornicated with a harlot upon the Holy Scriptures, then seized the holy vessels and hauled them back to Rome. Mid-journey, his ship hit a powerful storm. Titus instructed his sailors to tie him to the top of the mast, where he shouted at the sky, "So the God of the Jews only has power in the water! I dare Him to fight me on land!"

Immediately the sea was calm, and the next morning the joyous sailors reached the shore. The second Titus's sandal hit the sand, a gnat flew up his nostril and lodged in his brain. It pecked there for seven years. When Titus died, his baffled doctors opened up his skull and found an insect the size of a wild bird weighing two *selah*s.

In his will, Titus asked that his body be cremated and the ashes scattered over the sea, so that the God of the Jews would not be able to bring him to judgment.

Titus's son Telemachus visited a sibyl devoted to the goddess Isis, who conjured up his father's spirit with incense and lamb's blood.

"Who is the most important nation in the world to come?" asked Telemachus.

"The Jews," his father replied in a gloomy voice.

"Should I join them?" asked Telemachus.

"No!" said Titus. "They have too many laws. You wouldn't be able to keep them all. It is better to fight against the Jews and be a leader in your world."

"Dear Father," wept Telemachus. "How do you fare in the world to come?"

"I suffer the judgment I decreed on myself" was the response. "Every day I am burned and my ashes are scattered over the sea."

"I had this f-f-feeling you'd come for me," Noam said, pulling Jeremy away from the other yeshiva students ashing their cigarettes over the balcony railing. His sport coat hung over his free arm, and his white shirt was open at the neck.

"Oh, it's you," said Jeremy, somehow not surprised. He was getting the sense that everyone in Jerusalem was connected to everyone else. "What's up?"

"I'm sorry I ran off the other night." Noam lowered his voice. "Thanks to Ha-Shem you came. I was afraid I'd never see you again, and I need your help."

"I'm not very good at helping people, but I'll try," Jeremy said. "Do you know where we could get some lunch? Your friends ate everything in sight downstairs."

"I know where we could grab something quick," said Noam, patting his beard. "It's owned by a friend of Daddy's." He linked arms with Jeremy and took him around the corner of the building to a staircase leading to the street. They flattened themselves against the banister to make room for yeshiva students hurrying back down to class.

"Don't you have class now, too?" Jeremy asked.

"I m-m-may not be returning to class," Noam said. "That's what I wanted to talk to you about. C-c-come on. I can't wait anymore." He clutched Jeremy by the elbow and pulled him through the crowd until they were safely out of the main gate. "You were right when you said I can't deny myself forever. I don't want to end up miserable."

"You might want to think twice before taking advice from me," said Jeremy. "I seem to be bad luck for people."

"It's not just your advice. I've been thinking this over for a long time and I want to change, but . . . Oh fudge! This is a dead end."

They stood in a shady courtyard with a single young tree stuck in the middle like an afterthought. Its rubbery branches stretched upward like a person asking, Why? Through a window, Jeremy spied a class of children, all boys, reciting the Hebrew alphabet together in a classroom with the lights out.

"Did I tell you my roommate's going back to the States?" Noam asked as they turned around. The street was wide enough for them to walk side by side, but Noam kept bumping into Jeremy. "I've been thinking. Maybe I ought to go, too—if not to the States, then at least to Tel Aviv, since that's pretty much the same thing."

"What for?" Jeremy was daydreaming about throwing himself on the mercy of George's parents, then explaining away to his own indignant mother the black eye and broken nose he'd suffer as a result. He imagined the catastrophe that might ensue if his mother and George's mother ever met. In a war of mothers, who would win?

"You know, you're much better looking without your n-n-nose ring," said Noam.

"I think we've messed up again," said Jeremy, starting to feel anxious. They were looking down a staircase with a metal detector at the bottom and, beyond it, the Wall plaza.

"How is that p-p-possible? I'm sure we turned left on Misgav Ladach."

"I don't know what you mean," said Jeremy, about to cry. "Please, I just want to get out of this awful place."

"I know, I know. Wait a minute. I'm thinking."

"Can't we turn around and go in the opposite direction?"

But keeping to one direction proved impossible, because of all the winding streets. We'll never get out of here, Jeremy thought. We'll just stay here until we rot. Oh well, wasn't that what life was anyway, a constant state of rot?

They ended up in front of a wall with a spray-painted arrow labeled TO THE WALL. "Let's go the opposite way," Jeremy said.

"But that way leads out of the J-J-Jewish Quarter."

"Good."

"But I thought you wanted food."

"Don't they have food in the Christian Quarter?"

"Not k-k-kosher food," Noam said.

"I don't keep kosher."

"Still . . ." Noam said. "Okay, look. Since this Oslo business, the guys and me kind of stay out of Arab areas. They just want to make trouble with us."

"Don't worry, I'll protect you."

Noam followed close behind Jeremy as they passed under the arched entrance to the Arab market, which was guarded by two Israelis with submachine guns. They were young, pretty soldiers with stern eyes but gentle noses and soft cheeks. What was a soldier, anyway, but some pretty boy behind a gun? Much too pretty to kill anyone, Jeremy thought. I bet their guns aren't even loaded. George would have liked them. We could have been out cruising soldiers today, seducing them away from their guns.

The stalls in this part of the market were crowded with locals, dark men picking through racks of T-shirts and jeans. The stone roof was festooned with a tangle of knotted power lines, and the air trapped underneath stank of sour milk and bitter Turkish coffee, perhaps centuries old.

Maybe when I tell George's parents the truth, I could offer to hire them a lawyer, Jeremy thought. Oh yeah, sure, with all my big-time legal connections in Israel. It'd be easier to visit George in jail and slip my passport through the bars so he can pretend he's American and just waltz on out of there like a movie star. Or, better yet, dynamite the bars and then he could simply jump through the gap. Yeah, why not? Why not just blow up the whole fucking country and start from scratch?

The smell of meat grilling at a roadside stand reminded Jeremy that he was hungry. A group of Arab men stood and feasted on shwarma beside the hunk of lamb rotating on a metal spit. They wiped the juice streaming down their lips with wax napkins.

Noam said, "Rabbi Goldstein says he who eats on the street is like a dog."

"Arf, arf," said Jeremy, lining up behind the Arabs, who made room for him to approach the meat. "Hi there," he said, trying to act as if he belonged with them.

"You want stand or sit?" said the man shaving the meat in English.

"I didn't realize it was possible to sit," Jeremy said.

With his knives, the carver pointed to a restaurant across the street, where a shirtless boy sat on the front step and sold coffee beans out of a sack.

The wobbly notes of a flute wafted out of the restaurant, a dark, smoky grotto with plaster walls painted muddy brown. A slim, handsome waiter in a black uniform yawned by the cash register. There were no menus. The waiter strolled over and informed them in a high nasal voice what they could and could not have.

"I want to eat whatever you guys eat." Jeremy pointed to an old man spooning brown lumps out of a bowl filled with oil and bits of orange fat.

"Lamb soup," the waiter sniffed, batting his heavy eyelids.

"One of those and a beer," said Jeremy. "Cold."

"I'm happy with just a F-F-Fanta," said Noam, adding under his breath, "I don't think they have anything kosher in this place."

"He'll have a falafel," said Jeremy.

The waiter yelled something in the direction of the kitchen, yawned, and then fell back into his chair by the cash register.

"Make sure it's vegetarian," Noam called out, waving grandly.

"Falafel is vegetarian," said Jeremy. "Haven't you ever had one?"

"Of course not. They don't serve us Arabic food at the y-y-yeshiva."

A boy with a pleading look on his face approached them with cigarette lighters decorated with American flags. Only five shekels. A special price. Jeremy bought one out of guilt, but when he tried to light it, a fat blue spark flew out and might have burned the place down if Jeremy hadn't stubbed it out with his foot. He clicked the lighter a few more times, but nothing else happened and the boy was gone.

"I like that yarmulke you're wearing," Noam said.

Jeremy turned white. "Jesus! I keep forgetting to take this off in public!" He yanked it off his head and threw the offending article across the table. "You want it?"

"D-d-don't do that." Noam snatched up the blue yarmulke and dusted it off. "It's a beautiful one. Are you sure you want to give me this?"

"I'd only throw it away. I've decided to resign from being

Jewish. Next time you talk to God, you can tell Him for me. He can go His way and I'll go mine."

Noam laughed. "Ha-Shem's inside you. You can't just resign from Him. That's like trying to cut out your heart with a p-p-pencil."

"Maybe that's true for your Ha-Shem," Jeremy said, fanning himself with his napkin. "Mine isn't lodged inside anything. He waits to be invited first."

"More on this later," said Noam as the waiter backed out of the kitchen with their food, letting out a cloud of steam and several flies. Jeremy's soup came in a brown bowl, while the falafel was served on a paper plate. The waiter opened their drinks and let the caps fall on the floor.

The first two bites of soup were satisfying, but the rest tasted like sludge. Noam sipped his Fanta but didn't touch his falafel. "Try one bite," Jeremy said. "For me."

Turning his pita inside out, Noam picked out the wrinkled lettuce and held his tomato up to the light, with hummus-greased fingers, to search for any traces of non-kosher meat.

"Go on," Jeremy said. "Indulge me." He felt like Noam's Auntie Mame.

Noam took a tiny nibble of pita and lettuce. "Good, but spicier than what I'm used to," he bleated, and accidentally knocked over his Fanta. "S-s-sorry." He got down on the floor and dabbed at the puddle with his wet napkin. The waiter ignored him, picked up the bottle with his fingertips, then mopped the floor with a sponge on a stick, using short, jerking strokes that made his forearms ripple. Nice ass, Jeremy thought as he drained his peppery, cool beer, then lit a cigarette. It was delicious to light up in a restaurant without your parents or anyone to remind you it was against the law, the way they would have in New York. A soldier walked by with a machine gun; Jeremy pretended it was a piano keyboard. Life tasted very sweet at that moment. He was tempted to throw it all away and forget that innocent Palestinian kid he'd met a few times who was now languishing in prison.

"So I t-t-told Daddy the truth," Noam said. "I said I hadn't done anything yet, but I had these urges. He asked if I was trying to kill him, and then he laughed and said, 'Okay, we'll cure you.' But I d-d-don't want to be cured. That's why I think I should go to T-T-Tel Aviv."

"I don't know," Jeremy said. "I've been to a couple of bars in Tel Aviv. They were pretty lame. Have you ever thought you'd be better off getting cured? I wish they could do it to me, zap me with electrodes until—voilà—I'm a productive, well-balanced young man who shops at Ralph Lauren on his way to work at some downtown investment firm where he earns enough money to support a nice Jewish family."

The waiter finished cleaning the spilled soda and brought Jeremy a second beer. An Arab sitting next to Jeremy looked at the beer and asked for one, too. The waiter asked to see his money first.

Noam looked confused. "I thought you, of all people, would understand."

"I was just kidding. I guess you're right," Jeremy said sadly. It was better to be alive than to be dead and peaceful. Better to prolong the torture for as long as you could—although there were times when it wasn't torture, even if not so many of them as he would have liked. But why was it better to be alive? Sex, drugs, and rock and roll? Family? Money? True love? Because God said so? Because there was no God and you had to seize the day like Robin Williams in *Dead Poets Society*? There was no good reason, which was what made everything so hard. Life was better than death for no reason.

Or maybe looking for a reason was the wrong way to think of it. That had been his mistake. It was more like this: there you were, alive, and more than you needed something to believe, you needed something to do. Or something to believe might work, if it gave you something to do.

"D-d-do you think I could try your beer?" Noam said. He took a sip, pursed his lips as if he'd just tasted vinegar, and handed the bottle back to Jeremy, who took a long, deep drink. He liked the way it lined his stomach.

"My mother thinks I'm an alcoholic," Jeremy said, tearing the label off the bottle. "But there's a difference. Alcoholics drink for the sake of drinking. I drink to escape my problems." His father had explained that difference to him, and at the time it had seemed entirely reasonable. Jeremy snorted. "I guess that's not much of a difference."

"What problems could you have?" Noam asked. "I thought you were free."

"Not true." The beer and the heat left him feeling sleepy and a bit silly. "Not true at all." He began prattling about George, the whole short, stupid, and sloppy history of him. "I know it's hard to believe, because I still have trouble believing it, too, but I really felt something for that guy, maybe even love. Yes—definitely, love. So I went to ask Dave for help. You know him?"

"Sure," Noam said. "Everyone knows Dave. He's a friend of Daddy's."

"Well, I asked him to help me, but he wouldn't. I fucked up."

"But it's not your f-f-fault. None of this is your fault."

"Who cares?" Jeremy took another deep swallow of beer. "It happened, and I was there. Now there's only one thing I can do: Tell his parents that I fucked up their kid's life. The trouble is, I'm scared shitless."

"You know what the most-repeated commandment in the Torah is? 'Don't be afraid.' " Noam unfolded a small black cell phone. "You have their number? Go ahead. Take as long as you want. My cousin's in the business. He gets me great rates."

"No, I have to do this in person. I ought to give them the option of killing me." His stomach gurgled; he stirred the fat in his soup, then pushed the bowl away. How sad, he thought, that a lamb had to die for my shitty lunch.

The waiter reached up to the stereo above the cash register, turned off the Arabic music, and put on the new Moby album.

"Would it help if I c-c-came with you?" Noam asked.

Jeremy wasn't sure he'd heard him right. "Why would you come with me?"

"W-w-well . . ." Noam smiled, and then suppressed a burp that came out as a hiccup. "I mean, we're fellow homosexuals. That counts for something."

Jeremy laughed.

"Now you're laughing at me. I feel stupid."

"No, no," said Jeremy. "It's good of you to want to help, though I don't deserve it. I was only thinking, if I showed up with a Hasidic Jew in this village where George lives, this Palestinian slum, how much worse that would be than going alone."

"I could change," Noam said. "I could wear a baseball cap and a Nike sweatshirt like a regular American tourist."

"Really, I'll be fine," Jeremy said, but Noam wouldn't give up the idea.

The sleepy waiter pointed them toward the Jaffa Gate as they left the restaurant. "Look here," Noam said, grabbing a muslin shirt with a drawstring collar from one of the stalls and holding it up to his chest. "T-t-tell me I couldn't pass for an American tourist."

"It doesn't look bad on you," Jeremy had to admit. His loyalty is impressive, he thought, even if the guy is certifiable.

A voice called out from the stall: "This is a very cool-looking shirt. You will be popular with the ladies where you are from. Where you from?"

The shopkeeper emerged pressing a black cotton smock against his broad chest, which he puffed out proudly. A handsome sickle-shaped scar ran down the side of his left cheek. The gold around his neck and wrists and on his fingers, the gel in his spiked hair, his Sergio Tacchini jogging suit zipped halfway down his furry chest—all of him seemed to glisten. "You from New York? I love New York," he told Jeremy. "My cousin lives in Brooklyn. I visited the Brooklyn Bridge, Statue of Liberty, Empire State Building, World Trade Center. You want to come inside?"

"I want a shirt," said Noam.

The shopkeeper scratched his spiked hair and looked at Jeremy. "Him, it's not his clothing."

"He wants a shirt," Jeremy insisted. "Pants too."

The shopkeeper shrugged and retreated inside.

"Maybe we should go," Noam said under his breath. "Bad idea."

"No, we're going in," Jeremy said. "What'll he do? Kill us?"

He selected a shirt and pants and went up a step into the shop, which smelled heavily of the shopkeeper's cologne and was crowded with shirts, pants, and dark-blue-glass eyes staring from light-blue strings. The shopkeeper stood at the back, behind his cash register. A poster of Jennifer Lopez hung loose from his desk, like an apron.

"My friend needs a place to change," Jeremy said.

The shopkeeper stretched out his gym shoe and pulled over a pink plastic shower curtain hanging from a rusty brass ring.

So the yeshiva student stepped behind the shower curtain and then metamorphosed into a hippie in a plum-colored smock and baggy muslin pajamas. "A definite step forward," Jeremy said, folding Noam's pants and dress shirt over his arm. "Let's burn these."

"You're kidding, right?" Noam made a grab for his clothes, but Jeremy held them out of his reach.

"You don't want some clothes for yourself?" the shopkeeper asked Jeremy. "I can make you good price." Jeremy said no and produced his father's Visa card, which unleashed a torrent of clucking and scolding until Jeremy agreed to pay a 3 percent surcharge. *"Y'ala, habibi!"* the shopkeeper yelled, snapping his fingers at a boy playing with a radio outside. The boy scurried a few stalls down to borrow a credit-card press.

"See, that wasn't so bad," Jeremy said. "Why don't you two shake on the deal?"

"Sure, sure," said the grinning shopkeeper. Such big hands, Jeremy thought. He must be big all over. "I love Jews, no problem."

"I'm paying you back for these," Noam said afterward as they passed under an arch, out of the covered market, and into the sunlight. He'd replaced his velvet yarmulke with Jeremy's bright blue one and carried his old clothes in a black plastic bag.

"Consider it a gift from my dad," Jeremy said, wondering why his father had never bothered to cut off the card, even after Jeremy had used it to buy a three-hundred-dollar bottle of champagne that tasted like shit.

A mother in a head scarf, with a baby strapped to her chest, bumped past Jeremy. So many babies, he thought. The world could use a moratorium on babies.

"How do I look?" Noam twirled in his light muslin and giggled.

"Like a different person."

Jeremy stopped in front of a white-tiled barbershop and looked at Noam again. "Something's still missing." He touched Noam's side curls.

"I can tie up my *payess* under my yarmulke. I do it all the time—"

Jeremy interrupted him. "Let's go in."

"Oh no," Noam said.

"If you go to Silwan with that hair, we'll both get stoned to death. Let's face it, your hair is a walking provocation."

"No, Jeremy. I have to draw the line here," he said, turning around.

"It's just hair. It'll grow back." Surprised at how much he cared, Jeremy grabbed Noam's flimsy sleeve. "Please, Noam. I'm afraid to go there alone. It'll only be a bit off the top and the sides, so it won't stand out as much."

"Y-y-you need me?" Noam said. "Really?"

"Of course I do," Jeremy said, embarrassed he'd admitted it. He pulled Noam toward the door. "Come on."

The shop was as hot as a sauna and smelled of rubbing alcohol, body odor, and coffee. A brass pot sizzled on a portable electric coil plugged in beside a row of razors. The light from the fluorescent lamps overhead bounced off the white tile floor, which was spotless except for a mound of cut hair resting in the corner like a sleeping animal.

There were no customers, just three barbers sipping coffee out of doll-size teacups and huddled around a TV where five Semitic beauties in hot pink leotards performed aerobics to an Arabic song spliced to a thumping house beat.

One of the barbers grunted in their direction and the others turned their heads too.

"My friend needs a haircut," Jeremy said, his face and neck turning red. Noam tucked his side curls behind his ears.

The barbers stared, stony-faced. A clean-shaven one, who had dyed the few strands of hair he had left tar black, stepped forward. "Excuse me, we are closed."

"Then why isn't your door locked?" Jeremy asked.

"Go out and we will lock it," said the barber, shooing them out with his fingers.

"Don't you want money?"

"Sir," said the barber. "This man has the beard. The curls." He pointed to one of Noam's side curls, which had come loose. "We don't want trouble."

"How much do you charge for a haircut?" Jeremy asked.

"If he wants to cut his hair, let him go out from the Old City. There he can go to many places. We can only go here, with our brothers. This shop is for Arabs," he said, waving his nose in the air like a flag.

"This shop is for people," Jeremy maintained. "Come on, enough bullshit."

"Please"—another nose wave—"get out, sir."

Noam reached for the doorknob, but Jeremy took out his wallet and peeled off the bills. "One hundred shekels to cut this man's hair."

"We don't care about money."

"I don't either. One-fifty."

The first barber turned around and looked at them again, then said something to his friends in Arabic. "First he must take off his hat."

Jeremy swiped the yarmulke off Noam's head. "Oh!" said Noam, covering his bare head with his hand.

"Go on," Jeremy said, giving him a little push. "I bet there's a hottie hiding under all that hair."

Noam thought for a second. "D-d-do you really think it

would help you?" he asked in a low voice, so the barbers couldn't hear.

"Yes. I already told you so."

"Because I like you, Jeremy, I really do. I'd do anything to help you, actually."

"But I want you to do this to help you, not me. Once you do this, you'll realize that you can do anything you want. Go to Tel Aviv, go to New York, get up on some sleazy bar and dance naked. Do it for yourself. Set yourself free."

Noam sat in one of the chairs, tucked his hands under his thighs, and stared into his reflection. Pictures of dark men cut out of Italian fashion magazines were taped around the mirror, a frame of firm-looking faces, stern eyebrows, windswept hair.

The clean-shaven barber swiveled the chair around and pumped the pedal until Noam tilted flat on his back. "Not too much," he begged, shutting his eyes.

"They're professionals. Relax," Jeremy said as the barbers converged around the chair. One of them spread a plastic apron over Noam's new clothes and tied the strings tightly at the neck.

"I can hardly breathe," Noam gasped.

"It's normal," said Jeremy like a father. He stood in the middle of the room, not part of the scene and not outside of it, either. A stoop-shouldered old grandfather with a trim white beard and slippers appeared from the back carrying a child's pink sand pail, which he filled with steaming water from the tap. The clean-shaven barber stood by and lit a cigarette. After soaping up their hands, the other two barbers rubbed through their victim's hair and pulled it out into spikes. Noam tried to raise his head, but the barbers pinned him by his chest to the chair.

The old man shuffled over with his bucket as one of the barbers rinsed off his hands, then dipped a towel in the water and wrung out a few drops over Noam's forehead. "It's burning!" Noam yelped, and the barbers laughed.

"I'm sure it's all right," said Jeremy, noticing for the first time a large Palestinian flag hanging on the back wall. "It's supposed to feel good."

"Nice," Noam said through clenched teeth.

A small, ineffective table fan buzzed furiously on one of the empty barber chairs. Jeremy brushed away the sweat pooling at his throat and on his eyelids. His lungs hurt, like he'd been holding his breath under water. Too tired to stand, he picked up the fan, set it on his lap, and sank into the chair.

When the two barbers finished rinsing Noam's hair, they pumped him back to an upright position and retreated to the back of the shop. The clean-shaven barber stubbed his cigarette out in his teacup and turned to Jeremy. "How do you want me to cut?"

Noam's eyes were still shut.

Jeremy wondered if he'd passed out. "Short like mine," Jeremy said, talking through a yawn. "And a shave. Lose the curls." He had trouble hearing himself above the fan, buzzing ever louder as it vibrated against his crotch.

"You know, maybe we shouldn't," Noam said, coming back to life and tucking his side curls behind his ears. "L-l-look, no one will notice they're there."

He tried to push himself up, but the barbers leaped into action. One grabbed his arms while another secured his legs. The old man shuffled to the windows and drew the blinds. "No!" Noam squealed, trying to raise his head, but the barber pushed his forehead back against the chair. Jeremy raised a finger but felt too light-headed to get up. The clean-shaven barber stretched out one of the side curls like a spring and, with a soft snip, separated the lock of hair from Noam's head. Jesus, Jeremy thought. What have I started? The barber ambled around the chair and cut off the other side lock in the same way.

Noam's body went limp, and he let out a strange whine, like a tire losing its air. The Arabs let go of his arms and legs while the old man crawled under the chair and brushed the two side curls into a dustpan.

As the barber's scissors flashed and twittered through Noam's soft hair, Jeremy's eyelids drooped and for a minute he imagined he and not Noam was the one getting the haircut. He could smell the old men's aftershave and feel their stiff, sweaty fingers bracing him against the vinyl chair. The cool blunt edge of the scissors grazed his skin, the hair fell away, and the load on his skull lightened. He shifted the fan on his lap to hide his erection.

When Jeremy opened his eyes, the barber with the mole was sharpening a long knife against a leather strap, worn shiny like seal skin. The blade swung back and forth like a sword while the old man pummeled Noam's cheek with frothy shaving cream.

The barber turned back to Noam. "Don't move," he warned, and held up the knife.

All along the road to Silwan, Noam kept checking his profile in the side-view mirrors of parked cars. "My face feels wet," he said, touching his clean cheeks and then the short bristles of hair on top of his head.

Jeremy wanted to touch the hair, too. It turned out that under the beard and the side locks, there really was a hottie, with high cheekbones, a bold jaw, and a lovely kiss of a mouth with a dimple at the top. "You look good," he said, squeezing

Noam's arm and then rubbing his back. "Hey, you've got muscles!"

"I used to be on the wrestling team in Baltimore," Noam explained. "You know what, I'm glad I did this," he added, though he didn't sound glad exactly.

Jeremy felt shy and tongue-tied that afternoon, awed by Noam's newfound beauty as well as his own resolve as they marched down the hill past the Old City, down into the valley of hell. He wished they didn't have to go.

"This place is really depressing," Noam said as they stepped over the crushed carcass of a bird missing its head, a feast for a tribe of ants. "It's like a slum."

"I guess so," said Jeremy, kicking up little rocks as he walked. *What the fuck am I doing here?* he wondered as they walked among the shabby houses, the torn fences and garbage dumps. *Was I really in this place before or was it only some nightmare?*

"We should help them," Noam said. "Not just you and me personally. All of us."

"Oh shit." Jeremy stopped. They were just outside the gate to the City of David archaeological site. He'd completely forgotten his appointment with his mother. "She'll kill me," he thought aloud. "She's going to put me on a leash for the rest of my life."

"I'm sure George's mother will be reasonable," said Noam, misunderstanding. "From what you've told me, they seem to be a good family."

"I've got to get back to the hotel as soon as we can. Let's hurry."

"Fine," said Noam. "Which way?"

They walked through the market, deserted for the afternoon. The shops were shut and dark inside except the butcher's, where they were mopping up blood and dumping the red water into the road. This place is so cold, Jeremy thought, so alien and Arabic. Helen must think I've really lost it, inviting her to this place. He hoped his mother hadn't waited long for him.

Maybe he ought to forget this whole visit. Wouldn't it be an insult to show up at George's house unannounced and deliver the bad news? Look at how the old lady had jumped when he'd simply said good morning and she wasn't looking. Imagine how she'd react when he appeared out of the blue to let her know that her beloved George, or rather Ahmad (or was it Ahmed?), was in jail.

"I'm sorry," Jeremy said to Noam. "What did you say? I wasn't listening."

"I didn't say anything."

The road turned. They were on George's street now— Jeremy was sure of it. So why did nothing look familiar? An old man with a wrinkled mouth sat on the steps in front of one of the houses and watched them pass. "I think this is it," Jeremy whispered, pointing to a narrow house. The windows were covered with dark blue curtains. Jeremy didn't remember the curtains. Were they really at the right house?

"Just march up and knock," said Noam. "Don't even think."

Exactly the kind of advice you'd expect from a religious person, Jeremy thought: Don't think. Still, he didn't have any better ideas.

He knocked twice, hard and loud. No one answered. He thought he saw one of the curtains move, and he peeked into the window, but he couldn't see anything. The old man up the block stood and watched them.

So I'm not going to save the world, Jeremy realized. Anyway, there's no point in saving it one person at a time. If you really want to do something, you've got to attack the system at its core. I've been very silly and romantic and I've ruined everyone's life—George's, my mother's, and now this yeshiva kid's too. "This is hopeless," he said.

"Try knocking again."

He knocked once more, though not very loudly. "There's no point. George'll be all right. He probably knows the system better than I do. He can take care of himself better than I could. Anyway, you were right before. It wasn't my fault."

"C-c-couldn't you leave a note somewhere?" Noam suggested. "To let them know you were here?"

"Where would I put it? And what would I say?" Jeremy peeked through the window one last time. He wished he could break down crying, but he didn't feel anything, not right then. "This was a stupid idea."

"At least you tried. That counts for something. That's all Ha-Shem could expect from any of us."

"I suppose." Unexpectedly, Jeremy felt a surge of joy as he stepped away from the door and brushed the top of Noam's fuzzy new haircut with his hand. The bristles tingled against his fingers. All he wanted was to go home and touch and be touched. "I've got to get back to the hotel." He looked up hopefully at Noam. "You want to come?"

"This is the best day of my life," said Noam as they walked back uphill.

IT IS FINISHED

MRS. MICHAELSON MAKES UP HER MIND

Mr. Michaelson smiled. "So you've chosen?" he asked.

"Yes. I've made up my mind."

Their wrinkled hands met. Their fingers locked. She rested her head on his chest.

"What was it that convinced you?"

"My taste of freedom," she said. "Because I wasn't free, just out of control. But then I slammed on the brakes and now everything fits so neatly."

Her husband leaned in closer and kissed her. He whispered, "Open your eyes."

Mrs. Michaelson obeyed. She found herself back in her hotel room, propped up against the pillows like a decorative doll. Her bed, with its starchy sheets and heavy blanket bunched up at her bare feet, was surrounded by a crowd of mourners speaking in hushed voices.

Rabbi Sherman sat next to her in the chair that was usually pushed against the writing table. Sherry Sherman, standing behind him, argued with a stranger, who was packing bandages and white tape into a little white suitcase.

"Believe me, g'veret, I know. Because that's what I went to school for," he said, then shook the hands of the men nearby and left the room.

Yocheved and Janis—the latter sporting a tiny Band-Aid above her mouth like a mustache—stood off in a corner and talked quietly. Two young men, one of them Jeremy, sat on the couch by the window and rubbed knees. Dave the tour guide stared pensively into his cell phone. Aliza the rabbinic intern stood by the TV with Baruch the bus driver and three Israeli men Mrs. Michaelson didn't recognize, one in a sport coat, the other two in navy-blue policemen's uniforms. They watched a Knesset debate playing live.

The TV cut to a close-up of Shimon Peres, and Mrs. Michaelson leaned forward.

Sherry Sherman said, "Everyone stay calm, but I think she's having a spasm."

While the rabbi assured his mother that Mrs. Michaelson

wasn't having a spasm, Yocheved and Janis poked her shoulder. They seemed to think she wasn't quite awake.

"Someone should call my dad," Jeremy said.

"Give me his number," Sherry Sherman replied. "I'll do it."

In a thick accent, the Israeli in the sport coat said to Rabbi Rick, "But the son looks normal. You said he had a pin in his nose and color in his hair."

"Helen, how are you *feeling*?" the rabbi said, waving to get her attention. "Listen, I've got good news. The detectives say they can catch the men who did this to you if you just give them a description. They know every resident of Silwan—man, woman, and child—and they can find the perpetrators if you give them even a few clues."

"What perpetrators?" Mrs. Michaelson said groggily.

"What did she say?" Rabbi Rick asked Yocheved and Janis, but they hadn't understood, either.

"Can't you remember anything?" the detective in the sport coat asked Jeremy. "Why was your mother in Silwan?"

"What did she tell you?" Jeremy asked.

"I want to know what you say."

"I wanted to see the City of David, that's all," Mrs. Michaelson said, straining to make herself heard.

"I guess she wanted to see the City of David," said Jeremy.

"You see?" the detective told Jeremy. "You are contaminating the witness."

"She went to meet his friend," said Rabbi Rick. "He has a friend there, a special friend."

"You mean a b-b-boyfriend?" said Jeremy's companion, who had a military haircut and was rather good-looking. Maybe he was a soldier. "I'm his boyfriend."

"Donkeys!" one of the policemen shouted in Hebrew at the TV screen.

"Sons of donkeys!" said Baruch the bus driver.

"It says the number's been changed," said Sherry Sherman, cradling the phone.

"That's right," said Mrs. Michaelson and tried to explain, but no one listened.

"Here, let me dial," said Jeremy, grabbing for the phone.

"Please relax, everyone," said the detective, then turned to the rabbi. "Who told you he had a lover in Silwan?"

"No one," stammered the rabbi. "Not in so many words. It was obvious."

"I'm telling you, it says the number's been changed and there's no new number listed," Sherry said, enunciating extra clearly, as if she were talking to an old person. She tried to hang on to the phone, but Jeremy took it from her.

Aliza sat on the bed and patted Mrs. Michaelson's hand.

Julie Solznick appeared. "I've got us a fruit platter!" she announced, and ran out of the room.

"Why was your mother in Silwan?" the detective repeated.

"To meet your boyfriend, right?" said the rabbi.

"To see the City of David," said Jeremy, trying to dial his parents' number.

"I've always wanted to see the City of David," said Jeremy's friend.

All this talk, Mrs. Michaelson thought, and for nothing. Why couldn't they shut up? Their noise would get them nowhere. There were no perpetrators. Only misguided boys young enough to learn to do better, to change the way she'd hoped Jeremy would change.

Janis came over and sat on the bed with Mrs. Michaelson.

The detective pushed on the mattress with his index finger. "These people are killing us in our backyards. They kill children." He pointed to Mrs. Michaelson. "Who were these men?"

"There were no men," she said, crying now. She turned to her son and grabbed him by the wrist, the way she used to when he was a toddler and about to run into the street. "Get rid of them, please," she said. "My head hurts." She wished her husband were there. He might have done something.

Jeremy looked at her strangely, then faced the others. "Leave her alone," he said in a squeaky voice, and cleared his throat. "You asked questions and she answered them. Let her rest. Everyone go. Get out of here. We don't want any of you." He turned off the television. "Let's go, now."

The detective shrugged, then barked something in Hebrew at the policemen. "We may visit you again tomorrow."

Janis stood up slowly. "I think you're very brave," she said, kissing Mrs. Michaelson on one cheek and then the other. They smiled at each other, as if they'd reached an understanding.

"We are all tired," Yocheved said with a last look at the TV. "Come on, Janis. We will go find your parents."

"I'll pick you up tomorrow morning, Shoshana," Baruch called out on his way to the door, "and then we'll fly to the Riviera, okay?"

Sherry Sherman slipped something cold and plastic into Mrs. Michaelson's hand. "The maid must have knocked your name tag into the wastebasket. I rescued it for you."

"You'd better go too, Noam," Jeremy said to his friend.

"Can I wait for you downstairs?"

Mrs. Michaelson didn't hear the answer, but she watched them hug, and then Jeremy kissed Noam on the cheek. She'd never seen two men kiss each other on the cheek except for European diplomats on TV. It made her uncomfortable for a minute, but then she thought she could get used to it. "See you sometime, then," said Noam, touching the spot on his cheek where he'd been kissed.

Jeremy stood by the door until everyone was gone except the rabbi, who stood with his arms folded and studied her face. He made her feel as if she'd wet her pants and he knew, as if he were holding the soiled underwear as proof. "I'm not ready to go," he said.

"Why do you keep bothering her?" Jeremy said. "What do you want from us?"

"Is that how you feel, Helen?" Rabbi Sherman asked.

"Of course," she said, shutting her eyes and squirming in bed.

"But this morning," he whispered, "I thought we were going to . . ."

"Stop, stop. I don't want to hear this now. Go already," she said, covering her eyes with the crook of her arm.

"All right, then." The rabbi moved away from the bed and knocked over one of the chairs. "You're afraid of me," he said, setting the chair upright. He cleared his throat like he was going to give a sermon, but instead he left the room.

As soon as Jeremy locked the door, Mrs. Michaelson shut her eyes and smiled. "It's so quiet," she said. "Like none of this has happened. We can start over."

"But it has happened," he said.

"As soon as we get home, I'm making a long list of everything we need to do next and then I'm going to do it. But right now my head aches. Don't bother trying to call your father back. I'll do it myself."

"But what happened to our phone number? And why was the rabbi so weird?"

"I'll explain later." She lay back against the pillows and wiped her nose.

Jeremy was talking. It sounded like he was trying to make an apology, but she didn't have the strength to listen. "Nothing now," she said drowsily. "My head hurts."

"Then let me get you your Valium. No, wait. Aren't you the lucky lady. They gave you Percocet. Damn, if you don't want these, I'll take them."

"No, I'll take them," she said grouchily, grabbing the bottle before he could open it. "Bring me some water, please. Not too warm."

———

Standing in front of the bathroom mirror the next morning, she was shocked to see the bandage attached to her skin by three strips of tape. It looked like a giant white grub crawling up her neck. When she pulled it off there was only a small scab underneath, a red worm hardly worth all the fuss.

Worn out from her trip to the bathroom, Mrs. Michaelson went back to bed and nodded off for a while until the phone rang. She picked it up and heard the rabbi. "I'm sorry, that guest isn't here anymore," she said, hanging up. The phone rang again, but she ignored it.

Jeremy came in with coffee and a roll. He set her breakfast on the nightstand and opened the curtains.

"Ow!" she said, falling back against her pillow.

"I'll adjust it." Jeremy pulled one of the curtains. "Did you call David?"

He handed her the phone and she dialed the new number.

"I'm glad you called," Mr. Michaelson said. "I've been making an inventory of everything we own: the silverware and china, the rugs and the clock from Czechoslovakia from my mother. We have to decide now who gets what, or the boys will fight over it."

"I had a small accident, but I'm fine now," she told him. "Absolutely fine. Don't worry. We're leaving this afternoon."

"Well, that's good then," he said. "One of us has to stay healthy." His voice changed. "Are you sure you're all right?" He sounded genuinely concerned.

"Perfectly fine. How are you?"

"The usual. Just terrible."

"I wish you could have been here," Jeremy said when it was his turn to talk. "Practically the whole Mission was in the room." Strangely, neither he nor she mentioned that she'd been hit by a rock, as if the rock were her affair with the rabbi. So now she and Jeremy shared a secret.

"I need your help," she said after he hung up. "I still feel dizzy, and I need you to finish packing for me." She laughed a little. "I need you to take care of me."

"Of course." Jeremy dragged her suitcase out of the closet and began throwing her worn clothes into it. He made a mess of the folding, but she didn't mind. It was all going into the wash anyway. "I'm sorry," he said as he packed. "I was an asshole not to show up at the City of David yesterday. It could have turned out much worse."

"It was my fault for being late and then wandering off instead of staying put," she said as he picked up her sneakers from the closet floor. "Don't forget to check the drawers."

His hands trembled as he handled her bras and the worn silk panties by his fingertips. The phone rang again and he moved to pick it up, but she shook her head. "I'm not here," she said.

"This looks in pretty bad shape," he said, holding up a shriveled silk dress.

"Throw it away, please," she said coldly. "I can manage the rest. Do you want to go say good-bye to your boyfriend? I'm sorry I won't meet him, but he'll understand."

"That's finished," he told her. His voice sounded old all of a sudden. "It's this nasty habit I've picked up, pushing everyone away, and I can't stop."

"I don't think that's true," she said. "Don't keep putting yourself down."

"I met someone else, but it won't work out with him, either."

"You never know." It slipped out, a reflex, too ingrained to control.

"How could it work out? We're going home in a couple of hours," he said, then added, "Mom." Instead of "Helen."

"I suppose," she sighed, looking at the dress straps hanging over the rim of the wastebasket.

"Why can't you stop pretending things are the way they're not?"

"Why can't you stop lying?" she said. "You lie all the time."

Jeremy smirked. "I guess we're the same." He left the suitcase and sat down on the bed next to her just where her husband would sit when they used to stay up late together reading in bed. "You know, I'm thinking, maybe I should come back here. To visit, or maybe for a longer time when I finish school. It's weird, but I like this place. It feels alive to me. Fighting social hypocrisy in New York makes me feel like some big, dumb cliché. But here, everything seems to matter more. The people are awake. I mean, these two guys, Noam and George, they really understood me," he said. "I told them everything—even about my night in the hospital—and they didn't have to ask questions or make sympathetic noises. They got it. I mean, they got me. No one at home gets me. Not even my shrink."

"I wish I got you," she said. "I've been trying to."

"Then keep on trying. Listen instead of talking so much."

She turned to him and patted his hair. It felt soft, and she noticed a few traces of green dye on the sides. This one moment was worth all the trouble, she thought, but how long would it last? How long will he let me do this?

"Promise me you'll learn from my mistakes instead of repeating them with your kids," she said. "I've got to believe there's such a thing as progress."

"But I'm not having kids."

"That's right. You're the end of the line." That fact used to upset her, but today it came as a relief. Her neck felt sore and she pressed on the scab. "I'm sorry I brought you here, put you through this."

"But I just told you," said Jeremy. "I'm glad you made me come. Anyway, never mind. Here, let me." He reached over and massaged her neck.

"I've got some peppermint foot lotion from that hotel in Eilat. That might feel soothing. The lotion's in the nightstand." He found the bottle and began spreading it on.

His hands felt cold but soft. The room itself was a little cold, actually. Too much A/C. "Are you all right?" she asked, turning around. "Really?"

"I'm all right enough," he said, and put down the bottle of lotion. "You know what I'd like? Sing for me."

"Sing what?"

"The kiddush. Do you remember it?"

"Of course. But why . . . ?" She stopped herself. "Okay."

He rested his head on her shoulder. She put her arm around him and stroked his hair as she sang. Off-key. Worse than ever. Still, he seemed to like it. Why was it that when she set out to please, he pushed her away but when she humiliated herself like this in front of him, she made him happy? Embarrassed, she stared out the window at the sky, an empty, cloudless band of blue. The sun was already too high to see.

So they were going back to the old life, but not quite.

After the song was over, Jeremy lay with her for a while, until the phone rang. "Don't get it," she said.

"I won't." He sat up, smoothed his hair into place, and went back to packing. Mrs. Michaelson excused herself to the bathroom and began to wash.

All day, the staff of the Jerusalem Hilton was a bit sleepy, because they'd stayed up late watching Barak's no-confidence vote on TV and arguing about the result afterward. They were relieved he'd survived, ever so narrowly, and they were nervous too. Immediately after his victory, Barak boarded a plane to Camp David to save the life they'd gotten used to, of full hotels, markets crowded with tourists, Internet cafés with espresso machines and stainless-steel counters, where you could buy coffee from Africa or Ecuador, pastries from France, and ice cream from Vermont. Still, they were worried. Barak had promised to divide Jerusalem, but how could anyone divide Jerusalem? Where would he put the line? What kind of line would it be? A high wall or a friendly fence? A strip of blue paint, or perhaps the Western Wall itself? Or would it be one of those imaginary psychic boundaries, like the ones in the States, that divided neighborhoods without fanfare, though everyone knew to keep to his own side?

"Michaelson?" repeated the front-desk clerk at the Jerusalem Hilton as she sipped her double macchiato with skim. She looked again at the piece of paper given to her by the chubby Palestinian with the trusting eyes. "All gone."

She dug her red nail into the plastic lid of her macchiato while waiting for the Palestinian to write something else on the paper. "NO ADDRESS?"

Actually, there was one, provided by the *g'veret* in case of luggage left behind or gone astray. However, the woman at the desk didn't think she ought to give it out to a suspicious-looking case like the one in front of her. She shook her head, covered a yawn with her fist, and then smiled for the next person in line. A paying guest from Miami.

The Palestinian gave her a bashful smile and left the way he had come, through the revolving door. Outside, a searing wind from the east blew sand into his eyes. More brutal heat. Probably a new record. The night before, sweaty and miserable with thirst, he'd lain awake on a mat without a sheet in the stuffy Russian Compound. His age, his disability, his identity card, his proof of employment, his lack of a criminal record, his family's pleading—none of these facts had made a difference.

Finally, the principal of his school came. Her brother was a policeman. When they left the compound, she explained he would only be out for a short time, that he might have to go back. He told her the story, explained that nothing had happened.

"The problem is, there are witnesses," she said. "They say they saw you in Independence Park on the night of the disturbance. Were you with anyone who saw it too, who saw that you were not involved?"

He went home, and his father said what else could you expect from the imperialist Zionist oppressor. Then George's father called his old friend Menachem Levy, who knew lawyers.

Yes, yes, there was a witness. And now the witness had disappeared without a word.

As he left the property of the Hilton, George laughed one of his silent, choking laughs. It made a chilling sound that disturbed a pair of tourists from Philadelphia who were on their way out for a frozen yogurt at TCBY across the highway. They only made it as far as the end of the hotel drive before turning back, because of the heat.

"Are you sure this is a safe neighborhood?" they asked each other.

George laughed some more. It felt good to be free, even for a short time. He threw his head back to catch the sun. How unfair, he thought. How positively God-like.

Acknowledgments

I would like to thank the following tireless readers of this novel in its various stages for their criticism and crucial encouragement: Maureen Brady, Mark Derenzo, Paul Fischer, Lauren Grodstein, Mike Heppner, Binnie Kirshenbaum, David Levinson, Gordon Powell, Brian Rubin, Jessica Shattuck, Meggin Silverman, and Robert Williams. Thank you to Melanie Jackson and Andrea Schaefer for their work on my behalf. To everyone at Random House, especially Adam Korn, Veronica Windholz, Brian McLendon, and Bruce Tracy, who helped me realize my vision for this book with adroit questioning. To the Edward F. Albee Foundation, where a portion of this book was written. To Jeff Jackson, without whom I'd be completely lost in cyberspace. To the many people who lived within the dominion of Israel during the summer of 2000 and took the time to talk to me, especially Nathan Englander, Yigal Sadeh, and Martin J. Wein, whose insights continue to inspire me. To my cousins in Israel for their hospitality. To Alaine Waldshan for introducing me to the world of "the Mission." To the staff of Café Strudel, who provided a welcome refuge from Jerusalem's steamy streets. To the Jerusalem Open House for their determined advancement of human rights. All the members of my family here in the States: Mom, Dad, Sheldon and Eva, Paul and Nancy, Daniel and Denise, and my eleven wonderful nieces and nephews have been the most loyal supporters a writer could ever hope for. Thank you also to my co-workers at the Family Support Center in Sunset Park, especially for the one and only "View from Stalin's Head" cake! To my number-one fans, Heather and Maggie Binns. And to Mary Gordon for her constant support.

Articles, books, and other sources that were helpful to me in getting a feel for the places, people, and tone of this book include: the poetry of Yehuda Amichai; *Between Sodom and Eden* by Lee Walzer; *Independence Park*, edited by Amir Sumaka'i Fink and Jacob Press; *Boychiks in the Hood* by Robert Eisenberg; *One Palestine, Complete* by Tom Segev, as well as Anita Shapira's biting critique of Segev's book, "Eyeless in Zion," in the December 11, 2000, issue of *The New Republic*; *The Wisdom of Israel*, edited by Lewis Browne; *IT* magazine; the Aish HaTorah website; *Backpackers and Tourists* magazine; *Ha'aretz* online; *Ha'zman Ha'varod* magazine; Kareem Fahim's and Sylvana Foa's essays on Israel in *The Village Voice*; "An Impossible Occupation" by Scott Anderson in *The New York Times Magazine*, May 12, 2002; "The Apology" by Laura Blumenfeld, *The New Yorker*, March 4, 2002; too many tourist brochures to mention by name; "Holy Orlando" by Matt Labash, *The Weekly Standard*, March 5, 2001; *Jewish Heroes*, books one and two, by Sadie Rose Weilerstein; *The Meaning of the Glorious Koran*, an explanatory translation by Mohammed Marmaduke Pickthall; *A Child's Bible in Colour*, rewritten for children by Anne Edwards; *Israel Diary* by Bernard M. Bloomfield; *Great Jewish Women* by Elma Ehrlich Levinger.

ABOUT THE AUTHOR

AARON HAMBURGER is the author of *The View from Stalin's Head*. He was awarded a fellowship from the Edward F. Albee Foundation and won first prize in the David Dornstein Memorial Creative Writing Contest for Young Adult Writers. His writing has appeared in *The Village Voice, Poets & Writers, Out, Nerve,* and *Time Out New York*. He teaches writing at Columbia University and lives in New York City.

ABOUT THE TYPE

This book was set in Walbaum, a typeface designed in 1810 by German punch cutter J. E. Walbaum. Walbaum's type is more French than German in appearance. Like Bodoni, it is a classical typeface, yet its openness and slight irregularities give it a human, romantic quality.